FAUST

PART TWO

JOHANN WOLFGANG GOETHE was born in 1749, the son of a well-to-do citizen of Frankfurt. As a young man he studied law and briefly practised as a lawyer, but creative writing was his chief concern. In the early 1770s he was the dominating figure of the German literary revival, his tragic novel *Werther* bringing him international fame.

In 1775 he settled permanently in the small duchy of Weimar where he became a minister of state and director of the court theatre; in 1782 he was ennobled as 'von Goethe'. His journey to Italy in 1786–8 influenced the development of his mature classical style; in the 1790s, he and his younger contemporary Schiller (1759–1805) were the joint architects of Weimar Classicism, the central phase of German literary culture.

Goethe wrote in all the literary *genres* but his interests extended far beyond literature and included a number of scientific subjects. *Faust*, written at various stages of his life and in a variety of styles, became a constantly enlarged repository of his personal wisdom. His creative energies never ceased to take new forms and he was still writing original poetry at the age of more than 80. In 1806 he married Christiane Vulpius (1765–1816), having lived with her for eighteen years; they had one surviving son, August (1789–1830). Goethe died in 1832.

DAVID LUKE is an Emeritus Student (Emeritus Fellow) of Christ Church, Oxford. He has published articles and essays on German literature and various prose and verse translations, including Goethe's *Selected Verse*, Stifter's *Limestone and Other Stories*, Kleist's *The Marquise of O and Other Stories*, *Selected Tales* by the brothers Grimm, Goethe's *Iphigenia in Tauris* and *Hermann and Dorothea*, a volume of Goethe's erotic poetry (*Roman Elegies* and *The Diary*), and Thomas Mann's *Death in Venice and Other Stories*. His translation of *Faust* Part One was awarded the European Poetry Translation Prize in 1989.

THE WORLD'S CLASSICS

JOHANN WOLFGANG VON
GOETHE

FAUST

PART TWO

Translated with an
Introduction by
DAVID LUKE

Oxford   New York
OXFORD UNIVERSITY PRESS
1994

Oxford University Press, Walton Street, Oxford OX2 6DP

Oxford New York Toronto
Delhi Bombay Calcutta Madras Karachi
Kuala Lumpur Singapore Hong Kong Tokyo
Nairobi Dar es Salaam Cape Town
Melbourne Auckland Madrid

and associated companies in
Berlin Ibadan

Oxford is a trade mark of Oxford University Press

British Library Cataloguing in Publication Data
Data available

Library of Congress Cataloging in Publication Data
Data available
ISBN 0-19-282616-6

1 3 5 7 9 10 8 6 4 2

Typeset by Pure Tech Corporation, Pondicherry, India
Printed in Great Britain by
BPCC Paperbacks
Aylesbury, Bucks

τοῖς ἀγγέλοις εἰρήνης,
πιστοῖς ὁδηγοῖς καὶ φύλαξιν

CONTENTS

CONTENTS

PREFACE

'*Faust, Part Two*' (or as Goethe calls it *Faust, der Tragödie zweiter Teil*) may arguably be regarded either as a loose, almost independent sequel to '*Faust, Part One*', or (as the word 'part' suggests and as many critics insist) as the continuation of a single work called '*Faust*'. Readers will differ as to which approach makes better sense; in any case, largely for practical reasons, I have not tried to integrate this translation and edition of Part Two with that of Part One in a single bulky '*Faust*' volume. I have assumed, however, that those who read this sequel, if such it is, will probably be acquainted with Part One in some form or another, and perhaps with my own version of it which was published by Oxford University Press in 1987. In this hope I here occasionally refer (by page or line or scene number) to the Part One text or to my introduction and notes to it. (In both translations I have preserved the standard line-numbering of the German text, and for greater clarity added editorial numbers to Goethe's scenes; a scene-index appears on p. lxxxiii.)

As with Part One, the German text is so well established that it makes no significant difference which of the many standard editions one translates from, but I have in fact used the relevant Reclam volume (Reclams Universal-Bibliothek, Stuttgart, 1986), which is itself based on volume 15 (*Faust*, II Teil, ed. Erich Schmidt, 1888) of the venerable Weimar Edition of Goethe's works (1887–1919). I have also frequently consulted the *Faust* volume (vol. 8, ed. Gotthard Erler, 1965) of the more modern Berlin Edition, in which Goethe's different *Faust* texts, peripheral writings, and other relevant material are presented in a rational and accessible way. The 'Weimarer Ausgabe' and 'Berliner Ausgabe' are referred to as WA and BA. For the complex problem of the genesis of Act V, which (as in the case of the genesis of Part One) must affect any interpretation of the conclusion and indeed of the whole of Part Two, an indispensable aid has been Ulrich Landeck's recent text-critical edition of this Act (*Der fünfte* Akt von Goethes Faust II: *kommentierte kritische* Ausgabe, Artemis Verlag, Zürich 1981).

As in the Part One edition, I have tried to condense what seemed to be the most important points for discussion into the introductory essay, using asterisks to relegate specific miscellaneous details to the 'Explanatory Notes'; the Notes are placed after the text since they annotate it as well. They are also preceded by a few extracts from Goethe's unpublished sketches and other material on the periphery of Part Two: the so-called paralipomena, which are, so to speak, a penumbral extension of his official text of *Faust*, without reference to which it is difficult to understand his developing (and therefore his final) conception of the whole work. The Notes are followed by a short bibliography of sources used or mentioned in the Introduction or in the Notes themselves; since I also frequently quote from Goethe's letters and conversations, an index of names is included in this section, giving brief details of his correspondents and conversation-partners. (A more extended bibliography of translations and other literature concerning *Faust* and Goethe generally, together with a chronological table of relevant events, appears after the Introduction to Part One.) Since Acts II and III of Part Two supposedly take place in Thessaly and the Peloponnese respectively, and contain numerous mythological or other classical allusions, I have also added an index of classical mythology and a map of Greece. Here and elsewhere, with regret but for the sake of consistency, I have in nearly all cases adopted the conventional Latin spellings of Greek names and place-names (Achilles for Akhilleus, Patroclus for Patroklos, Peneus for Peneios, etc.; Helen/Helena has inevitably been Anglicized as well as Latinized).

I am particularly indebted to Dr John R. Williams of the University of St Andrews, not only for his various specialized published writings on *Faust* Part Two but also for his kindness in reading my introductory essay and notes, which have benefited considerably from his expertise. Valuable suggestions arising out of the Introduction have also been made by Dr R. W. Truman, Professor Dimitri Obolensky and Mr R. L. Vilain. Mr Vilain was also kind enough to double check the proofs of the whole edition. For the classical material I owe much to the erudition of Professor P. J. Parsons as well as to M. C. Howatson's *Oxford Companion to Classical Literature* (1989). My remaining errors, in these addenda and in the translation, must await later correction or at least exposure.

D.L.

INTRODUCTION

1 GOETHE AND *FAUST*

In the spring of 1827 Philippe Albert Stapfer, a retired Swiss diplomat living in Paris, who a few years earlier had published a successful translation of Goethe's dramatic works in four volumes, was planning a new, separate French edition of *Faust*, Part One, to be illustrated by Delacroix. He had heard that the nearly 78-year-old Goethe was about to publish a sequel or second part, and wrote to him for information. Goethe had in fact recently decided to begin preparing a final collected edition of his works, the so-called *Ausgabe letzter Hand* (ALH), and this indeed had been the main practical stimulus for his resumption of work on *Faust*. He was including in it what we now know as Act III of Part Two, the 'Helena' Act, printed as a separate dramatic poem; this would be the first published piece of *Faust* material since the appearance of the 'First Part of the Tragedy' in 1808. It duly appeared in April 1827, in volume 4 of the ALH, under the title 'Helena: a classical-romantic phantasmagoria. Intermezzo (*Zwischenspiel*) for *Faust*'. Goethe replied to Stapfer's letter on 3 April, explaining that for the time being he had nothing to add to Part One, in which no changes were to be made; the forthcoming 'Helena' was

an intermezzo [*un intermède*] belonging to the second part, and this second part is entirely different from the first in its conception, its execution and its scene of action, which is set in higher regions. It is not yet finished, and I am only publishing this intermezzo as a sample, to be fitted into the rest later.

Stressing the total stylistic difference between 'Helena' and Part One, Goethe assures Stapfer that he will be able to satisfy himself when he reads it that the Helen drama 'cannot be connected in any way to the first part', and that the French publisher will prejudice the success of his proposed edition if he attempts to do so. On the other hand, he, Goethe, would of course be happy to see a French edition of 'Helena' appear in a separate volume.

The complete Part Two, the long-awaited 'sequel', was unveiled in December 1832, having been deliberately withheld by Goethe until after his death. One other instalment had appeared during his lifetime: the first three and a half scenes of Act I, published in 1828 alongside Part One in volume 12 of the ALH. But 'Helena', as he emphasized from the start to Stapfer and others, was a different matter:* how different, for instance, were Faust's dealings with Helen of Troy from his affair with poor Gretchen, that youthful story from which the author now distanced himself with remarkable asperity. In March or April 1827, just as 'Helena' was seeing the light of day, he wrote a review of a now forgotten academic work on ancient drama, in which, referring in passing to *Faust*, he describes the central tragic theme of Part One dismissively as 'that earlier relationship, which came to grief in the chaos of misunderstood learning, middle-class narrow-mindedness, moral disorder and superstitious delusions'. By contrast, Faust's relationship with Helen is one 'presenting itself in a freer domain of art and pointing to loftier views'. Notwithstanding the strong probability that in his youthful Frankfurt period he also conceived and planned a Faust–Helen story in some form,* the Goethe of 1827 clearly wishes to lay all possible emphasis on the autonomy and self-sufficiency of his newly published version, to keep it pure from all contamination by the tragic *Urfaust* material which he now seems to regard as belonging almost to a pre-Goethean previous existence. And it is indeed now almost literally true that 'Helena' *'ne peut en aucune façon se rattacher à la première partie'*. The old Dr Faustus legend, to be sure, had from its sixteenth-century beginnings included the motif of the return of Helen from the dead to be Faustus's 'paramour'.* But even apart from Goethe's deliberate classical Greek and operatic stylizations, which differentiate 'Helena' not only from Part One but from most of the rest of Part Two as well, its story would make almost as much sense on its own if the hero's name were not Faust but, say, Roland or Rinaldo or Walther von der Vogelweide; Mephistopheles has in any case changed both his name and his sex. A spectator or reader who knew nothing of Part One or of the Faustus legend would be at no great disadvantage. He would be more puzzled by the remaining Acts; but here, even if we know Part One and the legend, some perplexities remain. Why, for instance, is this Second Part called 'the Second Part *of the Tragedy*'? The word 'tragedy' would be appropriate if the fatal Pact, the 'blood-scribed document' which the Devil (for it is he) waves in the face of the dead Faust at the end (Sc. 22) of Act V, were to turn out to have remained in force all along; if the hero, for all his great creative exploits and his visions of beauty in nature and art, were nevertheless utterly destroyed in the end by some ingrown taint, the inescapable perduration of an original decision or curse. But no: that scene is written like the comic ending of a medieval mystery play in which the Devil is foiled after all, in this case by the ambiguous small print of his contract plus the distracting ribaldry of a verbal romp with come-hitherish boy angels.

Answers to this can be offered: we can point out for instance that the 'Prologue in Heaven' at the beginning of Part One, in which the non-tragic ending is predicted, is in fact not printed as a prologue to 'the First Part of the Tragedy' but to *Faust* as a whole. We can then maintain that the two scenes following Faust's death (Sc. 22 and 23 in the present edition) are jointly an epilogue to the whole drama, which thus becomes a tragedy in two parts framed within a mystery play. Nevertheless, confronted with a 'Second Part' which the author himself insists is '*complètement différente de la première*', and which turns so decisively away from the ultimately naturalistic consistency of tragic drama towards epic and lyric digressiveness, towards the operatic mode, towards allegorical disguise and masquerade, pageant and festival, and not least towards comedy,* only the most persistently naïve commentator will seek to interpret it from beginning to end, or indeed at all, in terms of such concepts of traditional dramatic naturalism as the unfolding of a consistent action or Faust's moral progress; still less should we cling to reading it in terms of the traditional devil's-bargain story to which the 'blood-scribed document' belongs. This much-discussed Pact or Wager, as we saw, already creates much confusion in Part One, its terms having been devised by Goethe about a quarter of a century after he wrote the Gretchen tragedy, with which they are flatly inconsistent; and another quarter-century was to elapse before his main work on Part Two was even begun. In fact the Wager scene only really makes sense if we forget about it completely during the Gretchen tragedy and during Part Two, Acts I–IV.* In Act V, Scene 22, it at last comes into its own, and Goethe consents to close the ring of dramatic form by bringing back a motif that had, essentially, been devised as belonging to the ending. Faust is not 'damned' by the 'loss' of the Wager, because the contrary outcome had been built into both the Wager scene and the 'Prologue' when they were written at the turn of the century; his 'salvation', already foreseen in the 'Prologue' and enacted at the end of Act V, is the Wager's proper and only intelligible context.

Goethe wrote *Faust* intermittently over a period of about sixty years, in four widely separated phases of composition which have already been partly considered in the context of Part One.* The third of them was at the turn of the century: the *annus mirabilis* 1797 and a few years after that, during which both Goethe and his close intellectual partner Schiller published or wrote or began, and intensively discussed with each other, much of their finest work. These were the 'classical' years, the Schiller years, which Goethe later called his 'best period' (conversation with Boisserée, 3 August 1815); they were the years in which he was most strongly under the influence of Greek tragedy and epic, and in which he began to write 'Helena'. In June 1797, when he again resumed work on *Faust*, nothing of it had been published except the puzzling and truncated 'Fragment' of 1790. It was now that he wrote the 'Prologue in Heaven' and decided to divide the whole drama into two parts. He concentrated for the time being on supplying the missing material for the first, but also produced some fragments for the second, writing *c*.1800 a version of the first 269 lines of 'Helena' and sketching, or at least planning, some of the scenes of Act V. His correspondence with Schiller during these years contains not only a number of exchanges on *Faust* but also, in 1797, an important discussion of the nature of dramatic and epic form and their differentiation. According to their agreed theory, drama as such is characterized by logical consistency and economy, the precipitation of the action towards the denouement, the subordination of the parts to a single purpose which the end will bring to fulfilment. In the epic style, on the other hand, 'sensuous breadth' is of the essence: a certain discursive lingering over pleasing detail and episode for its own sake, a tendency of the parts to pursue their own enjoyable autonomy rather than remain functions of a tightly controlled, end-directed whole. All the evidence suggests that whereas Schiller's instincts inclined him in practice towards drama, and specifically towards tragic drama in which the form is at its purest, Goethe was by nature an epic and lyric writer. Or, more exactly, what Goethe really wanted to do was to write dramatically nuanced epic, or epically and lyrically enriched drama. In the former genre he published, also in 1797, his idyllic short narrative poem of German middle-class life, *Hermann and Dorothea*, which was a brilliant popular and artistic success. He did not repeat this achievement, but its influence is evident in some of the new scenes for Part One written at this time.* They reflect a shift towards a more liberal, less austere style of drama, including a tendency towards opera, a form of which both Goethe and Schiller approved for its decisively anti-naturalistic character. With his songs, chants and choruses of soldiers, dancing revellers, angels, demons, and witches in the 1797–1801 scenes, Goethe introduced an element that was to come further into its own in Part Two. Drama does not drop out of sight, but it moves still further from naturalism, and drifts increasingly into epic and other more relaxed modes. His willingness to publish separate instalments of Part Two is itself significant. Even the advance announcement of a non-tragic or supra-tragic denouement in the Prologue could be counted as an additional epic feature; such a procedure (as he had written to Schiller on 22 April 1797) must remove a work from the vulgar sphere of dramatic suspense. As an example he cited Homer's *Odyssey*, in which the hero's eventual safe return from his wanderings is implied in the opening lines.

Goethe evidently found that the 1797 theory of epic form accommodated his deepest artistic instincts; but for Schiller, whose classical dramatic masterpieces were written in these last years of his life, logical integration and a carefully constructed overall unity remained essential to dramatic form as such. To the author of *Maria Stuart*, Goethe's dramatic work seemed (as he frankly remarked to him in a letter of 26 December 1797) 'epically flawed' rather than truly tragic. Under his influence, Goethe made serious efforts to think of *Faust* as a work which, when finished, would be an intellectually integrated whole, as required by the official theory; and in his letters to him, as we have seen, he often refers apologetically to his doubts on this score.* In the summer of 1797, probably at Schiller's prompting, he appears to have worked out a plan for the unfinished two-part drama and to have set down a detailed written scheme, from which however only a brief and highly obscure fragment has survived (see paralipomenon BA5 and note). Schematic analysis was uncongenial to the creative process by which this unclassifiable work came into being. Nevertheless, on the evidence of remarks attributed to him by conversation-partners at this period and later, Goethe remained ambiguous on the question of whether *Faust* is an intellectual unity, with a central theme or idea running through both parts. He is on record as claiming both that there is (but he will not say what it is) and that there is not (or at least that he does not know of one). Heinrich Luden, for instance, a young history professor from Berlin, visited him in the summer of 1806, shortly after he had finished Part One and sent it off to his publishers; Luden of course knew only the 1790 'Fragment', but claimed to be able to quote most of that by heart. With great obsequiousness he ventured to express some scepticism as to whether this 'fragment' could ever become part of a whole. Goethe, very much on the defensive, insisted that it was and would be so, that there was a central point, a basic idea, and that if Luden found contradictions in the 'Fragment', it was because he did not appreciate sufficiently that in poetry there are no contradictions, only in real life. How strange an idea Luden must have of the way *Faust* had been written: did he suppose the poet 'simply did not know what he was about, but started writing at random and straight into the blue, merely using the name of Faust as a thread on which to string one bead after another in case they got lost'? (conversation with Luden, 19 August 1806). Later, more than twenty years after Schiller's death, when he was no longer under his rationalizing influence and had written and published 'Helena', Goethe was talking to his young and pedantic companion Ecker-mann (conversation with Eckermann, 6 May 1827): he reverted to the point on which he had expressed himself so emphatically to the young and pedantic Luden, and even used the same metaphor to say what appears to be the exact opposite:

(German readers) come and ask me, for instance, what 'idea' I tried to embody in my *Faust*. As if I knew that myself and could put it into words! . . . And a fine thing it would have had to be, if I had taken the rich and colourful and varied life I had expressed in *Faust*, and tried to string it onto the thin thread of a single idea running through it all! . . . It has not been my way as a writer to try to embody *abstractions*.

In a later conversation (13 February 1831) Eckermann earns Goethe's emphatic endorsement by taking up the same point, 'thread' metaphor and all, and giving an excellent summary of the theory of the epic mode.* None the less, Goethe's remarks in 1806 to Luden and his remarks in 1827 to Eckermann are plainly both expostulations against one or other sort of academic philistinism (pulling a poem to pieces or hanging it on an abstraction), and need not be taken to represent a radical change of view. In any case, both in the Schiller period and in the last years, he would often retreat into a convenient irrationalistic position, declaring that *Faust* is 'fragmentary' or 'incommensurable', and that this indeed is how poetry should be in any case: 'the more incommensurable and elusive to the understanding a work of literature is, the better it is' (conversation with Eckermann, 6 May 1827; cf. also their conversation of 3 January 1830 and Part One, Introd., p. xlvi).

A possible identification of the missing central 'idea' in *Faust* suggests itself if we consider further Goethe's paradoxically non-tragic, 'salvationist' treatment of the old Dr Faustus story: paradoxical in that it reverses a tradition going back to the legend's beginnings and which has revived since Goethe's time. From the sixteenth until the later eighteenth century the unquestioned assumption of the story was that Faustus was to be 'damned'.* It is not clear at what stage Goethe decided otherwise. When writing his youthful version of it, the *Urfaust*, in the 1770s, he may well have intended a more traditional conclusion: the stark ending of the Gretchen tragedy, when she bids Faust an eternal farewell and Mephistopheles drags him off with the terrible and untranslatable cry (added in the 1808 text) of '*Her zu mir!*', could be read in this sense. It may be that his instinctive aversion to even such an approximately hellish denouement, and the difficulty he had devising one that would be more modern and optimistic, together account for his long delay and hesitation in continuing and completing *Faust*. In the 1797–1801 period he seems to have felt that he had at last solved the problem; we might say that the drama, or epic- dramatic poem, now had a centre, a dominating if not strictly unifying theme. The complex modern hero, the 'superman' as the Earth Spirit has mockingly called him, the creative personality beyond good and evil, who has thrown himself into earthly experience of all kinds and inevitably incurred serious guilt, this *magnus peccator* was at the very end to qualify for divine endorsement—but in some paradoxical and mysterious manner, quite unconnected (or as unconnected as was artistically possible) with the ordinary Christian ways of salvation. Eudo Mason (1967, 312) suggests with some plausibility, though perhaps with some overstatement, that during all the stages of the composition of *Faust* this issue was Goethe's central preoccupation, the unchanging 'essential purport' of the work. How was the superman, the Earth Spirit's protégé, the Devil's disciple, to be 'saved'? The ultimate fate of Faust was certainly a matter of public curiosity after the publication of Part One, and Goethe in embarrassment or irritation would decline to gratify it. Unable, perhaps, to cast off the last vestiges of Christian belief, he may still have thought of the question in theological terms, certainly in terms of some kind of metaphysical realism, such as the theory of the selective survival of the more powerful entelechy or monad.* Perhaps we may in any case rephrase the question as a psychological one: How does a complex and creative human psyche achieve maturity? What are the integrative, relaxing, 'epic' processes of growth in an exceptional and developing personality? What kind of poetic or spiritual journey (an *epic* journey, comparable to that undertaken by Dante in the *Divine Comedy*) must be made by this new explorer? Was such an exploration the central 'idea' which Goethe declared he did not know or could not put into words?

The gradual creation of the text of *Faust* is something like an analogue of the gradual creation of the 'text' of Goethe's own life. It would be convenient if we could with confidence add here 'and that of his hero', but the distinction between author and 'hero' must not be overlooked. In considering the later stages of Goethe's work on Part One during his mature 'classical' period, we have already noted that the poet's own development involved the emergence of a certain ironic distance between himself and the figure of Faust.* In Part Two, the distance is least in Acts I–III, where Faust's development symbolically but recognizably parallels Goethe's own, and greatest in Acts IV and V, where Goethe's ambiguous presentation of Faust is such as to have provoked much critical controversy. Many earlier commentators discerned in the poem as a whole a unilinear progress of its hero, through both Parts and the successive Acts, towards moral perfection, maturity, and enlightenment, a point at which his salvation would be 'deserved' (and therefore, indeed, unnecessary). Such a view, whether relying on Marxist theories of perfectibility or on the unassailable optimism of the Lord in the 'Prologue in Heaven', will now scarcely bear examination. But, while avoiding simplistic identifications, we can still say that the poem grew with the poet, even if the poet grew away from the hero. All three (the hero, the work, the author) intertwine in this dimension of *growth*, of living development: an area having less to do with logic or morality or artistic design than with a complex, only partly conscious inner evolution of the genius of a personal existence. We can still apply Goethe's own much-quoted words to *Faust* and call it yet another 'fragment of a great confession', or endorse his description of it as the expression of 'a rich and colourful and varied life' (whether we read that 'life' as Faust's or Goethe's or that of humanity). In all this, the critic must proceed delicately, inspecting, but not putting asunder, these unique symbioses. We should note, moreover, not only the *Entstehungsgeschichte* or genetic history of the text but also the fact that *Entstehung*, genesis, the process of coming into being, is itself a major theme *in* the text, perhaps its central theme. This gives an added tilt to the continuing debate in *Faust* criticism between the 'unitarian' or aesthetic-integrationist tendency and its opposite, the historicist-genetic method.* That we might claim Goethe's own endorsement for the latter (a thought suggested by the 'Dedication' preceding Part One, which entwines the poem with his biography, as well as by the prominence of the theme of development in Part Two) seems confirmed by his remark in a letter of 1803: 'We do not get to know works of nature and art as end-products; we must grasp them as they develop (*im Entstehen*) if we are to gain some understanding of them' (to Zelter, August 1803). (The implied comparison of a poem to a plant here is noteworthy.) A genetic approach does not in any case commit us to extreme 'fragmentarianism': it is compatible with the working assumption, which respect for the author requires of us until proof of the contrary, that *Faust* does have both some degree of unity overall and some coherence or pattern within its component parts. Actually, it is less difficult to maintain this assumption in the case of Part Two, which apart from some tentative beginnings was essentially written in Goethe's last six years, than in the case of Part One, on which he was intermittently engaged for about three decades; and this throws some light on his retrospective assertions that Part Two was designed to be 'less fragmentary', more rationally coherent than Part One (letter to Meyer, 20 July 1831, and conversation with Riemer, ? 1831). His method in Part Two is, however, deliberately enigmatic and allusive, operating with hints and half-hidden parallels (letter to Iken, 27 September 1827, and to Meyer, 20 July 1831). If interpretations are to be offered that will, in Nicholas Boyle's welcome phrase, 'stand the test of common sense' (Boyle 1982–3, 136), they must usually take account of matters external to the finished and published text, such as the author's earlier versions and variants, his known intentions and reading, events in his life or in history. The biographical method and the traditional enquiry into sources (*Quellenforschung*) have been decried as theoretically outmoded and merely 'positivistic' for much of this century, but were brilliantly vindicated by Katharina Mommsen, whose 1968 study in particular (*Natur- und Fabelreich* [The Realm of Nature and the Realm of Fable] *in Faust II*) is a landmark in *Faust* studies. Concentrating on Goethe's treatment of the Helen story, and especially on the extraordinary and fantastic second Act, Mommsen adduces in an interpretatively fascinating way his earlier versions of the material, his sources in classical Greek mythology, and notably also his sources in the *Arabian Nights* tales, which he reread intensively in a new translation just before resuming work on *Faust* in 1825. By scrupulous examination of the text against this background, she identifies a number of underlying themes, parallels, and patterns that might otherwise pass unnoticed, and reveals an unexpected degree of unity and continuity in Part Two which has usually been lost in the general mass of conjectural exegesis. I here follow gratefully in her footsteps.

In the same letter to Meyer (20 July 1831), written eight months before his death, Goethe states that he had carried the Part Two material about with him for many years 'as an inner fable [*inneres Märchen*]'. His use here of the word *Märchen* (fable, folk-tale, tale of magic; the usual debased translation 'fairy-tale' is misleading) has been given added significance by Mommsen's investigations. The 'many years' extended at least from the turn of the century, when some of Part Two was written or sketched, to the last creative period (1825–31) when the whole work was finished. So far as we know, not a line of the published text was composed between April 1801 and February 1825. In 1816, however, Goethe dictated to his secretary Kräuter a scenario or synopsis (see paralipomenon BA 70) of the 'tale' he was carrying in his mind; this interim report (or perhaps final report, if he did decide then, at the age of 67, that he would never be able to finish *Faust*) was at first meant for inclusion in *Poetry and Truth*, the autobiographical account of his early life (up to 1775) which he was then writing. The scenario was in fact left unpublished, but survives as a fascinating record of Goethe's early plan for what we now know as the contents of Acts I, III, and IV of Part Two. It is not clear how early this raw material is; some or all of it may even have existed since the 1770s, as the intended context of *Poetry and Truth* seems to suggest. It also differs markedly from the fragmentary opening of Act III written *c.*1800, which closely resembles the final version; this too suggests that the 1816 scenario perhaps records a conception dating back to Goethe's youth (for which the term '*Ur*-Helena' should really be reserved). In any event, it is one of the two most extensive and important documents to have survived among the unpublished earlier versions and variants, the many notes, sketches, and fragments that Goethe kept until his death for the benefit of future editors and commentators: a mass of manuscript material collectively known as the 'paralipomena'.* The 1816 scenario is referred to in the present edition as BA 70 (using the numbering of the paralipomena adopted in the Berlin edition*). The other item of special importance is paralipomenon BA 73 (q.v.), the much longer and more detailed sketch or scenario for Act II only, dictated in December 1826 and probably conceived at that time, although Act II itself was not finished until nearly four years later. These two prose scenarios are indispensable, especially the first, for the insight they give us into the metamorphoses undergone by Goethe's 'inner *Märchen*' over a period of anything up to fifty or sixty years between its initial conception (whenever that was) and the last few years of his life; and we should take note of these metamorphoses not merely by way of historicistic pedantry, but because the process of creative change, the *process* of Goethe's life and work (and more generally of life, of nature, of European culture) may itself be regarded as the 'essential purport' of the final version of Part Two, the version published some months after its author was no longer in a position to change it.

2 ACT I

One very notable passage that underwent this process may serve as an example of what happens many times in the genesis of Part Two.

The opening scene ('A beautiful landscape') is officially the first scene of Act I, but stands out sharply from the rest of the Act, and has rather the character of a prologue to Part Two generally, as I have editorially suggested. It was written partly in the spring of 1826 and partly in the summer of 1827, but its germ was the brief and crude prose version, conceived at least ten years earlier, which we find in BA 70 (q.v.). At the beginning of Act I, or to introduce it, Goethe needed an intelligible transition, a way of breaking the connection with Part One and continuing the Faust story in a quite different style and milieu; the tragic ending of the Gretchen drama must be decisively left behind, and Faust launched on a new career. A hero haunted by remorse would not suit Goethe's purposes; but one who could simply put the matter callously out of his mind would not do either. The solution, as Goethe explained to Eckermann in 1827,* was to plunge Faust into a trance-like or death-like sleep in which he would forget his recent experiences completely; and as had been done more than once in the 1797–1801 stratum of Part One, a chorus of spirits could be introduced, to practise on him a kind of suggestion therapy or hypnopaedia, after which he would wake refreshed and in a mood for the positive resumption of life. All this is common to both versions, the early sketch and the finished prologue. In the former, however, the spirits are merely tempting demons, urging Faust on to great deeds with dreams of worldly power and glory; their flattering propositions are 'in fact ironical'. Moreover, in this relatively banal earlier narrative, everything happens indoors, in an unidentified town from which Faust and Mephistopheles at once travel to Augsburg to present themselves to the Emperor Maximilian. In the final version, by contrast, the scene takes place quite literally 'in higher regions'. Faust lies asleep in a beautiful mountain landscape, watched over by nature-spirits whom Goethe identifies as elves, and who are compassionate and beneficent (Eckermann, same conversation). The theme of worldly action has disappeared (unless we read 4662–5 as a faint echo of it); the imperial court is not mentioned, and Mephistopheles is conspicuously absent. A different theme has developed, or (as other evidence from the paralipomena suggests) has suddenly taken over after long unconscious preparation,* and now dominates the material: that of the beauty of nature and its healing, integrative powers, which Goethe celebrates here in two of his greatest passages of lyric poetry, the elves' chorus evoking the passing night and the reborn Faust's speech hailing the sunrise. The theme of natural processes, including that of Faust's unconscious growth and healing, is thus identifiable as the important—indeed, central—element in the finished scene, in which the basic situation has been retained, but has undergone an inspired transformation and enhancement.

The rest of Act I (Sc. 2–7) is entirely concerned with events at the imperial court. About two-thirds of it was written between the summer of 1827 and February 1828, and two months later Goethe published this fragment in a new volume of his collected works, ending at line 6036 with the laconic statement 'To be continued'. He then turned to other work, and did not finish the remaining third of the Act until the latter part of 1829. With the exception of certain poetically outstanding passages, notably in Scene 5, the court scenes of Act I must probably be for most readers (to say nothing of translators) the least rewarding part of Part Two; the disproportionately lengthy Carnival scene (Sc. 3), in particular, is something of a literary embarrassment, and a producer would not be wrong to treat it less reverently than many scholars have done. Nevertheless, it is interesting to trace the *development* of what Goethe was apparently trying to do in this Act, and here again we can profitably compare the early prose sketch BA 70 with the end-product. In the former, Faust and Mephistopheles make their way to Augsburg, where Maximilian I is holding court (in the final version these specific identifications are dropped, and the Emperor becomes a stylized, composite figure). The Emperor receives the now famous magician graciously; but their meeting is a comic social failure, obliging Mephistopheles to come to Faust's rescue by magically replacing him as his *Doppelgänger*.* The Emperor makes the traditional request for Helen to be conjured up for him, and Faust disappears for a time 'to make the necessary preparations' (a point left unexplained). During this interval Mephistopheles, still disguised as Faust, ingratiates himself with the court ladies by magically curing their freckles and other physical defects. The tone of facetious comedy is maintained when Paris and Helen appear and are criticized respectively by the male and female spectators. Unspecified 'bizarre complications' lead to the sudden disappearance of the magical scene; 'the real Faust' falls in a swoon, Mephistopheles vanishes, and the company is left in confusion. There is no Carnival in this scenario, and no mention at all of certain themes that assume great prominence in the finished and vastly expanded Act I: the economic crisis in the Empire and the invention of paper money (Sc. 2, 4) or Faust's mysterious journey to the 'Mothers' in search of Helen (Sc. 5). This last scene, especially, is characteristic of Goethe's later and more serious conception, contrasting notably with the trivialities retained from the old scenario (such as Mephistopheles' role as quack cosmetician) or added in the first half of the Carnival scene.

As finally executed, the Court sequence in Act I falls into two unequal parts, the first and longer dominated by the theme of the Empire's bankruptcy, the second by that of the conjuration of Helen. Both are symbolic, and the first may be referred to any or all of various historical situations, such as the anarchic conditions in the Holy Roman Empire in the sixteenth century under Maximilian I, its terminal decay in the late eighteenth century, or the parlous state of the *ancien régime* in Louis XVI's France.* Equally, in Goethe's time there were a number of financial scandals and crises, in Germany and in England and France, resulting from the issue of paper credit.* In Act I, and indeed in Part Two generally, Goethe is in the last resort reflecting events of his age and especially patterns in his own life, and this makes it natural that before we come to Faust's search for classical beauty, we should have a 'political' sequence, just as Goethe's politically active career at the ducal court of Weimar began in 1776 and continued until 1786, when he made the journey to Italy with which the 'classical' phase of his development may be said to have begun. But over and above the merely autobiographical unity in Act I, its two main themes (the quest for wealth and the quest for 'Helen') can be seen as symbolic parallels. In an important letter written at the time when he was working on Scenes 2–4, Goethe refers to passages in his earlier and later poetry that have been considered obscure, and remarks (letter to Iken, 27 September 1827):

Since there is much in our experiences that cannot be clearly expressed and directly communicated, it has long been my practice to juxtapose images and let each of them, as it were, be a mirror to the other, in such a way as to reveal the more hidden meaning to attentive readers.

This method of allowing the intended theme to express itself indirectly and discreetly through parallels or contrasts is much used in *Faust*, in Part Two especially. Act I, despite its excessive length, gains a certain overall unity or continuity if we look upon its two main themes in this way. The Emperor's search for buried gold, on Mephistopheles' advice, ends in the specious substitution of paper money; Faust's search for Helen in perilous underground regions, also on Mephistopheles' advice, ends in her brief appearance as an insubstantial phantom. Goethe seems to insert a 'delicate hint' (letter to Meyer 20 July 1831) of this parallel in 6191 f. and more particularly in 6197–8:

> . . . conjuring Helen out of time
> Like phantom paper-money from the air

and 6315–16:

> Beauty's like buried treasure: where it lies
> Is known by art and magic to the wise.

A close association, or indeed symbolic equivalence, between the magical acquisition of wealth and the creation of beauty by the magically gifted poet is also suggested in the latter part of the Carnival masquerade (Sc. 3), which may thus also be integrated to some extent into the general sense of Act I.

Goethe had already written more than one masked pageant or revue of this kind for the Weimar court, he had witnessed the Carnival celebrations in Rome, and commentators have noted various other models or sources. He follows the conventions of the genre until about half-way through the scene, when the character of the events changes and they become magical happenings. The Herald, as master of ceremonies who describes what is taking place, is puzzled, and control of the proceedings seems to pass to Faust, who enters masked as Plutus, the god of riches. With him comes, as Goethe also explains to the puzzled Eckermann,* a figure from Act III (which he has already written but which has not yet officially happened): Faust's son Euphorion, here disguised as a young Charioteer. Both Euphorion and the Charioteer are allegories of Poetry, as we learn from the same conversation between Goethe and Eckermann and from the Charioteer himself:

> I am Profusion, I am Poetry
> (5573)

Both his kinship with Plutus and his word 'profusion' (literally 'prodigality') suggest a close association between poetic creativity and wealth, both of which seem to be combined in Plutus at the end of the masquerade, though at this earlier point (5610–29, 5689–708) the theme is perhaps rather the poet's gratitude to the rich patron on whom he depends. Here too we may detect an allusion to Goethe's own experience at Weimar, including his attempt to repair the finances of Karl August's duchy by reopening the Ilmenau silver-mine and his frequent desire for creative solitude amid his duties at court (5696). A further function of the scene (as often in such theatrical court entertainments) is to administer a discreetly allegorical moral lesson to the ruler himself: Faust is perhaps trying to educate the Emperor about the true nature and right use of wealth, as contrasted with Mephistopheles (Avarice), who can only put gold to vulgar uses (5779–94). Faust's treasure-chest seems to turn into a vat of molten gold (5739–51) and then into a fountain of fire (5920–5); as the Emperor stoops over this vision which should enlighten him, his beard catches fire, and a general conflagration and panic are averted only by Faust-Plutus's magic intervention (5926–86). The fire might be seen as a symbolic warning to the Emperor of the danger of war or revolution. Goethe's main source for this incident was an old chronicle which tells of a similar disaster at the court of Charles VI of France.* Mommsen has demonstrated, however, that in this part of Scene 3 and at the beginning of Scene 4 he is also making use of *Arabian Nights* story-motifs.* It is very significant that the Act I fragment published in April 1828 ends with the Emperor (6031–6, in Sc. 4) congratulating Mephistopheles on his imaginative inventiveness and comparing him to Scheherazade, the Sultan's wife in the frame-fiction of the *Tales* who prolongs her forfeited life by entertaining him with her inexhaustible fund of narrative. Taken in conjunction with the magic climax of the masquerade, this one express mention of the *Arabian Nights* tales and their narrator at the end of the 1828 fragment amounts (as Mommsen suggests) to a concluding celebratory homage by Goethe to the power of poetic imagination, and reinforces the thematic linkage between imaginative creativity and true wealth, the vision of classical beauty and the vision of hidden treasure.

The second phase of the court sequence in Act I begins with the 'Mothers' scene (Sc. 5, written in the autumn of 1829), which is also the opening point of the central Faust–Helen story in the finished Part Two as a whole. Faust's first attempt to capture the supreme

beauty is instructively unsuccessful. He 'descends' in search of her,
counselled by Mephistopheles in strange and compelling words
(6211–17, 6239–48, 6275–91), to those timeless, spaceless goddesses*
who are the ineffable origin of all living forms or all that was once
living; they are surrounded by the images of all creatures, their
business is metamorphosis and rebirth:

> Formation, transformation,
> The eternal Mind's eternal delectation.
>
> (6287–8)

From them, perhaps, Faust can retrieve for a while, as a poet might
do, a beauty that belongs to the past, enchanting it into a new kind
of life out of the flux of time. His speech in the conjuration scene
itself (Sc. 7, 6427–38), echoing the impressive obscurity of the
speeches he has just heard from Mephistopheles, confirms Goethe's
half-concealed intention to cast him in the role of a poet: in an earlier
draft for 6435 f. he had written not 'the bold magician' but 'the poet
boldly'. (Similarly, he had planned to make 'the poet' intervene
during the magic conclusion of the masquerade, but then decided
that Plutus with his magic staff was symbolically explicit enough.)
As Faust discovers, however, classical beauty cannot be truly recre-
ated within the Gothic constraints of medieval Christendom. Helen,
as Mephistopheles says of her, is 'not my period' (6209), and the Holy
Roman Empire of the German Nation is not hers. She will appear
only long enough for Faust to glimpse her and fall in love with her.
He must try again, set out on a still longer perilous quest. To be
sure, even after he has then found her, his union with her will be
brief; but a lesson will have been learnt, a point will have been made,
a great experience (10054) will have marked Faust (or Goethe or
humanity) for ever.

3 ACT II

We should remember that Act III, the 'Helena' Act, was not only
the first part of Part Two to be published, but also (apart from
possible fragments of Act V) the first to be written: the 'Mothers'
scene and all the events of Act II were major afterthoughts, added
four years later (in 1829–30) and designed retrospectively to provide

a basis or rationale for the already published Helen story. As we have seen, Goethe for a long time regarded the latter as almost a foreign body in Part Two: a 'phantasmagorical intermezzo', an episode, even as 'my *opus supererogationis*' (letter to Boisserée, 10 December 1826). But in the end, as he worked on the first two Acts, he tried to play down this whimsical and accidental character of 'Helena' and to integrate it into the action as a whole. In 1828 he told Zelter how anxious he was to finish Acts I and II, so that 'Helena' will be 'properly prepared' and follow naturally from the rest 'in an aesthetic and rational sequence' (letter of 24 January 1828). In the final Part Two the slightly apologetic subtitle 'classical-romantic phantasmagoria' is dropped, but in 1826–7 it was retained for the interim publication of 'Helena', and in presenting so extraordinary a piece to the public, Goethe felt that an explanatory advance blurb or preface was called for. The long prose sketch of Act II (paralipomenon BA 73, December 1826) was intended for this purpose, and in its concluding sentence Goethe advises his readers to study these 'antecedents' of the forthcoming 'phantasmagoria' with care. As he then changed his mind about publishing it, they were unable to follow this advice; but we can with advantage do so today for the better understanding of Act II as well as of Act III. (Since Act II is all late material, the earlier scenario of 1816, BA 70, contains nothing at all that corresponds to it, and passes straight from its equivalent of the end of Act I to its equivalent of the beginning of Act III, as we shall see later on.)

   Act II deals, though rather incompletely in its final version, with Faust's second quest for Helen, his long journey in space and time to the classical underworld. Having made the mistake of conjuring her into the wrong environment, he is himself taken back into the gloomy, medieval world of his former study, where he lies in a trance dreaming of her mythical begetting by Zeus, who in the form of a swan visits Leda as she bathes with her maidens. From this point, before he can 'draw back into life that unique form' (7438 f.), he must find his way to where Helen really belongs.* Here again Goethe uses *Arabian Nights* sources, but since the two cultures now to be symbolically contrasted with each other are those of the Germanic Middle Ages and of Greek classical and pre-classical antiquity, it is not possible to introduce Oriental material overtly, and he therefore masks it with Greek names and Greek mythology.* The central motif is that of the lovesick hero's long and difficult journey to win an apparently unattainable prize, such as the love of a spirit-princess. One story on this model is that of Prince Asem or Hassan and the Princess of the Flying Islands of Waak al Waak, whom he first saw bathing with her maidens; he has captured her for a time, but she has disappeared into another world, and to reach her he must pass through a region inhabited by strange monsters, warned and coun-selled by successive advisers, etc. In order to develop this motif in Greek style, Goethe invents (in BA 73 and Act II) the extraordinary 'Classical Walpurgis Night', an ironic counterpart to the Germanic 'Walpurgis Night' of Part One, the witches' sabbath on the Blocks-berg (Sc. 24, 25). The 'classical' version is a Greek rite of passage celebrated in Thessaly on every anniversary of the battle of Pharsalus in 48 BC: the decisive victory of Caesar over Pompey which sealed the fate of the Roman Republic and led to the establishment of the Empire under which the provincialization of the Greek world became complete.* Faust must attend this ghostly festival and there find an entry to Helen's world. Since Mephistopheles has proved incompetent in this matter, a new magical link is required, a new adviser or 'helper' who can remove Faust from the world of Rome's successor, the Holy Roman Empire, and take him back to classical Greece. It is at this point that Goethe introduces the second extra-ordinary feature of the Act II material: the figure of the alchemical mannikin or 'homunculus'.

As he knew from his youthful reading, the alchemists of the late Middle Ages believed that it was possible to create artificial miniature human beings by mixing human sperm with other ingredients according to mysterious and disgusting recipes;* the homunculus would resemble a tiny human body, but would be transparent and incorporeal. The difficult *opus* of making such a creature was closely associated with the search for the Philosophers' Stone which would turn base metals into gold; the homunculus was indeed often symbolically identified with the Stone. He was usually born with some deficiency, such as the lack of a solid body or an unintegrated sexual duality, and thus signified potential metamorphosis, growth to full stature or to a higher, more perfect state. This is already enough to suggest that the Homunculus and Faust are intended as parallel figures, but Goethe's development of this point is com-plex. Both Faust and the Homunculus are also associated, in his conception, with what (very loosely adapting a term from Aristotle's metaphysics, with some Leibniz thrown in) he called the 'entelechy': the unit or monad of discarnate spiritual force which survives the death of the body or precedes physical existence. In the final scene of Act V, after Faust's death, the angels are carrying his 'immortal part [*Fausts Unsterbliches*]', which in a manuscript variant Goethe here also calls 'Faust's entelechy'; and he is reported to have told Eckermann that the Homunculus represented 'the pure entelechy, the intelligence, the spirit as it comes into being before all experience; for man's spirit is already highly gifted when it arrives here'.*

But Goethe's original Homunculus, in the 1826 sketch BA 73, does not have this lofty symbolic role. For one thing, the 'chemical mannikin' (not yet dignified by his Latin name) has here evidently been 'begotten' by Wagner, Faust's pedantic research assistant whom we encountered in Part One, who still works in his former master's quarters and has taken to alchemy. Wagner's function in Part One was to be the target of the young Goethe's constant satirical parodying of dry academic learning, scholarship remote from life; his progeny, therefore, is in the first instance fittingly conceived as the embodiment of excessively cerebral qualities. The original Homunculus's approach to classical antiquity is historicistic, greatly preoccupied with dates; as he flies to Greece on the magic carpet with Faust, Wagner, and Mephistopheles, he entertains them on the way with 'an unending flood of geographical and historical detail on every place they pass over'. He knows not only the correct date of the battle of Pharsalus but also its chronological coincidence with the recurring Classical Walpurgis Night; we are told that 'his head contains a general historical universal calendar'. He is in fact uncannily like what we now call the *idiot savant*, the autistic prodigy with a freakish gift of memory or calculation. It may be that Goethe perceived this (could he ever have encountered the phenomenon or read about it?) as the initial defect of a purely 'spiritual' or cerebral, not yet physical, being. The point is not developed further in the prose sketch, where indeed the mannikin's only real function seems to be that of proposing the trip to classical Greece, in which as a scholar he is naturally interested. All this has led some commentators to suggest that the 'learned' Homunculus satirically represents the intellectually limited scholars of Goethe's time, busily travelling for their professional self-improvement. The mannikin of the prose sketch travels in his learned progenitor's breast pocket, and seems to share Wagner's hope that a female homunculus can perhaps somehow be scraped together out of the dust of the Thessalian battlefield. Both he and Wagner disappear from the narrative at an early stage.

The final version of the 'Classical Walpurgis Night', written in the earlier months of 1830 about three and a half years after the BA 73 sketch, greatly enhances and elaborates the role of the Homunculus, increasing its prominence and seriousness. Although still presented with a trace of irony, he is now no longer simply the offspring of Wagner: Goethe makes it clear, or almost clear (6683 f., 7003 f.*) that Mephistopheles has had a hand in his making. He now (Sc. 9) has magical vision enabling him to see Faust's dream about Helen's parentage as Faust is dreaming it (6903–20*). He instinctively understands Faust's longing for classical Greece, and feels actively impelled to travel there with him. Wagner, the mere antiquarian, is left behind in his Gothic surroundings. The Homunculus's story is similar to Faust's: he pursues a distant goal, not a princess but the bodily existence which he still lacks. His freakish artificiality is emphasized by the fact that he does not at once break his glass retort and step out of it, as in the sketch, but floats carefully about inside it.* There are repeated, slightly comic expressions of his apprehension that the glass might break (6881, 8093, 8235 f.): this must not happen until the right moment comes, and yet he is impatient for that moment (7832). The philosopher Thales, seeking advice on his behalf from Proteus, the god of metamorphosis, explains that the Homunculus '*möchte gern entstehn*' (8246 in the German text)—he would dearly like to come into being, to be born properly, to acquire a body:

> His intellectual qualities are many,
> But earthly solid life he has hardly any.
> This glass retort's still all that gives him weight;
> His wish now's to become incorporate.
>
> (8249–52)

He will achieve this only by undergoing the natural processes of evolution, beginning in the sea. His programme, as Thales puts it, is to

> Move onward by eternal norms
> Through many thousand thousand forms,
> And reach at last the human state.
>
> (8324–6)

The moment at which the Homunculus begins this long journey is the moment of his sudden passion for the goddess Galatea, as she comes riding Venus-like over the waves. Moved by 'Eros, first cause of all' (8479; literally, 'Eros who began it all'), he leaps on the back of Proteus, who has now changed into a dolphin, and shatters his glass against Galatea's chariot, in creative self-immolation. The final version culminates in a kind of pageant of the elements, a festive setting for this 'marriage' between the Homunculus and the sea.

Both the Homunculus and Faust, on their parallel but diverging journeys, encounter a series of advisers (the 'helpers' of the *Märchen* tradition), and in this respect they both resemble the questing hero of the *Arabian Nights* tales. The characteristic pattern is that each of the helpers (they are usually older figures, called in the *Tales* 'spirit teachers' or 'spirit uncles') passes the hero on to the next, until finally he is shown how to reach his goal. Faust is carried by Mephistopheles to his first effective helper, the Homunculus himself: a magic omniscient creature suspended, like Petronius's sibyl, in a glass vessel. (In an *Arabian Nights* story one of the helpers or talismans acquired by the heroine is a magic omniscient talking bird which never leaves its cage.) Arriving in Thessaly (the land of magic *par excellence*, as the ancients believed), he recovers consciousness, and first consults the Sphinxes, who advise him to ask Chiron, the divine centaur, wise pedagogue to so many heroes. Unseduced from his quest by the nymphs of the river Peneus, he meets the galloping Chiron, who carries him down the Peneus to a temple near Mount Olympus, where he hands him over to the aged prophetic sibyl Manto, recommending him to her as a psychiatric patient. Manto, like Erichtho, is also a Thessalian sorceress with necromantic powers, and at one stage (according to another of the 1826 fragments) Goethe's plan was to have Helen's release negotiated at a high level with Persephone, the queen of the dead, by 'daemonic sibyls' from the mountains of Thessaly. The final version, modifying this, has Manto conduct Faust into a dark cavern in the mountain base, an entrance to Hades which (as BA 73 tells us) gapes open every year on the anniversary of Pharsalus, remembering how many dead it swallowed up on that day. By this route Faust and Manto will descend to Persephone and together plead with her to let Helen go, citing various precedents in Greek mythology for such a dispensation. Here the *Arabian Nights* parallel and source is again the story of Prince Asem: nearing the end of his quest, the prince is helped by an aged woman who takes him to the court of the Spirit Queen. There his beloved is being held captive, and is about to be condemned to death for marrying a mortal; but the old woman, who is the queen's nurse, defends the princess and secures her release.

Goethe evidently attached importance to the similar dramatic climax of his own hero's journey; but for reasons which have been much debated by critics, the Faust–Manto–Persephone scene was never written, with the result that, about a third of the way through the 'Classical Walpurgis Night' sequence, Faust merely disappears underground with his guide, and we lose sight of him for about a thousand lines. Instead, we witness the foolish adventures of Mephistopheles in this unsuitable Greek setting, until he too disappears underground (8033) two-thirds of the way through the sequence. The last third of it is dominated by the continuation and elaboration of the story of the Homunculus, which has thus effectively replaced that of Faust as the centre of attention. As late as February 1830 Goethe still planned to end Act II with the scene in Hades; in June he thought of transferring it to Act III as a prologue; but in the end he simply left it out altogether. The easygoing view of this omission or rearrangement, adopted by some critics, is to accept it as another 'epic' licence, whereby (in defiance of the classical laws of dramatic proportion) Goethe omits what might be thought to be dramatically central material but digresses elaborately at other points. Or we may call it a further example of Goethe's occasional cavalier treatment of the 'characters' in *Faust*, who are at times not so much psychologically realistic persons as convenient mouthpieces uttering whatever general theme may at the time be in the forefront of the author's interest: an instance in Part One is Faust's dramatically irrelevant soliloquy about natural phenomena at the beginning of the 'Forest Cavern' scene (Sc. 17). This tendency is especially pronounced in Part Two, and is indeed one of the features that mark it as a product of Goethe's old age. It has been pointed out, by Anthony Storr for instance (1989, esp. ch. 11), that in his 'last period' a writer or other artist will characteristically be less concerned with empathetically creating an interpersonal 'drama' than with expressing his thoughts, setting up and exploring an inward synthesis of his own. As well as the move from the dramatic to the epic mode which we have already noted, we thus have in *Faust* Part Two a move from realistic drama to allegorical or symbolic expression. In the present instance, Goethe seems in the latter part of the 'Classical Walpurgis Night' to be chiefly concerned with the theme of natural processes and metamorphoses: did he judge that it could be better expressed with Faust absent and the Homunculus doing duty for him? Or that it might seem repetitious, since Faust has been down to mysterious lower regions once already, to lay undue emphasis on a second such descent? In any case, he seems to have felt that the missing link between the Sea Festival and Menelaus's palace, like that between the Act I prologue and the Emperor's court and other such transitions, could be left for the reader to supply.*

And this may be all there is to it. Reporting the completion of the 'Classical Walpurgis Night' to Zelter (letter of 4 January 1831), Goethe writes: 'Enough! At the beginning of Act III Helen enters without further ado.' On the other hand, it may be that the Homunculus's adventures in search of *Entstehung* are not so much a spontaneous digression from the story of Faust as a calculated symbolic continuation of it. The latter view is sustainable in so far as we can broadly establish the already noted parallel or equivalence between the alchemical sub-hero and the official hero himself, notwithstanding the former's Mephistophelian provenance, or perhaps even precisely because he is a cross between Wagner and Mephistopheles. Both the Homunculus and Faust, we might say, are moved by the sudden erotic vision of a unique and Hellenic beauty to embark, each in his own way, on a quest which is to bring about the *Entstehung* or self-fulfilment of each of them, and in Faust's case also the *Entstehung* of his beloved. The process is similar, though the Homunculus ends at the point of his vision and Faust begins with it, at Helen's phantom appearance in Act I. After this fiasco in the world of the imperial court and Wagner's laboratory, the helpless Faust must accept the assistance of the Homunculus, who is making a similar transition from the sphere of mere learning to that of the central mysteries of life. Both of them, each in his own way, have to experience a kind of education or growth. This, incidentally, means that the old satirical interpretation of the Homunculus as a caricature of mere learning is not basically incompatible with the official interpretation of him as the symbol of the striving 'entelechy': as such, he represents the desire to become what he potentially is, to grow out of cerebrality into a bodily and emotional self. The

Homunculus is, so to speak, a doctor to Faust who heals himself as well.

There can be little doubt as to the significance of these themes on the autobiographical level. In 1828-9 Goethe was putting together and editing, from old letters and diaries, the third and last part of the *Italian Journey*, his own record of an experience (1786-8) that had been not only the threshold of his mature 'classical' work as a poet and dramatist, but also probably the most important turning-point in his personal life. On the 'classical soil' of Italy, as he was to call it in the *Roman Elegies* of 1790, he had felt transformed, healed, reborn; his memories of that time were clearly alive as he began writing the 'Classical Walpurgis Night' early in 1830. Faust's reaction as Mephistopheles and the Homunculus set him down on the soil of Greece is similar: reviving again out of his death-like state, as in the Prologue, and finding himself in Greece as if by a miracle, he feels like the giant Antaeus, whose strength was increased every time he touched his mother Earth (7070-7). At this point the three travellers separate, and each moves off in a different direction. Faust and the Homunculus are both still questing heroes, but there is a difference of emphasis between them in the series of helpers they consult. In Faust's case the recurrent theme is that he needs 'healing' or 'cure' (a suggestion which he himself of course indignantly repudiates, 7459 f.): Mephistopheles has already referred him to the Homunculus for this purpose (6901), Chiron judges him to be mentally deranged (7446-8, 7487), and in order to emphasize this motif Goethe has in the finished version deliberately changed the traditional mythological parentage of Faust's final helper Manto, making her a daughter not of Tiresias but of the god of medicine Aesculapius and a sister of his aptly named daughters Iaso, Hygiea, and Panacea. The Homunculus, on the other hand, consults the natural philosopher Thales, the wise sea-god Nereus, and lastly Proteus, who is both a sea-god and the god of transformation. They all advise him about physical *Entstehung*, the process of coming into being, the natural birth of form out of the unformed. And it is noticeable that this enquiry into natural laws is now extended from the organic to the inorganic sphere: into the geological argument about the formation of the earth's crust. The sea, as the creative element in which all things originate, is now in the forefront of attention. The philosophers Thales and Anaxagoras, representing respectively the rival geological theories of 'neptunism' and 'vulcan-ism' in Goethe's day,* were already ironically played off against each other in the prose version; in the final text the neptunist Thales has gained greater prominence and seriousness as the Homunculus's preferred mentor, who introduces him to Proteus and thus to his marine and evolutionary destiny. Even the name 'Proteus' is a small clue to the connection between all this and Goethe's own scientific interests. Quoting, in 1829, what he had written from Italy in 1787 about his botanical theory of the 'primal plant' and his hopes of discovering it in the luxuriant gardens of Palermo or Naples, he recalls his sudden insight (as he believed it to be) into leaf form as the unifying principle underlying all plant morphology: his realiza-tion that in it 'the true Proteus lies hidden, able to conceal and reveal himself in all possible shapes'. 'Proteus', in this comment written not long before the Homunculus scenes, is Goethe's meta-phor for the natural processes, their personification. Incorrect though his botanical theories may have been, there is no denying the importance for Goethe, and to some extent also scientifically, of his intensive preoccupation with a number of natural sciences from about 1780 onwards. The list of them, extending through the rest of his life, included geology, mineralogy, comparative anatomy (leading to his discovery in 1784 of the human intermaxillary bone), botany, optics, and meteorology. His scientific writings occupy many volumes of his collected works, and he was even inclined to value his controversial *Theory of Colours* (1790–1810) more highly than anything else he had written. His Italian journey, offering him as it did a wealth of new observations, was a landmark on the scientific as well as the literary side of his development. It was in the context of this visit to Italy that he wrote the already mentioned 'Forest Cavern' soliloquy of Part One, Scene 17; here it was not so much Goethe the dramatist as Goethe the natural historian who spoke through Faust, giving thanks to the Earth Spirit for revealing its secrets to him.

All this suggests that if we are to interpret the similar yet divergent figures of Faust and the Homunculus autobiographically, they must be held to represent the development and education of, respectively, Goethe's poetic and his scientific genius. The symbolic role of Faust as the poet was already hinted at in Act I, as we have seen, and the hints continue in the 'Classical Walpurgis Night', both in the finished text and in the 1826 sketch. In both, Faust's descent into the underworld is compared to that of Orpheus, the mythical inventor of song and poetry. In the final version, his guide Manto is also associated with the Castalian spring, sacred to Apollo and the Muses and thought to turn men into poets; Chiron (7461) urges Faust to drink from it. In the 1826 sketch Manto at one point, during their descent to Hades, suddenly casts her veil over him to protect him from the sight of the Gorgon (see Paralipomena, p. 249); this is a deliberate allusion to the similar remarkable incident in Dante's *Inferno* (ix. 55–60), where Virgil saves Dante's life in the same way as he is guiding him down through Hell. In other words, Faust is indirectly identified not only with the poet Orpheus but also with the poet Dante, who under the tutelage of another poet is making, like Faust, a spiritual or psychotherapeutic journey. Faust, as the Homunculus remarks 'must thrive in this *myth-land*' (7054 f., emphasis added; literally, 'in the kingdom of fable', *im Fabelreich*). He must be healed by becoming a true poet; whereas the 'chemical mannikin' is to be made whole by becoming a scientist, by existentially discovering nature's hidden yet manifest laws. The Homunculus–Galatea action is the scientist's almost mystically passionate pursuit of insight into the natural world; the bodily fulfilment of the 'entelechy' is the maturing of this insight. The parallel between the Homunculus and Faust is thus complex and differentiative, without amounting to an out-and-out negative parallel or contrast. There is no need to turn the distinction between the scientist and the artist into a polarized antithesis, to the disadvantage of the latter, as Mommsen seems inclined to do. The 'fable-kingdom' of aesthetic vision, of poetic imagination, is not necessarily inferior to the 'real' world of natural existence and natural law; the 'magician' and the natural historian complement each other. In an essay* written not long after his return from Italy, Goethe had argued that a mature, truly classical 'style' (he seems to have meant style in the visual arts, but with possible application to literature) can develop only on the basis of a deep study of the natural world: '*Style* rests upon the deepest foundations of knowledge, on the very essence of things, in so far as we are permitted to behold it in visible and tangible forms'. It must have been his wish to achieve a synthesis, or at least a working accommodation, between these two sides of his nature; whether he fully succeeded in doing so is another matter.

If the complex affinity between Faust and the Homunculus lends a certain unity of structure to Act II, can this unity also subsume the scenes involving Mephistopheles? The notion of bringing the Christian Devil into the world of Helen and Greek mythology, in the stylistically appropriate disguise of an aged hideous hag, belongs properly to the 'Helena' Act; the motif appears in paralipomenon BA 70, and the hag had already been identified in the 1800 'Helena' fragment as one of the Phorcyads or Graiae. In the finalized 'antecedents' for Act III, Mephistopheles must be shown finding his way to this necessary transformation. In Wagner's laboratory, the percipient Homunculus has predicted not only that Faust will be 'in his element' in the classical world, but that Mephistopheles will also encounter the notorious witches of Thessaly (6977 ff.). Accordingly, much of the 'Classical Walpurgis Night' has been devoted to his unfunny lustful adventures (a vein of half-hearted publishable indecency in which Goethe is not at his best); but he has been obliged to recognize that he is quite out of place in a remote pre-Christian world which knows nothing of good and evil or conventional morality. Thus Scene 10 as a whole, if it is a whole, may be said to follow out three thematic strands: Faust's pursuit of Helen, the Homunculus's pursuit of bodily existence and eventually of Galatea, and Mephistopheles' pursuit of the Lamiae and other monsters, as if to demonstrate at his cynical level that all enterprises broadly describable as sexual are much the same. His lengthy contribution to the events ends in his *badinage* and comical negotiation with the Phorcyads and his metamorphosis into the appearance of one of them. The daughters of Phorcys, so old that they have only one eye and one tooth left between them, live in a place where the sun never shines, and embody a kind of absolute ugliness and squalor, the polar opposite of the absolute beauty represented by Helen. They describe themselves as daughters of the original Chaos, and as a spirit of negation Mephistopheles feels himself instantly akin to them. In Part One, after all, Faust had called him 'strange son of chaos' (1383), and he had defined himself as part of the original Darkness (1350). He has, so to speak, returned to his original void to discover a new identity as 'Phorcyas' (i.e. 'a Phorcys-daughter'), and sardonically redefines himself as 'the well-beloved son' of Chaos—or possibly its daughter, since, as he also notes, he is now hermaphroditical (8029) like the Homunculus (8256). It is interesting, however, that in the

Phorcyad episode Goethe is making a possibly very significant use
of a classical Greek parallel, the story of Perseus. The hero Perseus,
a son of Zeus, is persuaded by his false friend Polydectes to bring
him the head of the Gorgon Medusa, and first seeks out the Phor-
cyads, who have ancient and powerful connections and are related
to the Gorgons; he compels them to help him in his dangerous task
by snatching their eye and tooth from them. As Mommsen conjec-
tures, Goethe is here perhaps tacitly suggesting (to readers learned
enough to catch the allusion) that Mephistopheles has after all
discovered a way of obliging Faust in the matter of Helen by fetching
her from Hades himself (8032 f.). In BA 73 there is, in fact, an allusion
to important unspecified terms in the agreement between him and
the Phorcyads, over and above the loan of the eye and the tooth;
and it may be that this explains the degree of magical power* he
appears to have over Helen when he reappears in Act III in the
Phorcyad mask.

4   ACT III

There is a certain mystery about the abrupt dramatic transition from
the 'Classical Walpurgis Night' to the opening of the 'Helena' Act,
which we should not try too hard to dispel. Some earlier commen-
tators even sought to bridge the gap by identifying Helen with the
(hermaphroditic) Homunculus, on the assumption that he will by
now have undergone the 'thousand, thousand forms' of his evolution
and become 'the beautiful human being' which Goethe had long
ago, in his essay on Winckelmann (1805) called 'the supreme product
of nature's perpetual self-enhancement'. While accepting the relev-
ance of this Goethean remark, we need not be over-literal. As Goethe
explained in the letter quoted above, his method was to be content
with suggestive juxtaposition. Act III is at least structurally connected
to its 'antecedents' (as Act II can unofficially be called) by a strong
effect of contrast: the creative chaos and flux of the Sea Festival, a
half-lit, lost-and-found scene of waves and moonlight, an operatic
riot of voices speaking and singing in rhymed verse, suddenly give
way to the static, sunlit figure of the heroine, emerging in high relief
against this background, the single voice of the protagonist opening
her Attic drama in stately trimeters. And there are other contrasts

and anticipations: the paradoxical world of the 'Classical Walpurgis Night' is not so much classical as pre-classical, archaic, pre-heroic, a pageant not of Olympian gods or Homeric heroes but of figures from earlier stories and a stranger demonology, Sphinxes who confess that Helen is not their period (7197 f.), Galatea who is not the great Aphrodite but her lesser heir, unobtrusive attendants who celebrate the timeless nature-rite regardless of passing centuries and cultures (8370–8); to say nothing, if Mommsen is right, of the hidden Oriental influence. This is a betwixt-and-between world, a condition between reality and fantasy, in which Faust re-experiences his vision of the begetting of Helen, but cannot decide whether he is seeing or dreaming or remembering (7271–312). Helen is, as it were, still in the making, not yet born, not yet ready to step ashore out of the rocking, intoxicating sea (8489 f.). The style is ambiguous, shifting ironically between lyric seriousness and persiflage (7080–98, 7426 ff.). Except for the sinister opening trimeters of the witch Erichtho (7005–39), the incongruous rhymed verse prevails: the ancient trimeter will not resume until Helen herself speaks and a drama in the fully classical style comes into being.

Although the 1826 narrative (BA 73) casts light on the events of the 'Helena' Act in certain important respects, it was intended as a preface to these events, and therefore stops short of the beginning of them. For comparison with an earlier (perhaps the earliest) version of what happens after Helen actually appears, we must go back to the 1816 document (BA 70). This relatively brief sketch (which, as we have noted, may represent an even earlier conception than the 1800 'Helena' fragment) tells a fairly straightforward story, foreshadowing the final version at certain points. Faust, infatuated with Helen's apparition at the imperial court, demands bodily possession of her: he is filled, we are told, with 'infinite longing for the supreme beauty he has now recognized'. He does not, however, have to make a long journey in time and space to the classical Greek underworld in search of her. Helen, restored to life by the old device of a magic ring, meets him in a medieval German castle which she mistakes for her husband's palace in Sparta; Faust is disguised as a crusading knight and Mephistopheles as an aged female housekeeper (not yet Hellenized as Phorcyas). A male caretaker with magic powers is also present. The theme of magic is prominent, though the symbolic implications have not been developed. The most important antici-

pation of the final version is that in the 1816 scenario a magic circle
has been drawn round the castle, and Helen can continue her
'half-real' existence only if she remains within it. Goethe's final
treatment of this motif of prohibition or restriction will be to take
up an ancient Greek parallel: the legend according to which Helen
was allowed to return from the dead on condition that she remained
on Leuce, an island in the Black Sea. This dispensation had been
obtained for her by the hero Achilles, himself now also dead, but
permitted to meet Helen on Leuce and there beget from this ghostly
union a son called Euphorion. Goethe will adopt the essentials of
this story: Achilles as the classical precedent* for Faust's post-mortal
union with Helen, Euphorion as the name of their son,* and the
similar stipulation restricting her to a particular territory (in this case
Sparta).* In the 1816 scenario the son (not yet named) is also subject
to a prohibition: he may go anywhere he likes within the precincts
of the castle, but must not cross the magic circle. Prohibitions are of
course a very well-known motif in the *Märchen* and myths of the
world (as when Bluebeard's wife is allowed to open every door in
his castle except one, or Adam and Eve may eat of every tree in the
garden except one). In the final version, the one constraint on
Euphorion is that he must not attempt to fly. In both versions the
son disobeys and is killed, whereupon Helen vanishes (in the 1816
scenario because, wringing her hands in grief, she loses the ring on
which her bodily shape depends). The 1816 version ends with a war
between Faust and the monks who have dissolved the magic circle
and tried to seize the castle;* he defeats them and acquires 'great
possessions', which seem to foreshadow on a simpler level the lands
he eventually wins from the sea in Acts IV and V.

This early 'inner *Märchen*' about Faust and Helen is the relatively
simple basis of the enriched, enhanced, elaborately allegorical final
version: the three scenes (11, 12, 13) of Act III. Nor should we lose
sight altogether of Goethe's two earlier subtitles for 'Helena', both
of which disappeared in the final edition. The 1800 fragment was
called 'Helena in the Middle Ages. A satyric drama. Episode for
Faust': this reminds us that the Helen affair is an 'episode', that it
will span the centuries in a fantastic manner, and that it is not prima
facie a tragedy (the classical Greek 'satyr play' was performed
immediately after the tragic trilogy as a piece of vulgar light relief).
The 1827 'Helena', as we have seen, was announced as 'a classical-

romantic* phantasmagoria'. The term 'phantasmagoria' is entirely appropriate, since the poet has chosen to operate wholly outside temporal constraints (7433). As Goethe himself pointed out (letter to Boisserée, 22 October 1826), the whole Act spans a period of some three thousand years, beginning with the supposed return of Helen from the Trojan War and ending with the death of Byron which the fall of Euphorion is supposed to symbolize. During all this compressed non-time Helen is 'alive' and can bear Faust a son, though at certain moments she wonders whether she is in fact 'real' or merely a phantom, as Mephistopheles tauntingly suggests (8876–81, 8930 ff.). These existential doubts give her a certain dramatic pathos, but we need not demand an exact ontology of her status in this Act, by comparison with her phantasmal manifestation in Act I, as some critics have done, insisting at one extreme that the Helen of Act III is real Greek flesh and blood born in the way of nature, or at the other that the whole thing, and perhaps Act II as well, is no more than a dream in Faust's mind anyway. The point is not whether the Helen of Act III is 'real' enough, but whether Faust is by now educationally mature enough, whether he (or Goethe or the European mind) can now achieve a creative union with 'Helen', whether he is now qualified to reinstate for a time the fragile classical beauty and classical culture that she represents.* Above all, it is not necessary to dismiss Faust's encounter with Helen as merely a tragic, ghostly illusion. The basic logic of the traditional story demands in any case that Helen should appear to Faust twice and vanish twice, at least if the motif of the long quest is to be used and if this is to be an episode and not the end of Faust's adventures; there is no question of her staying with him permanently, and a way must be found of returning her sooner or later to wherever she came from. This does not detract from the symbolic value of their meeting. On the allegorical level, it is a celebratory homage, the final homage of Goethe's life, to that culture of Greek antiquity which for so long and so profoundly influenced the culture of modern Europe, not least the literary classicism of Weimar which was Goethe's own personal version of the Renaissance. A celebration, yet also an elegiac recognition that there cannot be a lasting synthesis of ancient and modern. A meeting and mingling of two cultural traditions is allegorized as a magic love-story. The 'union' of the lovers could be called short-lived, if it were taking place in time. Nevertheless, the ideal is restated; the high noon of Goethe's experience, and of German cultural history, becomes that of the symbolic hero.

In the first scene, that of Helen's supposed homecoming to ancient Sparta, Faust is not present, but is waiting for her to be brought to him, as the tenuous link with the old Faust legend still requires. Scene II opens unambiguously in the manner of an Aeschylean or Euripidean tragedy: the heroine and her chorus of captive Trojan women outside the palace, her expository monologue in iambic trimeters, the chorus answering with lyric odes in triadic form, a foreboding of doom, a monstrous prophetic figure confronting the heroine and the chorus, single-line altercations ('stichomythia', as in 8810–25), passages of agitated trochaic tetrameter (8909–29, etc.).* As the situation and the role of Phorcyas-Mephistopheles develop, the style shifts towards comedy (9010–24, 9044–8, and very notably Mephistopheles' mock-macabre preparations for Helen's execution, 8937–46). On her consenting to seek the stranger's protection, the scene clouds over and changes, overleaping the centuries but not moving far in space, and Helen comes to Faust in his medieval castle. In this central scene (12) of the play as well as of Act III, Goethe combines, with great subtlety and originality, the immediate story and its allegorical significance as a marriage of classical and modern cultures. This is done very simply by prosodic metamorphosis. The ancient rhymeless trimeter has been retained until the moment of Faust's ceremonious entry, but here, hardly perceptibly at first, it begins to disappear: Faust speaks in the iambic pentameters of Shakespeare's 'blank verse', which had become the classic line of Goethean and Schillerian drama, and Helen instinctively answers in the same metre. From this point on, the dialogue is further and progressively enriched with medieval and modern verse forms. Faust's watchman Lynceus speaks in rhymed quatrains like a *Minnesänger*; Helen, puzzled by the recurring sounds that so strangely beautify the ends of his lines, must be instructed by Faust on 'the way our peoples speak'. As they draw nearer together, she answers him in lines first end-rhymed (9377–84) and then internally rhymed as well (9411–18). This extraordinary poetic courtship also has an Oriental source, revealed by its precedent in Goethe's own work: one of the poems in the *West-Eastern Divan* tells the legend of the Persian poet Behramgur, whose beloved mistress Dilaram helped him to invent rhymed verse by echoing his words.* This poem (1818) had in its turn enshrined a personal memory, that of his brief happiness in 1814–15 with Marianne von Willemer, the 'Suleika' of the *Divan*: by a curious interaction of inspiration, their love had also moved Marianne to write love-poems echoing those sent to her by Goethe, in the same style and of a quality equal to his.* In the Faust–Helen passage the dramatic meaning, the autobiographical meaning, and the allegory ('so far away and yet so near . . . long past and yet so new') are perfectly blended.

At the culminating point of Faust's love-dialogue Phorcyas-Mephistopheles, absent for the last 400 lines since rescuing Helen and her women from the vengeance of Menelaus, bursts in to warn them that the outraged husband is approaching at the head of his army. Unitarian critics who cannot forget Faust's Wager* in Part One argue that Mephistopheles chooses this moment to interrupt because Faust has just, in effect, blessed the passing moment (9417 f.) and thus probably lost his bet (1699 ff.). But while it is true that the Faust of Act III is the Faust not so much of perpetual striving and divine discontent as of maturity and fulfilment, it would for reasons already mentioned be implausible to press the point about consistency. Nor need we consider too curiously the question of the 'reality' or otherwise of the threat from Menelaus which Mephisto-pheles reports or invents for obvious dramatic reasons. More difficult questions arise when we consider the historical and allegorical aspects of Faust's supposed presence in Greece and the warlike role he and Menelaus now assume.

Goethe's earlier plan, sketched as we have seen in the 1816 para-lipomenon, was that Helen should appear by magic in a castle in Germany, occupied by Faust while its owner fights in one of the Crusades. When he came to work on the final version in 1825, he modified and developed this idea in the light of his researches at that time into the early history of the Peloponnese (or the 'Morea' as it was also called in medieval and later times). In one of the *Elegies* that celebrate his own rejuvenating contact with the 'classical soil' of Rome in 1788, he had ironically compared himself to a barbarian from the north, taking possession of Rome in the person of his Roman mistress 'Faustina'. What he learnt now about the successive invasions of Greece by various northern barbarian tribes, before and after the sack of ancient Sparta by Alaric the Goth in AD 395, provided him with a similar motif which could be vaguely based on historical fact. The 'northern' Faust was to go to the Peloponnese in search of Helen; he might thus be compared not only to the southward-migrating Germanic tribes of the Dark Ages but also to the not essentially dissimilar crusading settlers from various parts of Western Europe who, in the early thirteenth century, carved up the peninsula, set up usurping principalities all over what was after all a territory of the Christian Byzantine Empire, and built military strongholds at various points. The descriptions by Lynceus (9281–96) and by Faust himself (9446–73) of Faust's army and its activities identifies him loosely with all these invaders. He is of course a composite and generalized figure, like the Emperor in Acts I and IV, and the same goes for his symbolic 'Gothic' castle (9017–30), which need not be thought of as corresponding to any specific place. Goethe adopts a violently compressed time-scale, and treats the events in a highly selective manner, changing historical and geographical facts at will for the sake of his broad general purpose of bringing about some kind of encounter, as his story demanded, between a Greek classical heroine and a German medieval knight. Some details suggest, how-ever, that he may have particularly had in mind the Fourth Crusade and the period immediately following it. At this time, members of the Frankish Villehardouin dynasty, on their way from Palestine to share the spoils of the infamous sacking and desecration of Constan-tinople in 1204, were blown off course and landed near Pylos (9454 f.). They subdued the whole region, styled themselves 'princes of Achaea', and in 1249 their successors finished building a fortress a few miles west of Sparta, at Mystra (Myzethra, modern Greek Mystras, otherwise usually Latinized as Mistra). It has been common to 'identify' this as Faust's castle, although the latter (8994–9002) is considerably further north, near the source of the Eurotas. A more serious discrepancy, however, is that between Faust, as the agent of a high cultural synthesis, and the Villehardouins who were after all little more than brutal adventurers. Their lordship in Mystra was in any case short-lived, since they were decisively defeated by the Byzantine Emperor Michael VIII Paleologus shortly before he also, in 1261, recaptured Constantinople from Western occupation. By the peace settlement, the Frankish invaders were able to remain in the Morea for the time being, but Byzantine rule was restored in Mystra and certain other strongholds (Maina and Monemvasia); cadet members of the imperial family became 'Despots' of Mystra, and in the following century Byzantium reconquered the rest of the peninsula. During the 200 years of the Paleologan dynasty, ending with the fall of Constantinople to the Turks in 1453, the Empire was territorially much reduced and politically in terminal decline; but Mystra became and remained the centre of a great intellectual and artistic revival, which increasingly asserted its debt to the ancient 'Hellenic' tradition.* This cultural golden age developed not under Frankish rule or any other Germanic or Western influence, as *Faust* commentators (Beutler and D. Lohmeyer, for instance) have usually asserted, but as a result of the Byzantine reconquests.

It seems bizarre that Goethe, who must have had some knowledge of these facts, should in what amounts to a symbolic cultural history of medieval Greece leave wholly out of account the only medieval Greek civilization remotely qualifying to be described as a Renaissance. There is a baffling ambiguity (or perhaps some deeper ironic intention) in the position of Faust as commander of an army of pillaging barbarians (8999 ff., 9281–96, 9450–7; Mommsen has also compared them to the forces of Arab warlords) who are nevertheless receptive to the classical heritage of Greece, personified by Helen, as their Greek-named spokesman Lynceus appears to be (9273–80, 9313–32, 9346–55). In Faust's final speech to them, after dividing up the whole Peloponnese between the Germanic tribes of the earlier incursions (who seem to be synchronically identified with the thirteenth-century Frankish settlers), he orders them to surround and protect Helen and to establish her as queen of Sparta and overlord of them all, who will bring about an age of gold, plenty, and justice (9474–81). He thus seems strangely poised between the role of a recoverer and re-creator of culture and that of a destroyer. It is not really clear what the precious 'classical heritage' is being retrieved from, assimilated to, and defended against, or by whom; and the role of Menelaus (if it is to be interpreted allegorically at all) remains obscure and far-fetched.*

The 'Mystra' scene nevertheless reaches a positive climax when in his closing speech (9506–73) Faust magnificently evokes the idealized Arcadia where he now proposes to settle with Helen. This is probably the greatest piece of pastoral poetry in German literature, and another of the outstanding lyrical passages with which Part Two from time to time rises above allegorical obscurity and learned dispute. The 'Arcadia' here described bears little resemblance, of course, to the arid central region of the Peloponnese that still goes by that name; the safe haven to which Helen is now spirited away is the traditional *locus amoenus*, or earthly paradise, of poetic fancy.* Another long but unspecified lapse of historical time (9574) is reduced to an instant, and the third scene of Act III takes place in what appears to be the early nineteenth century. Except for the opening and closing passages, which revert to ancient metrical conventions, Scene 13 not only uses rhymed verse but is meant to be staged as an opera, with singers replacing the acting cast (conversation with Eckermann, 25 January 1827) and continuous music from the birth until the death of Euphorion (9679–938). It must presumably have been Goethe's intention to present the allegorical figure of Faust's son in the medium of an enhanced, second-order art; the reader, however, is here at a disadvantage, since in the absence of music much of the text fails to rise above the level of an unaccompanied libretto of average quality. (Its style of jingling versification, indeed, has been shown by Arens to resemble that of *Erwin and Elmira*, an operetta or *Singspiel* which the young Goethe wrote in his Frankfurt days.) Goethe claimed at different times to have had different models or parallels in mind for Euphorion (some critics have proposed Mozart in this connection, or even Goethe's own son August). In 1827 he told Eckermann that the identification with Byron had not been his original plan but an afterthought stimulated by the news of the poet's death in 1824. He explained that Euphorion, like the Charioteer in Act I, is 'the personification of Poetry', and that Byron was his only possible choice 'as a representative of the most modern poetic period' and as unquestionably 'the greatest talent of the century' (conversation of 5 July 1827). The appropriateness of Byron was further heightened by his special enthusiasm for the cause of Greek liberation from the Turks, which led to his death at Missolonghi (not, admittedly, in battle, but from malaria) and his continuing status as a Greek national hero. In general he must have appealed even to the elderly Goethe as a romantic rebel, a scorner of convention who had probably committed incest with his sister, an exile from England who lived in Italy for his last eight years; appealed as a reminder, perhaps, of Goethe's own youth, of a *Geniezeit* remembered with ambivalent nostalgia. All this is summed up in the Chorus's (dramatically impossible but poetically noble) lament for Byron in 9907–38. Dramatically, however, there is an obvious parallel between Euphorion's salute to the Peloponnese (9823–6), his timeless call to the warriors of Greece to fight for its freedom (9843–50), and Faust's own summoning of his warriors in Helen's defence. Once again, the noblest Greek heritage must be defended against its destroyers.

The story of Helen and Achilles on Leuce is Goethe's main classical Greek parallel for his Faust–Helen–Euphorion drama, though the latter also has some affinity to the myth of Orpheus and Eurydice. In both these sources the motif of prohibition is central: the beloved must return to Hades and be lost for ever if a certain stipulation is infringed. In Mommsen's interpretation, this already happened when Faust persuaded Helen to leave his castle and come with him to 'Sparta's near neighbourhood, Arcadia' (9569): his Faustian arrogance and discontent have breached the condition, and Helen is doomed to vanish. This is not entirely persuasive, as Persephone's stipulation that she must not leave Sparta has not been made explicit in the final text, only in the unpublished paralipomena; moreover, Helen has in any case already left Sparta when she joins Faust in his northern castle, despite which the two of them are allowed an Arcadian idyll of uncertain duration (9574). Goethe may have intended, in the final version, merely to hint at the underlying prohibition and to impose only an approximate obedience to it, for which Sparta's 'neighbourhood' would suffice; or even to apply it not to Sparta but to Arcadia itself. The leafy groves and underground caverns in which Faust and Helen find themselves give the impression of being a kind of secluded and protected royal demesne, a designated island of refuge which they will leave at their peril.* The further law binding Euphorion himself is more easily interpreted: from the old *Märchen* motif of the 1816 sketch which forbids him to pass over a magic circle, an interesting and significant symbolic idea has developed. His father explains to him why he must not attempt to fly, and it is no accident that the myth of Antaeus, invoked by Faust himself as he touched the Greek earth (7077), here reappears:

> In the earth lies the resilient
> Power that drives you upwards; touch the soil, on tiptoe merely touch it,
> And like the earth's son Antaeus you will grow at once in strength.
>
> (9609–11)

Poetry (or romantic poetry, or classical-romantic poetry, or poetry inspired by the Greek classical tradition) must not lose contact with

the maternal earth, with that life-giving nature which is the eternal
bedrock of true culture. The great synthesis in which 'separate
worlds unite' is possible only 'where the laws of purest Nature rule'
(9560 f). Ironically, it is Euphorion's vision of the defence of these
values that destroys him. The 'unwinged genius' (9603) forgets that
he is unwinged, and perishes like Icarus; it is left to the Chorus to
speak the only consolation, which again is from nature:

> For this soil has bred for ever
> Greatness it will breed again.
> (9937–8)

Helen disappears, the music stops, and the maidens of the Chorus
revert to ancient metres. Their leader Panthalis, the only one
dignified by a name, follows Helen and Euphorion to Hades after
commenting caustically (9962–5) on the spell of 'drunken tangled
notes' that has been worked on them by 'that old Thessalian hag'.
The rest, as Goethe puts it (conversation with Eckermann, 25 January
1827) 'cast themselves on the elements', dividing into four groups as
they transform themselves into nymphs associated with different
aspects of elemental nature. Their final celebratory lines (9992–
10038) are trochaic tetrameters, as in the concluding chorus of a
Greek drama; these must rank, with Faust's greeting to the sunrise
in the Prologue and his evocation of Arcadia in Scene 12, among
Goethe's greatest lyric achievements. The first group of maidens
represent the forests as dryads; the second, the echoing mountain
cliffs as oreads; the third are naiads haunting the streams and rivers;
and the fourth, maenads or bacchantes, the followers of the wine-
god. This last and longest section (10011–38) celebrates the ripening
of the grapes in the sun-god's fire and the treading of the new wine;
it develops magnificently into the evocation of a Dionysian *orgia*, as
the god reveals himself to his worshippers. Act III, like Act II, ends
with a great pagan mystery: the old wine is drunk, the grape's new
juice replaces it, the earth passes again through its eternal self-
renewal and self-transformation.

5 THE COMPLETION OF *FAUST*

The fact that the five Acts of Part Two were almost entirely written
between late February 1825, half-way through Goethe's seventy-sixth

year, and late July 1831, shortly before his eighty-second and last
birthday, is already so astonishing that we need not be unduly
surprised by his method of working. This was, as we have seen, to
take up particular Acts or scenes in no particular order but as mood
and instinct dictated and then to piece them together, leaving gaps
and filling them in in due course. Something like a record of the
progress of this work can be constructed from the letters and
conversations and from manuscripts of the text or paralipomena in
so far as these are datable; this evidence is sometimes clear,
sometimes scanty or obscure, sometimes contradictory. Soon after
the publication of Act III in the spring of 1827 Goethe confided to
Zelter (letter of 24 May 1827) that he had now reached the beginning
of Act IV, and that he intended to continue the work from this
point, the point at which Faust, carried out of the world of classical
antiquity by the cloud formed from Helen's garments, has been
deposited again in the world of 'his evil genius'. It is not clear from
this or from any other external evidence that Goethe actually wrote
at this time Faust's important opening soliloquy (10039–66). It would
have been an appropriate moment to do so: the speech, still in
classical trimeters, is a pivotal passage, both an epilogue or valedic-
tion to the Helen experience (10050–4) and a prologue to Acts IV
and V, a turning back to the medieval, 'romantic' world of Mephis-
topheles, the Emperor, and Gretchen, whose image stirs in him now
as a deep memory of the heart (10055–66).* Nevertheless, certain
affinities between this soliloquy and the final scene of Act V (Sc. 23,
'Mountain Gorges', written probably in December 1830) suggest
that it may indeed have been written after Scene 23 or at about the
same time, and therefore probably in February 1831, when the main
work on Act IV is known to have been started, as Eckermann
confirms (conversation of 13 February 1831: 'Goethe told me he is
continuing the fourth Act of Faust and has now successfully writ-
ten the beginning in the way he wished'). This was after the
completion of the first three Acts and not quite all of Act V. In 1827,
soon after the letter to Zelter of 24 May, he had changed his
mind about continuing with Act IV and taken up Act I instead: the
elf scene and Faust's first dealings with the Emperor. As we saw,
this material was carried forward as far as line 6036, and then
hurriedly published in 1828 as the Act I fragment, rather as if
Goethe had decided to serialize the rest of Part Two. But a curious

gap of about eighteen months then followed, in which he turned to the completion of his novel *Wilhelm Meister's Journeyman Years* and the autobiographical *Italian Journey*. In the latter part of 1829 *Faust* was again resumed, and by the end of that year he had finished Act I and the opening scenes of Act II (Sc. 8 and 9). The 'Classical Walpurgis Night' (Sc. 10) then occupied him until well into the summer of 1830, when Act II was at last declared to be finished (letter to Eckermann, 9 August 1830). For some months after this the record is incomplete, but seems to suggest that the concluding scene of Act V (Sc. 23, 'Mountain Gorges') was mainly written in December 1830, though like much of the rest of the Act V material it may have been planned, if not actually sketched on paper, very much earlier.

The genesis and dating of the last four scenes (Sc. 20–3) thus remain controversial. Goethe states repeatedly, over the years, that Act V is already finished or 'as good as finished' or was finished long ago,* though its first three scenes (Sc. 17–19, the Philemon and Baucis episode) are still missing at the beginning of April 1831, and their addition during that month is documented; Goethe remarked of them, however, that '[their] intention too is more than thirty years old' (conversation with Eckermann, 2 May 1831). Revisions to the final scenes 20–3, were apparently also made in the first few months of 1831. As for Act IV (Sc. 14–16), it is clear that it was begun or resumed in early February 1831 and then again in early May, and that it was finished on 22 July. Eckermann was often told of Goethe's determination to complete this Act and with it the whole work; in February for instance Goethe informed him (conversation of 17 February 1831):

I have had the whole manuscript of the Second Part bound, in order to have it visibly there before me as a physical object. I have filled the place where the missing fourth Act should be with blank sheets, and there is no doubt that completed material acts as an enticement and stimulus to finish what has still to be done.

He had made a resolution to complete the whole of Part Two by his eighty-second birthday on 28 August (letter to Zelter, 4 August 1831); in the event he did it with a month to spare, and could then say to Eckermann (late July 1831, anticipated by Eckermann in his record of a conversation of 6 June):

From now on, I can look upon the remainder of my life as a gift pure and simple, and ultimately it no longer matters at all whether I still do anything or what it may be.

Goethe then sealed up the manuscript, only to open it yet again in January 1832, two or three months before his death, and enter a few minor afterthoughts. Apart from these, the last work that he did on *Faust* was the completion of Act IV and the insertion of the Philemon and Baucis scenes of Act V, which are closely related to the events of Act IV. The difficulty of discussing these two last Acts separately is increased by the fact that Act IV is related to Act V in much the same way as Act II is to Act III: in both cases the structurally preceding but later written Act is designed to explain or set the agenda for the structurally following Act which has been written already (and in the case of Act III published already). In each case the historically later Act is both a postscript and an 'antecedent'. In order to understand Act IV, we must therefore first consider, so far as it is known, the development of Goethe's plan for Act V, and in particular the changes it seems to have undergone, under the influence of certain external events, between February 1825 and May 1831.

Among Goethe's various statements claiming or implying that the 'ending' of *Faust* has already been written, two are of particular importance; and although their exact meaning is in dispute, their authenticity as evidence has never been challenged. One is his conversation on 3 August 1815 with Sulpiz Boisserée (reported in the latter's diary), in which he says of the ending: 'I shall not tell you about it, I must not tell you about it, but it too is already finished, and it turned out very good and grandiose, something from my best period.' The other is the closing sentence of the narrative sketch BA 70, which, as we know, was written down in December 1816. This early outline of Part Two takes us up to the death of Euphorion, Faust's ensuing war with 'the monks', and his acquisition of 'great possessions'; Goethe then remarks in conclusion that the events of Faust's later life will be revealed in due course, 'when at a future date we assemble *the fragments, or rather the separately composed passages*, of this Second Part'. This is usually taken to imply that various sketches of the concluding part of the play (presumably Act V) were in existence not later than December 1816 and probably long before (there is no *terminus a quo*). Boisserée's report is clearer about the dating, since it is agreed that 'my best period' certainly means Goethe's years of collaboration with Schiller at the turn of the century. The dispute centres on what Goethe meant in this conversation by 'the ending', and to a lesser extent on whether he meant that he had already, about fifteen years earlier, committed some version of the concluding scenes to paper or whether they were merely in his head. The scenes he is thought most likely to have been referring to are the three so-called 'core' scenes of Act V: that of Faust's encounter with Care (Sc. 20), that of his death (Sc. 21), and that in which Mephistopheles is defeated and Faust's 'immortal part' carried aloft (Sc. 22). All three qualify for the description 'very good and grandiose'. So indeed does 'Mountain Gorges' (Sc. 23); and Mason (1967, 317 f., 349–56) seeks also to assign this mysterious last scene of all, in its essentials, to the c.1800 phase.* Stylistic and manuscript evidence make 1830–1 seem the likelier date, but Mason is right to stress that 'Mountain Gorges' must not be seen as an unimportant afterthought or optional extra, a piece of senile mystical babbling not integral to the main conception. The three 'core' scenes preceding it are, as it happens, extant (though incompletely) in an important manuscript (known as H2 or VH2) which represents Goethe's penultimate version of these scenes and was written out as an interim fair copy in March and April 1826, almost entirely by Goethe's amanuensis Johann August John. H2, in its turn, is based on a number of untidy autograph fragments, datable to 1825, which together represent a less coherent and even less complete version of the same scenes. Opinion differs as to whether Goethe first wrote these fragments in 1825 or whether they were much older material, perhaps from c.1800, which he for some reason, in 1825, copied in his own hand, destroying the originals. For present purposes, however, we need only consider the 1826 penultimate version (H2) of Scenes 20–2. Both this and the version briefly sketched at the end of the 1816 paralipomenon (BA 70) can be revealingly compared with the definitive version of the last two Acts, of which the final fair copy was made in the spring and summer of 1831, comprising: (1) Scenes 20–2, now revised and extended; (2) Scene 23 (probably December 1830, a few passages added later); (3) the new Philemon and Baucis scenes (17–19), added in April 1831; and (4) the new Act IV, added between February and July 1831. How did this final version of the closely connected last two Acts develop?

Goethe's diary first notes his resumption of work on *Faust* in February 1825. Various factors no doubt combined to prompt him to take it up again at this time, including the practical demands of the forthcoming final edition of his works and the literary stimulus, for Acts II and III at least, of his rediscovery of the *Arabian Nights* tales in 1824–5. At the beginning of February, however, a public event occurred that made a profound impression on him: the catastrophic tidal floods that struck the North Sea coast from Belgium to Jutland, devastating hundreds of square miles of land and killing 800 people. Goethe had recently become fascinated by the then relatively new science of meteorology, and in the short treatise on it that he was now writing (*Essay on Meteorology*, 1825), he refers to this natural disaster in words that are strikingly relevant to both Act IV and Act V of *Faust* Part Two:

Evidently, however, that which we call the elements is impelled to follow its own wild and disordered course. Now in so far as man has taken possession of the earth and is under a duty to preserve this status, he must prepare himself for resistance and constant vigilance. But particular precautions are insufficient: we must rather strive to counter anarchy with law, and here nature has set us a splendid example by opposing the forms of life to formlessness. We must therefore look upon the elements as gigantic adversaries with whom we have to fight unceasingly, conquering them in particular cases only by courage and guile and the highest energy of our spirit.

In the final 1831 version of Acts IV and V, the ageing Faust's last enterprise is to challenge 'the elements' by mastering the sea: this is now the essential agenda of the two Acts. The theme is only partly developed in the 1825–6 H2 material, inconsistently juxtaposed with a related but less impressive motif which may be earlier still: that of a land drainage scheme, apparently some way inland and not connected with coastal floods, but designed to reclaim habitable territory for large numbers of people and to earn Faust posthumous fame. The North Sea disaster of February 1825 evidently suggested to Goethe his final grandiose transformation of this plan, and the lines indicating the change are the one autograph passage in John's transcript H2, inserted by Goethe in 1826 in his own hand to put his new idea on record. The latter is then fully developed in Faust's last speech as revised in 1831 (11559–86). Here, Faust's project is not merely to drain waterlogged land, but to conquer 'the lordly sea'

(10229) itself: to drive it back from the shore and create 'green fields, so fertile', a 'new pleasant earth', 'an inland paradise' (11565–9), the protection of which from the wild surrounding sea will be a constant challenge (11564, 11570 ff., 11575–8). This vision is the underlying symbolic theme of the final version of the last two Acts. In Part Two as a whole we now have what might be called two macro-sequences: the first extending from the 'Mothers' scene in Act I through the 'antecedents' in Act II to the final chorus of Act III, and the second comprising Acts IV and V. If the overarching, unifying theme of the first (the Helena macro-sequence, to which the Act I Prologue is closely relevant) is that of classical beauty embedded and rooted in the timeless life of nature, that of the second is the heroic self-asser-tion of the human spirit against nature's negative forces: its destruc-tive wastefulness, the physical power of chaos. We might also say that these two macro-themes hold each other in balance, as do the 'entelechy' of the Homunculus which disappears mystically into nature, and the 'entelechy' of Faust which disappears into a realm transcending nature.*

The theme of man's struggle against elemental chaos, begin-ning historically in the *Meteorology* essay and the 1825–6 Act V material, is (in the structural dramatic sequence) first announced in the 'antecedent' Act IV, the function of which is to show how Faust comes to be in a position to execute his plan of mastering the sea. But here another problem arises. In the final, 1831 stage of the work, in the months in which he wrote the whole of Act IV and the Philemon and Baucis scenes, Goethe presents Faust in so negative a light that the effect of the macro-theme is prejudiced, and in the view of some critics destroyed. In this 1831 stratum (and here Goethe may again have been influenced by external contem-porary events) Faust appears, despite the impressiveness of his project, as the very opposite of mature or 'perfectible'; indeed, the sharpest expression of this view would be to say that in the last stage of his career he becomes a criminal or a madman. Nevertheless, in the paradoxical final conclusion which many readers have found unacceptable, Faust is 'saved': Goethe thus adheres to his earlier 'salvationist' plan which goes back certainly as far as 1825 and probably much further. In considering the events of Acts IV and V, we must bear both sides of this paradox and final ironic ambiguity in mind.

In the opening scene of Act IV (Sc. 14) the two serious poetic high points are the already mentioned transitional soliloquy (10039–66) and the speech (10198–233) in which Faust expounds 'with passionate excitement' his vision of driving back the sea. In between, we return to the basically comic mode of contemptuous *badinage* between Faust and Mephistopheles, familiar from Part One and from the 'Mothers' scene in Part Two. Mephistopheles, having borrowed another magic object from the *Märchen* tradition, arrives on seven-league boots to meet his client among high mountain peaks, a landscape not unlike that of the Prologue to Act I, a previous significant turning-point. The venue prompts Mephistopheles to some incidental geological discussion with Faust, echoing the dispute between Anaxagoras and Thales (7851–72). Faust's view is instinctively 'neptunistic': to him it is self-evident that nature's creative processes are slow and gradual, and that the theory of violent volcanic upheaval is of the Devil. In the context of the rest of this Act we may say that the corresponding view of political change is metaphorically implied here as well. Mephistopheles then asks for his further instructions, and the dialogue proceeds, again along familiar lines, to contrast Faust's high-mindedness with Mephistopheles' cynicism. The most important parallel with Part One, however, is the development of this diabolic role into its practical corollary: as before, Faust's passionate wishes, the very expression of which gives them a certain nobility, must be not only mocked but corrupted in the very process of their fulfilment, vitiated in their translation into reality. As before, Goethe's Devil is the spirit not only of negation, but also of realization: the shadow that in the tragic interpersonal world of humanity falls between the vision and the act. In the present case, Faust first scorns the offer of princely wealth and a life devoted merely to luxury and pleasure (10136–54, 10160–75); he then outlines his plan, which involves the acquisition of property and power, but as the means to a great deed. Again he accuses Mephistopheles of being incapable of understanding the needs of the human spirit, which are essentially creative; and again Mephistopheles need not argue with this, since he will now immediately begin to corrupt Faust's project, to turn his creativeness into destruction.

At the end of the BA 70 sketch we read that Faust acquires great wealth after waging war on the monks who had tried to seize the castle in Germany into which (in this early plan) he had magicked the Helen episode; there is no mention here of the Emperor, whose only role in BA 70 was to receive Faust at court and request the Helen and Paris apparitions. In the 1831 version the Emperor is reintroduced with great prominence, his story being taken up from the point at which Faust and Mephistopheles left it in Act I. The introduction of paper money has of course led to inflation and economic chaos, and the right of the pleasure-seeking Emperor to rule has been called in question. In the hope of replacing him with a prince who will bring about stability and justice, a faction of the high nobility and clergy has elected a rival Emperor (*Gegenkaiser*). The resulting war has reached a critical point, and Mephistopheles now inveigles Faust into magically intervening on the legitimate Emperor's side, in the expectation of being rewarded with the lands along the sea-coast. Great emphasis, partly sinister and partly comic, is laid on the diabolic character of Faust's military intervention. Basically Goethe is here reviving material from the old Faust legend, according to which Dr Faustus used his magic arts to win battles for the Emperor Charles V. Mephistopheles now appears to be largely in control of events, as in Act III. Presumably briefed by him, Faust presents himself to the beleaguered Emperor as the agent and emissary of a notorious magician whose life the Emperor once spared when on a progress through Italy at the time of his coronation; the 'necromancer of Norcia' (a place in the Sabine Hills long associated with the black arts) is now supposedly repaying his debt of gratitude for having been snatched from the stake at the last moment (10439–52). The battleground is mountainous terrain, and among the helpers and servers provided or proposed by Mephistopheles and Faust are mysterious earth-wights referred to as 'the mountain people' (10320) and as 'ancient human powers from primal mountains' (10317 f.); this theme is strikingly developed by Faust in 10425–36.* Mephistopheles conjures up a phantom army by sending demons to animate suits of medieval armour (10557–64*), and the enemy is further terrified at crucial moments by magic floods (10717–41) and magic fire (10742–62). He also produces three monstrous fighting-men with (in the German text) biblical names*: these go back to the BA 70 version, and appear again in the Philemon and Baucis episode (written at the same time as Act IV), as if to make a symbolic link between the violence of the war and the unintended violent criminality of Faust's eviction of the old couple. They appear to have demonic powers, and their activities help to complete the rout of the enemy forces.

The rightful but weak and foolish Emperor is restored to his throne by these dubious means; he has risen above his weakness and foolishness at only one point, when he learns that a rival Emperor threatens him.* The latter, whom we are perhaps meant to think of as a Napoleonic figure and a potentially just ruler, has been utterly destroyed. The first act of the restored Emperor is the ceremonial granting of titles and offices of state to the four princes who have officially assisted him in the war; their functions will include that of electing future emperors. This scene is a foreshortened and ironic expression of the basic constitution of the Holy Roman Empire, as promulgated by Charles IV in his Golden Bull of 1356.* Written in the formal alexandrine metre of the French classical drama and its German imitations, the scene appears to be intended to present the restored Emperor as a ruler hallowed by centuries of tradition and legitimacy, while at the same time suggesting his actual dependence on the princes he purports to create; in particular, he is under the power of the Church. The Lord Chancellor, speaking as Archbishop, affects concern for the young ruler's spiritual welfare in view of the 'satanic' means he has used to re-establish his throne, and demands as penance an enormous gift of property in the form of an ecclesiastical foundation (10981–11002). This rich comic vein of anticlerical satire was one of which Goethe had never tired since the early *Urfaust* days (see Part One, Sc. 12); the Act even ends with one of the stock devices of classical comedy, when the Archbishop makes his reverential exit but returns twice with ever more rapacious afterthoughts, including the demand that the entire revenue of the lands reclaimed from the sea by the accursed sorcerer be paid to the Church. In Goethe's plan, this last part of the Act was to have contained a scene showing Faust's formal enfeoffment with the coastal lands: curiously, however, he omitted this important dramatic moment, just as he had omitted the (as one might have thought) equally important scene at the end of Act II in which Faust was to have been granted permission to remove Helen from the underworld (see above, p. xxxiii f.). Once again, a significant dramatic link, a piece of story-line, is left to the reader's imagination. In each case, Goethe may have felt that such a scene was out of keeping with the essentially comic, perhaps 'epic' character of the rest of the Act, or that the link was too obvious to need spelling out; in any event, in both cases it was left in the form of fragmentary sketches.* Nevertheless, the underlying theme of Faust's acquisition of vast tracts of land still remains central to Act IV, and Goethe seems to suggest that by the way in which this has been done it is Faust, as much as the Emperor, who becomes morally vulnerable.

This whole last-written part of *Faust* needs to be seen against the background of Goethe's political views in general and the European events of 1830 in particular. Goethe, who from the age of 26 had been in the service of the Duke of Saxe-Weimar, an absolute but enlightened ruler, was always strongly anti-revolutionary. His poetic answer to the first French Revolution was *Hermann and Dorothea* (1797), with its idyllic picture of small-town or semi-rural German bourgeoisie, set against the turbulent background of the Revolution and its international consequences. Notoriously, he professed great admiration for Napoleon, but with reservations which are also on record. After 1815, when in the general settlement his patron was created Grand Duke and the Weimar territories were enlarged, Goethe was more of a restorationist than ever. It was his conviction that revolutions are to be blamed in the first instance on the rulers, on their failure to be sufficiently enlightened autocrats to introduce necessary social reforms at the right time and the right pace. But under no circumstances was violent popular intervention to be countenanced: it was 'unnatural', like a volcano or an earthquake. The 'revolutionary mob' is motivated in practice only by the basest self-interest (conversation with Eckermann, 27 April 1825), and the young and ignorant should keep out of high matters of State (conversation with Eckermann, 21 March 1831). The so-called July Revolution of 1830, by which the last legitimate Bourbon king of France was deposed, was deeply shocking to him, seeming as it did to threaten a repetition of the tragedy of 1789; nor was he much reassured by the brevity of the upheaval and the precarious replacement of Charles X by Louis Philippe, a relatively liberal and very bourgeois prince from the Orléans branch of the dynasty. There were also minor repercussions in Germany—student riots and uprisings, for instance—as near home as Jena. But Goethe also felt that moral responsibility lay with the King, for not having adopted the right reforming policies: Charles X, like Louis XVI before him, had let down the cause of progress, and betrayed his duty as a prince.

Goethe's philosophy of political and social change seemed to be in ruins: was any other programme on offer?

Here we must note that in the years before the July Revolution, and especially in the last year and a half of his life that followed it, Goethe had acquainted himself with the teachings of the so-called Saint-Simoniens or Saint-Simonistes, the followers of Claude-Henri, Comte de Saint-Simon (1760–1825), the eccentric scion of a ducal family more famously represented by the memorialist Louis, Duc de Saint-Simon, the caustic observer of Louis XIV's court. Claude-Henri, turned social philosopher, instructed his valet to wake him every morning with the words 'Souvenez-vous, Monsieur le Comte, que vous avez de grandes choses à faire'. Goethe, an assiduous reader of *Le Temps* and *Le Globe*, had his attention drawn to this man by an obituary published in 1825, the year of his resumption of work on *Faust*. Five years later he was prompted by the July Revolution to delve more deeply into the ideas of what was now a flourishing intellectual sect, professing a new and radical programme of socio-political reorganization. In May 1831, just as he was working on the last stratum of *Faust*, he read Armand Bazard's official *Exposition de la doctrine saint-simonienne*, which disturbed him even more than the Revolution itself. The 'Saint-Simoniens', starting from a meritocratic work ethic, advocated the introduction of social equality and the abolition of hereditary land tenure and all other hereditary rights; property was to be distributed by an enlightened oligarchy of 'leaders' on the basis of merit, rather as in the Soviet Communist system of the twentieth century the party authorities moved writers (for instance) into smaller or larger apartments according to their productivity. The Saint-Simonien movement also developed a strongly religious colouring, with an 'église', a special symbolic costume, and a 'père suprême' for whom a 'holy bride' was to be selected. Eventually the French authorities banned the brotherhood in the interests of public morals, and about six weeks before his death Goethe learnt with satisfaction of the arrest of its leader.

It is probable that Scenes 15–20 of *Faust* Part Two reflect to some extent Goethe's sceptical and pessimistic reaction to these political and ideological developments. The Emperor appears as not wholly unsympathetic, but as idle and irresponsible; the clergy and aristo-cracy are cynical and self-seeking; at the other end of the scale, Buster, Bagger, and Hugger, the three *'allegorische Lumpe'*, as the

German text calls them (10329), who end up plundering the defeated rival Emperor's treasure, probably represent the detested *Lumpen-proletariat*, as Goethe might have called it at a later date. All this could well be read as a gloomy and sardonic symbolic commentary on what Goethe, in his remarkable last letter to Wilhelm von Humboldt written five days before his death (17 March 1832), describes as 'a bewilderment of counsel (which) rules the world, urging bewildered action'. Can we interpret the final actions and speeches of Faust himself in the same way? In this context it is worth noting that existing and proposed laws concerning property, posses-sion, and dispossession were a central theme in the Saint-Simonien system; also, that in 1821 Saint-Simon himself, in one of his pamph-lets, had called for the radical agricultural reorganization of France, the recultivation of barren areas, the draining of swamps, and the building of roads, bridges, and canals. It was probably fairly common for forward-looking intellectuals early in the industrial era to imagine future large-scale civil engineering projects of this kind; at any rate, Saint-Simon's disciple Barthélémy-Prosper Enfantin was one of the first to suggest a canal through the isthmus of Panama. Such a plan was also described by Goethe's friend the scientist Alexander von Humboldt (Wilhelm's brother), and Goethe himself, to judge by a conversation with Eckermann in 1827, was fascinated by the thought not only of a Panama canal (which he was sure the Americans would eventually build) but also of a British Suez canal and a German Rhine–Danube canal, though he was doubtful about the likelihood of the latter. He would be glad, he said, to live another fifty years for the sake of witnessing such achievements (conversation of 21 February 1827). The organization of nature, the mastery of the sea by the human mind: something of this futuristic excitement may have been present in Goethe's imagination as he envisaged Faust's final project—and some misgiving as well, for reasons which nearly two centuries of industrial and technological development since Goethe's time have made all too obvious.

The negative aspects of Faust's role in the 1831 scenes are plain enough. For the sake of his 'higher aims' and 'noble purpose' (10302 f.), he has needed no persuasion by Mephistopheles to ally himself with a corrupt, anti-reformist regime, with the forces of reaction and absolute power. He could, after all, have intervened on the side of the (possibly more enlightened) 'rival Emperor' instead, but his war profit might then have been less secure. By the beginning of Act V he has achieved his ambition 'to rule and to possess' (10187), and notwithstanding his theoretical status as a vassal of the Emperor owing tithes to the Church, his control over the new coastal territories appears to be unrestricted. At the beginning of Scene 18 he is said to be 'in extreme old age'; Goethe remarked to Eckermann on 6 June 1831 that he had intended him to be exactly 100 years old. Some critics have calculated from this symbolic age that the reclamation project must have been in progress for about fifty years; the text, however, tells us nothing further on this point. Nor does Faust's symbolic status as, to all intents and purposes, owner and master of the coastal lands lend itself to exact realistic definition. We can think of him as a medieval or *ancien régime* feudal lord, an independent prince, an eccentric aristocrat trying to turn utopian theory into practice, a ruthless landowner carrying out clearances, a cynical industrial entrepreneur, or a totalitarian dictator (of the left or of the right) forcing through a five-year plan. Incidental links with Saint-Simonism seem probable in view of Goethe's documented interest in it at the time; but the Saint-Simonistes were not the only proto-socialist visionaries of the early nineteenth century or the only ones who could have been known to him. In any case Goethe cannot have wished to tie the denouement of this symbolic drama to a specific allegorical-satirical meaning, and it would be absurd to see it exclusively as a prophetic denunciation or glorification of this or that future historical development, whether Marxist or Wilhelmine-expansionist or National Socialist, as critics of various persuasions have done. If we are looking for modern parallels to the intended forceful eviction and resettlement of Philemon and Baucis, one that might well suggest itself today would be the policy of the infamous Ceauşescu regime in Romania, which in the 1980s embarked on the wholesale destruction of traditional culture and architecture in the interests of a brutal and soulless reorganization. But Faust does not in fact seem to be driven by a paranoid political ideology of this or any other kind. The dimension we are in here is psychological. The old couple's cottage and the chapel beside it offend Faust by the very fact of not belonging to him, of representing an innocent tradition not dependent on his will. His impulse seems not so much political or social as perversely artistic: a vision of controlling the elements, of creating a world, a landscape in real space and time:

> . . . those few trees not my own
> Spoil the whole world that is my throne.
> From branch to branch I planned to build
> Great platforms, to look far afield,
> From panoramic points to gaze
> At all I've done; as one surveys
> From an all-mastering elevation
> A masterpiece of man's creation.
> I'd see it all as I have planned:
> Man's gain of habitable land.
>
>   (11241–50)

(cf. also 11153–8.) The vision is tainted with perfectionism, corrupted with the fantasy of omnipotence, and yet there is still something noble about it: the artist's pride and ruthless absorption in his own work.

Shortly after writing the Philemon and Baucis episode, Goethe told Eckermann, not quite correctly, that his story of the old couple whose names he had borrowed from classical legend had nothing to do with the old Greek story (conversation of 6 June 1831). He also told him a month earlier (conversation of 2 May 1831) that the 'intention' of these scenes was about thirty years old. As usual, it is not clear what this early conception or intended treatment of the story can have amounted to; but a piece of external evidence from 1802 does tend to confirm the dating, and also sheds some light on the otherwise obscure connection between Scenes 17–19 and the classical Philemon and Baucis. Goethe, who was in fact particularly fond of idyllic motifs all his life, had known since his youth Ovid's story of the simple old couple who gave shelter to Jupiter and Mercury without recognizing them and were rewarded by the gods for their hospitality (see Index, **Philemon**). In 1802, in a minor theatrical work written for the opening of a new theatre, he had used the story, inventing his own variant of it. This otherwise quite unimportant occasional piece expressly compares the husband and wife to Philemon and Baucis, and includes two motifs that reappear in the *Faust* scenes: that of the magical transportation of the couple to a fine new dwelling (11278 ff.) and that of the wife's suspicion that evil forces are at work (11111–14).* In the finished *Faust* episode of 1831 (by whatever stages it may have come to be written) Goethe's main emphasis is undoubtedly on the contrast between idyllic rustic simplicity and Faust's ruthless organization, his overbearing and, as the old couple see it, 'godless' power (11131). As Goethe further develops the story in Act V, another classical name rather strangely recurs: that of Lynceus the far-seer, the watchman who played a part in the Helen episode (Sc. 12) and was also mentioned in the 'Classical Walpurgis Night' as one of the mythical Argonauts (7377). He now (Sc. 19) reappears to perform the classical dramatic function of witnessing a violent off-stage event 'from the walls' (teichoscopy). His opening lines (11288–303), immediately preceding his description of the burning of the old couple's cottage, are the famous lyric piece 'Zum Sehen geboren . . .' which is often quoted out of context as the aged Goethe's final positive pronouncement on life; in fact, it is the first example of the clearly intended ironies of context that pervade Act V. Faust, unaware that his instructions have been exceeded, muses on the favour he is doing the old couple by resettling them in a new house. Mephistopheles appears, with the three monstrous servants, to complete the picture of the catastrophe by his narrative.

At this point there occurs a series of developments that raise difficult interpretative questions. First, Faust curses the 'reckless, savage deed' (11372, literal version), and by implication curses Mephistopheles and the Three. Does this amount to a renunciation of Mephistophelean magic, as 11404 ff. will seem to suggest? When he next speaks to Mephistopheles (11551), he is blind, and apparently takes him for his clerk of works. Secondly, does line 11382 in Faust's next and last speech in Scene 19 ('A rash command, too soon obeyed!') amount to an expression of remorse, an acknowledgement that he cannot shake off responsibility for the murder by blaming his agent? Thirdly, how exactly is Scene 19, and the Philemon and Baucis episode generally, related to Scene 20 ('Midnight', the first of the three 'core' scenes), in which Faust is confronted by the spectral figure of Care? Faust's last six lines (11378–83) seem intended to link the two, but Scene 20 was written in 1825–6 and Scene 19 in 1831, which calls in question the usually assumed relevance of the Care scene to Faust's feelings about his crime. (It is not even clear that the Care scene was originally conceived as taking place immediately before Faust's death (Sc. 21); the reference to 'our brother . . . Death' (11397) by the Four Grey Women can be read as meaning that he is approaching, but still distant). As against this 'disconnection' of Scene

20, we have to bear in mind Goethe's piecemeal way of working and the fact that both Scene 20 and the Philemon and Baucis sequence may go back in 'intention' to c.1800, and consequently that their present dramatic continuity in the final text may be as Goethe intended. The point has a certain importance in that it is relevant to how the mysterious figure of Care is to be understood.

One of the puzzles in the lines spoken by the Four Grey Women at the beginning of 'Midnight' (11384–91) is the meaning of the word *Schuld* in 11384 (the name of one of the apparitions) which I have translated 'Debt'. Some critics are inclined to take it in its other German sense as 'guilt': that is, moral or criminal responsibility for a wrong action, with or without an awareness or feeling of culpability (*Schuldgefühl*). Since *Schuld*, like Want and Need, declares herself to be unable to enter the house of a rich man (11386–9), the commercial sense seems prima facie more likely, especially in view of the uncertainty as to whether this scene was originally conceived as having any connection with the Philemon and Baucis episode—that is to say, with Faust's crime. In any case 'debts' (ὀφειλήματα) are a metaphor for sins ('trespasses') in a text even more famous than *Faust*; also, the inability of 'guilt' to enter Faust's palace would merely mean that the objective guilt for his crime cannot be brought home to him. It is notable that after line 11382 there is not the slightest allusion to the death of the old couple, in Scene 20 or anywhere else; indeed, Faust in 11438 ff. even congratulates himself on having become more wise and circumspect in his old age. Some commentators, concerned to raise Faust's moral status by insisting that he is capable of remorse, seize upon an observation by Goethe, made in a quite different context (*Wilhelm Meister's Journeyman Years*, book I, ch. 7), to the effect that *conscience* is 'closely akin' to care (that is, to brooding anxiety); but in that passage Goethe was merely remarking that 'conscience' tends to degenerate into 'remorseful anxiety [*reuige Unruhe*] that can embitter one's life', and this is precisely what Faust in Scene 20 is repudiating. If Care is supposed to personify his moral conscience, it is strange that nothing she says to him contains any hint of moral prompting or accusation. What she does instead is to recite, without even really addressing him, a relentless description of her dark power over mankind (11424–31, 11453–66, 11471–86). Faust recognizes her as a hostile, life-poisoning demon (11487–91), and ends by defying her in an attitude clearly intended to be seen as

heroic (11493 f.). She responds by cursing and blinding him, as witches
and demons were reputedly able to do; and he replies, again in heroic
mode:

> Night seems to close upon me deeper still,
> But in my inmost soul a bright light shines.
> I hasten to complete my great designs.
>
> (11499–501)

Care's evocation of the symptoms of paralysing neurotic anxiety is
so terrifyingly realistic as to suggest that this pathological state was
one well known to Goethe, the hidden shadow of his constant
advocacy of 'action'. *Sorge* ('anxiety' might in some ways be a better
translation than 'care') has already been compellingly evoked in Part
One, in one of the scenes written at the turn of the century:

> Care makes its nest in the heart's deepest hole
> And secretly torments the soul;
> Its restless rocking motion mars our mind's content.
> Its masks are ever-changing, it appears
> As house and home, as wife and child, it will invent
> Wounds, poisons, fires and floods – from all
> These blows we flinch before they ever fall,
> And for imagined losses shed continual tears.
>
> (644–51)

The theme of *Sorge* as the enemy of the creative, heroic-daemonic
personality was also prominent in the historical drama *Egmont* (1788).
In 'Midnight' (which is in all probability one of the scenes also
planned or sketched at the turn of the century) Care has become an
aspect of the elemental chaos against which Faust must struggle.
With Mephistopheles in disgrace, she comes to haunt him instead.
There seems to be a link between her visitation and his dismissal (if
that is what it was) of Mephistopheles; above all, it is linked to his
important soliloquy at the beginning of this crucial scene 'Midnight',
after Care has entered his house but before he has noticed her
presence (11398–419). Musing on what he has partly heard the Four
Grey Women say and on their mention of death, he looks inwards
and back at his career, remembering the despairing curse he had
pronounced on the world and himself (1587–1606; cf. 1607–26). He
now sees the words he spoke then as criminal, as an offence
against life; and for the first time he formulates the wish to renounce

magic (11404–11). By implication, this decision (repeated in 11423 when he is tempted to repel Care with a magic command) amounts to renouncing the services of Mephistopheles; if he can do so, he will have 'broken through to freedom' (11403) and be confronting nature as a man without special advantages, a man 'all alone' (11406). If we are looking for the positive, even noble, features in Goethe's final portrayal of Faust, then this new resolve must count as exceptionally significant. Psychologically it represents growth away from the illusion of omnipotence, the acceptance of a world over which he has only limited control and in which he is susceptible, for instance, to the infirmities of old age. Sudden blindness does not reduce him to despair or even to inactivity. He will continue with his symbolic project: the imposition upon nature of a shaping, civilizing will.

We are perhaps meant to assume that the tragedy of Philemon and Baucis has inwardly opened Faust's eyes to the corrupting character of his partnership with Mephistopheles; in any event, this is one of the few cases in which we might speak of moral progress or increased insight on Faust's part. Both his major speeches in 'Midnight' (11398–419 and 11433–52), in which he retrospectively and not uncritically reviews his life, are important in this way. But they are almost certainly both built into Goethe's early and continuing conception: there is not really any evidence that this essential conception changed, even during the completion of Act V, as has sometimes been suggested. In the 1825–6 H2 core material (and therefore, for all we know, in the original c.1800 conception) Faust's decision to renounce magic is already present; and so are both the swamp-draining project and the philanthropic motive, though these two appear in more rudimentary form. In H2, as well as damming back the sea, he is also draining inland swamps with a 'vast ditch'. The drainage project (which seems to have been an earlier plan of Goethe's, going back to before the North Sea floods) is expanded and explained in the final 1831 revision (11559–62), but is not first added at that stage to suggest a new philanthropic, social purpose, as some commentators have supposed. Lines 11559–62 are merely inserted to make the drainage scheme consistent with the dike scheme. As to Faust's philanthropy, in the shorter H2 version of his last speech he is already declaring that he will make a place in which millions can settle,

> . . . and live among them there
> On my true territory, my own land.

In the 1831 version this last line (11580) is movingly enhanced to

> With a free people on free land.

The 'millions' who dwell there will be subject to the constant danger of new inundations, but this very fact will make them 'active' and 'free' (11564, 11570–8). Life and freedom must be earned by unceasing vigilance, the daily reconquest of the 'elements' which in his meteorological essay Goethe had called our 'gigantic adversaries'. This imaginative revised version of Faust's project suggests, in its overtones, a kind of titanomachy between the earth and the sea, a vast mythical struggle

> The alienated earth to reconcile,
> To keep the ocean and the land apart,
> To rule the unruly waves once more.
>
> (11541–3).

The symbolic potential of the Faustian image seems to have been recognized by Freud, who in a lecture of 1933, discussing his theory of the dynamic organization of the psyche, epigrammatically sums up his own therapeutic project and ends with essentially the same simile: 'Where id has been, there ego must come to be. It is a civilizing work, comparable perhaps to the draining of the Zuider Zee.' Thomas Mann, quoting this passage in his 1936 lecture to celebrate Freud's eightieth birthday, rightly underlines the Goethean connection.*

Faust's 'civilizing work' demands from the critic something of a moral and interpretative balancing act, but not an impossible one. The fact that in both versions (H2 and 1831) he predicts that the reclaimed land will be a lasting memorial to him (11583 f.) has been taken by some as proof that his motive is mere self-aggrandizement; but since he believes neither in God nor in an afterlife (11442 ff.), it seems fair enough that he should look forward to the only kind of immortality available. It is also true that his work will probably not last for ever. Significantly, Mephistopheles claims (11549 f.) that the elements themselves are his allies, and predicts with relish that Faust's 'foolish dams and dikes' will all be swept away when 'Neptune, the water-devil' reclaims his own (11544–8). But a human enterprise can be noble even if it fails in the end. It would be simplistic to acclaim Faust's final actions and utterances as the heroic expression of a wholly admirable philanthropic vision; but to dismiss them as merely futile and deluded would be to accept that Mephistopheles' cynical and nihilistic final assessment (developed further in 11587–93 and 11595–603) is the last word on Faust and indeed on humanity.* It would be to say that the admittedly dubious hero of Goethe's life's work must be seen, in the end, as a criminal or a madman. The text as a whole (notwithstanding all the dark ironies of Scene 21, such as the blind Faust mistaking the digging of his grave for the progress of his excavations, 11539–58) will not support such a view, precisely because Goethe's essential and very realistic point, the premiss indeed for his whole Faust story, is that the Devil is half right but also half wrong.

Goethe's statement to this effect occurs as early as 1820 in his reply to a letter from Karl Ernst Schubarth, a classical scholar from Breslau whom he had recently met and whose comments on the yet-to-be-completed *Faust* he particularly valued. The relevant passage is worth quoting more exactly:

Your sense of the ending is also correct. Mephistopheles must only half win his wager; half the blame sticks to Faust, but the good old Lord's prerogative of mercy is exercised at the same time, giving the whole story a very happy conclusion. (Letter to Schubarth, 3 November 1820)

Unlike most of Goethe's comments on Part Two, this one was made some years before his main work on it began, and is therefore, like his already quoted remark to Boisserée in 1815, of particular interest. Two points in it are worth noting: first, that it reflects an earlier plan (which Goethe still seems to have had in mind at this time but later abandoned, probably in 1825) to submit Faust to a divine court of judgement, rather as the question of the hero's guilt in Aeschylus's *Oresteia* is decided in the end by the goddess Athena. A brief jotting from those years (paralipomenon BA 112) alludes to this idea: 'Heaven. Christ, his Mother, the evangelists and all the saints. Judgement on Faust.' Evidently the 'good old Lord [*der alte Herr*]', like Athena, was to have the casting vote in this difficult case. Secondly, of course, this very Goethean statement to Schubarth about Mephistopheles is made in terms of the story of the Wager. The ending, as Schubarth rightly sensed Goethe to be envisaging it, demands that Mephistopheles shall 'only half win his wager'. This could refer either to his wager with God in the 'Prologue in Heaven' (see Part One, Introd. pp. xxviii–xxxv) or to his wager with Faust in Part One, Scene 7; or to both of these, since they are essentially the same. At the end, as Goethe intends it, Mephistopheles will have made his point about Faust and about mankind, but God and Faust will have made theirs as well. The correspondence with Schubarth shows that if Goethe did retain in his mind, through the years and decades, a general schematic conception of how *Faust* was to be concluded, the Wager motif was meant to play some part in it. In the event, in Scene 21, Goethe reverts formally to the terms of the Faust–Mephistopheles wager (1699–1706): namely, that Faust will die if he ever reaches the state of contentment he believes to be impossible, and blesses the passing moment. Considerations of dramatic form now seem to constrain Goethe to bring the 100-year-old Faust's life to an end on the utterance of his self-forbidden words. In the H2 (1825–6) version of his last speech, looking ahead to living with a multitude of others on his 'true territory', he declares (my emphasis):

> [Now] to the moment I *may* [*darf*] say:
> Beautiful moment, do not pass away!

In the elaborated 1831 version Goethe reformulates this with careful ambiguity, to underline his conception of a wager half won and half lost: Faust speaks the forbidden words not to the present moment but to the imaginary future moment at which his vision will be realized and he will contemplate the new land and its inhabitants:

> Then to the moment I *might* [*dürfte*] say:
> Beautiful moment, do not pass away!
> (11581–2, my emphasis)

But since in this version he is still not saying it, it can be argued legalistically that he has not yet lost his bet, and may therefore still qualify for salvation. The verbal device is a means to Goethe's end, a subordinate function of his general intention of 'saving' Faust anyway. It is entirely in keeping with his 'half and half' adjudication between Faust and the Devil (or God and the Devil), as well as with his admixture of noble and heroic and even self-critical elements into Faust's closing speeches. Everything about his treatment of the salvation issue betokens a both ways approach, a mentality of *et . . . et* rather than *aut . . . aut*. The same applies to the theological position he now also finds it convenient to adopt for purposes of the denouement of his poem: a Goethean (and if anything Catholic rather than Protestant) variant of the traditional doctrinal balancing act between 'salvation by works' and 'salvation by faith'. The concept of 'works' he retains as 'activity'; 'faith' does not come into his discussion of Faust at all, and is replaced by divine grace, which in this case seems more particularly to mean grace mediated by loving intercession, and perhaps transferred merit. At the end, she who was 'once known as Gretchen' will be faithful and loving enough to save Faust (12069–95), just as later (in the conscious imitation by Ibsen) Solveig will be faithful and loving enough to save Peer Gynt.

Clearly, if it had really been Goethe's intention that Faust in the end should be seen as evil or deranged, a kind of Ceauşescu figure or negative King Canute, then his 'salvation' would be entirely a paradoxical operation of this kind of grace, having no perceptible continuity with his nature and actions. But Goethe characteristically insists on the two-way view: neither works nor grace can be presumed to be sufficient without the other, but grace can make good what works lack. In June 1831, in the very act of finishing *Faust*, he clearly professes this formula to Eckermann in a much quoted conversation. Reminding him first of the words of the angels in Scene 23 (11934–41) as they ascend with Faust's soul, to the effect that the man who never gives up striving 'can' be redeemed, more especially if love from on high has intervened on his behalf,* Goethe comments that this is

the key to Faust's salvation: in Faust himself an ever higher and purer activity continuing right to the end, and from on high the eternal Love coming to his aid. This is entirely in keeping with our religious conception, according to which we are not saved by our own strength alone but by supervenient divine grace. (Conversation with Eckermann, 6 June 1831)

The 'striving' referred to in the text (11936) seems as always to be merely a more poetic word for what to Eckermann Goethe calls 'activity'. As if to acknowledge, however, that to describe Faust merely as having never ceased to act would be a morally neutral truism, he adds that his activity has also been 'ever higher and purer'.

This qualification remains one of the irreducible obscurities in Goethe's discourse about *Faust*, despite the attempts of some commentators to demonstrate that the hero's pursuit of Helen is higher and purer than his pursuit of Gretchen and that his doings in Acts IV and V are higher and purer still. We are perhaps on safer ground if we merely credit him with tireless action as such, especially in the light of two further, much quoted passages in Goethe's conversations with Eckermann. In these, although they do not expressly refer to Faust, Goethe formulates his reasons for believing in human immortality (*Unsterblichkeit*) or survival (*Fortdauer*) after physical death; neither, of course, is quite the same thing as salvation (*Erlösung*).

Man should believe in immortality, he has a right to, it is natural to him, and he may rely on religious assurances. . . . For me, the conviction of our survival is derived from the concept of activity; for if I continue unceasingly active till the end of my life, nature is under an obligation to provide me with another form of existence when my present form can no longer keep pace with my mind. (Conversation of 4 February 1829)

I have no doubt of our survival, for the entelechy is indispensable to nature; but we are not all immortal in the same way, and in order to manifest oneself as a great entelechy in that future state, it is also necessary to be one.* (Conversation of 1 September 1829)

By 'entelechy' (as we have already partly seen, cf. p. xxx above) Goethe meant the spiritual energy innate in the physical self, uniting itself to the elemental substance by a process both mysterious and natural; this is to all intents and purposes what more popular parlance calls the 'soul', a word which Goethe tends to avoid; in Scene 22, for instance, he leaves it to Mephistopheles. In a manuscript variant in Scene 23, Faust's soul or 'immortal part' is called 'Faust's entelechy'. On Goethe's premises, his never ceasing activity has been the necessary and sufficient condition for his survival, though in so far as salvation is distinct from survival, grace appears to be necessary as well. Accordingly, it is under the influence of grace that in the final scene (23) Faust's entelechy detaches itself from its earthly substance and moves into an unknown realm of transfiguration, drawn onwards by an intervening love by which divine grace is mediated to him.

It should be noted that in so far as Goethe uses Catholic doctrines and imagery in these last scenes, they are not to be taken as indications of belief, but simply as a poetic device, impressive though the poetry may be. This is made clear by what Goethe says to Eckermann in another passage of the conversation on 6 June 1831:

You will understand that the conclusion, with the upward journey of the redeemed soul, was very difficult to write, and that in dealing with such supernatural, scarcely imaginable matters I might very well have lost my way in a nebulous void if I had not used the sharply defined figures and concepts of Christian and ecclesiastical tradition to impose on my poetic intentions the salutary limitation of a certain form and solidity.

The traditional forms are 'used', but what is offered is a personal and aesthetic synthesis of Christian and pagan elements. The concepts of divine grace, divine love, and earthly love are blended: from 11938 f. it is not immediately clear whose love it is that has looked down from on high to take Faust's part. It should be remembered that 'Mountain Gorges' and the 'Classical Walpurgis Night' were written in the same year (1830) within months of each other; and it is probable (as Williams points out*) that the latter was intended as a 'complementary mirror-image' of the former, or more particularly of the Sea Festival with which it ends. Goethe's greatest *et . . . et* or balancing act of all is his juxtaposition of the world of pagan sensuality, of Galatea and Helen, of 'Eros, first cause of all [*Eros, der alles begonnen*]' (8479), with that of the purified entelechy, of the penitent female sinners, of the Mater Gloriosa and the erotic-mystical call of the Eternal Feminine ('Eternal Womanhood', 12110). Such synthesizing nuances belong to the world of poetry, in which, as Goethe liked to remark, there are no contradictions.

Love as a cosmic force, the divine Eros, the divine Caritas, which intervenes to save Faust and may even save the Devil, is in fact the unifying theme of the two concluding scenes which follow Faust's death: the scherzo 'Burial Rites' and the mystic finale 'Mountain Gorges'. The former (Sc. 22) is the last of the three 'core' scenes of 1825–6, and nearly all of it was certainly written between February and April 1825, as the manuscript fragments show; twenty lines were then added in 1831 to Mephistopheles' last speech. It also almost certainly represents Goethe's original conception (*c.*1800) of how Faust's soul was to be rescued from Mephistopheles and the latter comically defeated (the classical years of his 'best period' were also those in which Goethe was most inclined to literary ribaldry). Both in 'Burial Rites' and in 'Mountain Gorges' he adopts the method he was to explain to Eckermann in the passage quoted above, and makes vivid use of medieval Christian imagery. A particular source is known to have been Lasinio's engravings of the fourteenth-century frescoes by Orcagna in the cloister of the cemetery (the 'Campo Santo') next to the cathedral in Pisa; on one of these, 'Il Trionfo della Morte', many details of Scene 22 are based. He also takes the opportunity, however, to satirize traditional dualistic notions of the 'soul' as a gaseous or butterfly-like entity distinct from the body and located in some specific part of it such as the alimentary canal or the navel (11664–9). Mephistopheles' assistant devils, summoned from a theatrical hell as reinforcements, are instructed to keep watch for it at every orifice of the dead Faust. Using old and popular stage traditions, Goethe creates in this scene a remarkable and sophisticated effect of alternation and musical dissonance, reminiscent of the first garden scene in Part One (Sc. 15) in which the two contrasting couples (Faust and Gretchen, Mephistopheles and Martha) enter by turns. The angels dramatically appear from above in a 'flash of glory', interrupting Mephistopheles' sardonic drivelling monologue; the comic and lustful tone of his subsequent speeches is similarly interrupted by their metrically contrasting, unironic lyrical choruses. Mephistopheles tries to dismiss this music as epicene choirboyish stuff, which reminds him of an unsuccessful infernal plot to halt the breeding of the human race by sterilization (11689 f.), an invention which had merely made male sopranos fashionable and led to the use of castrato boys in church choirs such as that of the Sistine Chapel (11691 f.*). But what the visitants sing about is love, symbolized by roses, which also seem (on the evidence of 11942 ff. in the next scene) to represent grace mediated by the Penitent Women. The roses burn the assistant devils and put them to flight; Mephistopheles stands his ground, but the divine Eros unexpectedly and grotesquely takes possession of him, distracting him from his business as he studies and comments on the charms of the adolescent male angels and wonders whether they are devils in disguise. Recovering himself only to find that they have vanished with his supposed victim's 'immortal part', he is left with his rueful reflections which end with a grudging acknowledgement: the power of this cosmic amorous folly must indeed be great, if in the end it could overcome even such a cynic as himself (11840–3). A trace, clearly, of the intention half-seriously hinted at in a conversation of 1816 recalled by Johannes Daniel Falk:

a passage, Goethe promises, will be found in *Faust* after his death in which 'the Devil himself finds grace and mercy before God'. And that, he adds, will be something for which his German readers will not easily forgive him (conversation of ?21 June 1816).

In the last scene, Goethe drops the mock-naïve mystery-play style; '*der alte Herr*' (as God has irretrievably become) does not make a personal anthropomorphic appearance as in the 'Prologue in Heaven', or in the intended Epilogue in which he was to sit in judgement over Faust and give him the benefit of the doubt. Asked by the (not wholly reliable) Friedrich Förster in 1828 whether that would not indeed be the right way to end the drama, Goethe is reported to have shaken his head and replied: 'But that would be in the spirit of the Enlightenment. Faust ends as a very old man, and in old age we become mystics.' Instinct rightly guided him to change the plan, to take us not into heaven but to the fringes of heaven, to a place both earthly and unearthly, a transitional region opening on the unknowable Otherness. This frontier is still visible at first, a landscape that will become a cloudscape: Goethe again uses the 'salutary form and solidity' of human art. The Pisan frescoes provided it, impressively portraying for him the first Christian hermits in their rocky desert near Egyptian Thebes (the ancient city on the site of Luxor). 'Gli Anacoreti nella Tebaide' showed the holy men poised between earth and sky, sitting in their caves, some with wild beasts at their feet, at different heights on the mountainside as if arranged in ascending order of spirituality. In Goethe's version the 'Pater Profundus' is in the 'lower region', the 'Pater Seraphicus' higher up, and the 'Doctor Marianus'* near the summit, 'in the highest and purest cell'. In the course of the scene this motif is developed in terms of the cloud symbolism, like that of Faust's Act IV soliloquy (see above, p. l and note), suggested to Goethe by his meteorological studies. Children who have died at birth, and are therefore innocent, rise into the ether in the form of clouds. Angels hover above the highest peak, carrying Faust's soul, which in an earlier sketch (BA 239) for Scene 22 was also enveloped in a cloud. Before long we lose sight of the mountain landscape altogether as the ascent continues. The whole picture is in motion, from the extraordinary opening stanzas ('Woods, hitherwavering . . .') to the causal verb of motion that ends the entire poem ('draws us on high'); a supreme object of love, like Aristotle's Unmoved Mover, imparts movement to all things (κινεῖ ὡς ἐρώμενον). The 'Pater Ecstaticus' levitates, 'hovering up and down', piercing himself with sensuous masochistic rapture (an experience for which words are found nowhere else in Goethe's poetry). Nature is flooded with divine energies, even stationary things seeming to be in motion: the Pater Profundus (11866–89) contemplates the downward thrust of the rocks and water, the upward thrust of trees, the cleansing thunderstorm, all of them 'love's messengers'. Being nearest to the earth, he prays for release from bodily and mental turmoil. The newly dead infants or 'Blessed Boys' look down on the earth for the first time through the eyes* of the Pater Seraphicus (11910–17); frightenened by what they see, they then soar away from his 'middle region' to the still purer air around the summit. All this indirectly expresses the purifying ascent and growth of Faust himself. His 'immortal part', now in a 'chrysalid' state (11982) already containing its further metamorphosis, is carried to the same 'upper atmosphere' by the angels who rescued him in Scene 22 (as they now report, 11934–53). Here he is handed over to the Blessed Boys, in whose company he will break out of his cloudy or cocoon-like integument (11985*); later (12076–83) we are told that they for their part will learn from his experience. It is interesting that the mute but still developing Faust, in his initiation process, is passed from hand to hand (the rescuing angels, the Blessed Boys, Gretchen) just as in Act II he was passed from mentor to mentor (the Homunculus, Chiron, Manto). This is one of the striking parallels between 'Mountain Gorges' and the 'Classical Walpurgis Night'. The Homunculus himself, as we have seen, is paralleled to Faust in various ways: he too is passed from one mentor to another (Anaxagoras, Thales, Nereus, Proteus), and he too is conceived in terms of Goethe's theory of the 'entelechy' (cf. pp. xxx and lxxii above). But the Homunculus entelechy is pre-incarnate and strives towards incarnation, bodily *Entstehung*, fusion with the fecund physical life of nature; his quest is accomplished when he is irresistibly drawn to Galatea. This is a pagan mystery, presided over (as Williams has interestingly shown) by the moon-goddess Luna, whom Galatea represents.* By contrast, the Faust entelechy is engaged in a Christian mystery of redemption and transfiguration: having survived physical death, he has still to cast off completely the bonds of earthliness from which the hermit fathers also seek release (11862 f., 11885–7). The Maturer Angels describe the purifying process he must undergo (11954–65; it is in a discarded stage direction to this speech that the variant reading 'Faust's entelechy' occurs). His 'powerful spirit-energy' (*starke Geisteskraft*) has attracted the physical elements to itself (11958 ff.), forming a 'subtle bond' (11962, *geeinte Zwienatur*, literally 'united dual nature'): this union can be unmade only by divine love (11964 f.), mediated in this case by Gretchen under the higher authority of the Mater Gloriosa. The Virgin Mother of God appears, like Galatea, only for a brief instant, at the climax of the scene, her epiphany dramatically prepared first by the ecstatic praises of the 'Doctor Marianus' (11989–12012), secondly by the prayers of her Penitent Women (themselves in cloud form) who recount their earthly experiences in the most moving stanzas of the scene, and thirdly by Gretchen, emerging from among the Penitents and herself interceded for by them. With her sorrow turned into joy, recalling and transforming the despairing words of her prayer in Part One (Sc. 21), she intercedes for her returning lover, asking and obtaining leave to continue his initiation (12092–5).

Many of the echoes here are of Dante, that other spiritual traveller, who is finally guided through the spheres of heaven by Beatrice, his beloved, and granted a vision of the Trinity after St Bernard has interceded for him with the Virgin. Even Dante's ending is dominated by the 'Virgin Mother, daughter of her Son'; God himself remains hidden in a flash of the unknowable. In Goethe the absence of God, and especially of Christ, is more pointed. His avoidance of the stylistic error of attempting the celestial judgement scene was certainly due to the fact that the Father and the Son were no longer viable for him as imaginatively serious symbols; on the other hand, something, so to speak, could be done with the Mother, notwithstanding her centrality in the Catholic cult. His attitude to Catholicism was on the whole hostile, though it softened to some extent under the influence (mainly in 1814–15) of Boisserée and the latter's enthusiasm for medieval art. It is conceivable (as I have tried to suggest elsewhere*) that he might have been less unsympathetic to Eastern Orthodoxy had he known anything about it. But what *Faust* expresses is a personal synthesis, a symbolic complex not to be construed as realistic in a metaphysical sense—not, that is to say, as corresponding to a system of transcendent realities, as having (in today's jargon) a transcendent referent. The poem embodies, without metaphysical commitment, the poet's sense of the real mystery of life; in this it borrows substance and resonance from the main traditions available to Goethe, of which two were pre-eminent. The myth complex of classical antiquity and the myth complex of medieval Christianity could be presented as equipollent alternatives; and this seems to be the sense of their juxtaposition in the 1830 stratum of Part Two, the additions made to it in that year: the 'Classical Walpurgis Night' (more especially the final Sea Festival) and 'Mountain Gorges'. Underlying both is Goethe's personal myth and mystique of the 'Eternal Feminine', of which Galatea, Aphrodite, Luna, and Helen are embodiments no less than the Mater Gloriosa and Gretchen. Even in the words of her most ardent devotee, Goethe's Virgin Mother is *'Göttern ebenbürtig'* (12011, literally 'born the equal of gods'); the phrase, used also of Helen in Act II,* is an unmistakable paganizing nuance. The synthesis is underlined by Faust's memorable soliloquy at the beginning of Act IV, a speech that may well, like the rest of the Act, have been written in 1831 (but see above, p. l) and therefore *after* 'Mountain Gorges', as the possible link between its last two lines (10065 f.), the words of the Virgin (12094 f.), and the last two lines of the whole poem (12110 f.) might suggest. The soliloquy is where Faust comes nearest to expressing both elements in Goethe's vision; in the final scene he is carried beyond what can be expressed.

Of the celebrated 'Chorus Mysticus' (which Goethe originally called 'Chorus in excelsis') Staiger has written that it is sung by no one, that it is 'only a voice filling the universe'. We are already far above the 'mountain gorges' among which the scene began: beyond this point lies only that of which the natural world and the world of human love are 'but a parable'. This is the reality that has been 'inaccessible' (*unzulänglich* probably in the old sense of *unzugänglich**) but will now be manifest (*Ereignis* probably in the old sense of *Eräugnis,* something grasped by the eye), the deed to which no description was adequate. The enigmatic force of these eight concluding lines (heightened immeasurably, but not explained, by Mahler's setting*) defies comment; like Faust, we are left wordless, but perhaps in an onward movement into the mystery.

Although the 'Helena' Act had been greeted with acclaim in some quarters when it appeared five years earlier, the posthumous release of Part Two as a whole in 1832 was a disappointment for the public.

After the strong dramatic meat of Part One, it was now offered obscure, pallid allegory and operatic extravaganza, the work, as it seemed to many, of an octogenarian poet who had outlived his own genius. The initial reception and exiguous stage history of 'The Second Part of the Tragedy' has been briefly sketched in the Introduction to Part One (pp. xlvii ff.); notably, it was not until 1876 that an integral performance of both Parts was given in any theatre. Critical reaction to Part Two in the first few decades after its publication ranged from ridicule (as in Friedrich Theodor Vischer's vulgarly facetious parody '*Faust*: the Third Part of the Tragedy', by 'Deutobald Symbolizetti Allegoriowitsch Mystifizinski') to moral or religious outrage (as with Wolfgang Menzel, who declared that if Faust deserved salvation after destroying Gretchen and her family, then every pig that rolls in a flower-bed deserves to be the gardener). Much attention, as the critical generations passed, was concentrated on the 'Faustian' nature as such. How was it to be defined? Was it an *exemplum horrendum* or an *exemplum ad imitandum*? What special vice or virtue of the German soul did it represent? A variety of idealizing interpretations came to be offered, more particularly in the heyday of German national self-consciousness, the years of empire between 1870 and 1918. The quasi-Christian ending, often a stumbling-block, could also be accepted as a merely symbolic endorsement by Goethe of whatever grandiose secular qualities the critic chose to ascribe to the hero. The terrible events of German history in the present century have made this line of interpretation difficult, at least for the ideologically uncommitted Western reader; increasingly, the critical solution has been to emphasize the 'dark' irony and ambiguity of Acts IV and V. But the author of the profoundest literary treatment of the Faust material in post-Goethean times, while retaining the theme (launched in effect, if not in intention, by Goethe) of Faust as a quintessentially German figure, was constrained for this very reason to abandon Goethe's accommodating and on the whole optimistic deflection of the story. Thomas Mann's tragic novel *Doctor Faustus* returns to the stark morality mode of the sixteenth-century legend. Fusing the two main elements of Mann's critical diagnosis of the fatality inherent in German culture as he saw it, his Faustus becomes both a composer of genius and a subtle allegorical embodiment of Nietzsche's creative and destructive contribution to twentieth-century values. His diabolic bargain is the mortal sickness that inspires his music, the most 'magical', most 'unpolitical', and yet least Goethean of the arts; his inevitable damnation is to collapse in the end into madness, as Nietzsche had done. It is the fate of 'my friend, my fatherland', for whose soul the appalled narrator's last words can only entreat mercy; *Doctor Faustus* was written between 1943 and 1947. In so far as it alludes to Goethe at all, it upholds him in the doomed hero's perspective as a model of 'classical' health, sanity, and balance.

The problems of translation in both parts of *Faust* are much the same, and have been discussed in the Introduction to Part One (pp. xlix–lv). For Part Two I have worked with essentially similar assumptions, which may be summarized as the principle, or dogma, that readable prosodic correspondence must be allowed priority over referential literalness. In Part Two, indeed, this priority gains added weight from the fact that Goethe deliberately gives the versification itself symbolic dramatic significance at certain points, especially in Act III. Fortunately the conventional constraints of ancient Greek metres, or rather of their German accentual imitations, are less severe than those of rhymed verse; it seems less difficult to devise English equivalents of Helen's iambic trimeters, or the chorus's trochaic tetrameters and triadic odes, than of Gretchen's folk-ballad quatrains, in which the enigma of simplicity becomes the greatest obstacle of all.

CHRONOLOGICAL SUMMARY OF THE COMPOSITION AND PUBLICATION OF *FAUST* PART TWO

*c.*1770–5 Goethe's earliest plans for *Faust* possibly include a conception of the Helen story and of Faust's salvation.

1790 Publication of the unfinished Part One as '*Faust.* A Fragment'.

1797 Goethe decides to divide *Faust* into two parts; schematic note (paralipomenon BA 5) indicating his overall conception at that time of Part One and Part Two.

*c.*1800 Unpublished sketches or notes (MS not preserved) for conclusion of Part Two, Act V (probably only for Scenes 20, 21, 22).

*c.*1800 Unpublished fragmentary version (269 lines) of the opening of Act III in iambic trimeters.

1808 Publication of Part One ('*Faust.* The First Part of the Tragedy').

1816 Early version of Part Two, Acts I, III, and IV (paralipomenon BA 70), dictated as a narrative sketch but not published (possibly conceived much earlier).

1825 (25 February–*c.*4 April) Act III, Scene 11 and beginning of Scene 12 written.

1825 (March) Revision of (?1800) material for Act V, Scenes 22, ?20, and ?21.

1826 Faust's speech in Act I Prologue possibly written in March/ April.

1826 (March) Resumption of Act III; Scenes 12 and 13 finished in early June.

1826 (December) Unpublished narrative sketch (paralipomenon BA 73) of Part Two, Act II ('Helena's antecedents').

1827 (April) Act III published as '*Helena*, an intermezzo for *Faust*' in Goethe's last edition of his collected works (Ausgabe letzter Hand, vol. 4).

1827 (?June/July) Act I Prologue finished.

1827 (July)–1828 (January) Act I, Scenes 2 and 3 written, and Scene 4 as far as line 6036.

1828 (April) Publication of this Act I fragment (ALH, vol. 12, with Part One).

1828 (February)–1829 (September) Work on other projects, including the third part of the *Italian Journey*.

1829 (September) Resumption of *Faust*: remainder of Act I (Scene 4 from 6037 and Scenes 5, 6, 7) and opening of Act II (Scenes 8 and 9) written by the end of the year.

1830 (January) 'Classical Walpurgis Night' (Act II, Scene 10) begun; continued in February, March, June; final completion perhaps later in the year.

1830 Act V, Scene 23, probably written in December, with some additions in 1831.

1831 (February) Act IV begun (but Faust's opening soliloquy possibly written in May 1827).

1831 (April) Scenes 17, 18, 19 (Philemon and Baucis episode) added to the otherwise essentially complete Act V.

1831 (22 July) Completion of Act IV and thus of the whole of *Faust*. Goethe seals the MS.

1832 (January) MS reopened (readings to friends; ?some minor revisions).

1832 (22 March) Death of Goethe.

1832 (December) Posthumous publication of Part Two ('The Second Part of the Tragedy') in ALH, vol. 41.

INDEX OF SCENES

Act One

Act Two

Act Three

Act Four

Act Five

FAUST

THE SECOND PART
OF THE TRAGEDY

ACT ONE

1 · [PROLOGUE]* · A BEAUTIFUL LANDSCAPE

[FAUST, *lying among grass and flowers, exhausted and*
restless, trying to sleep. Dusk.
SPIRITS, *graceful little shapes, hovering and circling*
round.]

ARIEL* [*his song accompanied by Aeolian harps*].

When the blossoms hovering
Rain on meadows green and new,
All earth's children feel the spring,
Bright with universal dew.
Come then, little elfin spirits,
All alike to help and bless;
Ours to heed no sins or merits
But to pity man's distress.   4620

You, round this mortal's head circling in air,
Heal now his heart, in noble elfin fashion:
Soothe its fierce conflict and the bitter passion
Of self-reproach's burning darts, make clean
His soul of all the horrors it has seen.
Four are night's vigils: now with fair
Contentment fill each one immediately.
First lay his head where it is soft and cool,
Then bathe him in the dew of Lethe: see,
His clenched limbs will relax, he will be free,   4630
As he gains strength and feels the day before him.
Obey the highest elfin rule,
And to the sacred light restore him!

CHORUS [*singly and in two or more voices, by turns and*
together].

When a fragrance has descended
All about the green-girt plain,
Richer air with mist-clouds blended,
Evening dusk comes down again;

Lulls to infant-sweet reposing,
Rocks the heart with whispering sighs,
And this wanderer feels it closing   4640
On his daylight-weary eyes.

Now to night the world surrenders,
Sacred love joins star to star;
Little sparkles, greater splendours,
Glitter near and gleam from far,
Glitter in the lake reflecting,
Gleam against the clear night sky;
Deepest seals of rest protecting
Glows the full moon strong and high.

Soon the hours have slipped away,   4650
Pain and happiness are past;
Trust the light of the new day,
Feel your sickness will not last!
Green the valleys, hillsides swelling,
Bushing thick to restful shade,
And the fields, their wealth foretelling,
Rippling ripe and silver-swayed!

Have you wishes without number?
Watch the promise of the dawn!
Lightly you are wrapped in slumber: 4660
Shed this husk and be reborn!
Venture boldly; hesitation
Is for lesser men—when deeds
Are a noble mind's creation,
All his enterprise succeeds.

[*A tremendous roaring sound heralds the approach of the
sun.*]

ARIEL.   Hear the tempest of the Hours!
          For to spirit-ears like ours
          Day makes music at its birth.
          Hear it! Gates of rock are sundering
          And the sun-god's wheels are thundering: 4670
          See, with noise light shakes the earth!
          Hear it blare, its trumpets calling,

> Dazzling eyes and ears appalling,
> Speechless sound unheard for dread!
> Quickly, into flowers deep,
> Into rocks and foliage creep,
> Hide where elves in silence sleep:
> Ear it strikes is stricken dead.

FAUST. How strong and pure the pulse of life is beating!*
Dear earth, this night has left you still unshaken,   4680
And at my feet you breathe refreshed; my greeting
To you, ethereal dawn! New joys awaken
All round me at your bidding: beckoning distance,
New-stirring strength, new resolution taken
To strive on still towards supreme existence.—
A gloaming-shine reveals the reborn world,
The forest sings with myriad-voiced insistence,
Through vale and dale the morning mists have curled,
But heaven's radiance pierces them, descending,
And branch and bough appear, revived, unfurled   4690
From the vaporous chasm, their slumber ending;
Now deep-down colours grow distinct, as flower
And leaf gleam moistly, tremulous pearls suspending.
Oh paradise again, oh encircling power!

Let me look up!—Each giant summit-height
Proclaims already this most solemn hour:
They are the first to taste the eternal light,
As we shall, when its downward course is ended.
Now the green-slanting meadow-slopes are bright
Again, each detail new and clear and splendid,   4700
And day spreads stepwise with the dark's downsinking:
See, the sun rises!—But my eyes offended
Turn away dazzled, from this great sight shrinking.

And thus, when with our heart's whole hope for guide
Towards our goal we have struggled on unthinking,
And find fulfilment's portals open wide—
From those unfathomed depths a sudden mass
Of fire bursts forth, we stand amazed: we tried
To set the torch of life alight—alas,
A sea of flame engulfs us, ah what flame   4710

Of love or hate, burning, consuming us
With pain and joy, which strangely seem the same!
We look back earthwards, hiding from this blaze
Behind a youthful veil of awestruck shame.

So be it! I will turn from the sun's rays.
At that rock-riving torrent, with increasing
Ecstasy at that waterfall I gaze:
From cliff to cliff it pours down never-ceasing,
It foams and streams a thousand thousandfold,
Spray upon spray high in the air releasing.   4720
But from this tumult, marvellous to behold,
The rainbow blooms, changing yet ever still;
Now vanishing and now drawn clear and bold.
How cool the moisture of its scattering spill!
I watch a mirror here of man's whole story,
And plain it speaks, ponder it as you will:
Our life's a spectrum-sheen of borrowed glory.

2 · AN IMPERIAL PALACE* · THE THRONE-ROOM

[*A Council of State awaiting* THE EMPEROR. *Trumpets
sound. Enter Court retinue of all kinds, in fine clothes.*
THE EMPEROR *takes his place on the throne;* THE
ASTROLOGER *stands on his right.*]

THE EMPEROR. Our greetings to you all, most dear
    And trusty friends from far and near.
    The sage is at my side, I see;   4730
    I had a fool too, where is he?

A COURTIER. Behind your train he tripped and fell
    Head-over-heels, Sire, on the stair;
    They lugged the load of guts somewhere—
    He's dead or dead drunk, who can tell?

ANOTHER COURTIER. And then, Sire, with strange
        suddenness,
    Another fool popped up in less
    Than no time: sumptuous in his dress,
    And yet grotesque—it quite alarms

One at first sight. Your men-at-arms'   4740
Crossed halberds bar him audience.
But here he comes, what insolence!

MEPHISTOPHELES [*kneeling at the throne*].*
What is both cursed and welcome? What
Is both desired and chased away?
Defended oftener than not,
Accused and railed at every day?
Who is the uncalled-for comer? Can
You name the name all love to hear?
What dares approach your throne? What ban
Keeps what, self-banished, far from here?   4750

THE EMPEROR. Come, spare your speech on this
     occasion;
I've riddling and equivocation
Enough from councillors like these.
Give me some anwers, if you please!
I fear my old fool's vanished without trace:
You'll do instead, come up and take his place.

     [MEPHISTOPHELES *mounts the steps and stands on*
     THE EMPEROR's *left.*]

MURMURS FROM THE CROWD.
               A new fool!—Now new troubles begin!—
               Where's he from?—How did he get in?
               The old one fell—Now he's off sick—
               He was pot-paunched—This one's a stick—   4760

THE EMPEROR. And so, right trusty friends, we say
Welcome to you from near and far.
We meet under a favourable star;
The heavens presage good luck today.
But tell me: in these glad times, when
We all cast off our cares again,
Put on our carnival masks, and try
Merely to take our pleasure, why
Must problems of the State torment us?
Yet, since you judge them to be so momentous,   4770
I gave consent; now give me your reply.

THE CHANCELLOR. About your head, Sire, like a halo, lies
One supreme virtue: none can exercise
It fully but the Emperor. It is known
As Justice!—All men love, desire, demand
To have it, all men sorely miss it—and the hand
Dispensing it to all is yours alone.
But what can wisdom still avail, alas,
Or the heart's goodness or the willing arm,
When raging through the realm wild fevers pass,   4780
And evils breed from evil's brood of harm?
Look down from this high place, look far and wide
Over the empire: it must seem
A nightmare of deformity, a dream
Of monsters, law to lawless power unfurled,
And rooting error spread about the world.

One man steals flocks, the next a wife,
A third the altar's treasury:
And yet can boast himself scot-free
From pains of law to limb or life.   4790
While plaintiffs throng the hall, and from
His sumptuous seat the judge looks down,
Rebellion like a gathering storm
Mutters and laps. Must justice drown
In these fierce waves? A miscreant
Protected by accomplices can vaunt
His crimes, while he whom only guiltlessness
Defends is pronounced guilty none the less.
And thus society falls to pieces,   4800
Order and decency decay;
How shall men not be led astray
As the true guiding instinct stunts and ceases?
So in the end good men and true
Succumb to bribes and flattery,
And judges can impose no penalty
For crime, but become criminals too.
I have painted a black picture, but I would
Draw blacker veils across it if I could.

[A pause.]

Your Majesty, decisions must be taken.
The imperial throne itself is shaken   4810
When all inflict, when all endure such harm.

THE ARMY COMMANDER. Sire, these are wild chaotic days.
Deaf to all orders, each man trusts his arm,
Every man for himself is slain or slays.
The burgher, snug behind his walls,
The knight, high on his rocky perch,
Vow they'll survive even though the Empire falls;
Their powers leave us in the lurch.
Our mercenary soldiers grow
Impatient, they demand their pay;   4820
But for the money we still owe
Them all, they'd all have run away.
And we can't stop them doing as they please;
That would stir up real trouble. So
The land they should protect, by these
Brigands it's plundered and laid low.
We let them rage and eat their fill:
Now half the world's already lost.
Some neighbouring kings are allied to us still,
But none of them thinks he should share the cost.   4830

THE TREASURER. Who'd boast of allies of that sort!
Where are their subsidies, their pledged support?
They're leaking pipes that have run dry.
Moreover, Sire, in your domains
What has become of property?
The new rich, living on their gains,
They set up house; they are ubiquitous,
And they seek independence. We look on,
And what else can we do, having foregone
So many rights? What still belongs to us   4840
By right? And parties, though they may
Call themselves this or that, no one today
Can trust them either. They commend
And they find fault, but in the end
Their love or hate's turned cold. The Ghibelline*
Lies low, the Guelph* has quit the scene.
They're in hiding, they're tired of helping neighbours;

It's for himself these days that each man labours.
The gates of gold are locked and barred.
They're digging for it, scraping, scratching hard;   4850
And our coffers are empty as before.

THE STEWARD. I too have to report calamities.
We're daily trying to economize,
And yet we're daily spending more;
Daily my problems are increased.
The cooks lack neither fowl nor beast:
Wild boar and stags and hares and deer,
Turkeys and chickens, geese and ducks—
Payments in kind, a steady flux
Of rents—all these we get, no problem here;   4860
But we are short of wine, I fear.
Our cellars, cask on cask, were once replete
With finest vintages; but this supply,
My lords, since we so endlessly compete
In our potations, is drained almost dry.
Even the town councils' stocks are tapped, they swill
From bowls and tankards with a will,
And feasts end up under the table.
As for the wages I'm supposed to pay—
The Jew will squeeze as hard as he is able;   4870
I get advances from him, years ahead.
We buy tomorrow what we eat today,
We slaughter pigs while they're still thin,
We pawn the very beds we're sleeping in;
In fact we are living, Sire, on mortgaged bread.

THE EMPEROR [after reflecting a little, to
      MEPHISTOPHELES].
Well, fool, do you too have some gloom to shed?

MEPHISTOPHELES. By no means, Majesty! Such light
      shines round us
From yourself and those near you! How could doubt
      confound us
Where such a lord wields such authority,
Such power to strike down any enemy?   4880
Where good will is made strong by wisdom, where

A host of hands is busy everywhere,
How could misfortune now or ill intent
Bring gloom to such a starry firmament!

MURMURS FROM THE CROWD.

> This sly rogue knows—what he's about—
> He'll be well in—till he's found out—
> He's up to something—I guess what—
> What do you guess?—Some scheme he's got—

MEPHISTOPHELES. Do we not all lack something, of one
    sort
  Or another? Here it's money that's run short.   4890
  It does not grow on trees, that's true, I fear;
  But from the depths wisdom can bring it here.
  There is gold in the earth, coined and uncoined,*
  Hoards hidden under walls, rocks precious-veined:
  This treasure's for the wise man to collect,
  By Nature's power and human intellect.

THE CHANCELLOR. Nature and Intellect! Who dares
    profess
  Such dangerous heresy to Christian ears?
  Atheists have been burnt for less.
  Nature is sin, the intellect's ideas   4900
  Are Satan's, and between them Doubt is bred,
  The mongrel offspring of their monstrous bed.
  Away with them!—The Emperor's lands are old,
  And here two native kindreds are alone
  The worthy guardians of his throne:
  The men of God, and all our bold
  And valiant knights. Against the storms of fate
  They are proof, and their reward is Church and State.
  There are confused plebeian minds in whom
  The spirit of revolt finds room: 4910
  Such men are heretics and sorcerers,
  The empire's ruined and the fault is theirs.
  And you, fool, with your insolent arts,
  Would smuggle them in here! They are close kin
  To fools, and quite depraved by sin.
  We cannot trust such black corrupted hearts.

MEPHISTOPHELES. I recognize a learned scholar's speech!
    What your hands cannot touch, lies far beyond your reach;
    What your minds cannot grasp or calculate,
    Does not exist for you; nothing has weight   4920
    If you have not first weighed it; and unless
    A coin was struck by you, you think it valueless.

THE EMPEROR. None of this solves our problems; I can
    see
    No point, sir, in your Lenten homily.
    I'm sick of all this endless hem and hum.
    We need more money: all right, get us some!

MEPHISTOPHELES. I will get what you need, I will get
    more;
    The way is easy, though the task is sore.
    The gold's already there for us to find,
    But that's the art: how shall it be divined?   4930
    Consider: in those days of terror, when
    A human flood covered the land, how then
    So many, here and there, in mortal fear,
    Secretly hid the treasures they held dear.
    Such is the custom, now as long ago;
    Since the Romans were great it has been so.
    All this lies buried in the Emperor's ground—
    And is the Emperor's property when found.

THE TREASURER. Well, for a fool, that's not a bad
    suggestion;
    The Emperor has these ancient rights, no question.   4940

THE CHANCELLOR. Satan lays golden snares to catch
    you all!
    The whole thing's impious and unnatural.

THE STEWARD. If I could give the court a decent dinner,
    I'd not mind all that much being a sinner.

THE ARMY COMMANDER. He's a sound fool; he knows
    what's good for us.
    As for his methods, soldiers mustn't fuss.

MEPHISTOPHELES. Perhaps you do not trust me? I refer
    You to this expert: ask the Astrologer!*

The heaven's houses he can scan, he can peruse
Its hours; come, tell us the celestial news!   4950

MURMURS FROM THE CROWD.
              A pair of rogues—So near the throne—
              Dreamer and fool—They speak as one—
              The Wise Man—(here's a tale we've heard!)
              Talks, and the Fool—prompts every word—

THE ASTROLOGER [*with* MEPHISTOPHELES *prompting*].
   The Sun itself, it is pure gold, they say;
   Mercury runs for favour and for pay
   As messenger; Venus who charms all men
   Gleams in the dawn and in the dusk again;
   The chaste Moon shines inconstantly, and Mars
   Smites you or threatens you with his fierce wars.   4960
   Jupiter is the fairest light of all;
   Saturn is great, but seems far off and small.
   As metal we do not esteem him much,
   For he is base, though heavy to the touch.
   But when the Sun and Moon have joined together,
   Silver to gold—then all the world's fine weather!
   When we have them, we can buy all the rest:
   Palaces, gardens, red cheeks, a plump breast—
   All this our learned scholar will provide,
   For he succeeds where no one else has tried.   4970

THE EMPEROR. I hear his whole speech twice, but I
      confess
   It sounds like nonsense none the less.

MURMURS FROM THE CROWD. What's all this bluff?—
              It's stale old stuff—
              I've heard such bosh—Alchemicaltosh—
              Andhoroscopes—They raise false hopes—
              He'd be the same—A swindler's game—

MEPHISTOPHELES. They stand around and gape, poor
      brutes;
   They doubt my high discovery.
   They blether about mandrake roots
   Or the black dog, denouncing sorcery,
   Showing their wits off; what will that avail   4980

When their sure-footed footsteps fail,
And when their soles begin to itch
With magic that can make them rich!

From her profundities do you not sense
Great Nature's timeless power, a living trace
Of her mysterious influence,
Her deep caress, the touch of her embrace?
When all your limbs are twitching so,
And you can smell the eerie air—   4990
Set to and dig, and hack and hoe:
The golden fiddler's buried there!

MURMURS FROM THE CROWD.
                    My foot's asleep—It's passed right out—
                    My arm's like lead—I must have gout—
                    I've got an itch in my great toe—
                    My whole back hurts—If we're to go
                    By these strange signs, this place must be
                    A wondrous buried treasury!

THE EMPEROR. Be quick then; you shan't wriggle out
    Of it this time, so try your fine words out: 5000
    Show us these noble places you know well!
    I'll lay my sword and sceptre down,
    If you're not lying, and my own
    Imperial hands themselves this work shall crown;
    If you are lying, then I'll pack you off to hell!

MEPHISTOPHELES. (I dare say I could find my own way
        there).
    But I must emphasize, this treasure's everywhere:
    It's ownerless, waiting to be discovered.
    The peasant ploughs his furrow, lifts the soil,
    And as it turns, a pot of gold's uncovered;   5010
    He scrapes saltpetre from his limestone walls
    And in his startled hand, all shrunk with toil,
    Finds to his joy a golden purse that falls
    From some forgotten hollow. And the initiate,
    What vaults he must blow open underground,
    What clefts, what passages are to be found,
    Close to the underworld! He'll penetrate

To spacious cellars, locked of old:
There tankards, plates and vessels of pure gold
All ranged in rows he will behold;   5020
There ruby-decorated goblets stand
Ready for use; for close at hand
Ancient elixirs still are stored.
Though here—you must believe my expert word—
The wooden staves have long disintegrated,
And yet the tartar crust such wine precipitated
Is now its cask. Wine's noble essence too
Must hide, as gold and jewels do,
Under a cloak of dreadful night.
But here the sage works on undaunted: 5030
Research is trivialized by too much light,
And night, not day, by mysteries is haunted.

THE EMPEROR. We want no darkness and no mysteries
    here;
Whatever is of value must appear
In daylight. In the dark, thieves slip away,
All cows are black and every cat is grey.
If there are pots of gold there, take your plough
And dig them up into the here and now.

MEPHISTOPHELES. You yourself must take tools and
    excavate;
Such peasant labour, Sire, will make you great,   5040
And a whole herd will come to birth
Of golden calves emerging from the earth.
Then with what joy you and your sweetheart may
Be instantly adorned with rich array!
On glittering stones the colours all will dance,
Beauty and majesty alike to enhance.

THE EMPEROR. At once, at once then! How long must I
    wait!

THE ASTROLOGER [prompted as before].
Let me entreat you, Sire, to moderate
Your fierce impatience till the merry feast
Is over! Order serves our purpose best.   5050
A penitent restraint first reconciles us,

Meriting heaven before earth beguiles us.
Who would enjoy good things, let him be good,
The pleasure-seeker cool his ardent blood;
Who calls for wine, ripe grapes he first must tread;
Who'd sup on wonders, let his faith be fed!

THE EMPEROR. So let us join in revels and in play!
I see tomorrow is Ash Wednesday.
Till then, in any case, I bid you all
Celebrate a still wilder Carnival!   5060

[*Trumpets, exeunt.*]

MEPHISTOPHELES. Merit and fortune interweave as one;
These fools don't know it. If they ever were
To find the famous Philosophic Stone,
They'd have a stone but no philosopher.

3 · THE CARNIVAL MASQUE*

[*A spacious hall with ante-rooms, embellished and
decorated for the festivities.*]

A HERALD. Forget you are in German lands, forget
Dances of Death, of fools and devilry:
These shall not mar our pleasant revelry!
Our noble Emperor, when he set
His course for Rome, and crossed the Alpine heights,
Conquered, for his advantages and your delights,   5070
A southern realm of gaiety.
There, at the Holy Father's stool,
He humbly stooped and claimed the right to rule;
A crown was what he went to ask,
But with the crown he brought us back the mask.
Now all are reborn in this garb of jest,
And every worldly man of us is glad
To pull it round his ears and head,
To look a clown and to be antic-mad,
Though under it he's sane like all the rest.   5080
I see already how they gather

And part, and fondly come together,
Chorus with chorus as they meet and mix,
As in and out and out and in they go.
Here we shall learn what we already know:
That with its hundred thousand foolish tricks
The world was always a great fool, and still is so.

FLOWER-GIRLS [*singing, accompanied by mandolines*].
　　　Siamo belle Fiorentine:
　　　All our finery we've brought,
　　　For we would be *signorine*   5090
　　　Worthy of the German court.

　　　Many flowers we are wearing
　　　On our dark and curly heads,
　　　Silken flakes and silken threads
　　　In their composition sharing,

　　　And their making is a special
　　　Skill, deservedly renowned:
　　　Though their beauty's artificial,
　　　It will blossom all year round.

　　　Many colours, tiny pieces,   5100
　　　All arranged in symmetry;
　　　Each one variously pleases,
　　　But the whole is harmony.

　　　Siamo belle giardiniere,
　　　And with men we're not contrary:
　　　For in every woman's heart
　　　Nature is akin to art.

THE HERALD. Baskets on your heads and arms,
　　　Richly loaded, match your charms;
　　　Show your wares! Let all make haste,   5110
　　　Each to buy what suits his taste,
　　　That a garden may appear,
　　　Paths and arbours all be here,
　　　Maidens and their merchandise
　　　Crowd into a paradise!

THE FLOWER-GIRLS. Let us sell, but let us not
  Bargain in this pleasant spot.
  Buyers shall be plainly told
  What they'll pay and what they're sold.

AN OLIVE BRANCH IN FRUIT.
  Fruit and flower wage no strife;   5120
  I need envy none of these,
  It is not my way of life.
  I, the strength of lands and fields,
  Am their guarantee of peace
  By my steady annual yields.
  Let us hope that I shall now
  Decorate some noble brow.

A GARLAND OF GOLDEN CORN SHEAVES.
  We are gifts the Earth Goddess sent:
  Add us to your jewellery!
  This most craved utility   5130
  Also charms as ornament.

A FANTASY GARLAND. Many-coloured mallows rising
  Strangely from the mossy ground!
  We are Fashion's own devising,
  Though in Nature seldom found.

A FANTASY BOUQUET. I am nameless, I was missed
  Out of Theophrastus' list;*
  Yet I hope to enrapture you,
  If not all, at least a few.
  Who will twine me in her hair   5140
  Lovingly to adorn her there?
  Who will raise me to her breast,
  Grant me there so sweet to rest?

A CHALLENGE OF ROSEBUDS.
  Let such motley fancies flower
  For the fashion of the hour;
  Strangest structures be invented,
  Though by Nature not intended!
  Stems of green and cups of gold

    In those tresses all behold—
    But we grow unseen, unbidden,   5150
    And when rosebuds first ablaze
    Hint at early summer days
    You may find us, fresh and hidden;
    Such a pleasure who would miss?
    Promise and fulfilment: this
    Law in Flora's kingdom binds
    Every eye, all hearts and minds.

[THE FLOWER-GIRLS *prettily arrange their wares in the leafy avenues.*]

GARDENERS [*singing, accompanied by bass lutes*].
    Flowers that seem to bloom and grow
    On your heads their beauties show;
    Fruit with living flesh and juices   5160
    Only for itself seduces.

    We, the sun-burnt workers, sell you
    Cherries, king plums, blushing peaches:
    Buy them! for your eyes will tell you
    Less than tongue or palate teaches.

    Come, this fruit is ripe and sweet;
    Taste, for it is good to eat!
    Poems to a rose are written,
    But an apple must be bitten.

    Let us join your pretty labours;   5170
    Richest youth is youth that shares!
    We'll display our mellow wares
    In abundance, as good neighbours.

    Arbours decked and garlands wound,
    Bowers blithe and convolute:
    All at once may here be found,
    Bud and petals, flower and fruit.

[*Singing in turns and accompanied by guitars and bass lutes, the two choruses continue to offer their wares and to arrange them in a display which mounts higher and higher. A* MOTHER *and* DAUGHTER *enter.*]

THE MOTHER. When you were but a mite, my lass,
                   I put you in a bonnet;
                   Your figure and your little face   5180
                   Were pretty as a sonnet.
                   Even then I saw you as a bride
                   With a rich husband by your side—
                   I set my heart upon it.

                   Ah well; now many a year's gone by,
                   Wasted and dissipated.
                   The wooers come, but off they fly,
                   And none of them has waited;
                   And yet you danced and did your best,
                   With nod and nudge your interest   5190
                   Was clearly indicated.

                   At all our parties, what went wrong
                   We never could discover—
                   Forfeits and Third Man all night long,
                   And all was vain endeavour!
                   But on a crazy night like this,
                   Open your legs now, little miss,
                   And you'll soon catch a lover.

[*They are joined by a number of pretty young playmates,
and all the girls begin gossiping intimately together.*
FISHERMEN *and* BIRD-CATCHERS *with nets, rods,
lime twigs, and other equipment enter and mix with the
pretty girls. Charming dialogues* * develop as they all by
turns try to woo and capture and escape and hold on to
each other.*]

HEWERS OF WOOD [*roughly bursting in*].
                   Make way! A clearing!
                   Space for us, please!   5200
                   We're felling trees;
                   The timber crashes;
                   The load we're bearing
                   Bumps and bashes.
                   You must understand
                   We want praise and esteem:

For if none in the land
Were hard of hand,
Where would they be,
The cream of the cream,   5210
For all their wit?
They'd freeze, if we
Didn't sweat, you see;
That's the nub of it.

PUNCHINELLOS* [*performing clumsily, almost inanely*].
You poor stupid hacks
Born with bent backs!
We are the sly ones,
The work-shy ones.
Dunce-caps sit lightly,
Our garb is flimsy;   5220
We can be sprightly,
Live by our whimsy,
Leisurely skippers
In comfy slippers.
Through street and square,
Through crowds we go;
We stand and stare,
We shriek and crow
To call each other,
Like eels we slither   5230
Right through the throng,
And dance together
The mad day long.
Whether you praise us
Or criticize us,
We never bother!

PARASITES* [*eagerly fawning*].
You stout log-bearers
And your near-brothers
The charcoal-burners,
You are our heroes!   5240
Would not our bowing,
Nodding and scraping,

Flattersome phrasing,
Hot and cold blowing
That bends to fancies
And suits pretences,
Be unavailing
(Though we were given
Supplies unfailing
Of fire from heaven)   5250
If logs were lacking,
No charcoal setting
The wide hearth blazing,
The hot flames cracking?
There the food's basted
And seethed and roasted;
The patroned picker,
The true plate-licker,
Smells fish and meats,
And comes to table   5260
Eager and able
For gastric feats.

A DRUNKARD [*oblivious*].

Now I'll have a jolly day,
Nothing getting in my way!
Look at what I've brought along:
High good cheer, a merry song.
So I'll drink! I'm drinking, drinking:
Come, drink with me, clink-a-clinking!
You back there, come join the fun!
Lift your elbows and it's done!   5270

My good wife turns up her nose,
Scolds me for these motley clothes,
Doesn't find my antics funny,
Tells me I'm a costume-dummy.
But I drink! I'm drinking, drinking:
Drink, my hearties, clink-a-clinking!
All you dummies, this is fun!
Fill your glasses and it's done!

If I'm lost, why, then I've strayed
To a most convenient spot: 5280
Credit from mine host, if not
From his wife or from the maid.
So I still am drinking, drinking;
Come on, you lot, clink-a-clinking,
Each to each! So on it goes;
Now we're all drunk, I suppose.

Be such revels where they may,
Let it always end this way!
Let me lie now where I'm lying;
I can't stand, it's no use trying.   5290

CHORUS.   Brothers, let's be drinking, drinking!
Raise a toast, a-clinking clinking!
This one's ended on the floor:
Keep your seats or there'll be more.

[THE HERALD *announces poets of various kinds: nature
poets, bards of chivalry and court life, tender minstrels
and rhapsodists. In this throng of miscellaneous
competitors none succeeds in making himself heard. One of
them slinks past, uttering a few words.*]

A SATIRIST.   If I might do the very thing
To give my poet's soul some cheer,
I would write and speak and sing
What no one wants to hear.

[*The Night and Graveyard poets* *send their apologies,
explaining that they are in the middle of a highly
interesting discussion with a freshly resurrected vampire,
from which a new poetic genre may perhaps be developed;*
THE HERALD *has to excuse them, and in the meantime
summons up Greek mythology, which loses none of its
character and charm even in modern costume.*]

THE GRACES

AGLAIA.   If you would learn graceful living,
Mingle grace with all your giving.   5300

HEGEMONE. To accept with grace be skilled,
                 When sweet wishes are fulfilled.

EUPHROSYNE. And from quiet sheltered days
                   Learn to thank in graceful ways.

THE FATES

ATROPOS.   As the eldest, I am bidden
                 Now to spin the thread of fate.
                 Many meanings here lie hidden,
                 Much for me to meditate.

                 Finest flax your lives has woven,
                 Soft and supple it must be,   5310
                 Ever slender, smooth and even;
                 Leave such skilful work to me.

                 But reflect: though bold your dances,
                 Rank the pleasures you may take,
                 Towards its end this thread advances;
                 So beware, for it may break.

CLOTHO.   Things have changed: in recent years
                 I have held the fateful shears.
                 She is old, and by her action
                 With them caused dissatisfaction.   5320

                 Useless lives dragged out their story,
                 Lingered on in light and breath,
                 But the hopes of youth and glory
                 She cut short by gloomy death.

                 Yet I too, I'm bound to say,
                 Made mistakes in my own day,
                 So my shears are sheathed for surety
                 In the interests of security.

                 And I welcome this restraint
                 On such festival occasions;   5330
                 Watching you, I am content
                 To prolong your celebrations.

LACHESIS. As the wise one of the three,
    Fate's disposal fell to me;
    Ever-even distribution
    By my reel's perpetual motion.

    Threads appear and threads are wound,
    And they never miss their way:
    Each I guide where it is bound,
    It must circle as I say.   5340

    And my vigilance must never
    Lapse, or all the world's disjointed.
    Years are measured, hours are counted;
    Twisted skein goes to the weaver.

THE HERALD. Now here come ladies you'll not know by
    sight,
    However well you've read the ancient books;
    They've done great harm—but judge them by their looks,
    And they'll be guests you're eager to invite.

    They are the Furies—you'll not credit this,
    Seeing them so attractive, young and kind;   5350
    But get to know them better, and you'll find
    How sharp as snakes these pretty doves can hiss.

    Yet though they are malignant, nowadays
    The foolish vogue's to boast of one's defects;
    So they'll not pose as angels to win praise,
    But own that they are ruin's architects.

THE FURIES

ALECTO. Try as you will, you'll trust us in the end;
    We're pretty pussies and good flatterers.
    If one of you has got a little friend,
    We'll pour caressing poison in his ears   5360

    Till he believes us when we tell him straight
    That she's come-hithering so and so as well,
    That she's lame, hunchbacked, or an addlepate—
    In fact, that he'll be marrying trash. We tell

Similar stories to the bride: we say,
For instance, that her friend, the other day,
Spoke to that other girl, or some such slight.
They may be reconciled, but never quite.

MEGAERA. That's a mere trifle; once she is his wife
My work begins. Their happiness I can   5370
Destroy with mere ill humour. Human life
Is various, various are the hours of man.

The lover may embrace what he desires,
But longs at once for something still more sweet;
Poor fool! He quits the joy of which he tires,
Seeks to warm ice, flees the sun's ardent heat.

All this well suits the tricks I have in mind.
My faithful demon Asmodeus* stands by,
We scatter well-timed mischief, he and I;
Thus, pair by pair, we ruin all mankind.   5380

TISIPHONE.   Death, not merely tittle-tattle,
                    Is my vengeance on the traitor!
                    Knife or poison, soon or later
                    Comes the adulterer's requital.

                    Moments of sweet love must all
                    Turn to froth and turn to gall;
                    Here no special plea assuages,
                    Guilt must pay its utmost wages.

                    Let none sing 'Forgive, forgive!'
                    'Justice!' to the rocks I cry;   5390
                    'Shall the fickle-hearted live?'
                    And they echo: 'He shall die!'

THE HERALD. Now move aside, make way, if you don't
      mind:
Something is coming that is not your kind.
A mountainous beast* approaches, if you please,
Its flanks bedecked with gorgeous tapestries;
Two tusks, a snake-like trunk hang from its head;
Mysterious! But such riddles can be read.
High on its back you see a slender beauty sit,

With a slim wand she guides and governs it.   5400
Up there, too, stands another, ringed with light
And splendour—I am dazzled by the sight.
In chains two women walk, of noble mien,
One at each side, one fearful, one serene:
One wishing, and one feeling herself free.
Let each state her identity!

FEAR.   Reeking torch and lamp and light
             Glimmer through this feast's confusion;
             Among faces of illusion
             I am bound, alas, so tight!   5410

             Foolish jokers thronging round me,
             Grinning false seductive smiles!
             All my enemies surround me
             On this night of treacherous wiles.

             This man was my friend: I see
             Through him now and his disguise.
             That man tried to murder me,
             Now he flees from my sharp eyes.

             Why can I not get away
             From the world? Yet I must stay: 5420
             Doom that hangs above my head
             Holds me here in murk and dread.

HOPE.   Greetings, sisters! You have spent
             These two days in merriment,
             In a pleasant masquerade;
             But tomorrow you'll prefer,
             I am sure, to be displayed
             As yourselves. Indeed, we care
             Little for this torchlight scene;
             We would wander our own ways   5430
             On the sunny summer days,
             Freely through the meadows green,
             Single or companioned, choosing
             To be active or reposing.
             Lacking nothing, free of care,
             All we seek is granted there;

Every one a welcome guest,
We may enter where we please,
Seeking happiness with ease,
Sure of finding what is best.   5440

WISDOM.   Let not Fear or Hope infect you!
See, I bring them chained and bound;
Thus—stand back, make way all round!—
From these scourges I protect you.

This great living lump of power,
On his back he bears a tower.
On he plods with steps enchanted,
Uphill, downhill, nothing daunted.

But above his turret's wall
Stands a goddess with swift wings   5450
Wide outspread; for so she brings
Ready benefit to all.

Glorious brightnesses surround her,
Flashing far and all around her,
And her name is Victory,
Goddess of all activity.

ZOILO-THERSITES.* Ho, ho! It seems I'm just in time
To curse the lot of you! But I'm
Particularly keen to sneer
At Lady Victory up here.   5460
With her white flapping wings she may
Well think herself a bird of prey,
And as she gazes down so grand,
Fancy she's queen of all the land.
But where there's honour and success,
They raise my hackles, I confess.
I'd lift what's low, put down what's high,
Make wry things straight and straight things wry:
That's the one thing that comforts me,
That's how I want the world to be!   5470

THE HERALD. Why then, my sacred staff, you low-
Born cur, shall strike a master-blow!—

Now writhe and squirm! Now you're in trouble!—
Ugh! Now that back-and-front dwarf-double
Shrinks to a dirty clod of earth,
Then to an egg; just fancy that!
It swells to bursting and gives birth
To twins: a viper and a bat
Hatch out of it! One slithers back
Into the dust; the other, black   5480
As night, flits to the roof. Somewhere
Outside, this ill-intentioned pair
Will meet; I'd rather not be there.

MURMURS FROM THE CROWD.
      Come, there's dancing, music's playing!—
      I don't like this, I'm not staying—
      This is creepy; don't you feel
      Spells being woven? It's not real—
      Something's whirring round my head—
      There, you see, my foot feels dead—
      We're not really hurt at all—   5490
      We're just scared to death, that's all—
      I call this a rotten joke—
      It's those swine, the trickster-folk.

THE HERALD. I have done, since I was made
  Herald of the Masquerade,
  Duty at each feast as sentry:
  Nothing harmful must gain entry
  To our place of celebration,
  And I stand firm at my station.
  Yet through windows, I admit,   5500
  Airy phantoms seem to flit;
  There are ghosts and magic here
  Which I can't keep out, I fear.
  First, that spooky dwarf; and now
  A whole flood of it somehow.
  As my office bids, I should
  Give you an interpretation
  Of these shapes; I wish I could!
  They defy all explanation.

Pray assist my ignorance! See,   5510
Through the crowd—how can this be?—
Floats a splendid chariot,* drawn
By four steeds, easily borne
Through their midst; they need not part
Or give way. What wizard's art
Does it?—Far-off glittering
Stars in many colours rise,
Flickering, magic-lanternwise.
What is this storm-snorting thing?
Now I'm scared! Make way now!

THE BOY CHARIOTEER.   Whoa-ah!   5520
Check your wings, my horses; so!
Feel the wonted reins you know;
Rule yourselves as now I rule you,
Leap like fire when so I school you—
Let us pause and pay respect
To this place. Look, they collect
Round us, the admiring crowd.
Herald, come; proclaim out loud,
While we're with you, who we are,
What we're like, etcetera.   5530
Since we're allegorical,
You, I think, should know us all.

THE HERALD. To describe you I might try;
But that's not to identify.

THE BOY CHARIOTEER. Try it, then!

THE HERALD. First, I must concede
You're a young, handsome, halfling boy;
Women must hope to have more joy
Of you when you are fully grown. Indeed,
You are a future lady's man, I'd say,
A born seducer anyway.   5540

THE BOY CHARIOTEER.
You are most kind; but pray continue.
Have you this riddle's pleasant answer in you?

THE HERALD. A jewelled ribbon beautifies
Your night-black hair above dark flashing eyes.

And from your shoulders to your feet, how fine
A garment flows, with gems ashine
And edged with purple! Some might say
You're like a girl; and yet, even today,
For better or for worse, you'd make a good
Impression on the girls—they would,   5550
I'm sure, teach you your ABC.

THE BOY CHARIOTEER.
   And this resplendent figure, who is he,
   Who on the chariot's throne sits royally?

THE HERALD. A prince he seems, rich and a generous
    giver:
   Lucky are those who know his favour.
   To gain their wish they cannot fail;
   To scan all needs his eyes avail,
   And giving is his purest pleasure,
   Greater than fortune or than treasure.

THE BOY CHARIOTEER.
   Good, but that's only half your task: 5560
   A full description's what I ask.

THE HERALD. Such dignity no words can praise.
   A moon-shaped visage bright with health,
   Full lips, red cheeks, a sun-like gaze
   Beneath his jewelled turban's wealth;
   A rich commodious robe. What shall
   I say of his demeanour? All
   The world must know him as a king!

THE BOY CHARIOTEER. Plutus, the god of riches (for
   That is his name) in triumph here I bring;   5570
   He is badly needed by the Emperor.

THE HERALD. But tell us now your own identity.

THE BOY CHARIOTEER. I am Profusion, I am Poetry,
   The poet who perfects himself the more
   He spends from his most precious store.
   I too am rich like Plutus, and I hold
   Myself his peer in wealth untold.

I enliven his feasts, adorn his dances:
Where his provision lacks, there mine enhances.

THE HERALD. To boast with charm's your proper part,   5580
But let us also see your art.

THE BOY CHARIOTEER.
I'll snap my fingers then; see how lights play
And flicker round the chariot straight away!
Here's a pearl necklace—out it jumps; and here
Are clasps of gold for neck and ear;

[*He continues to snap his fingers in all directions.*]

And combs, of course, and diadems,
And gold rings set with priceless gems.
Sometimes I offer flames as well
Where they may kindle, who can tell!

THE HERALD. Now watch it snatch, the foolish mob!   5590
Even the giver's having a hard job.
He snaps out trinkets left and right;
It's like a dream, and they all fight
And grab for them. But what new tricks
Are these? One catches something, picks
It up, and what, for all his pains,
Is the reward? Nothing remains!
The string of pearls has vanished, and
Black beetles scuttle in his hand.
He casts them down, and now instead   5600
They're buzzing round his silly head.
And all the rest are fooled likewise,
With monstrous moths their empty prize.
The rogue! He promised them a lot,
And now fool's gold is all they've got.

THE BOY CHARIOTEER.
It seems your herald's role is to proclaim
The hollow mask, but not to name
The true reality that lies behind;
That is beyond your shallow courtly mind.
But we'll not quarrel here. To you, my master, I   5610
Shall turn, and you will make reply.

[*Addressing* PLUTUS.]

Did you not give me my four steeds,
This chariot with its whirlwind speeds?
Do I not drive as you command me,
There in an instant where you send me?
And did I not triumphantly
Win you the palm of victory?
How often I have fought your wars,
And every time the day was yours!
The laurel that adorns your brow,   5620
I wove it, for my mind and hands knew how.

PLUTUS. You are, as I will gladly testify,
Spirit of my spirit, acting ever as I
Would wish; your wealth exceeds my own.
Acknowledging your service, let me bear
Witness that this green laurel bough I wear
Is precious to me like no other crown.
This word I speak to all, and it is true:
Beloved son, I am well pleased in you.

THE BOY CHARIOTEER [*to* THE CROWD].
Look, now I have distributed   5630
My greatest gifts: on many a head
A flame that spurted from my hand
Now flickers. Fiery tongues dance round,
Pausing on each of them in turn:
To one they cling, the next they spurn,
But seldom does the fire blaze high
In brilliant bloom that soon will die;
Few even recognize the spark
Before it fails and all is dark.

CHATTERING WOMEN.
              Who's that up there behind, asquat   5640
       The luggage-box? I bet he's not
       The genuine article. A clown,
       But hunger and thirst have thinned him down;
       We've never seen clowns that weren't fat.
       Try pinching him, he'll not feel that!

THE SKINNY FELLOW.*
  Disgusting females, let me be!
  I know you have no use for me.
  Once, Home and Woman meant the same,
  And *Avaritia* was my name;
  Those were the days! Good luck about   5650
  The house; lots in and nothing out.
  My coffers were well stocked with gold—
  I was a mortal sin, we're told.
  But in more recent years, this passion
  For saving's not been woman's fashion:
  Like all bad payers, she has more
  Wishes than ducats. It's a sore
  Plight for her husband, he's beset
  On every side by ruinous debt.
  Her spinning-money she'll soon spend   5660
  On clothes and on her fancy friend;
  She dines and wines with every sort
  Of squire who comes to pay her court.
  So I set greater store by gold, being wiser,
  And now my masculine name is Miser.

THE LEADER OF THE WOMEN.
  Miserly dragon! Let him stick
  To his own kind. It's just a trick
  To turn our men against us, though
  That's hardly needful, as we know.

THE CROWD OF WOMEN.
        You old straw guy! Old skin and bone!   5670
        How dare he threaten us? Come on,
        Give him a slap! That ugly frown
        Won't frighten us. Let's pull him down!
        The dragons are just wood and paper!

THE HERALD. My staff calls order! Stop this caper!—
  But my help's scarcely needed now.
  Look at those fearsome monsters, how
  Quickly they clear a space, and spread
  Their double wings, their claws of dread!
  Those scaly dragon-snouts, fire-spitting,   5680

Chatter with rage. The crowd's retreating;
It scatters. Now there's room.

[PLUTUS *dismounts from the chariot.*]

                              How like a king
He has dismounted! At his beckoning
The dragons set to work: the chest
Is lifted off at his behest,
Brought to him, set down at his feet,
With gold and miser, all complete.
Now this is a miraculous thing.

PLUTUS [*to* THE CHARIOTEER].
    You have laid down your heavy burden here;
    Now you are free to fly to your own sphere,   5690
    For here it is not. Here we are surrounded
    By grotesque motley shapes, wild and confounded.
    Only where you gaze clear into sweet clarity,
    Trusting yourself alone, there you should be:
    Where you are yours, the beautiful and the good
    Alone can please. There make your world—in solitude!

THE BOY CHARIOTEER.
    As your true envoy I esteem myself; so too
    I love you as my next of kin. Where you
    Dwell, there is fullness; and wherever I
    May be, there all I bless and gratify.   5700
    Confused by life, men often hesitate
    Whether to serve you, or commit their fate
    To me. Your followers of course enjoy
    A life of ease, but mine must constantly employ
    Their energies. My deeds I cannot hide:
    If I but breathe I am identified.
    Farewell then, since you grant my happiness: I go,
    But I'll return when you shall whisper so.

                    [*He leaves as he came.*]

PLUTUS. Now it is time to set the treasure free.
    To strike the locks I take the herald's stave;   5710
    And they fly open. In bronze vessels, see!

The golden lifeblood stirs, a seething wave,
And jewellery—rings and chains, a crown—
Which soon the metal flood will swallow and melt down.

THE CROWD [*yelling by turns*].
    Oh look, oh look, it's overspilling!
    Right to the edge the chest is filling!—
    See how they melt, the cups of gold,
    See how the rolls of coin are rolled!—
    The ducats dance as if new-struck;
    Oh joyful sight, oh great good luck!—   5720
    I watch my dearest wish come true!
    They're spinning on the ground now too—
    This is your chance, now use it quick,
    Stoop to be rich, and take your pick!—
    Our lot's the strongest, we're the best,
    We'll carry off the treasure-chest.—

THE HERALD. You fools, it's just a masquerade!
 What are you doing? That's enough
 Greed for one evening. Did you think this stuff
 Was gold and money? I'm afraid   5730
 You louts don't even qualify
 For gaming-counters in this game.
 A pleasant fancy: you think that's the same
 As the coarse truth? And indeed, why
 Should you know truth? You wildly snatch
 At any dull illusion you can catch.
 Oh mask of Plutus, lord of mummery,
 Scatter this rabble mob for me!

PLUTUS. For that, no doubt, your staff is fit,
 If I may briefly borrow it!—   5740
 I'll dip it in the soup of gold.—
 Now, mummers, have a care! Behold
 It flash and splash and spark and spit!
 Soon it's red-hot, see how it glows!
 Now anyone who comes too close
 Will be unmercifully singed. Stand clear!
 I must pace out a circle here.

THE CROWD [*crying out and pushing*].
>Oh! Oh! We're done for! Runaway!—
>Every man for himself, I say!—
>You there behind, get back, make way!—   5750
>It's spurting in my face, it's hot!—
>I'm crushed by the burning stick he's got!—
>Stand back, you mummer-mob, stand back!—
>Make room, make room, you senseless pack!—
>Now we're all lost, now we'll all die!—
>Oh, give me wings, and off I'd fly!—

PLUTUS. The encircling crowd must now retire;
>They seem to have escaped the fire.
>The mob takes fright,
>They're put to flight.   5760
>But I must draw an unseen border
>To guarantee this new-found order.

THE HERALD. A splendid work you now fulfil,
>Thanks to your power and your skill.

PLUTUS. We must be patient, noble friend;
>This tumult's not yet at an end.

THE MISER. Now, if we please, we may survey
>This charming circle: once again,
>As always, women take the forefront when
>Some sweetmeat tempts or something's on display.   5770
>My rusting-up's not yet complete,
>A female beauty's still a treat.
>So off I'll go and court some ladies;
>And I'm in luck today—it's *gratis*.
>But with such crowds of people here,
>Not every word is heard by every ear;
>So I will use my arts, and mimically express
>My meaning; this should bring me some success.
>Hands, feet and gestures here are insufficient:
>But in a ruder jest I'll be proficient.   5780
>My clay shall be this malleable gold,
>For it's a metal apt to every mould.

THE HERALD. Our walking skeleton, what's he up to now?
>Has hunger made him humorous somehow?

He's kneading all that gold like dough;
Between his hands it softens so.
He squeezes it: a lump, a ball
Shaped like no proper thing at all.
He shows it to the women: they
All shriek and try to run away,   5790
Making a great show of disgust.
The rogue shows malice in his lust:
The more he outrages decency,
I fear, the better pleased he'll be.
This must not pass! Give me my stave!
I'll drive him out, I'll teach him to behave.

PLUTUS. But now another threat draws near!
　　Leave him his antics; he has no idea
　　What's coming. There'll be no room for his fooling;
　　Law rules, but *force majeure* is overruling.   5800

TUMULT AND SINGING.
　　　　　The Wild Host comes from the high hills,
　　　　　Out of the wooded glens it spills:
　　　　　Who can withstand us now, who can
　　　　　Resist? We honour our Great Pan.*
　　　　　A secret known to none we know;
　　　　　The circle's empty, in we go!

PLUTUS. I know you well, and your Great Pan. Good
　　　　speed
　　Together you have made. I know indeed
　　That secret known to few; respectfully
　　I loose the circle's narrow boundary.—   5810
　　Now may good fortune still pursue them!
　　The strangest things may happen to them;
　　They cannot tell where now they tread,
　　For they have failed to look ahead.

WILD SINGING. You dressed-up mob, parading vainly!
　　　　　　　We come here bare, we come ungainly;
　　　　　　　See how we run and leap so far,
　　　　　　　How rough and rude and strong we are!

FAUNS. Now fauns advance
  In merry dance;   5820
  In curly hair
  Oak-leaves we wear,
  Among our locks each pointed ear
  Pricks up so neatly here and here,
  Our nose is blunt, our face is broad:
  All these are things that women applaud.
  A girl will dance and be delighted
  When by a faun's paw she's invited.

A SATYR. Up pops the satyr now, complete
  With scrawny haunches and goat's feet;   5830
  They must be lean and sinewy,
  For like a mountain chamois, he
  Delights in rocky heights to see
  The world. Refreshed in freedom's air,
  He mocks all humankind from there:
  Deep in their valleys' steamy stew
  They fancy they are living too,
  But high above all taint and throng
  Those regions to him alone belong.

GNOMES. Here come the Little Folk, trip-trot;   5840
  Not two by two, we'd rather not.
  In moss-green smocks, with lamps aglow,
  We helter-skelter to and fro,
  Each of us doing his own thing,
  Like glow-worms swarming, glimmering,
  Scuttling busily about,
  Hither and thither, in and out.

  Dwarves are like us, they're our close kin.
  Rock surgery we specialize in:
  We bleed the lofty mountains' veins,   5850
  And out pours treasure for our pains.
  We pile up metals we have struck,
  With miners' greetings wishing luck.
  All this is thoroughly well meant;
  Good men deserve our good intent.
  But we bring gold up so that they

May steal and whore, for that's their way;
With iron weapons we supply
The proud man for whom thousands die.
The three *thou shalt nots* men ignore   5860
Soon have them flouting many more.
All this is not our fault, and you
Must still have patience, as we do.

GIANTS. Here are the Wild Men, that's our name,
The Wild Men of Harz Mountains fame.
Natural-naked in full strength,
Each with his club a pinetree's length,
We come as giants big and tall
And thickly girdled one and all
With leaves and branches bound like thatch.   5870
No Pope has bodyguards to match!

NYMPHS IN CHORUS [*surrounding* GREAT PAN].
Great Pan is here!
In him is shown,
In him alone,
The great world's sphere.
You happy nymphs, surround him now,
Flitting and dancing round him now;
He's serious but benevolent
And a friend of merriment.
And he'd be wakeful all day too   5880
Under the heaven's tent of blue,
But by the breezes he's caressed
And streamlets murmur him to rest.
And when he is asleep at noon
No leaf or twig will stir too soon;
Life-giving plants are growing there,
Their fragrance fills the soundless air;
No nymph dare stay awake, we fall
Asleep still standing. But his call,
His sudden cry of fearful power,   5890
When it rings out in that same hour
Like thunder or the roaring sea,
Then none knows where to stand or flee,

Brave armies quail, the hero quakes
Hearing such tumult as Pan wakes.
So let us praise this lord who brought
Us here, and hail him as we ought!

A DEPUTATION OF GNOMES [*to* GREAT PAN].

Though the glinting treasures thread
Richly through the mountain's heart,
Only the diviner's art   5900
To that labyrinth is led.

Troglodytically living
In dark caves we hide away:
Yours the gold for gracious giving
In the purer airs of day.

Now this other spring divined
Most conveniently close by
Will miraculously supply
All we scarcely hoped to find.

You can bring this to completion: 5910
Take it, lord, and care for it;
Any wealth in your possession
Is the whole world's benefit.

PLUTUS [*to* THE HERALD].
We must be high in spirit, we must face
With resignation what will now take place;
And indeed you are valiant, as I know.
All will deny, even posterity
Will disbelieve this dire calamity,
But in your written record it must show.

THE HERALD [*grasping the staff which* PLUTUS *continues to
    hold*].
The Dwarves, with Great Pan following,   5920
Approach with care the fiery spring;
It boils up from its source, and then
Sinks down into the depths again;
Now dark it stands, the open jaw,
Till glowing broth spews out once more.
Great Pan, whom this strange toy amazes,

In high good humour stands and gazes,
As pearly foam from each side blazes.
Shall he believe his eyes? And low
He stoops, to see if it is so.   5930
But his beard drops into the vat!*—
Whose beard? And whose bare chin is that?
His hand conceals it. Now, alas!
A great misfortune comes to pass:
The beard bursts into flames, blows back,
Wreath, head and breast the flames attack,
And our rejoicing turns to grief.
All rush to quench, to bring relief,
But none escapes the leaping fire;
The more they smack and smite, the higher   5940
The inferno rages. An entire
Tangle of masqueraders, wrapped
In flames, by burning death are trapped.

But what is this report I hear,
From mouth to mouth, from ear to ear?
Oh ever wretched fatal night
That brings us to this dreadful plight!
What none can bear to hear or say
Will be proclaimed this coming day;
And now from loud cries I am learning: 5950
'It was *the Emperor* who was burning!'
Oh if it only were not true!
He burns, and his attendants too.
That cursed rout seduced his mind
And came with resinous twigs entwined
To bellow their wild song: now all
Into this general ruin fall.
Oh youth, youth, can you not constrain
Your joy into its purer measures?
Oh majesty, will you never reign   5960
All-powerful, yet with prudent pleasures?

And now the arbours are alight;
The pointed tongues lick upwards, right
Into the coffered ceiling. Why,

We'll all be burnt now, we'll all die!
Alas, I fear it will be so.
Who'll save us from this general woe?
One night, and the imperial state
Lies burnt to ash and desolate.

PLUTUS. Come now, that's enough alarm!   5970
You shall all be saved from harm.
With our staff now strike the ground,
Let its sacred power resound.
Let the wide air at our will
Now with cooling fragrance fill.
Come, you trails of drifting, sliding
Mist, enveloping and hiding
All this fiery chaos; curl,
Fleecy cloudlets, trickle, swirl,
Breathe your vapours, gently gliding!   5980
You can quench, you can assuage,
You can damp this false fire's rage:
Do so, and it all shall seem
But the summer lightning's gleam.—
Thus, when spirit-power assails us,
Magic's ancient art avails us.

4 · A PLEASURE-GARDEN

[*Morning sunlight.* THE EMPEROR *and* COURTIERS,
FAUST *and* MEPHISTOPHELES, *dressed in a becoming
manner, fashionable but unostentatious; both kneeling.*]

FAUST. Sire, for the pyrotechnics we apologize.

THE EMPEROR [*motioning them to rise*].
It was most entertaining; pray devise
Such sport more often! Suddenly it seemed
That I was Pluto, and a great sphere gleamed   5990
And burned about me. A dark rocky pit
Glowed as with fiery coals, and from the depths of it
And of the other, blazed wild flickering flame
Of many thousand tongues, which all became

A single vault, a supreme temple: higher
It rose, forming, unforming out of fire.
Whole peoples moved through the vast colonnade
All round me that the twisting flame-tongues made:
They thronged towards me, circling far and near,
And all, as hitherto, paid homage here.   6000
I recognized my court among these wonders;
I was prince of a thousand salamanders.*

MEPHISTOPHELES. And so you are, Sire, for the elements
All recognize your high pre-eminence.
The submission of fire you have seen first;
Plunge now into the sea at its wild worst,
And scarcely will you touch the pearl-strewn floor
Than a great dome will shape itself once more:
The mobile waves, light green and purple-fringed,
Into a kingly dwelling shall be changed   6010
Round you, its central point. Go where you please,
Each step you take, you take your palaces
Along with you. That globe's live walls will swarm
With flickering things all darting to and fro;
Sea-monsters, nuzzling at its strange mild glow,
Approach, but none can pierce the magic form;
Gold-squamous coloured dragons play, the wide-
Jawed shark lunges: you mock him, safe inside.
Your thronging court here takes delight in you,
But such a throng as that you never knew.   6020
Nor are you there debarred from sweetest wishes:
For curious Nereids (young and keen as fishes
Yet shy, or older and more circumspect)
Swim up, your deep-sea lodging to inspect
In its eternal lustre; Thetis too will wed
This modern Peleus and take him to her bed.
Next, high Olympus and the kingdoms there—

THE EMPEROR. Thank you: you may omit the upper air.
One mounts that throne quite soon enough, we're told.

MEPHISTOPHELES. And, Sire, the earth you already have
and hold.   6030

THE EMPEROR.
　　What lucky chance has brought you here, straight out
　　Of the Arabian Nights? You need not doubt,
　　If you can match Scheherazade's skill
　　In story-telling, that I will
　　Grant you high favour. Let me count on you
　　When the day's doings bore me, as they often do.

THE STEWARD [*entering hurriedly*].
　　Your Majesty! I never would have thought
　　I'd one day bring the news I now have brought
　　Of such good fortune to you! Here I bow
　　Before you with such joy! For how　　　　　　　　6040
　　Can it be true? The bills are paid,
　　The usurers' rage has been allayed
　　And from their hellish claws I'm free!
　　Can heaven offer such felicity?

THE ARMY COMMANDER [*quickly following him*].
　　The army debt has been half settled,
　　The oath resworn, the troops refettled,
　　Their mercenary morale restored,
　　Landlords all rich, the men all whored.

THE EMPEROR. How light of heart you both seem now,
　　The wrinkles vanished from your brow,　　　　　6050
　　A quicker step, and cast-off cares!

THE TREASURER [*who has also arrived*].
　　Sire, you must ask these two, the work was theirs.

FAUST. It is the Chancellor's office to explain.

THE CHANCELLOR [*approaching slowly*].
　　I am glad not to have lived so long in vain!
　　Hear then and see this fateful paper, which
　　Has changed our poverty and made us rich.

　　　　　　　　　　　　　　[*He reads.*]

　　'To whom it may concern: hereby be advised and told,
　　The present note is worth a thousand crowns in gold.
　　This sum secured and covered in full measure
　　By Imperial land's abundant buried treasure;　　6060

The same to serve as its equivalent
Upon recovery, as is Our intent.'

THE EMPEROR. My lords, this is some fraud, some vast
    deceit!
Who dared to sign my name in counterfeit?
Has no one yet been punished for this crime?

THE TREASURER. You wrote it, Sire, yourself; at Carnival
    time,
Last night! You were Great Pan, you will recall;
The Chancellor approached, as did we all,
Beseeching you: 'A few strokes of your pen
Will crown the feast and mend the realm again!'   6070
You signed: and thanks to prestidigitation
The night sufficed for ample duplication.
And in this general boon, to ensure fair play,
We printed the whole series straight away:
Tens, thirties, fifties, hundreds—all are ready.
See how the people all rejoice already!
This town, half mouldy-dead of late, now thriving,
Swarming with life, its appetites reviving!
Your name has blessed the world for many a year,
But never was so gladly read as here.   6080
The remaining alphabet grows valueless,
For in this sign all now find happiness.

THE EMPEROR. My people think it's gold? Well now,
    that's funny.
The court, the army, treat this as sound money?
Astonishing. But now what can I do?

THE STEWARD. No one could catch them, and away they
    flew;
It spread like lightning. Now on every side
The money-changers' doors are open wide;
They're honouring every note, both small and large,
With gold and silver, though of course they charge   6090
Commission. Butchers, bakers, landlords—good
Money for them! Half the world just wants food
And drink, the rest want fine new clothes to strut
About in; tailors stitch, cloth-merchants cut;

Meanwhile plates clatter, meats are stewed and roasted
In taverns, and 'The Emperor!' is toasted.

MEPHISTOPHELES. Walk then alone along the terraces:
See, a fair lady all in fineries,
Covering one eye with her proud peacock fan,
Come-hithering with the other any man   6100
Who bears this paper passport to her heart,
Which outpersuades all wit and wooer's art!
No need to lug a purse around; the best
Place for such *billets* is a lover's breast,
Among his *billets doux*. A priest may carry
Them piously inside his breviary;
As for the soldier, he's a nimbler fighter,
I dare say, if his money-belt is lighter.
Forgive me, Majesty, if I trivialize
By such examples our high enterprise.   6110

FAUST. The abundance of treasure buried deep
Under your lands lies frozen and asleep
Until we waken it. Thought's utmost scope
Sets a mean limit to such wealth; the hope
Of fancy in its highest flight must fail,
Try as it may, to tell so rich a tale.
Yet worthier spirits whom deep insights bless
Place trust unbounded in this boundlessness.

MEPHISTOPHELES. Such paper currency, replacing gold
And pearls, is most convenient: you can hold   6120
A known amount, no sale or bartering
Is needed to enjoy love, wine, or anything
You please. And there are banks to sell you coin;
If not, then temporarily you join
The diggers, sell a golden chain or cup,
And thus the paper debt's at once paid up
And all the mocking sceptics put to shame.
Everyone's used to this, they want the same
System continued; thus the Empire far and wide
With jewels, gold, and paper now is well supplied.   6130

THE EMPEROR. The Empire owes great benefits to you,
And a commensurate reward is due.

We entrust you with the ground in all our lands;
To guard that wealth, yours are the worthiest hands.
You know where we must dig, and at your word
We shall recover this great hidden hoard.
As partners now, joint masters of our treasure,
Fulfil your honourable task with pleasure!
For here two worlds to union are invited,
Upper with lower happily united.*   6140

THE TREASURER. Sire, there shall be no strife and no
        divisions;
    I like to have colleagues who are magicians.

                    [*Exit with* FAUST.]

THE EMPEROR. Now for some gifts; but you must each
        confess
    What use you intend to make of my largesse.

A PAGE [*receiving some money*].
    I'll have high life, song, dance and jollity.

ANOTHER [*likewise*].
    I'll go and buy my sweetheart jewellery.

A LORD OF THE BEDCHAMBER [*accepting a gift*].
    From now on I'll drink wine at twice the price.

ANOTHER [*likewise*].
    My fingers itch already for the dice!

A KNIGHT-BANNERET [*reflecting*].
    I'll pay the debts off now on my estates.

ANOTHER [*likewise*].
    I'll watch my fund as it accumulates.   6150

THE EMPEROR. I hoped it would inspire you to new
        deeds.
    But it's easy to guess your well-known needs;
    It's obvious that however rich you grow,
    Whatever you have been you'll still be so.

THE FOOL [*reappearing*].
    Is this a bounty? Shall I get a bit?

THE EMPEROR. So you're back! You'll just live by
        drinking it.

THE FOOL. They're magic papers! What do the words say?

THE EMPEROR. You'll misread and misuse them anyway.

THE FOOL. There are some more that dropped—what
shall I do?

THE EMPEROR. Just take them, it's a windfall, they're for
you. [*Exit.*]   6160

THE FOOL. Five thousand crowns! You mean all this is
mine?

MEPHISTOPHELES. So you rose from the dead, you
two-legged bag of wine?

THE FOOL. I often do, but this time's the best yet.

MEPHISTOPHELES. You're so pleased now, you're
breaking out in sweat.

THE FOOL. But look, is this worth money?

MEPHISTOPHELES.   It will buy
All your big maw and belly want; just try!

THE FOOL. You mean a house, livestock and farming land?

MEPHISTOPHELES. Of course! Just offer, they will
understand.

THE FOOL. A castle, hunting forests, fishing streams?

MEPHISTOPHELES. I'll soon address you as 'my lord', it
seems.   6170

THE FOOL. Oh luxury! I'll be a squire this very night!
[*Exit.*]

MEPHISTOPHELES. Call him a wise fool now, and you'll
be right!

5 · A DARK GALLERY

[FAUST. MEPHISTOPHELES.]

MEPHISTOPHELES. These gloomy passages! Why do you
 drag me here?
Was all that high society
Not fun enough? There's plenty of good cheer
Still to enjoy, and much fine trickery!

FAUST. No need to speak of it; in the old days
    You played that game a hundred tedious ways.
    Now stop your slithering to and fro
    And tell me what I need to know.   6180
    They're pestering me now for action:
    The Steward, the Chamberlain want satisfaction.
    The Emperor demands to see
    Helen and Paris, here, immediately;
    The ideal man and woman, to appear
    Before his eyes, in figures plain and clear.
    So get to work! I mustn't break my word.

MEPHISTOPHELES. You promised that? How frivolous,
    how absurd!

FAUST. Let me inform you that your pranks
    Have consequences, my good friend.   6190
    We made him rich and earned his thanks,
    And now he must be entertained.

MEPHISTOPHELES. You think this task's a simple one;
    But it's a steeper stair to climb,
    A stranger region than you've ever known,
    Which by your new commitments you now dare
    To tread, conjuring Helen out of time
    Like phantom paper-money from the air.
    Easy, you think?—Witches I can supply,
    Ghost-goblins, changelings, curious succubi;   6200
    But Satan-sweethearts, though quite charming in
        their way,
    Can't pass for Homer's heroines even today.

FAUST. So, here we go again, your old lament!
    With you there's never any guarantee;
    Nothing gets done without an extra fee,
    Everything is a problem you invent.
    She'll come at once, as I know very well!
    Two mumbled words from you will summon her.

MEPHISTOPHELES. Pagans are not my period, sir;
    They're lodged in their own special hell.   6210
    But there's a way.

FAUST.   Divulge it instantly!

MEPHISTOPHELES. I do not like to; this is high mystery.
    Enthroned in solitude are goddesses—
    No place, no space around them, time still less;
    I mention them with some uneasiness.
    They are *the Mothers.**

FAUST [*startled*].   Mothers!

MEPHISTOPHELES.   You dread the name?

FAUST. The Mothers! But how strange 'the mothers'
    sounds!

MEPHISTOPHELES. Indeed; we hesitate ourselves to speak
    Of these great goddesses, and your mortal minds
    Have never known them. Go to the depths to seek   6220
    Their dwelling! If we need them, you're to blame.

FAUST. Which is the way?

MEPHISTOPHELES. No way! A path untrodden
    Which none may tread; a way to the forbidden,
    The unmoved, the inexorable. Make preparation!
    There'll be no locks to unlock, no bolts to slide:
    On solitudes you will drift far and wide.
    Do you know solitude and desolation?

FAUST. If these are your wise saws, you might as well
    Not speak. They've a witch-kitchen smell;
    This is all stuff from long ago.   6230
    The world was with me, was it not? And there
    I learnt and taught nothing but empty air.
    If ever I talked sense, told what I know,
    They'd shout me down still louder; finally,
    Embracing desert solitude to flee
    From the vile tricks society played on me,
    Rather than have no company at all
    I invoked the Devil, as you will recall.

MEPHISTOPHELES. Yet even if you'd swum the ocean
        through
    And known its boundlessness, even then   6240

You would see waves roll by and roll again;
Even at the dreadful drowning-point, there too
You would see something. In the still sea-green
There would be darting dolphins to be seen;
There'd be the clouds, sun, moon and starry sky—
But in the eternal void you'll say goodbye
To sight, not hear the step that steps so far,
Not rest a foot on where you are.

FAUST. You talk like any ancient mystagogue
    Addressing neophytes with words to fog   6250
    Their simple minds; but here *per contra*. I
    Am sent into your void to magnify
    My art and strength there; I am to cat's-paw
    Your chestnuts from the fire. Come then! let's claw
    The meaning out of this. I hope to see
    Your Nothing turn to Everything for me.

MEPHISTOPHELES. My compliments, sir, as you take
    your leave;
    You know the Devil well, I do believe.
    Now take this key.

FAUST.   That little thing!

MEPHISTOPHELES.   First seize
    It firmly, and respect it, if you please.   6260

FAUST. It grows in my hand! It shines, it's all a-glitter!

MEPHISTOPHELES. Perhaps you now appreciate it better.
    Follow it downwards, for this key can read
    The hidden map: to the Mothers it will lead.

FAUST [*shuddering*].
    The Mothers! Every time it strikes such fear
    Into my heart, this word I dare not hear.

MEPHISTOPHELES. Are you so limited, that a new word
    Disturbs you, merely one you've not yet heard?
    Let nothing trouble you in sound or sense:
    By now you should be used to strange events.   6270

FAUST. Yet must I turn to stone? Not so I'll thrive!
    Our sense of awe's what keeps us most alive.

The world chokes human feeling more and more,
But deep dread still can move us to the core.

MEPHISTOPHELES. Descend then! I could say ascend;
   there's no
Distinction. Flee from all that has been born
To the unbound realm of empty shapes; return
To savour what has vanished long ago.
Like drifting coils of cloud they will approach you:
Brandish the key, for then they cannot touch you.   6280

FAUST [with enthusiasm].
   I seize it, and at once my spirits rise,
   I feel new strength for this great enterprise.

MEPHISTOPHELES. A glowing tripod will alert your fall
   That it has reached the deepest depth of all.
   And by that tripod's light you'll see the Mothers;
   Some sitting, as the case may be, and others
   Who stand or walk. Formation, transformation,
   The eternal Mind's eternal delectation.
   You'll pass unseen: the whole world of creatures
     swarms
   As images round them; they see empty forms   6290
   And nothing else. But you will be in great
   Peril still, and you must be bold: go straight
   To the tripod, touch it with the key.

   [FAUST strikes a decisive commanding attitude with the
   key.]

MEPHISTOPHELES [watching him].   Just so!
   Then, slave-like, it will follow where you go;
   Good fortune's wings will raise you, never fear!
   Before they miss it, you'll be back up here.
   And once you've got that brazier, then you may
   Summon the famous pair into the day.
   No one has ever dared before to do
   This deed, and it will be achieved by you.   6300
   The incense-cloud, with magic to compel it,
   Will assume any godlike shape you tell it.

FAUST. Well then, what now?

MEPHISTOPHELES.   Strive downwards; stamp, and you
    Will sink; you'll rise again by stamping too.

        [FAUST *stamps and disappears into the earth.*]

    I hope he's well protected by that key.
    Will he get back, I wonder? We shall see.

6 · BRIGHTLY LIT HALLS

    [THE EMPEROR *with* PRINCES *and* COURTIERS,
    walking to and fro.]

THE CHAMBERLAIN [*to* MEPHISTOPHELES].
    You still owe us that spirit scene; you're late
    With it. The Emperor doesn't like to wait.

THE MARSHAL. He's just been asking us when it's to be.
    Delay's an insult to His Majesty.   6310

MEPHISTOPHELES. My colleague's gone to see to it; he
      knows how
    It must be done, he's working on that now,
    With silent labour and peculiar skill.
    This occult task's not easy to fulfil.
    Beauty's like buried treasure: where it lies
    Is known by art and magic to the wise.*

THE MARSHAL. What arts you use is your affair; just
      hurry!
    The Emperor wants to see the show start, that's our
      worry.

A BLONDE GIRL [*to* MEPHISTOPHELES].
    A word with you, sir! My complexion's clear,
    But every summer horrid spots appear—   6320
    Hundreds of them, red-brown; it's such a pest,
    Covering my white skin! Can you suggest
    A remedy?

MEPHISTOPHELES. For shame! A bright young thing,
    Marked like a panther-kitten every spring!
    Take frogspawn, toads' tongues, mix, distil them well

In the full moonlight to complete the spell;
Wait till the moon wanes, then apply with care,
And when May comes, the spots will not be there.

A DARK GIRL. Look how these flatterers mob you, sir! I
    beg
  A remedy too. It's for my foot, my leg: 6330
  It's frozen! I can't move it properly,
  To walk or dance or curtsey.

MEPHISTOPHELES.   Allow me
  To give your foot a footprint of mine too.

THE DARK GIRL.
  Well, that's a thing that courting couples do.

MEPHISTOPHELES. My foot, child, has a more important
    function.
  All ills are cured by like to like's conjunction;
  Thus, foot heals foot, and so with other parts.
  Come now, keep steady! Don't reciprocate!

THE DARK GIRL [shrieking].
  Oh! Oh! You stamped so hard on me! It hurts!
  That was a horse's hoof!

MEPHISTOPHELES.   At any rate,   6340
  My dear, you're cured. From now on you'll be able
  To dance, and play foot-footsie games at table.

A LADY [struggling to reach him].
  Let me through! Let me through! I'm in such anguish;
  Deep in my heart I boil and burn and languish.
  I was his sweetheart only yesterday:
  Now he walks out with her, tells me to go away!

MEPHISTOPHELES. That's a problem; but now do as I say.
  Take this charcoal: steal up close to your man
  And mark him with it where you can —
  His sleeve, his cloak, his shoulder—and at once   6350
  He'll feel a prick of loving penitence;
  But swallow the coal immediately, don't take
  A drop of wine or water. That will make
  Him sigh this very night before your door.

THE LADY. I hope it's not a poison?

MEPHISTOPHELES [*indignantly*].

If you please,
  Show due respect! The flames around a stake
  Charred this rare relic; bonfires such as these
  Were commoner in days of yore.

A PAGE. I'm in love, but they say I'm still not old enough.

MEPHISTOPHELES. I'm at my wit's end, answering all
    this stuff.   6360

[*To* THE PAGE.]

The pursuit of young girls will certainly frustrate you.
  Try older ladies, they'll appreciate you.

[*Others crowd round him.*]

More cases to be dealt with! I don't know
  Which way to turn. In such a situation
  One has to tell the truth, in desperation.
  Oh, Mothers, Mothers, help me! Let Faust go!

[*Looking about him.*]

But already the lights are burning low;
  The whole court is assembling for the show.
  In seemly sequence they advance down long
  Passages, through far galleries, and throng   6370
  Into the great hall—such a crowd its old
  And noble space can scarcely hold.
  Its walls are rich with tapestry displays,
  And knightly armour stands in nooks and bays.
  I think no magic words are needed here;
  Now of their own accord the spirits will appear.

7 · THE GREAT HALL

[*Subdued lighting.* THE EMPEROR *has entered with his
court.*]

THE HERALD. My task was always to announce a play:
  Now, spirit-antics complicate the thing.

Their secret tricks I can't explain away
By common sense; it's most bewildering.   6380
The thrones and chairs are all in readiness;
Facing the wall, the Emperor takes his place;
Depicted on its surface he can see
Old battle-scenes very commodiously.
So here they sit, lords, ladies of the court;
Behind, on benches, are the commoner sort,
And for this ghostly show, amid the huddle,
Sweetheart and sweetheart find a place to cuddle.
Thus, all are seated, all's in order here,
We are prepared: the spirits may appear!   6390

[*A fanfare is sounded.*]

THE ASTROLOGER.* Then let our drama start at once.
   By high
Command, let the walls open, mastered by
A ready magic!* See, the hangings furl
Away, as if they were on fire; the whole
Wall splits, turns inside out; now I ascend
To the proscenium, as a deep stage
Appears before us by some sortilege,
And glimmering light mysteriously is feigned.

MEPHISTOPHELES [*appearing in the prompt-box*].
From here I hope to please the general taste;
As a prompter the Devil is well placed.   6400

[*To* THE ASTROLOGER.]

You know the starry motions in and out;
You'll understand my whisperings, I don't doubt.

THE ASTROLOGER. By magic power now before our eyes
We see a massive temple-structure rise;
And as old Atlas carried heaven, so
These many pillars stand in stalwart row,
Ample to bear a mass of rock so great;
Two alone would support a building's weight.

AN ARCHITECT. So that's the antique style! Well, to my
   mind
It's most ungainly, lumpish, unrefined.   6410

They call such coarseness grand and noble! Where
Are our slim columns striving through the air,
Our pointed arch that lifts the spirit high?
Such edifices truly edify.

THE ASTROLOGER. Welcome with reverence this
    star-favoured hour!
Reason, be bound by verbal magic's power!
And boldly, splendidly, from far and wide,
Let Fancy come here and be satisfied.
What you have dared to crave, your eyes now see;
Believe it *quia impossibile*.   6420

        [FAUST *rises into view at the other side of the*
                    proscenium.]

THE ASTROLOGER. In priestly robes and wreath, a
    miracle-man
Comes to complete the great work he began.
A tripod rises from the depths with him,
A whiff of incense from the brazier's rim;
His lofty task he now will crown and bless;
All will be well, all points to happiness.

FAUST [*with grandiose declamation*].
In your name, oh great Mothers, you whose throne
Is boundlessness: eternally alone
You dwell, and yet in company! Round the head
Of each of you, life's forms float, live yet dead;   6430
What once has been, what once shone gloriously,
Still stirs there, seeking evermore to be.
Your mighty power divides it; day's bright tent
Receives it, or the night's dark firmament.
Some images are merged with life's sweet flow,
And some the bold magician captures: so
With prodigal confidence he satisfies
Our wish, and brings wonders before our eyes.

THE ASTROLOGER. His glowing key touches the bowl,
    and all
At once a misty vapour fills the hall.   6440
Cloud-like it creeps and shapes itself, extended,

Compacted, parted, criss-crossed, double-ended.
Now for a masterstroke of spirit-art!
These moving clouds make music, touch the heart
With airy tones, some *je ne sais quoi* of sound,
And all is melody as they drift around.
They set the columns and the triglyphs ringing:
I do believe the entire temple's singing.
The mist subsides: from it, as if to dance,
We see a beautiful young man advance.   6450
The lovely Paris—but I'll say no more;
He needs no introduction here, I'm sure.

[PARIS *appears*.]

A LADY. Oh radiant youth, in fullest flower so sweet!

ANOTHER. How like a peach, juicy and fresh to eat!

A THIRD. His lips how delicate, yet full and pink!

A FOURTH. A shapely cup; wouldn't you like to drink!

A FIFTH. He's pretty, in a slightly vulgar way.

A SIXTH. Not quite enough deportment, I would say.

A KNIGHT. I recognize the shepherd-boy, that's clear,
    But not the prince; not one of us, I fear.   6460

ANOTHER. Oh, he's half-naked, looks all very well,
    But let him put on armour, then we'd tell.

A LADY. Now he sits down; how softly, with what grace!

A KNIGHT. You'd find his lap a pleasant resting-place?

ANOTHER LADY. How gently on his arm he rests his
    head!

THE CHAMBERLAIN. The lout! Such postures are
    prohibited!

A LADY. Why must you men find fault perpetually?

THE CHAMBERLAIN. To loll and sprawl before his
    Majesty!

A LADY. It's just his act, he can't see us or you.

THE CHAMBERLAIN. This is the Court; plays must be
    courteous too.   6470

A LADY. A gentle sleep envelops the dear creature.

THE CHAMBERLAIN. And now he snores; entirely true to
    nature.

A YOUNG LADY [*enraptured*].
    What can that fragrance in the incense be
    That moves my heart, that so refreshes me?

AN OLDER LADY. Indeed, it penetrates the soul, this
    breath
    That comes from him!

A STILL OLDER LADY.   It is the bloom, the growth
    Within him: the whole atmosphere is filled
    With this boy's youth ambrosially distilled.

[HELEN *appears*.]

MEPHISTOPHELES. So that's her! Pretty, but not what
    I'd call
    Exciting; she's just not my type at all.   6480

THE ASTROLOGER. I must admit it in all honesty:
    Though I had tongues of fire, here there would be
    No more for me to do than say: Behold,
    Now beauty comes! As poets sang of old,
    The sight of beauty maddens; to possess
    It is good luck in dangerous excess.

FAUST. Have I still eyes? Has beauty's fountain-head
    Itself flooded my inmost mind? So blest
    Is my reward after that fearful quest!
    How empty all the world was, closed and dead   6490
    To me until this priestly revelation
    Founded it fast, a timeless, loved creation!
    May life's breath fail me, if habituation
    Shall ever wean me back from you again!—
    What magic mirror was it long ago,
    What fair shape that bewitched me so?
    What vision now, what vaporous fantasm then!—
    To you I pledge my strength, my whole desire,
    Passion's quintessence, all the fire,
    The idolatry, the madness of my heart.   6500

MEPHISTOPHELES [*from the prompt-box*].
  Compose yourself, keep calm, stick to your part!*

AN OLDER LADY. She's tall, well-made; why is her head
  not bigger?

A YOUNGER LADY. How coarse her feet are! They don't
  match her figure.

A DIPLOMAT. She's just like many a princess I know;
  I think her beautiful from top to toe.

A COURTIER. Gently she steals towards the sleeping lad.

A LADY. Spoiling his youthful purity; it's too bad!

A POET. Now in her beauty's rays he seems to bask.

A LADY. Endymion and Luna, need one ask!

THE POET. Exactly so! And now the goddess stoops   6510
  Down to him, drinks the breath upon his lips;
  A kiss!—Ah, enviable consummation!

A DUENNA. In public! This is an abomination!

FAUST. Shall that boy be so favoured?

MEPHISTOPHELES.   Let them be!
  Ghosts will be ghosts—respect their liberty!

A COURTIER. She tiptoes from him; now he is awake.

A LADY. But she looks back at him, make no mistake.

A COURTIER. He is amazed, he can't believe his eyes.

A LADY. Amazed! Not she; for her it's no surprise.

A COURTIER. How modestly she turns to him again!   6520

A LADY. Oh yes, she'll educate him now with care.
  What fools they are in such a case, these men!
  No doubt he thinks he is the first one there.

A KNIGHT. Come, let's not carp. What majesty, what
  grace!

A LADY. The common slut! Just look! It's a disgrace!

A PAGE. What would I give now to be in his place!

A COURTIER. The man she can't ensnare's not yet been
  born.

A LADY. The pretty jewel's been so often worn,
    Even the gilding's getting less like gold.

ANOTHER. She started it at only ten years old.*   6530

A KNIGHT. We must be opportunists; I'd not say
    No to the good things others throw away.

A SCHOLAR. I see her plain, but I must say I feel
    A little doubtful whether she is real.
    To say she's here could be exaggeration;
    The text is what I go by, the narration
    In which I read that all Troy's greybeards fell
    Head over heels in love with her as well.
    This proves the point, I think; for I'm not active
    And young, and yet I find her most attractive.   6540

THE ASTROLOGER. Now he's a boy no more! A hero's
        arms
    Boldly embrace her scarce-resisting charms;
    With sudden strength he lifts her—seems to bear
    Her off, indeed—

FAUST.   Rash fool! How does he dare?
    Stop! Can't you hear me? I must intervene!

MEPHISTOPHELES. But it's all in your mind, the mad
        spooky scene!

THE ASTROLOGER. After all this, I've one more thing
        to say:
    The Rape of Helen's what I'd call the play.

FAUST. Rape! Do I count for nothing here? My hand
    Still holds this key, this key that was my guide   6550
    Through all the solitudes, through ocean-wide
    Chaos, and brought me back again to land!
    Here I set foot, here are realities,
    From here the spirit wars with spirits, here is
    The joining of the two great sovereignties.
    Far as she was, how nearer can she be!
    I'll rescue her, and she'll belong to me
    Twice over! Mothers, Mothers, grant this boon!
    Who that has known her lets her go so soon!

THE ASTROLOGER. Faust! Faust! What are you doing?—
    By main force   6560
  He has seized her, and her shape grows dim, of course.
  He turns his key against the young man—No!—
  It touches him!—We're done for now! Oh! Oh!

  [*There is an explosion,* FAUST *is struck to the ground.
  The spirits dissolve into mist.*]

MEPHISTOPHELES [*hoisting* FAUST *on his back*].
  So there, you see! Take up with fools, and you'll
  Regret it; even the Devil learns that rule.

        [*Darkness, general tumult.*]

ACT TWO

8 · A HIGH-VAULTED, NARROW GOTHIC ROOM

[*Formerly* FAUST's *study, unchanged.*
MEPHISTOPHELES *steps from behind a curtain. As
he lifts it and looks back, we see* FAUST *lying prostrate
on a bed of antiquated design.*]

MEPHISTOPHELES. Lie here, poor wretch! Ensnared
    again!
Who'll free you now, misguided lover?
When Helen paralyses men,
They don't so readily recover.

[*Looking about him.*]

I raise my eyes, I look around;   6570
It's as it was, not changed a bit!
The stained glass seems a trifle browned,
And the room has more cobwebs covering it;
The ink's congealed, the paper's yellow,
But all's in place—even the pen is duly
Displayed that Faust once used, poor fellow,
To sign his bargain with yours truly;
And here, dried up inside the quill,
That drop of blood I invited him to spill!
A valuable collector's piece;   6580
Unique, in fact. And, if you please,
Here's his old gown still on its hook,
To remind me of the pains I took
Teasing a student with my learned jokes—
He'll have grown up still feeding on that hoax.
Well, you warm, furry cloak! I'd really quite
Like to wrap up in you and play
The tutor once again today.
That splendid sense of being always right!
It's a fine art that scholars know;   6590
The Devil lost it long ago.

[*He takes down the fur-trimmed gown and shakes it;
crickets, beetles, and moths fly out.*]

CHORUS OF INSECTS. Our old master has come!
     Let us hover and hum!
     What a pleasure to meet you!
     We know you, we greet you!
     You planted us quietly,
     A few here and there;
     Now we swarm for our daddy
     And dance in the air!
     A man's wicked thoughts,   6600
     In his heart they will bide;
     But the bugs in his cloak
     Are less easy to hide.

MEPHISTOPHELES. What an agreeable surprise! My
  youthful brood!
One harvests in due course the seeds one sowed.
I'll give another shake to this old clout—
Now a few more of them come jumping out.
Fly up, fly round, my dears! Cover your traces!
Here you've a hundred thousand hiding-places.
Here's yellowing paperwork enough,   6610
Old dusty files where you can stuff
Yourselves, old broken pots; and there,
Those death's-heads with their hollow stare.
Where one's all mouldering, only half alive,
Bugs in the brain will always thrive.

      [*He puts on the gown.*]

Come, robe, cover my shoulders as before!
Today I am the boss once more.
But though I claim such a position,
What good is it without some recognition?

  [*He pulls the bell,* which rings with a high-pitched,
  piercing clangour, making the halls tremble and the doors
  spring open.*]

A FAMULUS [*tottering down the long dark passage*].
     What a clang that bell is making!   6620

Staircase shaking, walls all quaking!
Through the trembling windows' glimmer
I can see the lightning shimmer.
Splitting ceilings, cracking floors,
Plaster, rubble, down it pours!
And the door I locked so fast,
Opened by this magic blast.—
There! In Faust's old pelt, horrendous,
Stands a giant; heaven defend us!
How he beckons, how he eyes me,   6630
How his presence terrifies me!
Shall I stay or shall I flee?
What is to become of me?

MEPHISTOPHELES [*beckoning*].
Draw near, my friend!—Your name is Nicodemus.

THE FAMULUS. Most reverend sir, it is indeed—*oremus*.

MEPHISTOPHELES.
We'll leave that out.

THE FAMULUS.   So glad you recognize me!

MEPHISTOPHELES.
As your old mossy pate can yet apprize me,
You're still a student. What else can you do
But just read on! That's scholarship for you!
One builds a modest card-house, there to sit;   6640
Even great minds never quite finish it.
But your master, now he's a man of parts:
We all know Wagner,* doctor of all the arts,
A noble man, a prince of scholars! He
Alone sustains the academic mystery,
And contributes to knowledge day by day;
His eager hearers come from far away,
Crowding to listen, as in the lecture-hall
He shines unique! Saint Peter's key, with all
Its power to open secrets high and low,   6650
Is like the erudition he can show.
None before his renown can stand,

His fame's the brightest in the land,
Not Faust himself's now so well known;
Invention has been Wagner's gift alone.

THE FAMULUS. Most reverend sir, forgive me if I say,
  Venturing to contradict you if I may:
  All that is not at all my master's way!
  Humility's all he could ever learn.
  Since the great Doctor in mysterious fashion   6660
  Vanished, he has been suffering from depression;
  He'll be consoled and healed only by Faust's return.
  This study, since the Doctor left,
  Untouched, just as it's always been,
  For its old master waits bereft;
  I scarcely dare to venture in.
  What hour of destiny has struck?
  The walls all seem to shake with fear,
  The doorposts swayed, locks came unstuck—
  How else could you have got in here?   6670

MEPHISTOPHELES. Come now, where can your master
      be?
  Take me to him, bring him to me.

THE FAMULUS. Oh dear, he gave strict orders—how
  Shall I dare interrupt him now?
  For months the *Opus Magnum's* mewed
  Him up in total solitude.
  This learned man, so meek and mild,
  Looks like a charcoal-burner: wild
  Complexion, black from ear to nose,
  Eyes reddened by all the fires he blows.   6680
  Moment by moment he craves and longs;
  Music for him's the click of tongs.

MEPHISTOPHELES. My visit should be welcome to him;
  There are professional favours I could do him.

  [THE FAMULUS *departs*, MEPHISTOPHELES *sits
  down ceremoniously*.]

Now, when I've scarcely taken up my place,
I have a visitor; I know that face.

But this time he's the *dernier cri*;
Who knows how limitless his cheek will be!

THE GRADUATE* [*barging along the passage*].

> Open doors and free admissions!
> Here's some hope of new conditions.   6690
> As things were, one used to rot
> Like a corpse in such a spot;
> Life was mere disintegration,
> Death by slow anticipation.

> Walls and halls, you've had your day!
> Now you crumble and decay.
> Here's no place to stop; we'll all
> Squash to death here when you fall.
> Though I'm bold as brass, I fear
> They'll not educate me here.   6700

> But, bless me! This is the same
> Place—long years ago I came
> Here, a freshman fond and shy;
> What a silly boy was I!
> Trusted those old greybeard farts,
> Let them peddle me their arts.

> Lies they told me from a few
> Scabby books, that's all they knew,
> And they knew it's all moonshine;
> Thus they'd waste their lives and mine.   6710
> What's that?—Still, in this same room,
> One of them sits in the gloom!

> There he sits in his old gown—
> How amazing!—that same brown
> Furry robe I saw him wear;
> Just as when I left him there!
> Then, I thought him smart enough,
> Couldn't understand his stuff;
> But that trick won't work today.
> So here goes, I'll have my say!   6720

If, ancient sir, your bowed, bald head is yet
Unswamped by Lethe's turgid stream,

Recall a humble pupil you once met:
One who has now outgrown the rods of academe.
You've not changed much in that time-span,
But I've come back another man.

MEPHISTOPHELES. I am glad my bell has summoned you.
I had a high opinion of you too;
The grub, the chrysalis, can prophesy
The future many-coloured butterfly.   6730
Lace collars, curly locks—the charming style
You favoured, was a trifle puerile.
Perhaps you sometimes wore a pigtail?—But
Today, I see, it's a crew cut.
Very manly, I'm sure, and quite the hero.
Still, let's not send you home as Absolute Zero.

THE GRADUATE. My ancient sir, this place may be the
        same,
But times have changed; and, by your leave,
I'd just as soon be spared your verbal game
Of ambiguities. We've grown harder to deceive.   6740
When I was a poor innocent you played
Those jokes on me, and easy sport you made.
No one dares try that on today.

MEPHISTOPHELES. Greenhorns don't like to hear the
        honest truth.
One tells it plain to unsuspecting youth
Who will learn it themselves the painful way
Years later. Then of course they'll say
Their own brains were their only school
And their old erstwhile teacher was a fool.

THE GRADUATE. A rogue perhaps! What teacher's ever
        told   6750
The truth straight to our faces? They all mould
It to their docile childish hearers, smiling
So wisely, or so solemnly beguiling.

MEPHISTOPHELES. Well, there's a time for learning. You,
        I see,
Are yourself qualified to teach. Presumably,

After these many years, or months at least,
Your store of experience will have increased.

THE GRADUATE. Experience! Insubstantial stuff!
Unworthy of the intellectual.
What's long been known quite well enough,   6760
Why bother knowing it at all?

MEPHISTOPHELES [*after a pause*].
I see now I'm an idiot; I stand corrected;
A shallow simpleton, as I've long suspected.

THE GRADUATE. I'm glad you now show such intelligence!
The first old man I've ever heard talk sense.

MEPHISTOPHELES. I've searched for buried treasure in
          the ground,
And ugly dross was all the gold I found.

THE GRADUATE. Admit it then: your skull, bereft of hair,
Is just as hollow as those skulls up there!

MEPHISTOPHELES [*affably*].
No doubt you are politer when you try.   6770

THE GRADUATE. In German, sir, politeness is a lie.

MEPHISTOPHELES [*rolling his wheelchair nearer and nearer
          to the footlights and addressing the pit*].
I'm being crowded out here, as you see;
Perhaps down there you might make room for me?

THE GRADUATE. In dotage years, to keep up the pretence
Of being somebody, is sheer impertinence.
Man's life lives in the blood: where does blood stir
More strongly than in youth? That, ancient sir,
Is the young living blood, blood that creates
A new life out of life as it pulsates.
Here all's in movement, here's where things get done;   6780
The weak fall down, the strong take over. We
Have conquered half the world, as all can see,
While you've been nodding, dreaming, meditating,
Making your plans, plotting and ruminating!
Old age is a cold fever, it's an ague
That freezes, fancies that torment and plague you.

Once over thirty you're as good as dead:
We'd do better to knock you on the head
At once, and finish you off straight away.

MEPHISTOPHELES. So much for that; what can the Devil
    say?   6790

THE GRADUATE. The Devil needs my permission to exist.

MEPHISTOPHELES [*aside*].
    The Devil may yet give your young tail a twist.

THE GRADUATE. This is youth's noblest task! The world
    was not
There till I made it; it was I who brought
The sun out of the sea; the moon began to weave
Its changing circles when I gave it leave;
Mine was the morning's various ornament,
The earth turned green and blossomed where I went,
The stars on that first night unfolded all
Their splendour at my beck and call.   6800
By me you were released from the constriction
Of limited and philistine reflection.
I for my part, free as the spirit bids,
Pursue my inner light whither it leads,
And in the special rapture of my mind
Follow the bright day, leave the dark behind.   [*Exit.*]

MEPHISTOPHELES. Fantastic crank! Go on your glorious
    way!—
How you would hate to know that nothing wise
And nothing foolish can be thought today
That's not been thought for many centuries!—   6810
And yet, there's no great harm in our young friend;
A few more years will bring about a change.
The fermentation may be rich and strange,
But the wine's drinkable in the end.

    [*To the younger spectators in the pit, who do not applaud.*]

My words appear to leave you cold;
But never mind, my dears, I pardon you.
Remember that the Devil's old—
When you're his age, you'll understand him too.

9 · A LABORATORY

[in medieval style, with elaborate clumsy apparatus for
fantastic purposes.]

WAGNER *[at his furnace].*
    That dreadful bell's reverberation
    Comes shuddering through the sooty walls.   6820
    Too long my doubtful expectation
    Has waited for what now befalls.
    From blackness to illumination
    The deep alembic now has passed,
    And like a living coal at last
    A fine carbuncular fire is glowing,
    Into the dark its brilliance throwing:
    An incandescent white shines through!
    Let me succeed, just this once more!—
    Oh God, who's rattling at my door?   6830

MEPHISTOPHELES *[entering].*
    A well-meant greeting, sir, to you!

WAGNER *[anxiously].*
    Greetings, by this hour's ruling star!
    [sotto voce] But hold your words and breath: I am not far
    From a great work's goal, now to be displayed.

MEPHISTOPHELES *[sotto voce].*
    What great work's that?

WAGNER *[in a whisper].*
                A man is being made.

MEPHISTOPHELES.
    A man? So you have locked an amorous pair
    Up in your chimney-stack somehow?

WAGNER.
    Why, God forbid! That method's out of fashion now:
    Procreation's sheer nonsense, we declare!
    That tender point where life used to begin   6840
    That gentle power springing from within,
    Taking and giving, programmed to portray
    Itself, to assimilate what came its way

From near or far—all that's now null and void;
By animals, no doubt, it's still enjoyed,
But man henceforth, being so highly gifted,
Must have an origin much more uplifted.

[*Turning to the furnace.*]

See how it gleams!—Now we may hope to see
Results. The ingredients—our manifold
Materia anthropica, they are called—   6850
We mix in a retort most patiently,
With all due care, and so by perlutation
And proper double-distillation,
They quietly reach their consummation.

[*Turning to the furnace again.*]

It works! The moving mass is clarified,
And our conviction fortified:
These mysteries we thought only great Nature knew,
Our expertise now dares attempt them too!
Her way with living matter was to organize it,
And we have learnt to crystallize it.   6860

MEPHISTOPHELES. When we live long, we learn a thing
Or two; nothing surprises any more.
I have, in my long years of wandering,
Seen crystallized humanity before.

WAGNER [*who has been staring intently at the retort*].
It flashes, swells and rises! One
More moment and it will be done.
Great plans seem mad at first, but one day we
Shall laugh at what is bred haphazardly;
And one day, too, some great brain will create
A brain designed to think and cerebrate!   6870

[*Gazing at the retort in delight.*]

The glass is struck into harmonious sound.
Ah, now it cannot fail! It clouds and clears:
And moving daintily around
A well-formed tiny little man appears.
What more do I, what more does the world need?

The secret is at last made known.
Now hear this music: it has grown
To a voice, and into speech, indeed!

THE HOMUNCULUS* [*in the retort, to* WAGNER].
　　Well, dad! It worked, you see! And how are you?
　　Come now, embrace me tenderly—but do　　　　　　6880
　　Be careful, please, my glass must not be cracked.
　　That is the way things are, in fact:
　　For natural growth the world's too small a place,
　　But art must be enclosed in its own space.

[*To* MEPHISTOPHELES.]

　　So you are here as well, my mocking cousin?
　　I am much obliged; the moment was well chosen.
　　Our good luck brings this timely call by you.
　　Since I exist, I must find things to do:
　　I'd like to set to work this very day,
　　And you know how to set me on my way.　　　　　　6890

WAGNER. Just one word, please! It's so embarrassing,
　　The way I'm questioned on this sort of thing.
　　For instance: no one yet can understand
　　How soul and body seem to have been planned
　　To fit so perfectly and cling so tight,
　　Yet each torments the other day and night.
　　Furthermore—

MEPHISTOPHELES. Stop, stop! One should ask him rather
　　Why man and woman can't endure each other.
　　My friend, you'll never get such matters straight.
　　There's work to do here: our small guest can't wait.　　6900

THE HOMUNCULUS. What's to be done?

MEPHISTOPHELES [*pointing to a side-door*].
　　　　　　　　　　　　　　　　　A case for you to cure.

WAGNER [*still gazing into the retort*].
　　You are a little darling, to be sure!

[*The side-door opens,* FAUST *is seen lying on the couch.*]

THE HOMUNCULUS [*astonished*].
　　Remarkable!—

[*The retort slips out of* WAGNER's *hands, hovers over*
FAUST *and illuminates him.*]

    Delightful place!—Clear streams
In a dense grove, and women making ready
To bathe; enchanting! Better still already!
But one shines brighter than them all, she seems
Descended from great heroes, gods perhaps.
She sets her foot in the translucent pool;
Life's noble flame in her sweet body dips
Into the yielding crystal and grows cool.—   6910
But now, what flurry of quick wings, what whirring
Is this, in the smooth surface splashing, stirring?
The girls flee in alarm: the queen, calm-eyed,
Remains alone, but her heart fills with pride
And womanly contentment as she sees
The prince of swans come nestling to her knees,
Docile yet bold. He seems to like it there.—
And round them all at once has risen a veil
Of mist, thick-woven to conceal
The loves of this most charming pair.   6920

MEPHISTOPHELES. What a strange tale! Your fantasies at
    least
Are out of all proportion to your size.
I can see nothing—

THE HOMUNCULUS. Why should you! Your eyes
Are northern, steeped in medieval mist;
In that mad world of monks and armour-plated
Knights, naturally your vision's obfuscated.
Dark ages are your proper habitat.

[*Looking round.*]

Black mouldering stones, arches in Gothic style
And absurd curlicues—how drab, how vile!
If he wakes up here, like as not   6930
He'll drop dead on the very spot.
Nude women, swans and woodland streams
I saw in his prophetic dreams.
In this dank hole he'd have no future;

Neither would I, despite my unfastidious nature.
Away with him!

MEPHISTOPHELES. I welcome this solution.

THE HOMUNCULUS. Order a warrior to fight,
Or a young girl to dance all night,
And things soon reach their right conclusion.
And let me see—tonight is Classical   6940
Walpurgis Night, as I recall.
A lucky chance, I do declare!
He'll be in his own element there.

MEPHISTOPHELES. I know of no such date.

THE HOMUNCULUS.   Indeed!
You'll not have heard of it, you and your breed.
Romantic ghosts are all they know in hell:
A proper ghost is classical as well.*

MEPHISTOPHELES. But where do we go, where do we
        start exploring?
My ancient history colleagues are so boring.

THE HOMUNCULUS. Satan, the north-west is your
        stamping-ground!   6950
But for this trip, south-eastward we are bound,
To the great plain where the Peneus flows;
Tree-lined, bush-lined its moist meandering goes.
Out to the mountain glens the lowlands rise,
And up there, old and new, Pharsalus* lies.

MEPHISTOPHELES. Ugh! why do you remind me of
        those gory
Wars between slaves and tyrants? That old story,
How stale it is! Their battle is begun
All over again as soon as it is done;
They never guess they merely are the dupes   6960
Of Asmodeus,* who really rules the troops.
They call it fighting for their liberty:
Slaves against slaves in fact, it seems to me.

THE HOMUNCULUS.
Just let them squabble; men will never mend.
Each one asserts himself as best he can

From boyhood on, and so becomes a man.
The question here is how to cure our friend.
If you've a remedy, then try it now;
If not, leave it to me to find out how.

MEPHISTOPHELES. My Blocksberg* magic might be what
   he'd need   6970
  But pagan rules forbid me to proceed.
  The Greeks were never much good anyway!
  But you are charmed by their free sensuous play,
  They lure mankind to many a sinful blessing;
  The sins we sell are gloomy and depressing.
  And so, what now?

THE HOMUNCULUS.   But you do like some sport,
  I think; Thessalian witches* are the sort
  Of thing that might appeal to you.

MEPHISTOPHELES [lustfully].
  Thessalian witches! If I've heard aright,
  They're persons well worth meeting, that is true;   6980
  Not for concubinage night after night,
  I hardly think that that would do.
  But for a visit, for a try—

THE HOMUNCULUS.   We need
  Your cloak! And wrap it round our gentleman!
  This cloth will bear you, as you know it can,
  And carry both of you with speed;
  I'll light the way ahead.

WAGNER [anxiously].   And I?

THE HOMUNCULUS.   Why, you
  Must stay at home: you have great things to do.
  Study old manuscripts, learn from their lore
  How to collect life's elements together   6990
  And carefully compose them each to other;
  Consider what, consider how still more.
  I meanwhile, travelling the world about,
  Shall light on some essential point, no doubt.
  Then our great work will have achieved its end:
  Such striving merits such reward, my friend!

>Gold, honour, fame, health and longevity;
>Service to science, virtue too—maybe!
>Farewell!

WAGNER [*sadly*].
>   Farewell! This parting's pain
>And grief; I fear we'll never meet again.   7000

MEPHISTOPHELES. So, off to Greece then!—Judging
>   by your arts,
>Cousin, you are a mannikin of parts.

>   [*Ad spectatores.*]

>Just fancy that! One does depend
>On one's own creatures,* in the end.

10. CLASSICAL WALPURGIS NIGHT*

[10a · THE PHARSALIAN PLAIN. *Darkness*]

ERICHTHO.* Now as the dreadful ceremony of this night
>   begins
>I, dark Erichtho, make attendance yet again;
>Less loathsome than the poets tiresomely have claimed
>In hyperbolic slander ... For they never cease
>Praising and carping ... Now already right across
>The plain I seem to see grey tents, a pallid flood: 7010
>A second sight this night of grief and horror leaves.
>How often its self-repetition I have seen,
>Its never-to-end recurrence! Neither side accepts
>The other's rule; for none concedes a realm once seized
>By force, and governed so. A man who cannot reign
>Over his inner self, lusts fiercely to control
>His neighbour's will, imposing what his pride
>   dictates ...
>But here a great example by this fight was made:
>Of how a mighty power confronts one mightier still,
>Rending the full flowered garland of sweet liberty   7020
>And pleating iron laurels round the conqueror's brow.
>Here Pompey* dreamed of early greatness blossoming,

There Caesar* watched and heard the flickering scale
  of fate.
They will do battle now. The world knows who prevailed.
Watch-fires are glowing: as they scatter their red flames,
Out of the ground the long-spilt blood's reflection
  breathes,
And as the night's strange radiance works its spell
  on them,
They come, the assembling legion of Hellenic lore.
Round all the fires uncertainly they hover or
Commodiously they sit, those ancient fabled shapes . . .   7030
The moon, still not yet at its full, shines brilliantly,
And as it rises, sheds its gentle light afar;
The tent-mirage has disappeared, the fires burn blue.
But overhead, what unexpected meteor's this?
The globe it shines from and upon is bodily.
I can smell life. It is not fitting that I should
Approach a living thing, to which I must bring harm;
An ill repute attends such inexpediency.
Now it is landing. Prudently I will withdraw!

    [*She moves away. The aeronauts appear overhead.*]

THE HOMUNCULUS. Take another flight around   7040
        This great burning gruesome plain;
        Such a ghostly killing-ground
        You'll not often see again.

MEPHISTOPHELES. In my northern wastes I used to,
        Watch the denizens of hell;
        Ghastly ghosts are what I'm used to,
        Here I'm quite at home as well.

THE HOMUNCULUS. Some tall figure there is striding,
        Hurrying from us through the night.

MEPHISTOPHELES. Through the air she saw us riding;   7050
        Doubtless she has taken fright.

THE HOMUNCULUS. Let her go! Now put your seeming
        Dead man down here: he'll revive
        Instantly, for he must thrive
        In this myth-land of his dreaming.

FAUST [*as he touches the ground*].
  Where is she?—

THE HOMUNCULUS. There we're in some doubt,
  But here you'll probably find out.
  Explore these flames: you've time to go
  On a quick tour, till dawn appears.
  One who has ventured down below,   7060
  To the Mothers, need have no more fears.

MEPHISTOPHELES. I too have business here; but I
    suggest,
  For all our sakes, it would be best
  If each seeks out by his own whim,
  From fire to fire, whatever pleases him.
  And when we need to meet again,
  My little friend, shine out and sing out then!

THE HOMUNCULUS.
  You'll see a flash, you'll hear a sound like this.*

          [*The glass hums and flashes powerfully.*]

  Now off to our new mysteries! [*Exeunt.*]

FAUST [*alone*].
  Where is she!—But why ask! I should have known   7070
  The soil her feet have trod, the sea
  That lapped against them; even enough for me
  This very air whose language was her own!
  Here, by a miracle, here I am in Greece!
  At once I sensed the ground; what could release
  Me from my sleep but this fresh spirit's glow!
  And thus I stand: Antaeus was strengthened so.
  What wonders here in one place concentrate!
  This fiery labyrinth I will investigate.

          [*He moves away.*]

MEPHISTOPHELES [*sniffing around*].
  I must say that the creatures in this place   7080
  Among these bonfires, make me feel quite lost:
  Nearly all naked, some half-clad at most.
  Unblushing sphinxes, griffins a disgrace,
  And all the rest with their long hair and wings—

Whichever way I turn I see the things! . . .
Though we're no strangers to indecency,
In the ancient world life runs too high for me;
We should control it with our new ideas
And various modern, fashionable veneers . . .
A beastly tribe! But I must do my best   7090
To greet them decently, as a new guest.
Greetings, my gracious ladies, wise old greyfins!*

A GRIFFIN [*snarling gutterally*].
 Griffins, not greyfins! No one likes to hear
 His grey hairs mentioned. Words connote
 Their origins, these words stick in one's throat:
 Grey, grievous, grumpy, gruesome, graveyard, grim—
 Etymologically they agree,
 And disagree with us.

MEPHISTOPHELES.   Yet, all the same,
 Griffin's akin to *gripping,* a fine name!

THE GRIFFIN [*snarling similarly, and so throughout*].
 Of course! It's a well-tried affinity;   7100
 We are much blamed, praised more than equally.
 A griffin *grips* or *grabs*; girls, crowns, or gold—
 Good fortune favours those who take good hold.

ANTS [*the colossal species*].
 You mentioned gold: we'd gathered a whole hoard,
 In rocky caves we had it stuffed and stored:
 The Arimaspians, that sly thieving race,
 Boast now how they sniffed out its hiding-place.

THE GRIFFINS. We'll soon make them confess.

THE ARIMASPIANS.   But not tonight!
 Tonight we're free, it's carnival!
 (By morning we'll have spent it all;   7110
 This time we've done the job all right).

MEPHISTOPHELES [*who has sat down between* THE
   SPHINXES].
 How easy it is to acclimatize
 Oneself here! All your speech makes sense.

THE SPHINXES.* We breathe our spirit-utterance,
  Which your ears then corporealize.
  We'd like to know your name now, if we may.

MEPHISTOPHELES.
  I am called many names; legion, they say.
  The British, now—they're a much-travelled nation,
  They seek out battlefields and waterfalls,
  Musty old classic sites and ruined walls;   7120
  Have some come here? A worthy destination!—
  They'd recognize me from their mystery plays:
  My name was 'Old Iniquity' in those days.

THE SPHINX. Why should they call you that?

MEPHISTOPHELES.   I can't think why.

THE SPHINX. Well ... Do you know about the starry sky?
  How do you think the planets stand tonight?

MEPHISTOPHELES [looking up].
  Star shoots to star, the quartered moon shines bright.
  This is a pleasant place; I've seldom felt
  So snug as here against your lion pelt.
  Why wander up to heaven? It's absurd.   7130
  Let's play at riddles; come, think of a word.*

THE SPHINX. Think of yourself, if you want mystery.
  Resolve your own parts by deep cogitation:
  'Virtue and vice both need him: he must be
  A fencer's dummy for the ascetic's lunge,
  A boon companion to the wastrel's plunge,
  And both merely for Zeus's delectation.'

FIRST GRIFFIN [snarling].
  No, I don't like him.

SECOND GRIFFIN [snarling still louder].
                                No, he's odious.

BOTH. Doesn't belong. What does he want with us?

MEPHISTOPHELES [fiercely].
  Perhaps you think this stranger's nails can tear   7140
  Less well than your sharp claws? Try, if you dare!

A SPHINX [*amiably*].
>   If you feel so inclined, by all means stay;
>   You'll soon leave by your own choice anyway.
>   At home, no doubt, you flourish; but in these
>   Surroundings, I would guess, you're ill at ease.

MEPHISTOPHELES.
>   From the waist up you're an attractive sight;
>   The bestial bottom half, that's the real fright.

THE SPHINX. Deceiver, we shall punish that impiety;
>   Our paws are healthy. As for your
>   Deformed and shrivelled hoof, no wonder you're   7150
>   Uncomfortable in our society.

> [SIRENS,* *perched on trees, strike up a prelude.*]

MEPHISTOPHELES. Who are those birds cradled among
>   The branches by this poplared stream?

A SPHINX. Beware! Great heroes that sing-song
>   Has lulled into a fatal dream.

THE SIRENS. How perversely you are clinging,
>   To these dark grotesqueries!
>   See us gathering in the trees,
>   Hear how sweet our harmonies,
>   As befits the Sirens' singing!   7160

THE SPHINXES [*mockingly imitating their melody*].
>   First compel them to the ground!
>   Though they hide them in the branches,
>   They have claws like birds of prey
>   That will tear your heart away
>   If you listen to that sound.

THE SIRENS. Let all envious strife be banned!
>   Joys are scattered bright and clear
>   On the earth: unite them here!
>   Now on water and on land
>   Let us with our happiest   7170
>   Gesture greet this welcome guest.

MEPHISTOPHELES. So that is music nowadays!
>   A scrape of strings, a well-tuned throat,
>   All intertwining note with note;

    A pointless tra-la-la! It plays
    A tickle-tinkle on my ear,
    But leaves my heart untouched, I fear.

THE SPHINXES. Your heart, forsooth! What empty brag
    Is this? A dried-up leather bag
    Would be the appropriate organ here.   7180

FAUST [*entering*].
    How wonderful! I relish this great sight;
    Repellent, yet imposing. Am I right,
    And does this solemn scene portend for me
    Some unknown favourable destiny?

           [*Referring to* THE SPHINXES.]

    Before such beings did not Oedipus once stand?

           [*Referring to* THE SIRENS.]

    Ulysses before these writhed in his hempen band.

           [*Referring to* THE ANTS.]

    By these much golden treasure was collected,

           [*Referring to* THE GRIFFINS.]

    And by these guardians faithfully protected.
    Now a refreshing spirit moves me: how
    Great are these forms, how great these memories now!   7190

MEPHISTOPHELES. You'd once have cursed these
        creatures, I must say;
    Now you're in need of them, it seems.
    When lovers seek the object of their dreams,
    They welcome even monsters on the way.

FAUST [*to* THE SPHINXES].
    You who are women, you must tell me true:
    Has Helena been seen by one of you?

THE SPHINXES. We're not her period: long before her birth
    Hercules slew the last Sphinx left on earth.
    Ask Chiron:* on this ghostly night
    He's galloping around—perhaps he might   7200
    Consent to stop, then he will put you right.

THE SIRENS. We wish you success as well!
           Ulysses? He did not spurn

Our green shore, but stayed to learn
Many a tale he would retell.
Come with us, to where the wide
Sea-waves roll, and we shall hide
Nothing that you long to hear!

A SPHINX. Scorn, noble stranger, these false hopes.
As Ulysses was bound by ropes,   7210
By our good counsels now be bound:
Great Chiron's words, when you have found
Him, they will satisfy your ear.

[*Exit* FAUST.]

MEPHISTOPHELES [*in annoyance*].
What's this now, croaking, winging past?
They can't be seen, they move so fast,
All of them following beak to tail.
Here even a huntsman's skill would fail.

A SPHINX. Like winter storms that scour the sky
The Stymphalids come rushing by;
Hercules' arrows they outfly.   7220
They have hawks' beaks, they have goose-feet.
With well-meant croak they try to greet
Their cousins—for we count as such;
They seem to want to keep in touch.

MEPHISTOPHELES [*nervously*].
There's something else, I hear it hissing.

A SPHINX. The heads of the Lernaean Snake—
You needn't be alarmed, the rump is missing,
Though they still think they're on the make.
But tell us, why this agitation?
What, sir, is now your destination?   7230
What's to become of you? Why don't
You go? . . . You crane your neck—you want
To join that chorus over there. Feel free
To do so! Greet that charming company,
The Lamiae—subtle little tarts
With smiling mouths and shameless arts

Such as the satyrs like, designed
To please your lustful goat-foot kind.

MEPHISTOPHELES. But you will stay here? We shall meet
again?

THE SPHINXES. Yes! By all means, mix with that airy
throng.   7240
We are from Egypt, and our kind has long
Been used to its millennial reign.
And you must honour us: we calculate
The cycles of the sun, and the moon's state.
   Judges over nations, thus
   By the pyramids we sit;
   Wars, floods, peace—we watch it pass,
   Never blink an eye at it.

[10b · THE PENEUS. *The river-god is surrounded by tributary*
        streams and nymphs]

PENEUS. Gently stir, you whispering rushes,
Reeds, my sisters, make a breeze!   7250
Rustle lightly, willow-bushes,
Lisp, you trembling poplar-trees,
To my interrupted dream! . . .
For a fearful tremor wakes me,
A mysterious motion shakes me
From my wandering slumber-stream.

FAUST [*coming to the river's edge*].
Leaves and branches interwound,
Arbour-like, and murmuring,
If I hear aright, with sound
As when human voices sing.   7260
Are the wavelets not like speech,
Breezes fondling each and each?

NYMPHS [*to* FAUST].
    Oh come and lie down
    In this coolness, refreshed
    From your weariness, come,

For our counsel is best:
In this place you shall find
Your lost peace of mind;
Our murmuring, our whispering
Shall lull you to rest.   7270

FAUST. A waking vision!—Linger there,
Oh you sweet forms beyond compare,
Projected by my longing eyes!
What is this joy that fills me so?
I have once felt it, long ago:
Are these now dreams, or memories?
How fresh the leaves that gently move
On the dense bushes! Through this grove
Scarce-rippling streamlets steal their way
From all around; that shallow pool   7280
Unites a hundred springs, so cool
And clean, and there the maidens play!
Young healthy limbs, all mirrored clear
In the moist surface, so that here
My gaze redoubles its delight.
They bathe, a happy company;
The bold swim, some wade cautiously;
All ends in a shrill watery fight.
With these my eyes should drink their fill,
My mind should be content: but still   7290
It seeks what I have not yet seen.
My gaze would pierce that leafy wall,
That ring of verdure rich and tall,
That veil which hides the lofty queen.

And how strange! Now swans are coming,
From the streams and inlets swimming;
How majestically they drift!
Graceful, pure, in a gregarious
Motion, yet with calm self-glorious
Pride, as heads and beaks they lift . . .   7300
One alone, with swelling breast,
Seems serene above the rest,
Bold and swift his course prevails:

Plumage puffing and subsiding
Like the wave-tops he is riding,
To that holy place he sails . . .

The other swans swim to and fro,
Calmly their brilliant feathers glow,
But then in warlike style they tease
The maidens, and those timid beauties   7310
Are soon forgetful of their duties
As each her own pursuer flees.

NYMPHS.   Sisters, listen, lay an ear
                 To the river-bank's green ground!
                 If I hear aright, the sound
                 Of a horse's hooves draws near.
                 Who is this that gallops past,
                 Rides tonight with news so fast?

FAUST. On the earth I hear a drumming
        As of hurried hoof-beats coming.   7320
                 Far off I see
                 Good luck approaching me:
                 Can this already be
                 My wondrous destiny?
        It is a horseman; I can tell
        That he is bold and wise as well.
        The steed he rides is gleaming white . . .
        I recognize him—I am right—
        Philyra's great and famous son!—
        Stop, Chiron, stop! I have to speak to you . . .   7330

CHIRON. What's this? who? what?

FAUST.   Tame your wild pace!

CHIRON.   I run
        And never rest.

FAUST.   Then take me with you too!

CHIRON. Jump up! Now I can ask you freely: where
        Do you want to go? On the Peneus' banks
        I find you: we can cross if you prefer.

FAUST [*mounting*].
   I will go where you like! Eternal thanks! . . .
   Great, noble man, you who have won such fame
   As mentor to so many heroes—need I name
   The Argonauts' prestigious company,
   And all who built the world of poets' fantasy!   7340

CHIRON. Well, let that rest. Small credit even the wise
   Athene gets in her tutorial guise;
   One's pupils all just end as each is fated,
   You'd never know they had been educated.

FAUST. The learned healer, every plant you know
   By name, and how its deep roots grow;
   You soothe the wounded, heal the sick—and here
   I may embrace such strength, a mind so clear!

CHIRON. I treated many an injured friend
   In battle, helped them to recover;   7350
   But I gave up my practice in the end—
   The witches and the priests took over.

FAUST. You act as truly great men do,
   Disclaiming praise that is your due;
   With an evasive modesty you speak,
   Pretending you are not unique.

CHIRON. You do a wily flatterer's job;
   You'd please a prince or rouse a mob.

FAUST. Admit to me at least and say:
   You saw the noblest heroes of your day—   7360
   You longed for great deeds; how austere your life,
   A demigod's, an emulating strife!—
   Say now, of all those valiant men you knew,
   Which of them seemed the worthiest to you?

CHIRON. The Argonauts—all were magnificent;
   But in his own way each was excellent,
   Inspired by some particular energy,
   Outstanding in some special quality
   The others lacked. Zeus's Celestial Twins*
   Were always first where youthful beauty wins   7370
   Renown; when swift resolve and help were needed,

The winged Boreads all the rest exceeded;
Jason led well, sagacious, strong, and wise
In councils, and he pleased all women's eyes;
The contemplative tender Orpheus played
His lyre, and all with wonder were dismayed;
Steered by far-sighted Lynceus, night and day
The sacred ship pursued its perilous way.
Danger faced with companions—that's the test:
When one acts, and earns praise from all the rest.   7380

FAUST. And Hercules—did he not play a part?

CHIRON. Oh, do not stir that passion in my heart! . . .
Apollo I had never met,
Nor what's their names, Ares or Hermes yet,
When suddenly these eyes of mine
Beheld one whom mankind hail as divine.
Oh, he was born a king, and he
Grew up a youth most beautiful;
Yet humbly did his elder brother's will
And served fair women most devotedly.   7390
Earth will not bear his like again,
Nor Hebe carry heavenwards
Another such. Vain here are poets' words,
And sculptors hack their stones in vain.

FAUST. Yet in your own words he is most
Alive, for all the sculptors' boast.
Now of the finest man I've heard from you:
Describe the loveliest woman too!

CHIRON. What! . . . Female beauty's a mere mask,
Too often formal, cold and dead.   7400
Give me a living fountain-head
Of lively appetite for life, that's what I ask!
Beauty remains serene and self-sufficing:
But grace is irresistibly enticing.
As Helen was, when once she rode me.

FAUST. You carried her?

CHIRON.   Yes, she bestrode me.

FAUST. Oh, am I not enough confused

With joy! The very seat she used!

CHIRON. Indeed, and by the hair she grasped me tight,
    As you are doing.

FAUST.   Oh delight   7410
    Beyond endurance! Tell me, how—
    She is my only passion now!—
    When did she ride you, where and why?

CHIRON. That I can answer easily.
    It was when bandits took her prisoner;
    The Twins* came to her rescue. But those men,
    Unused to such defeats, gave chase again
    With renewed rage, nearly recapturing her:
    She and her brothers faltered in mid course
    At the Eleusinian swamp; I got across   7420
    Splashing and swimming, the Twins waded; then
    She jumped down, stroked my mane, all wet
    It was, and thanked me; how can I forget
    Her charming self-assurance, and how wise
    Her sweet youth was, what joy to my old eyes!

FAUST. A little girl of ten! . . .

CHIRON.   You, I perceive,
    Are misled by those scholars' make-believe.
    Mythical woman is a special case:
    The poets freely choose her changing face.
    She never need grow up, grow old,   7430
    Or lose her looks; abducted, so we're told,
    As a young girl, wooed as an aged crone.
    In short, the bard's not bound by time—he makes his own.

FAUST. So let it be with her: let no time bind her!
    On Pherae* did not great Achilles find her,
    Himself being outside time? What strange delight,
    To win such love, defying fate's dark might!
    And shall I not, by passion's power, draw
    Back into life that unique form I saw?
    Eternal, godlike being, tender as she   7440
    Is noble, lovely in her sublimity!
    You saw her once—I have seen her today;

She charms my eyes, she charms my heart away,
She rules me now, my fixed, my guiding star:
I cannot live till I find Helena!

CHIRON. My dear sir, as a man you are entranced;
    As spirits, we should call it an advanced
    State of derangement. Luckily for you
    It is my annual habit, for a few
    Moments, to visit Manto: she's the daughter   7450
    Of Aesculapius. Silently she prays
    To him that doctors in these latter days
    May at last do him honour, mend their ways
    And darkened minds, and cease their insolent slaughter
    Of patients . . . She's the Sibyl I like best:
    Not always in a fidget like the rest,
    But calm and a good influence. Stay with her
    A while: her medicines guarantee your cure.

FAUST. I want no weakling's cure! I will not be
    Like the contemptible majority!   7460

CHIRON. This noble healing fountain you should taste.
    Dismount now! We are here: no time to waste.

FAUST. Through stony streams you have carried me
    somehow
    On this wild night; where have I landed now?

CHIRON. Here Rome and Greece, Peneus on the right,
    Olympus on the left, fought their great fight;*
    A mighty empire vanished in the sand,
    Kings fled, the burgher gained the upper hand.
    Look! The eternal temple, close and clear,
    Looms over us in the moonlight here.   7470

MANTO* [in the temple, dreaming].
                With tremor of hooves
                My sacred threshold moves.
                Demigods are approaching.

CHIRON.   It is so!
                Open your eyes to know!

MANTO [*waking*].
　　Welcome! You keep your tryst, I see.

CHIRON. Your temple stands and waits for me.

MANTO. So tirelessly you wander still.

CHIRON. Yours is the peace by stillness bounded
　　I need to circle round at will.　　　　　　　　　　　7480

MANTO. I wait, by circling time surrounded.
　　What stranger's here?

CHIRON. 　　　　　　This night of ill fame caught him
　　Into its vortex and has brought him
　　To us. His mind is much elated:
　　With Helen he's infatuated,
　　And has no notion how to start.
　　The case deserves your Aesculapian art.

MANTO. On the impossible he sets his heart;
　　Such men I love.

　　　　　　　[CHIRON *is already in the distance.*]

　　　　　　　So enter with good cheer,
　　Rash wooer! Down through this dark passage here,　　7490
　　In Olympus' deep core, Persephone
　　Waits for forbidden greetings secretly.
　　I smuggled Orpheus in once this way too;
　　Use your chance better. Come now, down with you!

　　　　　　　　　　[*They descend.*]

　　　　[IOC · BY THE UPPER PENEUS, *as before*]

THE SIRENS. Plunge into Peneus' stream!
　　　　　　　We must play and we must swim
　　　　　　　And with singing long and loud
　　　　　　　Comfort this unhappy crowd.
　　　　　　　Where there's water there's salvation!
　　　　　　　Now let our whole company　　　　　　　7500
　　　　　　　Hasten to the Aegean Sea:
　　　　　　　All shall there be jubilation.

　　　　　　　[*An earthquake strikes.*]

Now the river churned to foam
Leaves the bed that was its home;
Earth is trembling, waters choke,
Banks and pebbles burst and smoke.
Flee this prodigy, come, hide!
Such a peril none can bide.

Come away, each noble guest:
By the sea our feast is best.   7510
Quivering waves that glint and gleam
Wet the shore in swelling stream,
And one moon shines out like two,
Moistening us with holy dew:
There is freedom, life and motion—
Here the shattered earth's commotion.
From the depths what terrors rise!
Leave this place, all who are wise.

SEISMOS* [*rumbling and banging in the depths*].
    One more heave and one more shove,
    And I'll be there, up above,   7520
    Out into the light of day;
    No one there gets in my way.

THE SPHINXES. How unpleasant is this quaking,
    Ugly shuddering and shaking,
    Sudden jolts and sudden shocks,
    To and fro the whole place rocks;
    How offensive a display!
    But we'll sit and not be shifted,
    Though the roof of hell be lifted.

    Now, how strange! an arch of stone   7530
    Heaves in sight. That old man's known
    Well to us: for it was he
    Who raised Delos from the sea,
    Leto's isle, that she might bear
    Phoebus and his sister there.
    How he strives and strains and presses!
    Atlas-like, with shoulders bent
    And stiff-armed, see, he has sent

Sod and soil up, earth in masses,
Stones and gravel, sand and clay—   7540
Tears our peaceful banks away,
Lifts the valley's quiet lid,
Interrupts the river's course,
Thrusting up with tireless force,
A colossal caryatid:
Monstrous stonework he has carried
On his head, though still half buried.
But here ends his upstart story:
This is sphinxes' territory.

SEISMOS. All this is my unaided work,   7550
And in the end they'll give me credit.
Without me here to quake and jolt and jerk,
Where would earth's beauty be? I made it!—
Where would your mountains be, that rise
Splendid in pure ethereal blue,
If I'd not reared them out for you
And shaped that picture to enchant your eyes?
My earliest ancestors of all
Were Night and Chaos; I was strong,
I grew up with the Titans; before long   7560
With Pelion and Ossa we played ball.
In youthful rashness on we sported,
Till for a lark we finally transported
Both of those mountains through the air
And gave Parnassus a twin cap to wear . . .
Apollo to this day amuses
Himself there with the blessed Muses;
And even for Zeus the Thunderer, I
Fashioned his throne and raised it high.
Just so, with monstrous efforts, as you see   7570
I have emerged from the abyss,
And now demand new life to go with this:
Happy inhabitants to live on me!

THE SPHINXES. Here's a mountain we should now
Judge to be of ancient birth,
Had we not just witnessed how

It was churned up from the earth.
New rocks in their convulsions still compound it
Even as dense forest grows already round it.
A sphinx need be no whit perturbed: 7580
We shall remain enthroned and undisturbed.

THE GRIFFINS. Gold in leaves and gold in slivers:
Through the fissures, look, it quivers!
Ants, come, claw this treasure free,
Seize your opportunity!

CHORUS OF ANTS. The giants thrust
This mountain up somehow:
Creepy-crawlies, we must
Climb up it now.
Quick, scuttle in and out!   7590
These rocks contain
A fortune: we must find
The smallest grain.
We must investigate
Even the tiniest
Cranny immediately:
Hurry, make haste!
Come, swarming host,
Swarm about busily!
Bring gold: the barren stone,   7600
Leave it alone.

THE GRIFFINS. Come, pile it up! Pile up the gold!
We'll stretch our claws and take good hold,
And it will be well locked and barred:
No treasure that our grip can't guard.

PYGMIES. Here's a spot to occupy.
Where we're from we've no idea.
No use asking how or why;
We just happen to be here.
Life is quick to find its place,   7610
Glad of any new terrain:
Give us cracks in the rock face,
And the dwarves pop up again.
Male and female, dwarfish twosome,

Toiling gladly cleft by cleft;
Was it thus in nature's bosom,
In the paradise we left?
We're content here none the less;
East and west, where's best to be?
Let us bless our luck, and bless   7620
Mother Earth's fertility.

FINGERLINGS. To these small folk the Earth
In one night gave birth;
Now the smallest appear,
Our kind too is here.

THE PYGMY ELDERS. Take up positions,
In this new country,
And be in readiness,
Strong by your speediness!
Set up your foundry   7630
To make munitions,
To turn out weapons
When the war happens.
Ants, we've a task for you:
Metals we ask of you.
Swarm and get busy!
And you tom-fingerlings,
You thousand tiny things,
Bring us whatever
Wood you can gather!   7640
Heap it together:
Our metal-smiths require
Its secret fire.

THE COMMANDER-IN-CHIEF. Now in good order,
Set out with arrows
And shoot those herons
Down by the water,
All at one swoop!
Thousands of nests there;
Puffing their breasts there,   7650
All cock-a-hoop.

        Fetch from that feathered breed
        The helmet plumes we need!

THE ANTS AND FINGERLINGS. Now who will save us?
        Iron for giants
        We make, and they make
        Chains to enslave us.
        Too soon to break them: we
        Must show compliance.

THE CRANES OF IBYCUS. Shrieks of murder, dying cries,   7660
        Wings' fear-stricken susurration,
        Moans and wails of lamentation:
        Through the air to us they rise.
        See, with blood the lake is red!
        All the herons now lie dead,
        Of their noble crests despoiled
        By a greed perverse and wild,
        And the plume already waves
        On those bow-legged pot-paunched knaves.
        You companions of our host,   7670
        Wedgewise wanderers of the coast,
        For revenge on you we call;
        These were kindred of us all.
        To the bane of that thrice-hated
        Race let all be dedicated!

        [*They scatter in flight with raucous cries.*]

MEPHISTOPHELES [*on the plain*].
    Up north, the witches would respect one's rights:
    I just can't deal with these damned foreign sprites.
    The Blocksberg—that's a snug spot, I must say;
    One feels at home there, wander as one may.
    Old *Ilse* on her *Rock* still waits up for us,   7680
    And so does *Heinrich* on his *Heights*; the *Snorers*
    Are snorting towards *Elend* as before;*
    It's all been there a thousand years or more.
    But here, where does one stand? That's the real trouble:
    One can't tell when the ground will burst a bubble
    Under one's feet. I'm calmly wandering

Down a wide valley—suddenly this thing
Pops up behind me; mountain one can't say,
But high enough. My Sphinxes, where are they?
Hidden behind it ... Here some fires still gleam
And flicker round; what wonders are downstream?   7690
That chorus—it still flirts invitingly,
Roguishly dancing, hovering, luring me
And yielding. Come! Lovers of tasty fare
Must take their chance to nibble anywhere.

THE LAMIAE [*drawing* MEPHISTOPHELES *after them*].
                    Now hurry! hurry!
                    Faster and faster!
                    Then pause a moment,
                    Chatter and comment.
                    It's so amusing   7700
                    To be seducing
                    This old whore-master
                    Who would seduce us!
                    He will be sorry.
                    He has a dud foot;
                    Look at his club-foot
                    Hobbling and limping,
                    Clumping and stumping,
                    As he pursues us!

MEPHISTOPHELES [*stopping in his tracks*].
    Oh, damned fate! Tricked and fooled again!   7710
    Since Adam's time, poor silly men!
    Older, but wiser not a whit;
    Even I often fell for it.
    One knows they're a completely worthless crew;
    All laced up, and their faces painted too;
    Unwholesome hags, no match for our advances—
    In every limb they crumble at a touch;
    One knows all this, eyes and hands tell as much,
    And yet when these sluts play the tune, one dances!

THE LAMIAE [*stopping*].
    Stop! He deliberates, he's in doubt.   7720
    Keep in his path, don't let him out!

MEPHISTOPHELES [*advancing again*].
　　But let's not be too sceptical;
　　It's foolish. Come, another try!
　　For if there were no witches, why
　　The devil be the Devil at all?

THE LAMIAE [*exerting their charm*].
　　Circle round this hero thus!
　　And his heart, we may be sure,
　　Will be touched by one of us.

MEPHISTOPHELES. Though the lighting is obscure,
　　You attract my wandering eyes;   7730
　　Pretty girls I don't despise.

AN EMPUSA [*thrusting herself in among them*].
　　Don't despise me either, please!
　　I'm as pretty as all these!

THE LAMIAE. Now she intrudes again; this bitch,
　　She always comes to queer our pitch.

THE EMPUSA [*to* MEPHISTOPHELES].
　　Your cousin, sir, begs leave to greet you!
　　Empusa Ass-hoof, pleased to meet you.
　　Your hoof's just from a horse, I know;
　　We're close relations even so.

MEPHISTOPHELES. I thought they'd all be strangers here;   7740
　　But they're my family, I fear.
　　How old a book I'm browsing in!
　　German or Greek, they're kith and kin.

THE EMPUSA. I can act quickly, too, and change
　　My shape at will: I've a whole range
　　Of shapes. But in your honour now
　　The ass's head seemed right somehow.

MEPHISTOPHELES. These people set great store, I see,
　　By kindred and affinity.
　　But come what may, it must be said   7750
　　That I disclaim the ass's head.

THE LAMIAE. Leave her alone, the hag! She scares
　　Beauty and charm away; who dares

Look beautiful and charming when
She shows her ugly face again!

MEPHISTOPHELES. These cousins too I must suspect:
They're *svelte* and slim, but I detect
Behind those cheeks as red as roses
An imminent metamorphosis.

THE LAMIAE. Why don't you try us? We are many.   7760
Just chance your luck; if you have any,
You may expect to snatch the prize.
This lustful litany—why, you
Poor fellow, that's no way to woo!
You'll need some cutting down to size.—
But now he's mixing with us all:
So gradually let your masks fall—
Be your bare selves before his eyes!

MEPHISTOPHELES. The prettiest now—this one I'll pick . . .

[*As he embraces her*]

Ugh! She's a dried-up piece of stick!   7770

[*Seizing another*]

Or this . . . What a disgusting face!

THE LAMIAE. And serve you right too! Know your place!

MEPHISTOPHELES. I'll catch that little lizard there . . .
But she slips through my hands! Her hair,
A pigtail slimy as a snake!
But here's a tall one I can take . . .
It's nothing but a thyrsus-staff;
Her head's a pine cone. What a laugh!
What next? . . . That fat one with the paps,
I'll get a squeeze from her perhaps;   7780
Come, one last try!—Ah, squashy, plump!
An Oriental prince for this soft rump
Would pay hard gold . . . But it explodes!
A fox-fart puffball, by the hellish gods!

THE LAMIAE.
Disperse now, flutter to and fro,
Swiftly and darkly round him, so,

This witch-man! Punish him, and rightly!
Uncanny circles, silent wings,
Bat-like, with half-seen hoverings!—
The rash intruder gets off lightly.   7790

MEPHISTOPHELES [*shaking himself*].
I've not learnt much from this experience,
It seems. The south, the north—neither makes sense;
Down here, back there, the ghosts are mad,
The common folk a bore, the poets bad.
Here too a masquerade, a dance
To give the senses one more chance.
I snatched at charming masks: they hid
Realities that really did
Make my flesh creep . . . Illusions are such fun,
If only they would stay with one.   7800

[*Losing his way among the boulders.*]

But now where am I? Here's more trouble;
There was a path, and now it's rubble.
I came this way on level ground,
Now these damned rocks are strewn all round.
This clambering up and down's no good.
Where are my Sphinxes? Who ever would
Have thought of such a crazy scene?
In just one night a mountain's been
Produced. Well done, that broomstick crew!
The Blocksberg's in their luggage too.   7810

AN OREAD [*from the natural cliff* *].
My mountain's old: come up to me!
Since earliest antiquity
I stand: respect my steep rock-bridges,
The extremities of Pindus' ridges.
This was my shape when Pompey fled
Over my unmoved watershed;
Whereas that lump, that phantom show
Will vanish at the next cock-crow.
I've seen such magic many times: it rears
Its head, and just as quickly disappears.   7820

MEPHISTOPHELES. All honour to your summit, crowned
    With noble oak-trees; they surround
    An inner darkness standing dense
    Against the moon's bright radiance.—
    And yet, close by the thicket gleams
    And moves a modest light, it seems.
    Well met by chance, I do confess!
    It's our Homunculus, no less!
    Where are you off to, little man?

THE HOMUNCULUS. I'm hovering about as best I can,   7830
    And what I want's to be born properly:
    I just can't wait to break my glass, you see.
    However, I'd not care to get
    Into the bodies that I've so far met.
    But between you and me, I'm looking
    For two philosophers: I heard them talking
    And they kept saying 'Nature, nature'! They
    Shall be the guides I cling to on my way;
    They surely know the secrets of the earth,
    And in the end, no doubt, I'll learn   7840
    From them which way I should be wise to turn.

MEPHISTOPHELES. You must find your own way to your
    own birth.
    Where phantoms gather, the philosopher
    Is welcome; he'll create a dozen more
    Phantoms at once, he can display
    His art and his good will that way.
    Only by error will you learn plain seeing.
    Find your own way of coming into being!

THE HOMUNCULUS. Good advice never comes amiss,
    who knows?

MEPHISTOPHELES. Off with you then, and let's see how
    it goes.   7850

             [*They separate.*]

ANAXAGORAS [*to* THALES].
    I see you're of the same opinion still:
    What more's required to bend your stubborn will?

THALES. The waves will bend at every wind's insistence;
    From the unyielding rock they keep their distance.

ANAXAGORAS. I say this rock by fire was created.

THALES. In moisture all that lives originated.

THE HOMUNCULUS [*appearing between them*].
    Allow me to accompany your debate!
    I too am trying to originate.

ANAXAGORAS. In one night, Thales, you I think would fail
    To make from slime a mountain on this scale.   7860

THALES. The peaceful flow of Nature's living powers
    Needs no constraint of nights or days or hours.
    She moulds and rules all forms, and even on
    The greatest scale no violence is done.

ANAXAGORAS. It was done here! Monstrous Plutonian
        heat,
    Aeolian explosive gas, replete
    With rage, burst through the earth's old flat crust,
        and so
    At once compelled this great new hill to grow.

THALES. Well, so you say; what then? The mountain came,
    And when all's said and done, that's no great shame.   7870
    We waste time thus disputing, and mislead
    The patient flock who pay our words some heed.

ANAXAGORAS. Those rocky clefts are habitation
    Already for a pullulation
    Of pygmies, ants and fingerlings—
    Myrmidon races, busy little things!

            [*To the* HOMUNCULUS.]

    You lack ambition; your career
    Is hermit-like. If you can here
    Adapt yourself to sovereignty,
    I will have you crowned king immediately.   7880

THE HOMUNCULUS. Does my Thales advise it?

THALES.   No; with small
    People one does small deeds, but with the great
    The small can rise to greatness. Contemplate

Up there the menacing black cloud
Of cranes: they threaten the excited crowd
And would be equal danger to a king.
With beaks and talons sharp as knives
They set the pygmies running for their lives;
The fatal storm is flickering
Already. As the herons stood   7890
About that quiet mere, their blood
Was murderously shed: that arrow-rain
Waters fierce vengeance for the slain.
Rage of the herons' kith and kin
Is roused against the pygmies' sin.
What shield or spear can now avail,
What dwarfish helm with heron plume?
The ants and thumblings hide and quail;
The army flees but cannot flee its doom.

ANAXAGORAS [*after a pause, solemnly*].*
The chthonic gods have favoured me till now: 7900
In this case to a higher power I bow.
Goddess, unageing on thy heavenly throne,
Thou of three names, three shapes in one:
Now in my people's woe I call on thee,
Diana, Luna, Hecate!
Lifter of hearts, deepest in wisdom, tranquillest
In shining, in strong passion innermost:
Open the dreadful gulf of thy dark shade,
And without magic let thy ancient power be displayed!

[*A pause.*]

   Is my prayer heard too soon?   7910
   By my imploring
   To heaven soaring,
   Is Nature's order overthrown?
And bigger, ever bigger, nearer looming,
The goddess's encircling throne is coming,
A monster to the eye, a sight of dread,
Its fire darkening to red! . . .
No nearer! Mighty menace, great round thing,
By you the land, the sea, we all are perishing!

So it is true: Thessalian witches once   7920
Sang magic spells in wicked confidence
That dragged you down from your celestial course,
And used you with destructive force!
But now the lustrous disc is darkling,
Suddenly cracking, flashing, sparkling!
I hear it spit, I hear it hiss!
What thundering, what monstrous gale is this?—
Prostrate I lie—forgive me, powers divine!
I called it down, the spell was mine!

[*He prostrates himself.*]

THALES. What curious things this man has seen and heard!   7930
I'm not quite sure what has occurred;
I noticed nothing, anyway.
These are mad times, one's bound to say.
As for the moon, it's still on high,
Floating as usual through the sky.

THE HOMUNCULUS. The pygmies' mountain, look! I'd
        swear
It was round-topped, now there's a peak up there.
I did feel a great crash or shock—
The moon had dropped that lump of rock.
It squashed to death both friend and foe,   7940
No by-your-leave for doing so.
But in one night, I must concede,
It took creative art indeed
To build this mountain quite spontaneously
From underground and from the heavens
        simultaneously!

THALES. Do not concern yourself; it was all fantasy.
We're well rid of that squalid tribe. What a good thing
They didn't choose you as their king.
Now for the festival, the great sea-treat!
Many a strange and honoured guest we'll meet. [*Exeunt.*]   7950

MEPHISTOPHELES [*climbing on the opposite side*].
So here I am, dragging myself up these
Steep ledges, past stiff roots of old oak-trees!

Back home in my Harz-land, the resinous smell*
Resembles pitch, which I like well,
As I do brimstone . . . In this old Greek place
There's not a whiff of either, not a trace.
Do they have hell-fire here? If so,
What fuel do they use, I'd like to know?

A DRYAD. Back in your native land, your native wit
No doubt sufficed; here, you seem short of it.   7960
Give up your homesick notions, they're home-made;
And reverence these oak-trees' sacred shade.

MEPHISTOPHELES. Things one was used to, they still
    haunt the mind;
Paradise is what one has left behind.
But tell me, what is in that cavern there,
In the dim light, a crouching shape, threefold?

THE DRYAD. The Phorcyads; approach them if you dare;
Speak to them, if your blood does not run cold.

MEPHISTOPHELES. Why not?—I see: now this is most
    bizarre.
In all humility I must avow   7970
I've never met creatures like this till now.
They're worse than mandrake-roots . . . How are
Even the blackest, oldest human sins
Still to seem ugly, if comparison begins
With this unholy trinity?
Even our most odious hells are places
Where we'd not let them show their faces.
How, in the very land of beauty, can this freak
Grow and be reverenced as antique? . . .
They stir, they seem to sense my presence; how   7980
They squeak! Like vampire bats they're gibbering now.

A PHORCYAD. Sisters, give me the eye, and it shall see
Who dares approach our temple-sanctuary.

MEPHISTOPHELES. Most honoured ladies, by your leave
    I'm here,
To seek your threefold blessing I appear;
I come a stranger still, but I could show you

That ramifying kinship binds me to you.
I have seen gods most ancient and most proud,
To Ops and Rhea deeply I have bowed,
The Fates themselves, sisters of Chaos, your   7990
Sisters indeed, I saw a day ago or more—
But on your like I never yet have gazed:
Words fail me now, I am delighted and amazed.

THE PHORCYADS. This spirit seems to be intelligent.

MEPHISTOPHELES. Yet no bard sings your praises!
   Wonderment
Fills me: how can this be? And I have never
Seen any likeness of you: sculptors should endeavour
To carve your venerable shapes, and not
Juno, Athene, Venus, and that lot.

THE PHORCYADS. Sunk in deep solitude, in still night
   pondering,   8000
We three have never thought of such a thing!

MEPHISTOPHELES. Indeed, why should you! Hidden
   from the world
You dwell, beholding none, by none beheld.
By rights you should live in some courtly place
Where wealth and art shed equal light and grace,
Where blocks of marble, hurrying to display
Themselves, rush into life as heroes every day;
Where—

THE PHORCYADS. Do not tempt us! Speak no more of
   this;
How would it help us, knowing what we miss?
Night-born, akin to darkest night alone,   8010
Known scarcely to ourselves, and by no others known.

MEPHISTOPHELES. That doesn't matter greatly, even so;
One can transfer to other selves, you know.
Your one eye and one tooth suffice for three:
Would it not then be good mythology
To squeeze your triune essence into two,
And lend the image of the third of you,
Briefly, to me?

ONE OF THE THREE. Well, sisters, shall we try?

THE OTHERS. Yes, let's; but keep the tooth and keep the
    eye!

MEPHISTOPHELES. But with those vital features
    disconnected,   8020
    How can a perfect likeness be effected?

ONE OF THE THREE. You must just shut one eye, no
    problem there;
    And one of your side-fangs you can lay bare.
    Your profile will at once accomplish thus
    A sisterly similitude with us.

MEPHISTOPHELES. Too great an honour; well, so be it!

THE PHORCYADS.   Done!

MEPHISTOPHELES [*with a Phorcyad's profile*].
    So here I stand, Chaos's well-beloved son!

THE PHORCYADS. We are her daughters, by undoubted
    right!

MEPHISTOPHELES. And to my shame, I'm a
    hermaphrodite.

THE PHORCYADS. Sisters, how beautiful! We're a new
    three,   8030
    Two eyes now and two teeth for you and me!

MEPHISTOPHELES. No eye must see me now, I must
    hide well:
    I'll dive right down and scare the fiends in hell.

[10d · ROCKY INLETS OF THE AEGEAN SEA.
The moon stands motionless at its zenith]

THE SIRENS [*reclining here and there on the cliffs, playing on
    flutes and singing*].

            Once, in Thessaly's deep night,
            By their wicked magic's might,
            Witches charmed you to the ground:
            Now from your dark orbit gaze
            Calmly on the tremulous
            Sea, where glittering radiance plays,

Swarming, scattering brightness round.   8040
Lady, shine upon your slaves
Leaping, tumbling from the waves:
Moon, look graciously on us!

NEREIDS AND TRITONS [*as marine prodigies*].
Let a shriller note resound
Through the seas with piercing sound:
People of the deep, appear!
From the storm's dark gulfs in dread
To these havens we have fled;
Your sweet singing draws us here.

Golden chains so rich and bright,   8050
See, we wear them with delight:
Crowns and gems adorn us too,
Bracelets, girdles—all these you
Gave us: for such treasures lay
Swallowed here in wrecks of ships
Lured to ruin by your lips,
You, the demons of our bay!

THE SIRENS.   Well we know where fish are gliding,
Through cool waters twisting, sliding,
Happy, swimming where they wish.   8060
Now we watch your festive motion:
Show us, creatures of the ocean,
Show us you are more than fish!

THE NEREIDS AND TRITONS.
We intended this before
We approached your rocky shore.
Sisters, brothers, come! To prove
We are more than fish, we'll move
Swiftly to the proper place,
Instantly to Samothrace.

[*They depart.*]

THE SIRENS. And vanishing so,   8070
Carried off by a fair breeze,
To that island they go
Where the lofty Cabiri* dwell;

What shall they accomplish then?
The Cabiri! Strange gods are these:
They beget themselves ever again,
But what they are they cannot tell.

Sweet Moon, stay graciously
Exalted, stationary!
Let night linger, let day   8080
Not drive us away!

THALES [*on the shore, to* THE HOMUNCULUS].
  I'd gladly visit Nereus with you,
  And the old fellow's cave's quite near here too;
  But he's a real curmudgeon, a thick-head
  And a sour-puss, it must be said.
  He's never pleased, he seems to find
  Fault with the whole race of mankind.
  Yet he has second sight, and so
  Everyone treats him with respect: they come
  To do him homage, and to some   8090
  He has done good services, I know.

THE HOMUNCULUS. Give him a knock, let's try it
    anyway!
  My glass and flame can stand it, I dare say.

NEREUS. Do I hear human voices? 'Pon my word,
  What rage they put me in! What an absurd
  Creature man is, striving to reach divinity,
  Yet stuck in his own image till infinity!
  I could have lived in blessed peace, and all
  Those years I felt the need to serve great men;
  But when they did their deeds, you'd have thought then   8100
  I'd never given them advice at all.

THALES. And yet men trust you, Old Man of the Sea;
  We need your wisdom, do not spurn us! See,
  This flame—in human likeness, it is true—
  Turns for advice devotedly to you.

NEREUS. Advice! When did men ever heed it? Wise
  Words merely freeze to death in ears of stone.
  Deeds self-discredited as soon as done

Still teach the headstrong nothing. When his eyes
Roved lustfully to Helen, Paris heard   8110
My fatherly warning. Boldly there he stood
On the Greek shore; I told him what I could,
For I foresaw it: fire and smoke upstirred,
Bloodying the air, roof-timbers all aglow,
Slaughter and carnage down below;
Troy's ordeal, captured in a poet's spell*
That binds three thousand years with dread and joy.
An old man's words amused that insolent boy:
He yielded to his whim, and Ilium fell—
A giant's corpse, great as the pains it bore;   8120
Its stiff flesh now wild birds of Pindus tore.
Ulysses too—did I not prophesy
Circe's deceits, the monster with one eye,
The folly of his men, his long-delayed
Return, and all the rest of it? It made
No difference, till the tossing sea upcast
Him on a hospitable shore at last.

THALES. As a wise man such folly gives you pain,
  But let your kind heart bid you try again:
  The pleasure of an ounce of thanks outweighs   8130
  The dull weight of a hundred thankless days.
  For our request's no trifle: this young creature
  Seeks wisely to acquire a bodily nature.

NEREUS. My mood was cheerful; must you spoil it for me?
  I had seen a quite different day before me:
  I have told the Graces of the sea, my daughters
  The Dorids, all to assemble in these waters.
  Neither Olympus bears, nor your dry land,
  Such lovely moving shapes, gracefully and
  Enchantingly from the sea-dragon leaping,   8140
  Mounting the sea-god's horses; gently thus
  The element takes them into its keeping,
  Even on the foam they ride victorious.
  Venus's rainbow-coloured chariot
  Of shell now brings the loveliest of the lot,
  Galatea: for since the Cyprian left us, she

Too is revered at Paphos equally.
As Aphrodite's heiress, chariot-throne
And temple-city now are both her own.
Away! A father's joy must fill this hour;   8150
My heart must not be hard, nor my tongue sour.
Ask Proteus! He has much strange information,
He'll tell you about birth and transformation.

[*He moves away towards the sea.*]

THALES. That didn't help; even if we had him here,
Proteus would just dissolve and disappear;
And even if one can hold him, all he'll say
Is merely meant to puzzle and mislead
The questioner. But, since it seems you need
Some such advice, come, let's be on our way!

[*Exeunt.*]

THE SIRENS [*on the rocks above*].
What's this towards us riding,   8160
Through the wave-kingdom gliding?
A wind-borne company,
White sails they seem to be:
Mermaids that shine so bright,
Transfigured with strange light.
Let us descend: you hear
Their voices drawing near.

THE NEREIDS AND TRITONS.
Look! In our hands we bring
You all a joyful thing!
In this great turtle-shell   8170
Are gods: now praise them well!
See how their stern forms shine,
Scattering light divine!

THE SIRENS. Tiny of stature,
Mighty in power,
Wrecked seamen's refuge,
Gods of an ancient age!

THE NEREIDS AND TRITONS. Now the Cabiri rule
This peaceful festival,

               The wild waves they can bind   8180
               And Neptune will be kind.

THE SIRENS. You are the stronger:
               When the sea's anger
               Wrecks ships, the crew
               Is saved by you.

THE NEREIDS AND TRITONS.
               We've brought you three of them;
               The fourth refused to come,
               He said he was the best
               Who thinks for all the rest.

THE SIRENS. One god may well deride   8190
               Another; beware such pride!
               Ever fearing to fall,
               You should revere them all.

THE NEREIDS AND TRITONS.
               Seven they should really be.

THE SIRENS. Where are the other three?

THE NEREIDS AND TRITONS.
               We've still not worked that out;
               In Olympus they'd know, no doubt.
               And the eighth subsists there somehow;
               He's not been thought of till now.
               They are favourably disposed,   8200
               But none is yet fully composed.
               They are peerless beings, each
               By an onward urge obsessed,
               Hungry with a strange unrest
               For a goal beyond their reach.

THE SIRENS. Let all reverence be done
               To the moon, to the sun,
               And where else it is due:
               This we think best to do.

THE NEREIDS AND TRITONS.
               How high now our fame flowers,   8210
               Who bring this festive pleasure!

THE SIRENS.   The heroes of ancient story
          Fell short of such glory,
          Though their high fame endures.
          The Golden Fleece was their treasure:
          The Cabiri are yours!

            [*Repeated in chorus.*]

          The Golden Fleece was their treasure:

          The Cabiri are $\begin{cases} \text{ours.} \\ \text{yours.} \end{cases}$

[THE NEREIDS *and* TRITONS *pass by.*]

THE HOMUNCULUS.   Misshapen things! They look to me
    Like dreary pots of clay.   8220
    But pundits probe this mystery
    With their blunt noddles to this day.

THALES.   Old pots are what they want! An old coin must
    Gain extra value from its rust.

PROTEUS [*unseen*].
    I like that! As an old romancer,
    I always find nonsense the soundest answer.

THALES.   Where are you, Proteus?

PROTEUS [*speaking like a ventriloquist, nearby and then from a
    distance*].
                   Here! and here!

THALES.   By all means play your old trick; but, my dear
    Friend, spare me idle words! I know
    You speak from where you're not.

PROTEUS [*as if from a long way off*]. Hullo!   8230
    Goodbye!

THALES.   He's very close. Now shine your light!
    He's as inquisitive as a fish;
    He's stuck now in some shape-shift, but a bright
    Flame will entice him where you wish.

THE HOMUNCULUS.
    My glass shall give its maximum radiation;
    But gently, to avoid disintegration.

PROTEUS [*in the shape of a giant turtle*].
    What's this that shines so prettily?

THALES [*covering up* THE HOMUNCULUS].
    Good! Take a closer look! You'll be
    Rewarded for your trifling pains. But you
    Must come, please, on two human feet; then we'll   8240
    Gladly, but on our terms, reveal
    This treasure hidden from your view.

PROTEUS [*appearing in a noble form*].
    You've not forgotten your old worldly arts.

THALES. You're still, I see, a man of many parts.

        [*He has uncovered* THE HOMUNCULUS.]

PROTEUS [*astonished*].
    A shining midget! This I've never seen.

THALES. He wants advice; he's only been
    Half born, it seems, in a most curious fashion.
    To be born fully, that's now his great passion.
    His intellectual qualities are many,
    But earthly solid life he has hardly any.   8250
    This glass retort's still all that gives him weight;
    His wish now's to become incorporate.

PROTEUS. A case of true parthenogenesis!
    Before he should be, he already is.

THALES [*sotto voce*].
    And there's another thing that's critical:
    He seems to me to be hermaphroditical.

PROTEUS. So much the better: he arrives
    In this world with a choice of lives!
    But here's no need for much discourse:
    In the wide sea you must begin your course!   8260
    At first one's small, but with great pleasure
    One swallows creatures of still tinier measure;
    Gradually one will thus augment
    And shape oneself for high accomplishment.

THE HOMUNCULUS. How soft and fresh the air! This smell
    Of moist fertility contents me well.

PROTEUS. That I can well believe, dear boy!
  And further on there's still more to enjoy.
  This narrow salient of the sandy shore—
  It has an atmosphere still more   8270
  Ineffable. And there we'll get the best
  Sight of the pageant as it floats in view.
  So come with me!

THALES.   I'll join you too.

THE HOMUNCULUS. March on then, our great threefold
      spirit-quest!

  [TELCHINES *from Rhodes, on hippocampi and
  sea-dragons, brandishing Neptune's trident.*]

CHORUS. The trident of Neptune, that rules the wild ocean:
  We forged it, we made it! When densest commotion
  Of storm-clouds unfolds in the Thunder-god's hour,
  Then Neptune responds to his terrible power.
  From heaven the lightnings flash jaggedly down,
  But skywards the spray leaps as waves are upthrown;   8280
  Seafarers in terror are tossed to and fro,
  Till the deep overwhelms them and sucks them below.
  And so he has lent us his sceptre today,
  And calm is the sea as we hover and play.

THE SIRENS.   Hail, you Helios devotees,
                     Sacred to calm skies and seas!
                     See, the moon too can excite
                     Homage on her festive night!

THE TELCHINES.
  Sweet goddess high up in the zenith, rejoice
  For your brother the sun is extolled with one voice!   8290
  From the blest isle of Rhodos his praises ascend
  To your listening ear in a hymn without end.
  When he starts his day's journey and when it is done,
  His face glows on us, the great fiery sun;
  On our mountains, our cities, our shore and our sea,
  The god's favour shines, they are lovely to see.
  No clouds linger round us; if any intrude,

With a ray and a breeze his pure sky is renewed.
Now his hundred reflections the god may behold,
The ephebe, the colossus his greatness unfold.   8300
For we were the first who such images made
And in man's noble likeness the high gods displayed.

PROTEUS. Let them sing on in vain self-praise!
    The sacred sun's life-giving rays
    Mock their dead handiwork to scorn.
    They carry on, they sculpt, they cast,
    A lump of bronze stands up at last,
    And they think something has been born.
    Why, these proud forgers, they're no good!
    Look now where their god-statues stood: 8310
    An earthquake knocked them flat! Since then
    They've all been melted down again.

    Say what you will, terrestrial life
    Is one long toil and one long strife;
    Water-life's better! Now I'll be
    Proteus-Dolphin. Come with me
    To the eternal deep!

            [*He transforms himself.*]

            It's done!
    Mount on my back, you'll be well carried,
    And all will turn out well. Be married
    To the great ocean from now on.   8320

THALES. Yield to your laudable temptation:
    Seek the beginnings of creation!
    Be poised to act, don't hesitate!
    Move onward by eternal norms
    Through many thousand thousand forms,
    And reach at last the human state.

      [THE HOMUNCULUS *mounts the*
        PROTEUS-DOLPHIN.]

PROTEUS. Come, as a spirit, to the wet
    Expanse! Full freedom there you'll get
    To live and move, to grow and be.
    But don't strive to a higher level: 8330

You'll go completely to the devil
Once you achieve humanity.

THALES. Well, that depends; it's no bad thing, I'd say,
To be a sound man in one's day.

PROTEUS. One of your sort, perhaps; they do
Last a while longer, that is true.
For many centuries I've seen your face
Among the pale shades in this place.

THE SIRENS [*on the rocks*].
See, a ring of cloudlets round it,
Shines the moon in rich display: 8340
Doves aflame with love surround it,
Silver-pinioned, white as day!
Paphian Aphrodite's favour
Sends her amorous love-birds here,
Lends our feast its fullest savour,
Makes our joy complete and clear.

NEREUS [*approaching* THALES].
That moon-halo's what the night-
Farer calls imagination,
But we spirits see it right,
Know the proper explanation: 8350
Those are sacred doves, attendant
On my daughter's shell-borne throne,
In mysterious flight resplendent,
Learnt of old and strangely known.

THALES. That is how I see it too:
An honest man's contented view
Of what is holy, what is best,
Snugly in his heart will nest.

PSYLLI and MARSI [*riding on sea-bulls, sea-calves, and
sea-rams.*]
In Cyprus's rude hollow caves,
Undrowned by seaquake waves,   8360
By earthquake shock unmarred:
As in days long ago
The deepest joy we know,

For ever the breezes blow,
The goddess's chariot we guard;
And where nights murmur and play
We bring through the weave of sweet water
The sea's loveliest daughter,
Unseen by eyes of today.
Our activity, quiet, incessant,   8370
Fears no Eagle, no Lion with wings,
Cares neither for Cross nor Crescent;*
Above us they dwell, these things
That war for their changing sway,
That rule and usurp and slay,
Sweeping crops and cities away.
But we, as ever before,
Bring the dear goddess here once more.

THE SIRENS. Circling swiftly, lightly moving,
    Round the chariot, in and out,   8380
    Line by line all interweaving,
    Coil by coil and turn about:
    Come, you stalwart Nereids, wild
    Buxom womenfolk! And you,
    Tender Dorids, bring her too,
    Galatea, your mother's child!
    She is like the gods, for she
    Has a deathless gravity,
    Though a mortal woman's grace
    Draws men to her lovely face.   8390

THE DORIDS [riding past NEREUS as a chorus, all on
              dolphins].
    Lend us, moon, your light and shade,
    For our father now must see
    These sweet youths with whom we played
    And have wedded instantly!

             [To NEREUS.]

    These young men we saved from death
    In the roaring breakers' greed,
    Warmed them back to light and breath,

Bedding them on moss and reed.
They give thanks for life restored:
Ardent passion's our reward—   8400
Look upon them favourably!

NEREUS. Excellent! Two advantages in one:
A work of mercy which is also fun.

THE DORIDS. Since you praise us, father, surely
You'll not grudge our well-earned joys:
Let us have and hold securely
Ever-young, immortal boys!

NEREUS. Enjoy your captives; fine grown men
You'll make of them. But why ask me
To grant them immortality?   8410
That's something only Zeus can do.
The sea-waves rock and cradle you:
Nothing lasts there, not even love.
So when it flits away, just shove
Them gently back ashore again.

THE DORIDS. Dear boys, we love you, but sad goodbyes
We must say, and our bonds must sever!
We asked for love that would last for ever;
The gods decree otherwise.

THE YOUTHS. That's quite all right for a sailor-lad!   8420
Just carry on kissing; we've never had
It so good before, such a time as this;
And what we don't have we don't miss.

[GALATEA *approaches, riding the shell-chariot.*]

NEREUS. It's you, my beloved!

GALATEA.   Oh father! I gaze
With such joy! Oh, how briefly the chariot stays!

NEREUS. Gone, gone from me already; out of sight,
Drawn past by the circling dolphin motion;
What do they care for the innermost heart's devotion!
Take me with you! Alas, if they might!—
And yet with that one look I am content   8430
For my whole year of banishment.

THALES. Hail, and all hail to you!
  How beautiful, how true
  This sense that flowers, that fills me through and through:
  In water all things began to thrive!!
  By water all things are kept alive!
  Grant us your bounty for ever, great ocean:
  Send us clouds, for if you did not,
  Abundant streams, for if you did not,
  And rivers in meandering motion,   8440
  And great waterways—for if you did not,
  Where would the mountains, the plains, and the world
    be then?
  By you fresh life lives and is sustained again.

ECHO [*from the general chorus of all present*].
  From you fresh life flows and is born again.

NEREUS. Back into the distance swerving,
  Their eyes and my eyes meet no more;
  In a great chain of circles curving,
  Dancing, in festive spirit moving,
  The countless host forsakes the shore.
  But Galatea's chariot-shell   8450
  I still see, yes, again I see:
  Bright as a star to me
  Through the crowd I know it well.
  What we love shines through
  The throng, far though it seems;
  Still it glistens, still gleams,
  Ever near, ever true.

THE HOMUNCULUS. In this sweet water-world,
                Wherever I shed my light   8460
                Is beautiful and bright.

PROTEUS.   In this, life's water-world,
                As never before, your light
                Makes music loud and bright.

NEREUS. What new mystery now in the midst of the
  dancing
  Reveals itself to us, our vision entrancing?

What flames round the shell at the goddess's feet?
It blazes up strongly, then gently and sweet,
As if touched by the pulses of love and desire.

THALES. The Homunculus, ravished by Proteus! . . . That
    fire
Is his powerful longing, its symptoms I know;   8470
I sense his loud anguish, the throb of his woe.
He will shatter his glass on her glistening throne:
Now he flashes, he gleams, now he spills and is gone.

THE SIRENS. What fiery wonder transfigures the sea?
The waves splinter and glitter, what storm can this be?
All shining and swaying, a progress of light,
Those bodies aglow as they move through the night,
And the whirl of the fire all about and around!
Now let Eros, first cause of all, reign and be crowned!

        Hail to the sea, the shifting tide,   8480
        By sacred fire beautified!
        Hail to the waves, hail to the flame,
        Hail, this event without a name!

TUTTISSIMI. Hail to the mild and gentle breeze!
        Hail, caverns rich with mysteries!
        Fire, water, air, and earth as well:
        You elements all four, all hail!

ACT THREE

11 · IN FRONT OF THE PALACE OF MENELAUS IN SPARTA*

[*Enter* HELEN *and the* CHORUS *of captive Trojan women.* PANTHALIS, *leader of the Chorus.*]

HELEN. So much admired and so much censured, Helena,
   Now from the sea I come; we are not long ashore,
   And drunken still with rocking upon the lively waves   8490
   Which on their high-uptossing backs, from Troy's wide
      plain,
   By great Poseidon's favour and by the east wind's force
   Brought us once more to harbours of our fatherland.
   Down there the king, my husband Menelaus, now
   With his most valiant fighters feasts his homecoming.
   But you must bid your queen here welcome, noble house
   Built by my father Tyndareus on his return,
   Nearby the slopes of Pallas Athene's lofty hill:
   Here with my sister Clytemnestra and the twins
   Castor and Pollux happily playing I grew up,   8500
   While he adorned it like no other in the land.
   All hail to you now, mighty doors of bronze! You once
   Stood open wide in hospitable welcome, when
   It came about that Menelaus, the elect
   Of many wooers, shiningly appeared to me.
   Let them once more be opened! for as a loyal wife
   I must fulfil an urgent bidding of the king.
   So let me enter, and let all the storms of fate
   That have been raging round me now be left behind.
   For since I crossed this threshold last, as duty bade,   8510
   All unsuspecting, visiting Cythera's shrine,
   And there was ravished by an adventurer from Troy,
   Much has befallen: far and wide men tell the tale
   And take their pleasure in it. But no tale can please
   One round whose name long legend spins its false report.

CHORUS. Most noble lady, do not despise
         What is yours with honour, this highest of gifts!
         For supreme good fortune is yours alone
         In the fame of beauty, excelling all.
         A hero's name before him resounds,   8520
         And he walks with pride.
         But even the most stiff-necked of men
         Before all-conquering Beauty will bow.

HELEN. Enough! My husband brought me back in his
      own ships
   And to his city sends me now ahead of him:
   But what his purpose may be, that I cannot guess.
   Do I come here as wife? Do I come here as queen?
   Or will the king avenge on me his bitter grief
   And all these long misfortunes that the Greeks have
      borne?
   I am a prize of war, perhaps a prisoner!   8530
   For by heaven's will, my reputation is two-edged
   As is my fate—and both, the ambiguous followers
   Of beauty, even now beset me with their dark
   And menacing presence, on this threshold of my home.
   For on the hollow ship, indeed, my husband looked
   Askance at me and seldom; no good word he spoke,
   But sitting opposite me, seemed to brood on evil things.
   Then, when the first ships' prows advanced into the deep
   Eurotas estuary and had scarcely touched the land
   In greeting, then he spoke, as if divinely moved: 8540
   'Here in due order all my men will disembark
   And on the sea's shore stand for me to muster them.
   You, for your part, proceed up-river, ride along
   Sacred Eurotas' fruitful banks, and travel on,
   Guiding the horses through the rich moist meadowlands,
   Until you reach the city in its noble plain:
   Here Lacedaemon, once a wide and fertile field,
   Was built in our grave mountains' far-surrounding shade.
   Enter the high-towered palace then, and muster all
   The women, our maidservants whom I left behind,   8550
   Also that wise old beldame, keeper of the house.
   Next bid her show you my rich treasury of wealth,

Bequeathed us by your father, which I have myself
Nurtured with constant increase both in peace and war.
All will be in good order, you will find it so;
It is the ruler's privilege, on returning home,
To find his house unchanged and all things faithfully
Preserved and in their place, as when he left them there;
For servants make no change without authority.'

CHORUS. Now feast your eyes on this ever-new   8560
                And most splendid treasure, refreshing your
                    heart!
                For here they lie, the bejewelled crowns
                And necklaces, self-complacent and proud;
                But enter, challenging them yourself:
                They will spring to arms!
                I watch with joy when beauty makes war
                Against gold and gems and pearls of great price.

HELEN. Thus then my lord spoke further with
            commanding words:
        'Next, having passed all things in orderly review,
        Take brazier tripods, judging how many are required,   8570
        And all such vessels as the celebrant may need
        To have to hand for sacred sacrificial rites:
        The pots, the dishes for the blood, the offering-dish.
        Let purest water from the holy spring be poured
        Into tall jars; and bring dry wood that rapidly
        Catches the hot flames; all this hold in readiness,
        And not forgetting, lastly, a well-sharpened knife.
        As for the rest, I must entrust it to your care.'
        So saying, he motioned me to leave; but careful though
        His orders were, they told me of no living thing,   8580
        No offering he would slaughter for the Olympian gods.
        This troubles me; and yet I put this care aside,
        Letting all these things lie upon the high gods' lap
        Who must and will accomplish all they have in mind,
        Whether by human reckoning it be counted good
        Or evil. We must bear it, being mortal men.
        Often it has happened that the sacrificial priest
        Has raised the sharp blade over the cowering victim's neck

But could not strike the blow, because his hand was
    stayed
By intervention of some enemy or some god.   8590

CHORUS.   To discern the future is not in our power;
           So with good courage, oh queen,
           Enter the house!
           Good and ill fortune come
           Upon man without warning;
           We disbelieve even what is foretold.
           Was not Troy burning, did we not see
           Death confronting us, shameful death?
           And are we not here,
           Your companions, serving you gladly,   8600
           Seeing the dazzling sun in the heavens
           And earth's loveliest treasure,
           Fortunate that she favours us?

HELEN. Be it or be it not so: whatever may befall,
I must without delay enter this royal house,
So longed for, lost for so long, almost for ever lost,
And which so strangely stands before me once again.
Less willingly my feet move now as they ascend
These lofty steps they tripped down lightly long ago.
    [*Exit.*]

CHORUS.   Sisters, you sorrowing   8610
           Captives, now cast away,
           Cast away all your suffering!
           Share in her happiness,
           Our lady's happiness:
           Helen has now returned with joy,
           To her hearth and her home she comes,
           Tardy her steps, yet all the more
           Firmly and surely they bring her.

           Praise to the sacred gods,
           They give us life again,   8620
           They grant blessed homecoming!
           For the freed prisoner
           Hovers like one on wings
           Over the harshest way, while there

In his bondage another grieves
Vainly in longing outstretching his
Arms over walls that enclose him.

But her exile ended when
She was snatched up
By a god out of Troy's   8630
Ruins and carried back here
To her ancient, newly adorned
Ancestral halls,
And after nameless
Joys and sufferings
To remembered youth
Brought to life once more for her.

PANTHALIS [*as leader of the Chorus*].
Step now aside from the delectable path of song
And turn your eyes to the great doorway of the house!
What is this, sisters? Is the queen not coming back   8640
To us, in agitation and with hasty steps?
Great queen, what is the matter? What alarming thing
In your own palace halls, instead of the greetings of
Your servants, can have encountered you? You do not
    hide
Your deep repugnance, for I see upon your brow
A noble anger written, fighting with surprise.

HELEN [*entering in agitation, leaving the doors wide open*].
To show base fear befits no daughter of high Zeus;
No fleeting slight alarm can set its hand on her.
But when some horror from the womb of ancient night,
Risen from the primal depths, is belched like burning
    cloud,   8650
Still manifold in shape, from the fire-mountain's maw,
Then nameless dread strikes even the heroic heart.
So it has been today: the gods of hell have marked
My entry to this house with terror, so that on
This once familiar, long desired threshold now
I turn my back, and flee it like a guest dismissed.
But no! thus far I yield, into the light: you shall

Not drive me further, whatever powers you may be!
I will reconsecrate the hearth: the fire will then
Be purified to greet its mistress and its lord.   8660

CHORUS. Most noble lady, your devoted servants stand
   Here to support you: tell us what strange thing befell!

HELEN. With your own eyes you too shall see what I
        have seen,
   If ancient night has not at once gulped back the shape
   Again into its deep dark womb of mysteries.
   But that they may inform you, listen to my words:
   No sooner had I solemnly, reflecting on
   The king's next order, entered the silent royal rooms
   And passages within, than their bleak emptiness
   Struck me. No sound of diligent footsteps could I hear,   8670
   I saw no busy haste of movement to and fro,
   No serving-maid appeared to me, no housekeeper,
   None such as welcomed any stranger in the past.
   But as I neared the bosom of the house, the hearth,
   There on the ground, where still some half-warm ashes
        glowed,
   I saw her sitting—some tall shrouded woman's form,
   Not like a sleeper, but like one who meditates.
   With stern commands I bade her set to work, for this,
   As I supposed, was the housekeeper whom perhaps
   My prudent husband left behind and set in charge;   8680
   But folded on herself she still sat motionless,
   Until at last, upon my threats, her right arm moved
   And seemed to motion me away from hearth and hall.
   I turned from her in anger, and approached the steps
   That lead up to the bridal chamber, festively
   Adorned, and close beside it stands the treasure-store.
   But the uncanny thing rose quickly from the ground,
   Barring my way commandingly, and there it stood,
   Tall and cadaverous, with hollow bloodshot eyes,
   So strangely shaped that it bewilders sight and mind.   8690
   Yet I waste breath; for ever vainly words attempt
   To recreate and recompose the forms we see.
   Look for yourselves! She dares emerge into the light!
   Here we are in control, until the king shall come:

   The sun-god is the friend of beauty, and he drives
   Vile night-born monsters underground, or masters them.

   [PHORCYAS *appears on the threshold between the*
   doorposts.]

CHORUS. I have seen much, although still my brows are
            Youthful, and youthful the locks that ring them!
            Many the horrors that I have lived through:
            War-harm's wailing, murk of the night of   8700
            Troy's fall.

            Through foggy clangour and through the dust-filled
            Tumult of warriors, I heard the dreadful
            Shouts of the gods, and over the field to the
            City's ramparts I heard the brazen
            Voice of strife.

            Ah, Troy's walls were not yet cast down,
            But already the blazing fire
            Leapt from neighbour to neighbour's house,
            Springing, spreading from here and there   8710
            Through the night of the darkened city,
            Blown by the wind of its own storm.

            Fleeing, I saw through the smoke and heat
            And the blaze of the writhing flames
            Gods approaching in hideous rage:
            Figures of wonder striding
            Giant-tall through the darksome
            Reek that swirled in the fire's glow.

            Did I see those things, or were they
            Mere phantasms born in my fear-   8720
            Tangled mind? That I never shall know;
            But that I truly behold
            This horror here and now with my eyes—
            Of this indeed I am certain;
            Even my hands could grasp it,
            If I did not shrink back from it,
            Sensing something of danger.

Which one are you among
Phorcys's daughters?
For I must liken you   8730
To that generation.
Have you come here perhaps as one of the
Grey-born hags, the Graiae, who take
Turns, the three of them sharing
One eye, one tooth, between them?

Monster, how dare you be
Seen beside beauty,
Seen by the sun-god
Whose gaze knows all things?
Yet, step forth if you will; for indeed, he   8740
Himself can behold no hideous sight,
Even as his sacred eye has
Never yet looked upon shadow.

But we mortals, alas, by our
Grievous fate, must endure this pain,
This unspeakable sight-affliction
Which all vile, all eternally abject
Things lay on lovers of beauty.

Hear then, you who in insolence
Have confronted us, hear our curse,   8750
Hear such threats and such dire abuse as
Can be formed in the mouths of the fortunate
Who have been fashioned by high gods!

PHORCYAS. The proverb's old, but still its meaning's high
        and true,
    That modesty and beauty never hand in hand
    Pursue their way together along the earth's green path.
    Between the two, ancient deep-rooted hatred dwells,
    So that wherever they may somehow chance to meet,
    Each of them turns her back upon her enemy.
    Each will press on then further with more vehement
        pace,   8760
    Modesty sadly, beauty flown with insolence,
    Till in the end hell's hollow night receives them both,

If they are not first subjugated by old age.
Thus now, you foreign hussies, shameless, arrogant as
You are, I find you swarming hither like a hoarse
And noisy flight of cranes, which in a straggling cloud
Above our heads sends down its harsh cacophony
On us, so that the peaceful wayfarer is moved
To glance aloft; but off they fly upon their way,
While he goes his; and so it shall be between us.   8770

Who then are you, who dare to rage around this high
And royal house with drunken maenad revelry?
Who are you then, who howl against the keeper of
The palace household, like dogs howling at the moon?
Do you suppose I do not know your pedigree,
You war-begotten, battle-nurtured bitch-whelp brood?
Man-ravenous all, seducers and seduced alike,
Unmanning warlike energy and civil strength!
I see you huddled there like some cicada swarm,
Dropping and settling, covering the green tender crops.   8780
You female jackals of the fruit of others' toil!
Dainty devourers of a germinating wealth!
You conquered slaves, you sold and peddled
    merchandise!

HELEN. To chide the servants when the mistress of the
        house
Is present, is to encroach upon their lady's rights,
For it is her prerogative alone to praise
What is well done, and punish what is done amiss.
Moreover, I am contented with them, for they gave
Me faithful service when the lofty power of Troy
Stood under siege and fell defeated; likewise when   8790
We bore a wandering voyage's vicissitudes,
Such as more often drive each man to serve himself.
And I expect the same here from these merry girls;
Not who one's servants are, one asks, but how they serve.
Therefore stop sneering at them now, and shut your
    mouth.
If on your mistress's behalf you have kept the king's
    house well

Till now, then you have done your duty; but since she
Is here again in person, keep your proper place,
Or you will merit punishment and not reward.

PHORCYAS. To threaten members of the household is a
    right   8800
Which the high consort of our heaven-favoured king
Has earned by long years spent in prudent governance.
Lady, since you, whom now I acknowledge, take again
Your former place as queen and mistress of the house:
Take up the reins that have so long grown slack, rule
    now
And repossess the treasure, repossess us all!
But chiefly I request protection for my years
Against this gaggle—for your swan-like beauty makes
Them seem no more—of poor, half-wingless, cackling
    geese.

CHORUS LEADER. How vile beside such beauty ugliness
    appears!   8810

PHORCYAS. And beside riper wits how witless witlessness.

[*From this point the members of the* CHORUS *step
forward one by one to answer.*]

FIRST CHORUS MEMBER. Tell of your father Erebus, tell
    of your mother Night!

PHORCYAS. Speak of the monster Scylla, your true sibling-
    child.

SECOND CHORUS MEMBER. How many monsters crawl
    about your family tree!

PHORCYAS. Begone to Hades; there you'll find your kith
    and kin.

THIRD CHORUS MEMBER. You'll not find yours there;
    none of the dead are old enough.

PHORCYAS. Find old Tiresias, try your harlot's wiles on
    him!

FOURTH CHORUS MEMBER. No doubt your great-grand-
    daughter was Orion's nurse.

PHORCYAS. Foul harpies fed you, I suppose, amid their
    filth.

FIFTH CHORUS MEMBER. What diet keeps your skinny
    figure as it is?   8820

PHORCYAS. At least not blood, the favourite fare for
    which you crave.

SIXTH CHORUS MEMBER. Corpses are your prey, a
    disgusting corpse yourself!

PHORCYAS. I see the vampire fangs gleam in your
    insolent mouth.

CHORUS LEADER. I can stop yours if I pronounce your
    proper name.

PHORCYAS. Pronounce your own first, and we'll share the
    mystery.

HELEN. In sorrow, not in anger, I must intervene,
    I must forbid this altercation's violence.
    Nothing does greater injury to a prince than if
    His loyal servants itch with hidden mutual strife,
    For his commands then can no longer echo back   8830
    Harmoniously, translated swiftly into deeds:
    Instead, disordered noise roars round him waywardly
    While in confusion he upbraids the empty air.
    Nor is this all. In your unseemly anger you
    Called dreadful shapes to mind and dismal images
    Which throng around me, so that I myself feel drawn
    Down hellwards, even on this my green and native earth.
    Is it a memory? Has delusion seized my mind?
    Was I all that? And am I? And shall I still be
    That nightmare image, Helena the cities' bane?   8840
    The girls all tremble: you alone, the eldest, stand
    Calm and composed: now show me wisdom in your
        words.

PHORCYAS. Long years of manifold good fortune make
    the gods'
    Latest and highest favours seem no more than dreams.
    But you, whom they have so extravagantly blessed,
    Saw in life's sequence only men whose hot desire

Inflamed them quickly to bold various enterprise.
You were a child still whom lust-maddened Theseus
  snatched;
A splendid shapely man, as strong as Hercules.

HELEN. He carried me off, a slender fawn, just ten years
  old,   8850
And I was held in Attica, in Aphidnus' halls.

PHORCYAS. But your twin brothers quickly rescued you;
  and soon
A choice array of heroes all were wooing you.

HELEN. And I confess, my silent favour chiefly fell
On one, Patroclus, great Achilles' lookalike.

PHORCYAS. But Menelaus won you, by your father's will;
He was a bold sea-rover and good housekeeper.

HELEN. He won the daughter, and the kingdom's riches
  too.
Then of our marriage-bed was born Hermione.

PHORCYAS. But when, to conquer Crete, he left you by
  yourself,   8860
You had a visitor whose attractions proved too strong.

HELEN. Why do you call to mind that semi-widowhood
And the appalling ruin that it spelt for me?

PHORCYAS. I suffered by that voyage too: free-born in
  Crete,
It brought me long imprisonment and slavery.

HELEN. You were brought back at once to keep his
  household here:
His castle and its hard-won wealth became your trust.

PHORCYAS. You left them both, to seek the towered walls
  of Troy
And to enjoy love's pleasures inexhaustibly.

HELEN. Do not speak of the pleasures! An infinitude   8870
Of bitter sorrow overwhelmed my heart and mind.

PHORCYAS. But you appeared, they say, in duplicated
  shape,*
Seen at the same time both in Egypt and in Troy.

HELEN. This is a superstition of dark-tangled sense!
    Which of them am I? Even now I do not know.

PHORCYAS. Then, as the story goes, out of the hollow realm
    Of shades Achilles too became your amorous
    Consort, his love defying all the decrees of fate.

HELEN. A phantom to a phantom, thus I joined with him.*
    It was a dream, for so the very words make plain.   8880
    I vanish, I become a phantom even to myself.

    [*She sinks back into the arms of the half-chorus.*]

CHORUS. Be silent, be silent!
        Creature of evil eye and evil tongue!
        From such hideous one-toothed
        Lips, what should be breathed
        Forth from so fearful a maw of horror!

        For I dread an ill nature that seems benevolent,
        The raging wolf in the garb of a sheep,
        And this to me is a thing more fearful
        Than the jaws of the three-headed hell-hound.*   8890
        We stand here and in fear we listen:
        When? how? where will it break out,
        This monstrous malignant
        Thing, from the ambush-depth where it lurks?

        See, you offer no words full of consolation,
        Oblivion-giving, speech gracious and mild:
        Instead, you stir up the past and all its
        Memories not of good but of evil,
        And you smother with darkness not only
        This present hour in its radiance   8900
        But also the gentle
        Gleam of the future's new-dawning hope.

        Be silent, be silent!
        That the soul of our queen,
        Almost slipping away already,
        May still hold fast, and hold fast
        This shape of all shapes, lovely
        Above all others the sun ever shone upon.

[HELEN *has recovered and stands in the centre again.*]

PHORCYAS. Come, from fleeting clouds emerging, lofty
    sun of this our day:
    Even your veiled form was rapture, reign in dazzling
      glory now!   8910
    See, the world unfolds before you, see it with your
      gracious eyes.
    Though for ugliness they chide me, yet I know true
      beauty well.

HELEN. In my swoon a desolation seized me, trembling I
    step free
    And would gladly rest again now, for so weary are my
      bones:
    But for princes it is seemly, and indeed for all men too,
    To stand firm, to face whatever sudden danger shakes
      the heart.

PHORCYAS. Now before us in your greatness, in your
    beauty here you stand,
    And your eye commands obedience: lady, say, what is
      your will?

HELEN. You must all compose your quarrel now, and to
    make good your fault
    Hasten, as the king has ordered, to prepare a sacrifice.   8920

PHORCYAS. All is ready in the palace: vessels, tripod,
    sharp axe-blade,
    Incense-fire and sprinkling-water: say, what shall the
      victim be?

HELEN. As to that, the king said nothing.

PHORCYAS.   Nothing? Oh, that word is grief!

HELEN. Why, what grief is this?

PHORCYAS.   You, lady, are the victim he intends.

HELEN. I?

PHORCYAS. These women too.

CHORUS.   Oh horror!

PHORCYAS.   By the axe-blade you must fall.

HELEN. Dreadful fate! And yet I guessed it.

PHORCYAS.   I can see no remedy.

CHORUS. What of us? Oh what will happen?

PHORCYAS.   She shall die a noble death:
As for you, from the high beam there that supports the
    gabled roof,
You shall hang and you shall wriggle like snared
    thrushes in a row.

  [HELEN and the CHORUS stand grouped in studied
  expressive attitudes of amazement and terror.]

Ghosts that you are! —Like frozen statues there you
    stand,   8930
Fearing the daylight's loss that is not yours to lose!
Mankind, for they are ghosts like you, the lot of them,
Renounce the sun's bright rays no less reluctantly;
But there's no prayer, no help for them against dark fate;
And this is known to all of them, but pleases few.
Enough, you all are doomed; let us make ready then!

  [She claps her hands, and masked, dwarf-like figures
  appear at the door, who quickly carry out her instructions
  as she speaks.]

Come out, you gloomy globular monstrosities!
Roll up, roll up; here's mischief to delight your hearts.
Bring first the gold-horned altar, set it in its place,
And let the axe lie gleaming on its silver rim;   8940
Fill up the water-jugs, for we shall have to wash
Away the black blood's hideous defiling stain.
Next bring the costly carpet, spread it in the dust,
For on her knees the royal victim here must die,
But then at once, wrapped up, though headless to be sure,
Have decent seemly burial, as befits her rank.

CHORUS LEADER. The queen, my mistress, stands aside
    and meditates,
The girls are wilting like mown grass on meadowlands;
But being the eldest I, as sacred duty bids,
Would speak with you now, great-great-ancient of us all.   8950
You are experienced, wise, and seem to wish us well,

Although these brainless creatures showed you scant
   respect.
Say, therefore, if you know some chance of saving us.

PHORCYAS. The answer's easy, for the queen alone may
   choose
To save herself and you too, her appendages;
But swift resolve is needed, there must be no delay.

CHORUS. Wise and venerated sibyl, oldest, noblest of the
   Fates,
Close your golden shears, and tell us rather how to save
   our lives,
For our little limbs already seem to sway and swing and
   dangle,
And the feeling is unpleasant: all their pleasure was in
   dancing   8960
And in some dear boy's embrace.

HELEN. Let these be fearful; I feel sorrow, but no fear.
And yet, if you could save us, we would show
   gratitude.
The wise and circumspect indeed may often find a way
To do the impossible; therefore tell us what you know.

CHORUS. Speak and tell us, tell us quickly: how shall we
   escape the dreadful
Deadly snares that now are hanging like a doleful
   necklace round us,
Knots of peril drawing closer? In advance, alas, we feel
   them
Choking, throttling us already: will you, Rhea, noble
   mother
Of the gods, not pity us?   8970

PHORCYAS. Have you the patience, as my long account
   unfolds,
To listen quietly? Many tales I have to tell.

CHORUS. Patience enough! To listen is to be still alive!

PHORCYAS. One who remains at home and guards the
   house's wealth,
Or keeps its high and noble walls in good repair

And can protect its roof from the intrusive rain,
Shall have good fortune and a life of many days.
But one who wantonly and lightly oversteps
The threshold's sacred boundary with fugitive feet
Will find, returning, that although the walls still stand,   8980
All else has suffered change or even been destroyed.

HELEN. What is the point here of these well-known
    platitudes?
Tell us your tale, and let vexatious matters be.

PHORCYAS. I speak historically, intending no reproach.
King Menelaus sailed piratically to and fro,
Attacking bays and shores and islands at his whim,
Bringing rich booty back from every port of call.
The siege of Troy, that venture took him ten long years,
And how much longer to return I cannot say.
But here at home, how stands the high-exalted house   8990
Of Tyndareus, how stands his kingdom round about?

HELEN. Is a censorious nature so ingrained in you
That your mouth opens only to upbraid and scold?

PHORCYAS. A mountain region, desolate for many years,
Rises to Sparta's north, with high Taÿgetus
Behind it; there Eurotas takes its origin,
A lively stream at first, then broad between the reeds
Down-rolling through our valley where it feeds your
    swans.
Unnoticed there among those sheltering heights,
    a bold
Invading race has settled: from Cimmerian night   9000
Southwards they pressed, and built unconquerable
    towers,
A fortress whence to plague our people as they please.

HELEN. It seems impossible: how did they accomplish this?

PHORCYAS. It took them twenty years or so, but they had
    time.

HELEN. Are they confederate bandits, or is one their king?

PHORCYAS. They are not bandits; one is ruler of them all,
And not ignoble, though I too have felt his power:

He could have taken everything, but was satisfied
Not, as he said, with tribute, but with a few gifts.

HELEN. What does he look like?

PHORCYAS.   Even I find him not at all   9010
Displeasing. He is well-proportioned, confident
And lively too, and more intelligent than most Greeks.
They call his people barbarous, but none of them,
I think, could match the cruelty of those cannibal-
Heroes, those many ogres at the siege of Troy.
He is magnanimous, I would trust myself to him.
As for his castle, that's a sight you should behold!
Quite different from these great crude lumps of
    masonry
Your forebears have thrown up here higgle-pigglewise,
In Cyclopean fashion hurling one gross rock   9020
Grossly upon the next! What he constructs is all
Straight lines across and up and down and regular.
Just look from outside, how it strives up heavenwards,
So rigid, so well-joined, and mirror-smooth as steel!
No climbing here, no foothold even for the thought.
Great courtyards too in the interior, with all kinds
Of buildings round them, for all manner of purposes:
Columns and little columns, arches large and small
You'll see there; balconies, galleries to look out and in,
And coats of arms.

CHORUS. Why, what are coats of arms?

PHORCYAS.   You will   9030
Recall the shield of Ajax, with its intertwined
Snakes, and how each of those seven fighters against
    Thebes
Bore such a shield-device of rich significance:
They showed the moon, the stars against the night-dark
    sky,
Goddesses, heroes, a siege-ladder, torches, swords,
And other such fierce perils, all good cities' bane.
Such emblems they have too, our northern warrior-host,
Bright-hued, to symbolize their ancient ancestors:

Lions and eagles you will see there, beaks and claws,
The horns of wild bulls, wings and roses, peacocks' tails,   9040
And stripes of gold and black and silver, blue and red.
Such things they hang in rows upon the walls, in halls
Vast beyond measure, halls as wide as all the world;
Halls good for dancing.

CHORUS.   Are there dancers there as well?

PHORCYAS. The very best! Fresh youngsters, boys with
    golden hair;
  They smell of youth; who else but Paris smelt so sweet
  When he approached the queen too closely?

HELEN.   It is not
  Your part to speak of that; finish your narrative!

PHORCYAS. The last word's yours: take thought, give
    your consent aloud,
  And I'll at once surround you with that castle.

CHORUS.   Say,   9050
  Oh say that brief word, save yourself and us as well!

HELEN. What, have I cause to fear the king my husband
    would
  Commit such cruel outrage as to injure me?

PHORCYAS. Have you forgotten the slain Paris's brother,
    your
  Deïphobus, who won you widowed, and in head-
  Strong lust, enjoyed you? And how monstrously the king
  Then mutilated him, cut off his nose and ears
  And various other parts? A dreadful sight it was.

HELEN. Indeed he did that to him, did it because of me.

PHORCYAS. And now because of him he'll do the same to
    you.   9060
  Beauty cannot be shared; who once possessed it whole
  Destroys it rather, cursing all co-partnership.

  [*Trumpets in the distance. The* CHORUS *starts in alarm.*]

  Sharp as the trumpet blares, ear-splitting, tearing deep
  Into our guts, just so the claws of jealousy

Clutch at a man's heart; for he never can forget
What he possessed, and lost, and now does not possess.

CHORUS. Do you not hear the sound of war-horns? Do
    you not see the weapons flash?

PHORCYAS. Lord and king, I bid you welcome! I will give
    full reckoning.

CHORUS. What of us?

PHORCYAS.   I told you plainly; her death stares
    you in the face,
And in there your own awaits you. There's no way you
    can be saved.   9070

                    [*A pause.*]

HELEN. I have considered what step now I dare to take.
You are a hostile demon, as I clearly sense,
And in your hands, I fear, evil will come of good.
But to the castle I consent to follow you:
That first. The rest I know; what thoughts in doing this
The queen may leave unuttered in her inmost heart,
These let no man discern. Old woman, now lead on!

CHORUS.   Oh how gladly we set out
            And hasten to follow her!
            Behind us is death,   9080
            And before us once again
            The unassailable wall
            Of a towering fortress:
            May it protect us safely,
            Just as safely as Troy's battlements,
            For they indeed were breached
            Only by contemptible cunning.

    [*Clouds envelop the background and foreground, spreading
    ad libitum.*]

            But what is this?
            Look about you, sisters!
            Was it not clear daylight?   9090
            Trails of mist are drifting up
            From Eurotas's sacred stream;

Already its delightful banks,
Garlanded with reeds, have vanished;
And the swans, so gently and
Freely gliding, so graceful and proud,
Swimming companionably together,
Alas, I see them no more!

And yet, and yet
I can hear them singing,   9100
Far away, with veiled voices—
A song that presages death, they say!
Oh let it not also foretell
Our own destruction in the end
Instead of the promised rescue;
Death for us all, the swan-like,
With our beautiful long white necks,
And for our lady, the swan-begotten.
Woe, ah woe to us all!

Mist already has veiled   9110
All that surrounded us.
We can no longer see each other!
What is happening? Are we walking,
Or merely hovering
With dainty steps over the ground?
Do you see nothing? Is Hermes perhaps not
Hovering ahead of us? Is that not the glint
Of his golden staff, beckoning, commanding us
Back again to that dismal place of grey dawning,
The place full of intangible shapes: 9120
Back to the overfilled, ever empty Hades?

Yes, a sudden gloom descending robs of light the mist's
    dispersal;
All is dark grey, brown as walls are; walls rear up against
    our eyes here,
Our free eyes, walled in so sternly: by a courtyard? by a
    dungeon?
Either is a dreadful prison! Sisters, once again we are
    captives,
Captive more than ever now!

12 · THE INNER COURTYARD OF A CASTLE

[Surrounded by buildings in a rich fantastic medieval style.]

CHORUS LEADER. How rash and foolish, truly womanish
  you are,
  Dependent on the moment, changeable as air,
  As luck and ill luck, bearing neither of the two
  With equanimity! Normally your squabbling tongues   9130
  Are all at variance with each other; only when
  Joy or affliction strikes you do you howl and laugh
  In the same tune. Be silent now, and wait to hear
  The queen's decision for herself and all of us.

HELEN. Where are you, Pythian priestess, or whatever
  you are?
  Come out to us from this grim castle's vaulted halls!
  If you have gone perhaps to announce me to the strange
  Warrior lord, that he may now receive me well,
  I thank you; take me to him quickly! All I want
  Now is an end to wandering. All I ask is rest.   9140

CHORUS LEADER. Vainly you search, oh queen; for that
  offending shape
  Has vanished from our sight, or stayed behind perhaps
  Deep in the fog, out of the midst of which somehow
  We have come here so swiftly, taking not a step;
  Or dubiously perhaps she wanders in the labyrinth
  Of this miraculous castle, many merged in one,
  Seeking its master for your royal reception's sake.
  But look, already many servants are astir,
  Up there in galleries, windows, portals, to and fro
  They move with haste: all this proclaims the guest shall be   9150
  Received with pomp and with a lordly welcoming.

CHORUS. My spirits revive! Oh look now, oh look
      How with solemn step, with seemliest gait,
      In formal procession those many sweet youths
      Come down towards us! How, and on whose
      Command do they appear, so swiftly assembled
      And ordered, this splendid host of young boys?
      What shall I admire most: their delicate tread,

Or the hair that curls round their shining brows,
Or their cheeks perhaps that are pink as peaches   9160
And covered like peaches with softest down?
I long for a bite, yet I dread it too:
I have heard of a fruit that could fill the mouth
Of the eater with horrible ashes.*

But the handsomest ones
Are approaching now;
What are they bringing?
Steps for a throne,
A carpet, a seat,
Curtains, a canopy   9170
Richly adorned;
Like clouds it surmounts
The head of our queen,
Like a cloudy garland;
For already she sits,
As invited, on the place of majesty.
Oh step by step
Let us now approach her
In solemn array.
Worthy, oh worthy, thrice worthy   9180
And thrice blessed be this noble reception!

[*All these actions have been taking place as the* CHORUS
*described them. After a long procession of pages and
squires has descended,* FAUST *appears at the top of the
stairway dressed as a medieval knight. He comes down
slowly and with dignity.*]

CHORUS LEADER [*gazing at him*].
Unless the gods have done here as they sometimes do,
Conferring on him only fleetingly a wondrous form,
A lofty dignity, a presence to enchant
But only for a while: then shall this prince succeed
In all he undertakes, whether in wars with men
Or in the lesser war with the fairest of our sex.
For truly he is to be preferred to many whom I
Have seen, though greatly I admired them none the less.

With slow and solemn, with restrained respectful pace   9190
This lord draws near; now turn your eyes to him, oh
   queen!

FAUST [*approaching, with a man in chains at his side*].
Not here the solemn greeting that was due*
The ceremonious welcome: instead I bring
To you that servant, closely bound in chains,
Who robbed me of my duty, failing his.
Kneel here, to make confession of your guilt
To this most noble lady! This, great queen,
Is the possessor of rare far-seeing eyes
Whom I appointed to the high look-out tower,
Thence to observe whatever showed itself   9200
In heaven's surrounding space and the wide earth:
He was to watch whatever stirred within
The circle of the hills, or in the valley,
Or near the castle, be it flocks and herds
Or an invading army; we protect
The former, stand against the latter. But
Today, what dereliction! You arrive,
And he does not announce you. No reception
Honoured so high a guest. This miscreant's life
Is forfeit, and his guilty blood already   9210
Should have been spilt, but that it is for you
Alone to punish or pardon, as you please.

HELEN. You grant high dignity, in making me
Both judge and ruler, even though it were
Only to tempt me, as I may surmise.
But I do my first duty as a judge
By hearing the accused. You, therefore, speak!

LYNCEUS THE WATCHMAN.
          Let me kneel and let me gaze,
          Let me die or let me live:
          To this lady, whom the gods give,   9220
          I devote my mortal days.

          I have watched a mystery:
          As I waited for the dawn,

Eastward peering, suddenly
In the south the sun was born.

And my eyes were drawn aside—
Not a peak nor valley there,
Sky nor earth they now descried:
Only her, uniquely fair.

Like the lynx on topmost bough   9230
With keen vision I am blessed;
But to wake I laboured now
As by some dark dream oppressed.

Where was I? What could restore me?
Towers, ramparts, where were they?
Such a goddess stood before me
As the mists were swept away!

Eyes and heart towards her turning,
I had drunk her gentle light,
And her beauty, dazzling, burning,   9240
Burned and dazzled my poor sight.

I forgot the watchman's duty
And my watch-horn's promised call.
Doom me now to death; yet beauty
Tames the anger in us all.

HELEN. I must not punish a misfortune I myself
   Have brought about. Alas, how pitiless
   Has been my fate, doomed everywhere to drive
   Men's hearts to madness, that they neither spared
   Themselves nor reverenced any other thing!   9250
   They ravished and seduced and fought and snatched
   Me hither and thither: heroes, demigods,
   Gods, demons, led me wandering to and fro.
   My single form confused the world, twice more
   My double; now I am threefold, fourfold ruin.
   Take away this good man and set him free;
   Let no shame strike one whom a god has crazed.

FAUST. A double sight, oh queen, amazes me:
   Your surely-speeding arrow, and its victim.

I see the bow that winged it on its way,   9260
And him who felt the wound. Arrows apace
Assail me now, I sense their feathering flight
At me from all sides, here within the castle.
What has become of me? My truest followers
You turn to rebels all at once, my walls
You weaken. Will my army now obey
Me, or this conquering unconquered lady?
What choice now, but to give myself and all
My supposed wealth to you in vassalage?
Let me then at your feet, freely and truly,   9270
Confess you mistress, who had but to appear
And take at once your place upon the throne.

LYNCEUS [*with a treasure-chest, followed by men bringing*
    others].

Queen, we return from near and far
To beg one glance, rich as we are!
What man is there that looks at you
And is not prince and beggar too?

What am I now? what have I been?
What must I will or do, oh queen?
My piercing sight, what can it see?
Your bright throne casts it back at me.   9280

Out of the east we came, and so
The west was conquered and laid low;
A weighty army, wide and strong,
From head to tail none knew how long.

The first would fall, the next would stand,
A third was ready spear in hand;
Each reinforced a hundredfold,
And a slain thousand fell untold.

So we rushed on like storm and flame,
Conquering and ruling as we came;   9290
One day I gave the orders, then
The plunder fell to other men.

We looked around with greedy eyes:
The loveliest woman was one man's prize,

Others took horses by the score
Or prancing bulls, as spoils of war.

But I would peer with my sharp sight
At all things rare and recondite:
I sought what no one else possessed,
Cared not a straw for all the rest.   9300

I hunted treasure's every trace,
Clear vision led me to the place,
No pocket hid its wealth from me,
Locked chests were glass, my eyes the key.

Mine it became, a hoard of gold
And precious stones. The emerald
Now of all gems is worthiest
To glow so green upon your breast;

And let a pearl from deepest sea
Now by your cheek hang tremblingly—   9310
So red it blooms, no rubies dare
To add their pale adornment there.

Oh queen, so great a gathering
Of riches to your throne I bring;
Much blood was shed in warlike fray,
Its harvest at your feet I lay.

These coffers all are full, and yet
More iron coffers I can get;
If I may be your slave, all these
Shall fill your vaulted treasuries.   9320

For scarcely were you here enthroned
Than all bowed down to you and owned
Their minds, their wealth, their power in thrall
To you, the loveliest form of all.

All this was mine, I held it fast,
I let it go, to you it passed.
I thought it worthy: now I see
This lofty treasure's nullity.

All's vanished now I called my own,
Withered it lies like grass that's mown.   9330
Lady, with one glad look restore
Its value to it all once more!

FAUST. Remove at once this burden boldly won;
Uncensured it shall be, yet unrewarded.
All that my castle's deep interior hides
Is hers already: a specific gift
Is otiose. Go, and lay out the treasures
In proper order. Raise on high the lofty
Image of unseen splendour! Let the vaulted
Roofs glitter like skies freshly starred; plant here   9340
Strange paradises of unliving life.
Where she will walk, let many carpets rich
With flowers unroll before her: let her feet
Fall upon softest ground, and brightest radiance,
Dazzling to all but gods, confront her eyes.

LYNCEUS.   Little, my lord, is this you ask,
                   Your command's a trifling task;
                   For this beauty all extol
                   Rules us all, goods, life and soul.
                   All the army now is tame,   9350
                   Every sword is blunt and lame;
                   And this form beyond compare
                   Dulls the sun and chills the air.
                   All's made empty, poor and base
                   By the riches of her face. [Exit.]

HELEN [to FAUST]. I wish to speak with you, but I would
    have you
Seated here at my side! This empty place
Calls for the master, and makes mine secure.

FAUST. First, as I kneel, accept my faithful homage,
Most noble princess! Let me kiss the hand   9360
That lifts me to your side; confirm me now
As the co-regent of your realm which knows
No boundaries, and let me be for you
Admirer, servant, guardian, all in one!

HELEN. Manifold wonders I have seen and heard,
    And in amazement I have much to ask.
    But tell me why the speech of that good man
    Had something strange about it, strange and friendly:
    Each sound seems to accommodate the next,
    And when one word has settled in the ear   9370
    Another follows to caress the first.

FAUST. It is the way our peoples speak; I know
    That if this pleases you, our music too
    Will charm your hearing, ravish your inmost heart.
    But it is best we practise it at once,
    Talking by turns, for that calls forth the skill.

HELEN. Then say, how shall I learn such lovely speech?

FAUST. It is not hard: say what your heart will teach.
    And when one's heart is full, one turns to see
    Who'll share the rapture—

HELEN.   Share it now with me!   9380

FAUST. No past recalled, no future time to guess;
    Only the present—

HELEN.   is our happiness.

FAUST. It is treasure and gain, possession and
    A pledge: but what must seal the pledge?

HELEN.   My hand.

CHORUS. Who would find fault with our queen for
      Granting this castle's lord
      Some signs of her favour?
      For we must confess that we all are now
      Captives, as we have been before
      So often already since the shameful   9390
      Fall of Troy, and our grievous
      Journey, labyrinthine, fear-haunted.

      Women accustomed to men's love
      May not be choosers, but
      Their knowledge is expert.
      For whether to golden-haired shepherd boys
      Or to swarthy bristling fauns,
      As the case may be or the occasion:

Equal rights will be granted,
Making them free of their soft limbs.   9400

Nearer they sit, closer already,
Leaning against each other;
Shoulder to shoulder, knee to knee,
Hand in hand they are cradled
On the soft cushions
Of the magnificent throne.
Our rulers do not forebear to make
Their secret pleasures
Proudly and exuberantly
Public before the gaze of their people.   9410

HELEN. I feel so far away, and yet so near;
   How willingly I say: Look, I am here!

FAUST. Breathless I seem, words tremble and lose power;
   This is a dream, in no place, at no hour.

HELEN. I am as one long past, and yet so new;
   To you bound fast, to an unknown stranger true.

FAUST. Why puzzle, why insist? Our unique role
   Bids us exist; one moment means the whole.

PHORCYAS [*bursting in*].
            Now's no time for childish riddling
            Amorous alphabetic fiddling   9420
            Idle puzzling and canoodling!
            Now there's other work to do.
            Can you hear the trumpets blaring,
            Hollow sounds of thunder nearing?
            Direst peril threatens you.
            Menelaus, battle-waging,
            Warrior-hosted, rides here raging:
            Arm yourselves for bitter strife!
            They'll outnumber you; he'll lop you
            Like Deïphobus, he'll chop you   9430
            Up for dallying with his wife.
            This slave-trash he'll hang; then, lady,
            For your neck an axe is ready
            Or a sacrificial knife.

FAUST. Offensive interruption! Insolently it intrudes.
I hate such headstrong folly, even when danger speaks.
Ill news disfigures even the fairest messenger,
And you, the foulest, you like best to bring the worst.
But you shall not achieve it this time: shake the air
With empty breath! There is no danger here, and if   9440
There were, it would be seen to be an idle threat.

[*Signals, explosions from the towers, trumpets and cornets,
warlike music, a powerful army marching through.*]

FAUST.   No! we shall stand, we shall not waver,
           As these my heroes now shall show.
           He alone merits woman's favour
           Who can defend her from the foe.

[*To the commanders, who step from the columns and
present themselves to him.*]

           You from the east, you from the north
           In youthful strength, in vigorous flower:
           Let your long silent rage burst forth
           And bring you victory in this hour!

           A steel-clad host, with glint of flame: 9450
           Earth trembles where it treads the ground,
           Kingdoms have crumbled where it came,
           It marches to the thunder's sound.

           In ancient Pylos from the sea
           We landed; Nestor ruled there once.
           The petty lordships fell, as we
           Warred on with wild unchecked advance.

           Now Menelaus comes: drive him
           Back to the waves without delay!
           Let him pursue his fate, his whim,   9460
           And go his wandering robber's way.

           As Sparta's queen commands, I greet
           You now as dukes; when you have laid
           These vales and mountains at her feet
           In princely kind you shall be paid.

Teuton, build ramparts on the shores
Of Corinth, and defend it well!
Achaia's gorges shall be yours,
Bold Goth, all comers to repel.

Let Elis be the Frank's to guard,
Let Saxons shield Messini, let
The sea-ways by the Norman's sword   9470
Be cleansed, and Argolis made great.

Thus each shall reign in his demesne
And outwards make his power known:
But she shall rule you all, the Queen
Of Sparta, from her ancient throne.

Under her sway an age of gold
And plenty on this land shall fall;
She shall enlighten and uphold   9480
And bless with justice each and all.

[FAUST *descends, the princes approach and surround him
to hear his further orders and dispositions.*]

CHORUS. He who desires the loveliest of women,
Let him above all wisely
Arm himself with redoubtable weapons.
For though he may have won by flattery
The earth's supreme treasure,
He will never possess it in peace:
Subtle enemies will seek to entice her,
Bold robbers to snatch her away from him.
Let him take heed to prevent this loss.   9490

Therefore I praise our prince and esteem him
High above others: for bravely
And with foresight he forms alliances,
And the strong stand loyally round him,
Awaiting his lightest gesture.
They will faithfully hear his commands;
Each will be serving his own advantage
And rewarding his prince with gratitude;
Both will win high honour and fame.

>   For now who can carry her off   9500
>   From her powerful possessor?
>   To him she belongs, and may he have joy of her;
>   This we doubly wish him, for with her
>   He has surrounded us too with a sure wall
>   And outside it with a mighty army.

FAUST. These fiefdoms which I here bestow—
>   To each a rich and thriving land—
>   Are great and splendid; let them go!
>   Here in the midst we take our stand;

>   These vying vassals shall make fast   9510
>   And sure our ambient realm the while—
>   So lightly linked and branched to Europe's last
>   Great mountain-chain, our wave-lapped demi-isle!

>   Above all lands beneath the sun
>   May this land flourish evermore,
>   Which for my queen we now have won:
>   Where first Eurotas' whispering shore

>   Looked up at her, when lovelier far
>   Than Leda and with eyes more bright
>   Than all her siblings, like a star   9520
>   She broke her shell to greet the light.

>   Lady, this land for you alone
>   Displays its beauty; the whole earth
>   Is yours, but this earth is your own:
>   Love this land more, which gave you birth!

>   The jagged summits on its mountain ridge
>   Suffer the sun's cold arrows sharp and clear;
>   But rocks blush green with scanty pasturage
>   And nibbling goats can seek their nurture here.

>   The springs leap up, down gush the mingling rills,   9530
>   Ravines and slopes are verdant now, the grass
>   Covers in turn a hundred fields and hills
>   Where the wide-wandering fleecy flocks may pass.

>   Horned grazing cattle, scattered, warily
>   Pacing, approach the brink of the sheer fall;

But darkly arching in the cliffside, see!
A hundred caves are shelter for them all.

There Pan protects them, there they lie at ease
In the moist wooded clefts where life-nymphs dwell.
With upthrust branches the close-crowding trees   9540
Aspire to higher regions. Mark them well,

These ancient forests! Mighty oaks extrude
Their stubborn and anfractuous limbs; here too
The maple, heavy with sweet liquid food,
Plays with its burden, soaring straight and true.

Here in the quiet shade a lamb, a child,
Sucks warm maternal milk with eager lips;
Here in the plains the fruit grows ripe and wild,
And from the hollow tree-trunk honey drips.

Contentment is a birthright here,   9550
A smiling mouth, a cheek that glows;
Each is immortal in his sphere,
No sickness, no disquietude he knows;

And thus the children grow in this pure day
To fatherhood. We ask again
As in astonishment we gaze: are they
Not gods indeed, or are they men?

Apollo lived with shepherds so, and passed
For one, and all were beautiful:
For where the laws of purest Nature rule,   9560
All separate worlds unite at last.

[*He sits at her side.*]

See, this is ours now; let our quest be ended,
The past behind us and beyond recall.
Feel from the highest god yourself descended;
Feel yours uniquely this first land of all!

And I will guard you where no walls enclose:
A place for ever young, not far
From here, shall now surround our sweet repose;
Sparta's near neighbourhood, Arcadia!

To this blest homeland, by Fate's happy power   9570
And my enticement, you shall flee.
These thrones become a leafy bower:
Let our joy be Arcadian and free!

13 · ARCADIA*

[*The scene changes completely. Leafy arbours grow by the
mouths of rocky caverns, a shady grove extends to the
surrounding cliffs.* FAUST *and* HELEN *are no longer
seen. The maidens of the* CHORUS *are lying about
asleep.*]

PHORCYAS. How long these girls have been asleep I do
    not know;
  Whether they could have dreamt what with my waking
    eyes
  I have seen clear and plain, that too I cannot tell.
  And so I'll wake them. The young fools shall be amazed;
  And so shall you, you greybeards, sitting there agog
  To see our riddling spectacle resolve itself.
  Come, girls! Come on now! Quickly, give your locks a
    shake,   9580
  Shake sleep from your eyes, stop blinking, listen to what
    I say!

CHORUS. We are listening, tell us quickly, tell us what
    strange thing has happened!
  Preferably tell us something that's so strange we can't
    believe it;
  For we all are bored to death here, sitting looking at
    these cliffs.

PHORCYAS. Why, your eyes are scarcely open, children,
    and you're bored already!
  Hear me then: our lord and lady have found shelter and
    protection
  In these caverns, in these grottoes, in these arbours; like
    a pair of
  Lovers in a pastoral idyll.

CHORUS.   What, in there?

PHORCYAS.   And quite secluded
  From the world. I was selected as their sole discreet
    attendant.
  So I stood there, highly honoured, at their side; but, as
    was seemly,   9590
  Looked elsewhere with eyes averted, turning this way,
    turning that way,
  Seeking roots and barks and mosses, for I knew their
    magic virtues;
  Thus our pair was left in peace.

CHORUS. Why, you talk as if those caverns had whole
    world-wide spaces in them:
  Forests, meadows, lakes and rivers; what unlikely tale is
    this?

PHORCYAS. But of course, you ignorant creatures! They
    are depths no man has fathomed;
  Many halls and many courtyards, which I subtly have
    explored.
  But I suddenly heard laughter echoing in the hollow
    caverns:
  And I looked, and from the woman's lap a boy leapt to
    his father,
  Then from him back to his mother; such caresses, such
    endearments,   9600
  Such a babbling fond affection! Peals of laughter, squeals
    of pleasure,
  Taking turns to deafen me.
  He is naked, like an unwinged genius, faun-like but
    unbestial;
  On the firm ground he is leaping, but the ground's
    elastic pressure
  Sends him springing, spinning skywards; two or three
    bounds, and already
  He has touched the vaulted roof.
  Anxiously his mother calls: Leap as you like, and go on
    leaping,
  But beware of flying freely, you are not allowed to fly!

And his loving father warns him: In the earth lies the
    resilient
Power that drives you upwards; touch the soil, on tiptoe
    merely touch it,   9610
And like the earth's son Antaeus you will grow at once
    in strength.
Thus he jumps about this solid cliff mass, from one
    rocky summit
To another and all round it: like a bouncing ball he
    jumps.
But a grim crevasse is gaping, and he suddenly is
    swallowed,
And we fear him lost. His father comforts his lamenting
    mother;
I stand by, nonplussed and anxious. But he reappears in
    glory!
Are there treasures in the abysses? Now his garments are
    like flowers,
He is robed in dignity.
From his arms hang tassels tossing, round his bosom
    ribbons flutter,
In his hand he holds the golden lyre; just like a young
    Apollo,   9620
He steps blithely to the cliff edge, to the precipice;
    amazement
Seizes us, the enraptured parents fall into each other's
    arms.
For about his head is brightness, a mysterious light, we
    cannot
Tell if it is gold, or flames of mighty spiritual power.
Thus he moves, and thus his gestures prophesy this boy
    the future
Master-maker of all beauty, through whose limbs the
    everlasting
Music is already flowing. Thus it is you all shall hear
    him,
And shall see him; there has never been so great a
    miracle.

CHORUS. Tell us, daughter of Crete,*
    Is this so wondrous?   9630
    Have you perhaps not listened
    To the instructive voice of poetry,
    Never yet heard the ancient
    Ancestral legends of Ionia
    Or of Hellas, with their rich treasure
    Of god-lore and lore of heroes?

    All that ever is done
    Nowadays is no
    More than a wretched echo
    Of the more glorious age of our forebears. 9640
    How can your tale compare with
    The song that a charming fiction,
    Less incredible than truth, sang of
    Young Hermes,* the son of Maia?

    Strong already though only just born,
    This tiny infant was wound in
    Cleanest, softest of swaddling-bands,
    Tied up firmly in sumptuous
    Wrappings by chattering nurses who
    Thought they knew their business.   9650
    But the young rogue, being tiny but strong,
    Very soon had most cunningly freed
    His elastic and supple limbs,
    Calmly discarding the royal purple
    Integument which so anxiously
    Had constricted them. Thus the full-grown
    Butterfly nimbly escapes, with its wings
    Spread wide, from the rigid prison
    Of its chrysalis, boldly,
    Wantonly fluttering ever higher   9660
    Into the ethereal sunlight.

    So too Hermes was nimblest of all
    And best fitted to be patron—
    Sprite for ever of thieves and rogues
    And all seekers of fortune.

This he at once made clear by the
Artfullest of exploits.
Quickly he stole the trident of the lord
Of the sea, and the war-god's sword
He soon slyly filched from its sheath;   9670
Likewise Apollo's bow and arrows,
As well as the tongs of the fire-god.
Even the thunderbolt of his father
Zeus he'd have taken, but dreaded its flame.
Yet he tripped and defeated Eros
When they wrestled, and for good
Measure he snatched Aphrodite's girdle
From her lap as she caressed him.

[*A delightful melody on stringed intruments is heard from
the cave. All pay attention, and soon seem deeply moved by
it. From this point until the pause noted below, the words
are continuously accompanied by fully harmonized music.*]

PHORCYAS. Hear these charming sounds, and let them
              Free you from this foolish lore!   9680
              Your old gods, you must forget them
              Now, for they are gods no more.

              Modern ears are closed to fables,
              We demand superior art:
              Only the heart's depth enables
              Any word to move the heart.

[*She withdraws towards the cliff.*]

CHORUS. If these melodies are pleasing,
              Ancient monster, to your ears,
              How much more must their sweet teasing
              Melt our new-born youth to tears!   9690

              Though the sun grow dark, we find it
              In our souls as bright as day:
              In our hearts we have enshrined it,
              What the world would take away.

[HELEN, FAUST, *and* EUPHORION *in the costume
described above.*]

EUPHORION. These are songs of children: hear them
                    With parental joy! And see,
                    To their rhythm I dance near them:
                    Do your hearts not leap with me?

HELEN.   Love uniting man and woman
                    Shapes a joy of two made one;   9700
                    Two, with rapture more than human,
                    Are made three; this love has done.

FAUST.   All is found, and it has found us:
                    I am yours and you are mine.
                    Sacred union now has bound us;
                    Is this not our fate's design?

CHORUS.   By this boy and by his splendour
                    Many years of blessing shine
                    On this pair; with bonds how tender,
                    Touchingly they intertwine!   9710

EUPHORION. Now I am freer!
                    Let me be leaping
                    Into the ether,
                    Skipping, escaping;
                    This is my craving,
                    This is my joy!

FAUST.   But not so hastily,
                    So overboldly!
                    They fall to ruin
                    Who leap so wildly: 9720
                    We dread to lose him,
                    Our dearest boy!

EUPHORION. I'll be no groundling!
                    Your hands detain me
                    With anxious fondling;
                    Let go my hair, let
                    Go of my clothing!
                    What's mine is mine!

HELEN.   Alas, remember,
                    You are our son: oh,   9730
                    Think of our sorrow,
                    Our bond so tender,

| | Our threefold union's | |
| | Delicate twine! | |

CHORUS.　　Soon it will sunder,
　　　　　　To grief and pine.

HELEN and FAUST.　For our sake, our sake,
　　　　　　Dear son, try harder
　　　　　　To curb this energy,
　　　　　　To check this ardour!　　　　　　9740
　　　　　　Let rural beauty
　　　　　　Content your heart.

EUPHORION.　My filial duty
　　　　　　Must take your part.

[*He weaves in and out of the* CHORUS, *drawing the
maidens into a dance with him.*]

　　　　　　These girls I hover round
　　　　　　Here are entrancing.
　　　　　　How does this music sound?
　　　　　　How is this dancing?

HELEN.　　　You have done well, indeed,
　　　　　　An artful dance you lead　　　　　9750
　　　　　　Them all, my son!

FAUST.　　　This fluttering trickery,
　　　　　　It has no charms for me;
　　　　　　Would it were done!

[EUPHORION *and the* CHORUS, *singing, move in a
complicated round dance.*]

CHORUS.　　You move your arms, how rare
　　　　　　And fine their motion!
　　　　　　You shake your curly hair
　　　　　　To bright commotion!
　　　　　　How light your foot can slide
　　　　　　Over the earth, how glide　　　　　9760
　　　　　　These limbs that to and fro
　　　　　　Around each other go!
　　　　　　Sweet boy, all this ensures
　　　　　　Your purposes, if they

                    Are to steal hearts away:
                    Ours all are yours!
                              [*A pause.*]

EUPHORION.   Is this too tame for you,
                    Lightfooted deer?
                    Here's a new game for you:
                    Run, run from here!   9770
                    I'll be your hunter,
                    You'll be my kill!

CHORUS.   You need not hurry,
                    We'll not outrace you;
                    We should be sorry
                    Not to embrace you;
                    Beautiful boy, your
                    Love is our will.

EUPHORION.   Come, to the woodlands,
                    Mountain and flood lands!   9780
                    I take no pleasure in
                    An easy capture;
                    Only what's hard to win
                    Fills me with rapture.

HELEN and FAUST. What a wanton mad performance!
                    Can they learn no moderation?
                    Now like horns in ululation
                    Through the woods and glens they call.
                    What a romp and caterwaul!

CHORUS [*entering quickly one by one*].
                    He ran past! Does he ignore us,   9790
                    Mock us, scorn us? He has chosen
                    One, and drags her here before us!
                    She's the wildest of us all!

EUPHORION [*carrying in a young girl*].
                    I have brought this little filly,
                    And I'll have her willy-nilly;
                    What a pleasure, what delight
                    To subdue and hug her tight,

And if she resists a kiss,
Show my strength and will like this!

THE GIRL.   Let me go! In my disguise   9800
There is strength and spirit too;
We have wills like yours, a prize
No less hard to snatch than you.
Do you think me helpless? How you
Trust your manly strength! Come, cling
Close to me, I'll singe you now, you
Fool! Such fiery sport you bring!

[*She bursts into flames and blazes up into the sky.*]

Follow me into the air,
To the abysses, follow there!
See, your goal is vanishing!*   9810

EUPHORION [*shaking off the last of the flames*].
Forest ravines, how steep
They loom around me!
Shall not my youth outleap
These cliffs that bound me?
Are these not winds that roar,
Waves from a distant shore?
They are too far from here;
I must be near!

[*He bounds higher and higher among the rocks.*]

HELEN, FAUST, and the CHORUS.
Chamois-like you leap, while we
Dread the inevitable fall.   9820

EUPHORION.   Ever higher I must be,
Seeing further, seeing all!
Where am I? Now I know:
Pelops' land here below,
The island of my birth,
Wedded to sea and earth!

CHORUS.   Cannot these mountains, these
Forests suffice you,
Gathering the grapes not please,

	Hillsides entice you,	9830
	Where vines stand row on row,
	Figs, golden apples grow?
	Stay in this lovely place,
	Live by its grace!

EUPHORION.   Dream, if you like, of dull
               Peace, dream of what you will:
               War is the word for me,
               The next is victory.

CHORUS.   Our wars are over:
               Can you want war again?   9840
               What hope shall ever
               Gladden you then?

EUPHORION.   Oh land that gave them life,
               Bore them to perilous strife,
               For you they shed their blood,
               Valiant and free they stood;
               Bless now these warriors
               Who in your name
               All are the carriers
               Of quenchless flame!   9850

CHORUS.   Look, how high he has ascended,
               Yet majestic still he seems,
               Like a conqueror: see, with splendid
               Bronze and steel his armour gleams!

EUPHORION.   By no walls, no ramparts shielded
               Each man stands and holds his own:
               Like a fortress never yielded
               Is his iron heart alone.
               Come for peace, for your delivery,
               Arm yourselves, your freedom take!   9860
               Women shall be fighters, every
               Child a hero for its sake.

CHORUS.   Poetry, art god-given,
               Let it leap up to heaven,
               Shine as the loveliest star
               Remote from where we are;

Yet still its sacred word
Finds us, its song is heard
Still from afar!

EUPHORION. I was not born here as a child: 9870
A young man armed I come to you.
The strong, the free, the bold and wild
Taught me the deeds I still must do.
Farewell!
They spell
My path to fame and glory too.

HELEN and FAUST. Scarcely are you born, ah scarcely
Given to the shining day,
And from those mad heights you fiercely
Long to find that dolorous way!   9880
Can our bond
Once so fond
Like a dream thus fade away?

EUPHORION. Hear, from the sea that thunderous call!
The thundering valleys make reply;
Through dust, through waves, those warriors all,
In mortal throng they strive and cry!
Fate has here
Spoken clear:
What other law but so to die?   9890

HELEN, FAUST, and the CHORUS.
Words of horror and despair!
Is your death then fate's decree?

EUPHORION. Mine their anguish, mine to share:
No mere spectator I will be!

HELEN, FAUST, and the CHORUS.
Oh heart too overbold,
Oh perilous pride!

EUPHORION. Yes!—And now wings unfold
Here at my side!
There! There! Now let me fly:
I must! I shall!   9900

[*He hurls himself into the air, his garments bear him up
for a moment, his head shines, a trail of light follows him.*]

CHORUS.   Icarus! From the sky
           Oh grievous fall!

[*A beautiful youth falls and lies dead at his parents' feet,
we seem to recognize his face as that of a well-known
figure;* but his body vanishes at once, the halo rises
skywards like a comet, his costume, mantle, and lyre
remain on the ground.*]

HELEN and FAUST.   Now into grief apace
           Our joy has grown.

EUPHORION's *voice* [*from the depths*].
           Mother, in this dark place
           Must I be left alone?

[*A pause. The* CHORUS *sings a lament.**]

CHORUS.   Left alone!—We seem to know you,
           And wherever death may take you
           When you haste to shades below you,
           Still our hearts will not forsake you.   9910
           And we scarcely can lament you,
           For we envy you your fate:
           Dark and bright the days it sent you,
           Songs and spirit, all were great.

           Born to high ancestral calling,
           Blessed with gifts, with noble name,
           Soon, alas, self-lost, and falling
           In the bloom of youth and fame!
           Wide the world to your discerning,
           To your heart the heart's depths known,   9920
           Women's love your love returning,
           And a music all your own.

           But in your impetuous coursing
           Free into strict snares you ran,
           Spurning all convention, forcing
           Wide the narrow laws of man.
           Yet a last high purpose forming

To pure courage lent its weight
To a noble task conforming;
But fulfilment comes too late.   9930

Who fulfils it?—There's no reading
This dark riddle fate must show
To a people dumbly bleeding
On this day of greatest woe.
Yet their spirit shall recover:
Sing new songs, forget your pain!
For this soil has bred for ever
Greatness it will breed again.

[*A complete pause. The music stops.*]

HELEN [*to* FAUST].
An ancient proverb proves itself in my case too,
Alas: that beauty weds not long with happiness.   9940
The bond of love is severed now, and so of life;
Bewailing both, I bid a sorrowful farewell
To you, and cast myself once more into your arms.
Persephone, receive us both, the boy and me!

[*She embraces* FAUST, *her body vanishes, her dress and
veil remain in his arms.*]

PHORCYAS [*to* FAUST].
Hold fast to what remains to you of it all.*
Her garment, do not let it go. Already
Demons pluck at the corners, for they long
To snatch it to the underworld. Hold fast!
The goddess you have lost it is no longer,
And yet it is divine. Use now this high   9950
Favour beyond all price, and rise aloft:
For through the ether swiftly it will bear you
Beyond all base things, while you yet have life.
I shall see you again, far, far from here.

[HELEN'*s garments dissolve into clouds which envelop*
FAUST, *carry him upwards, and drift away with him.*
PHORCYAS *picks up* EUPHORION'*s costume, mantle,
and lyre, and advances into the proscenium, holding up
these relics as she speaks.*]

PHORCYAS. Well, here's another lucky find!
        No sacred flame's been left behind,
        Of course, but I've enough to keep things going.
        With these, poets can still be consecrated,
        Professional envy generated,
        And though talent itself can't be created,   9960
        At least the outer garb I'll be bestowing.

[*She sits down in the proscenium at the foot of a column.*]

PANTHALIS. Be quick now, girls! At last the enchantment's
    at an end,
The crazy spell cast by that old Thessalian hag;
Likewise the strum of drunken tangled notes that so
Confused our ears, still worse befuddling all our minds.
Come, down to Hades! For the queen with solemn step
Has hastened there before us, and immediately,
As faithful servants, we must make her footprints ours.
At the Inscrutable Goddess's throne she waits for us.

CHORUS. For queens, indeed, any place is agreeable;   9970
        Even in Hades they have high positions,
        Proudly consorting with their peers,
        On familiar terms with Persephone.
        But our sort remain in a background
        Of deep fields of asphodel,
        Keeping company with gangling
        Poplars and infertile willows:
        How shall we pass the time?
        Squeaking like bats,
        An unpleasant, ghostly susurration.   9980

PANTHALIS. Those without noble purpose, who have
    acquired no name,
Belong to the elements. So begone, the lot of you!
For my most ardent wish is to be with my queen;
By loyalty, as by merit, we may be persons still. [*Exit.*]

ALL.   We have been restored to the light of day;
        To be sure, we are no longer persons,
        This we feel, this we know;
        But to Hades we shall never return.

We are spirits on whom ever-living
Nature makes an absolute   9990
Claim, as we do on Nature.

PART OF THE CHORUS.
We shall dwell amid this tremor of a thousand
    whispering branches,
Tease their roots to woo the life-sap softly up into the
    rustling
Tree-tops; there these floating tresses we shall deck
    with leaves and blossoms,
In extravagant abundance, free to thrive at airy heights.
When the ripe fruit falls, the people with their flocks
    will crowd here, eager
Hands will gather, mouths will nibble; thus they'll
    throng to snatch a harvest,
And they'll all bow down around us, as before the
    earliest gods.

ANOTHER PART. We shall linger by these cliffs with
    mirror-smooth far-shining faces,
Cling like gentle waves about them, flatter them in close
    caress;   10000
So to every sound we'll listen, songs of birds, the
    reed-pipes playing,
And though Pan's dread voice assail us, we shall
    instantly reply.
Even murmuring wind we'll answer, thunder we shall
    double-thunder,
Utter shattering iteration, mutter threefold, tenfold roll.

A THIRD PART. Sisters, we prefer more movement, we
    shall hasten with the streaming
Waters, lured by those well-wooded hills, those ranges
    in the distance.
Ever deeper down shall wander our meandering
    refreshment:
Now the pastures, then the meadows, soon the garden
    round the house.
There slim cypresses will mark us, tapering proud above
    the landscape,

By our banks and mirroring waters rising headup to the
   sky.   10010

A FOURTH PART. Wander where you like, the rest of
   you: our murmuring shall encircle
The close-cultivated hillside, where staked vines are
   growing green,
Tended daily, tended hourly by the vintager, whose
   toiling
Passion and devoted labour earn their ever-doubtful
   prize.
We shall see him hoeing, digging, heaping soil up,
   pruning, tying,
Praying to the gods to aid him, to the sun-god most of
   all.
The voluptuary Bacchus, careless of his faithful servant,
Rests in caves and lolls in arbours, flirting with the
   youngest faun.
All his dreaming, his half-drunken reveries have ever
   needed
Stands supplied for him in wineskins, stands in jars and
   hollow vessels,   10020
Right and left in cooling caverns, stored from
   immemorial time.
But when all the gods, and Helios first among them,
   giving breezes,
Giving moisture, warmth and fire, have heaped the
   grapes to horns of plenty:
Then at last, where quiet growers worked, all springs to
   life and motion,
All the leafy arbours rustle, all's astir from vine to vine.
Baskets creak and buckets clatter, groaning hods are fully
   loaded;
All to the great vat are carried, to the treader's lusty
   dance.
So by those rude feet the sacred bounty of the ripe
   unblemished
Grape is trodden, spurting grape-flesh crushed and mixed
   to foaming messes.

Now the ear is penetrated by the cymbals' brazen
    clangour: 10030
For the unveiled Dionysus from his mysteries comes
    forth,
Leaping with goat-footed satyrs, with goat-footed
    satyresses,
And among them wildly braying comes Silenus'
    long-eared beast.
No constraints now! Cloven hooves will trample down
    all decent custom,
All our senses reel, our ears are deafened with the
    hideous din.
Drunken revellers grope for liquor, heads and bellies
    overflowing;
Some still call for moderation, but can only swell the
    tumult;
For old wineskins soon are empty which the grape's new
    juice must fill!

> [*Curtain.* PHORCYAS *rises up as a gigantic figure in the
> proscenium, but steps down from her cothurni, removes her
> mask and veil, and reveals herself as* MEPHISTOPHELES,
> *who then as an epilogue to the drama adds such comments
> as may be appropriate.*]

ACT FOUR

14 · HIGH MOUNTAINS

[Rugged forbidding peaks. A cloud drifts up, leans against the cliff, settles on a projecting spur of rock, and divides.]

FAUST *[stepping out of it]*.

Gazing at those deep solitudes beneath my feet,*
I tread with circumspection this high mountain-brink,   10040
Dismissing now my cloudy vehicle, which has brought
Me gently through bright daylight over land and sea.
Slowly it has released me, yet does not disperse.
Towards the east it strives, a dense and vaporous mass;
The astonished eye strives after it in wonderment.
It parts as it moves on, in shifting, billowing change:
Yet seeks a shape.—Yes! now my eye is not deceived!—
On softest bedding, sun-gleamed, splendid there she lies,
A woman's form, most godlike, giant-like indeed:
I see it! It is like Juno, Leda, Helena;   10050
With what majestic charm it hovers in my sight!
Alas, already it drifts away: amorphous, broad,
Its icy summits towering in the distant east
Reflect the dazzling greatness of these fleeting days.

But round my breast and brow there hovers still, so cool,
So pleasing and caressing, a bright wisp of cloud.
Now lightly, hesitantly higher it ascends,
And shapes itself.—Does joy delude, or do I see
That first, that long-lost, dearest treasure of my youth?
They rise to view, those riches of my deepest heart,   10060
That leapt so lightly in the early dawn of love;
That first look, quickly sensed and hardly understood:
No precious jewel could have outshone it, had I held
It fast. Oh lovely growth, oh spiritual form!
Still undissolving, it floats skywards on and up,
And draws my best and inmost soul to follow it.

[*A seven-league boot touches the ground. A second follows
immediately.* MEPHISTOPHELES *dismounts. The boots
hurry on.*]

MEPHISTOPHELES. Well, that's quick marching, I must
    say!—
  Now, what are your intentions, pray?
  Why choose this savage place to pause,
  Where rocks upfang their dreadful jaws?   10070
  I know them, though from elsewhere, very well:
  This place was once, in fact, the floor of hell.

FAUST. Another of your foolish tales, no doubt;
  Such stuff you never tire of handing out.

MEPHISTOPHELES [*seriously*].
  When the Lord God—and I could tell you why—
  Hurled me and my lot headlong from the sky
  Into the fiery depths, the central flame
  For ever burning, evermore the same,
  We found ourselves, by this bright conflagration,
  In a most incommodious situation.   10080
  The devils all began to cough, to utter
  Much belching back and front, to sneeze and splutter;
  Hell filled with sulphurous acid fumes, expelling
  Its brimstone stench, like a great gasbag swelling!
  Until such monstrous force, as soon it must,
  Shattered the dry lands of the earth's thick crust.
  Now, things are upside down: the great abyss
  Of former times has become peaks like this.
  And on this, too, their orthodoxy's based,
  With nethermost by uppermost replaced;   10090
  For when we fled the hot pit's servitude,
  Our lordship of the upper air ensued.
  An open secret, kept till now with care;
  Lately revealed to the nations everywhere. (*Eph.* 6:12)*

FAUST. Mountains keep noble silence; let them be!
  Their whence and why's no puzzlement to me.
  When Nature's reign began, pure and self-grounded,
  Then this terrestrial globe it shaped and rounded.

Glad of their peaks and chasms, it displayed
Mountains and mountains, rocks and rocks it made;   10100
The soft-curved hills it shaped then, gentling down
Into the valleys; there all's green and grown.
Thus Nature takes her pleasure, never troubling
With all your crazy swirl and boil and bubbling.

MEPHISTOPHELES. Well, so you say; to you it seems just
     so.
But I was there, my dear sir, and I know!
I saw it all: the lower regions seethed,
They swelled and spilled, great streams of fire they
     breathed,
And Moloch's hammer,* forging rock to rock,
Scattered the fragments with its mighty knock.   10110
The land's still stiff with alien lumps of stone:
How's such momentum possible? The sages
Try to explain, but still untouched for ages
Those boulders lie, the answer's still unknown.
We rack our brains to death: what more
Can thinking tell us?—Only the old lore
Of simple folk has understood, they've read it
In their tradition's ripe unchanging store:
Wonders they see, and Satan gets the credit!
So on faith's crutch my hobbling wanderer goes: 10120
Devil's Rock, Devil's Bridge are all he knows.

FAUST. An interesting viewpoint, I must say,
To observe Nature's works the Devil's way.

MEPHISTOPHELES. Let Nature do its will; what do I
     care!
My word on it: Satan himself was there!
Our methods—tumult, mad upheaval—get
The best results; look round for proof!—But let
Me now speak plain: can we still offer you
No earthly joy? A panoramic view
Confronts you, far and wide you see unfurled   10130
The glory of the kingdoms of this world (*Matt.* 4):
And can your discontentment still
Discern no pleasing prospect?

FAUST.   Yes!
  A great thought has inspired me: guess
  It if you can.

MEPHISTOPHELES. That I soon will.
  In your place, I'd seek out some city for
  My capital. One with a nookshotten core
  Of streets where burghers munch, of Gothic gables,
  Of poky markets selling vegetables—
  Onions and cabbages and beet;   10140
  Benchfuls of fly-infested meat.
  Come here at any time, you'll sense
  The stink of ceaseless diligence.
  Wide avenues and squares then raise
  The social level of the place:
  And finally long suburbs sprawl,
  Impeded by no outer wall.
  There would be traffic, loud and fast,
  Such fun to watch! all bustling past,
  And to and fro the scuttling slither,   10150
  The swarming ants, hither and thither.
  And when I drove or rode, I'd be
  Their cynosure for all to see:
  A hundred thousand would revere me!

FAUST. All that, I fear, would fail to cheer me.
  One likes a growing population,
  Prospering, feeding, even taking
  Their ease, acquiring education—
  But they're all rebels in the making.

MEPHISTOPHELES. Then, somewhere suitable, to fit my
    state,
  A grandiose pleasure-palace I'd create.   10160
  Forests and hills, wide meadows, open land,
  Would be my garden, likewise very grand:
  Green walls and velvet greensward, avenues
  Straight as a die, precisely shaded views,
  Rocky cascades in even steps descending,
  And fountains in variety unending.
  Here, a great noble jet; there, bordering it,

A thousand jetlets hiss and piss and spit.
I would have maisonettes built, and instal   10170
The most delightful women in them—all
My time I'd spend most cosily enstewed
In such companionable solitude.
And I say 'women' quite advisedly:
Charm in the singular's no charm to me.

FAUST. Babylonian debauch, modern vulgarity.*

MEPHISTOPHELES. And what was your new project, may
          one ask?
    Some bold and noble striving, I'll be bound;
    Perhaps, since you've learnt to float above the ground,
    A mission to the moon is our next task?   10180

FAUST. Certainly not! This earthly sphere
    Is room enough for high deeds; here
    I still can achieve wonders. Never
    Have I felt such great strength for bold endeavour.

MEPHISTOPHELES. So, fame is what you want? One sees
          you've been
    Consorting with a heroine.

FAUST. I want to rule and to possess: what need
    Have I of fame? What matters but the deed?

MEPHISTOPHELES. Poets will come nevertheless,
    Your posthumous glory to profess;   10190
    Fools, kindling further foolishness.

FAUST. Mean spirit, you have no part nor lot
    In any of man's longings: what
    Can your embittered caustic mind
    Know of the needs of humankind?

MEPHISTOPHELES. Well, tell me—I'll be governed by
    Your will—what whim you now would satisfy.

FAUST. My eye fell, as I passed, on the high sea:
    It surged and swelled, mounted up more and more,
    Then checked, and spilt its waves tempestuously,   10200
    Venting its rage upon the flat, wide shore.
    And this displeased me: as when pride's excess

And angry blood and passion unconfined,
Rising too high, fill with uneasiness
A free and just and equitable mind.
I thought it chance, and looked more closely: then
The tide stood still, it turned, rolled back again—
From its high point's proud goal the flood retreated.
And later, the whole process is repeated.

MEPHISTOPHELES [ad spectatores].
   This is no news to me; I know that game,   10210
   For a hundred thousand years it's been the same.

FAUST [continuing with passionate excitement].
   Landward it streams, and countless inlets fill;
   Barren itself, it spreads its barren will;
   It swells and swirls, its rolling waves expand
   Over the dreary waste of dismal sand;
   Breaker on breaker, all their power upheaved
   And then withdrawn, and not a thing achieved!
   I watch dismayed, almost despairingly,
   This useless elemental energy!
   And so my spirit dares new wings to span: 10220
   This I would fight, and conquer if I can.

   And I can conquer it!—Flood as it may,
   It slinks past all that rises in its way;
   For all its gushing pride, a little hill
   Denies it passage, and against its will
   The least concavity lures it from its course.
   At once my plan was made! My soul shall boast
   An exquisite achievement: from our coast
   I'll ban the lordly sea, I'll curb its force,
   I'll set new limits to that watery plain   10230
   And drive it back into itself again.
   I've worked out every detail, and I say:
   This is my will, now dare to find a way!

      [A sound of distant drums and martial music is heard from
      behind the spectators, on the right.]

MEPHISTOPHELES. Why, that's no problem!—Distant
   drums; do you hear?

FAUST. A sad sound to the wise; more war, I fear.

MEPHISTOPHELES. War or peace it may be, but the wise
    man
  Turns both to his advantage if he can.
  He waits for the right moment, till he sees it.
  Now, Faust, your chance has come; be bold and seize it!

FAUST. Spare me this riddling rubbish and explain   10240
  Yourself! What's to be done? Just tell me plain.

MEPHISTOPHELES. On my way here I noticed, with
    distress,
  Our friend the Emperor is in a mess.
  You will recall, we entertained him well
  And fooled him with false gold—why, he could sell
  The whole world, he supposed. As a mere boy
  He was elected to the throne;
  And then, regrettably misguided
  Of course, he very soon decided
  To have it both ways: to enjoy   10250
  Both the imperial power and pleasures of his own.

FAUST. A great mistake. A ruler, to fulfil
  His duty, which is to command, must find
  Pleasure in the commanding. A high will
  Dwells in his heart, yet none must know his mind.
  He whispers it to intimates, and when
  It's done, the world can wonder at it then.
  That way, a lasting dignity allies
  Itself to supreme power. Mere pleasures vulgarize.

MEPHISTOPHELES. That was not his way. Pleasure,
    endlessly,   10260
  Was what he sought; the Empire's anarchy
  Is the result. Feuds between great or small,
  Criss-crossing strife, brothers exiling, killing
  Each other, castle against castle, all
  The cities daggers-drawn, the guilds rebelling
  Against the feudal lords, the bishops fighting
  Chapter and parish, every man despiting
  His fellow, throats cut in the church, no travellers
  Or merchants safe from highway murderers.

And all men plucked up courage, for life now   10270
Meant self-defence. Well, life went on somehow.

FAUST. Went on! Limped, fell, got to its feet, and then
Tripped up and fell head-over-heels again.

MEPHISTOPHELES. And no one did too badly; everyone
Tried to be someone; it was easily done.
Nonentities assumed sufficiency.
But the best and the strongest finally
Decided things had gone too far. They rose
In arms, and said: Let him be master who'll impose
Peace! This the Emperor cannot, will not do.   10280
We shall elect another, who'll renew
The Empire, bring things back to life,
Protect us all from war and strife,
Remake the world and give us peace and justice too.

FAUST. Very religious.

MEPHISTOPHELES. Priests, indeed, they were;
They played a leading part in this affair,
Protecting their fat bellies. The insurrection
Increased: it had their holy benediction.
And so our Emperor, whom we entertained of late,
Comes here to fight the battle that may seal his fate.   10290

FAUST. That's sad; he was a frank, good-natured man.

MEPHISTOPHELES. Come, while there's life there's hope;
    so let's do what we can!
This narrow gorge is trapping him: one bold
Rescue will rescue him a thousandfold.
Who knows how soon his luck may turn?
And with his luck, his vassals will return.

   [They cross the lower mountain range and survey the
   disposition of the army in the valley. Drums and military
   music are heard from below.]

MEPHISTOPHELES. A good position; he's quite well
    secured;
We'll join him, and his victory's assured.

FAUST. What help is ours supposed to be?
Fraud, sleight-of-hand, magical trickery!   10300

MEPHISTOPHELES. Stratagems to win battles! You
    Must keep your higher aims in view,
    Your noble purpose. If we save
    The Emperor's throne for him, restore his land,
    Then you will kneel before him and receive
    As your personal fief the wide sea-strand.

FAUST. Well, you have many talents, I don't doubt it;
    Now win a battle too, and quick about it!

MEPHISTOPHELES. No, you will win it; this time, sir,
    You're the commanding officer.   10310

FAUST. Oh yes, that suits me very nicely,
    My knowledge of war being nil precisely.

MEPHISTOPHELES. *Herr Feldmarschall!* Simply rely
    On your general staff, and you'll get by.
    I've smelt for some time there was war afoot,
    And so my council has been put
    On a war footing. Ancient human powers
    From primal mountains; allies, now, of ours,
    Fortunately.

FAUST.   What's that? I see armed men.
    Have you stirred up the mountain people,* then?   10320

MEPHISTOPHELES. No, but like Peter Quince, I've
       brought a mere
    Quintessence of the rabble here.*

    [*The* THREE MIGHTY MEN* *enter* (2 *Sam.* 23:8)]

MEPHISTOPHELES. Here are my lads; as you can see,
    Their age varies appreciably,
    As do their clothes and armour. You shall be
    Well served, I'll warrant, by all three.
    [*ad spectatores*] Weapons, these days, and knightly gear
    Are popular; these wretches here
    Will also widen their appeal
    By being more allegorical than real.   10330

BUSTER [*young, lightly armed, colourfully dressed*].
    If a man looks me in the eye,
    I bash his face in till needs repairs.

Escape my fist? Just let him try!
I'll have him first by the short hairs.

BAGGER [*mature, well armed, richly dressed*].
Picking an empty quarrel's not
My style; why waste the day with words?
Be bold and grab the goods first; afterwards
It's time enough to ask what's what.

HUGGER [*middle-aged, heavily armed, without a cloak*].
That's not much profit either; when
You've gained wealth, it's soon lost again;   10340
Life's current washes it away.
It's good to get, better to hold:
Let me take charge—I'm old and grey—
And then you'll keep it till you're old.

[*They descend together towards the valley.*]

15 · ON THE FOOTHILLS

[*Drums and martial music from below.* THE
EMPEROR's *tent is pitched.* THE EMPEROR.
THE COMMANDER-IN-CHIEF. GUARDS.]

THE COMMANDER-IN-CHIEF. This valley is convenient;
    to withdraw our force
And concentrate it here, still seems the proper course.
I am confident that it will prove
To have been a well-considered move.

THE EMPEROR. Well, we shall see. I'm sorry, I must say,
That we retreated, or at least gave way.   10350

THE COMMANDER-IN-CHIEF. Consider our right flank,
    your Majesty:
It's ideal fighting terrain. The hills neither
Too steep, the going not too easy either;
Favouring us, baffling the enemy.
This undulating ground half hides us: we're
Safe from a cavalry attack in here.

THE EMPEROR. All I can do is to approve.
Now we shall see how strong our arms and hearts will
    prove.

THE COMMANDER-IN-CHIEF. Mark too the central
    meadow's flat expanse:
  Our phalanx there in warlike fettle stands.   10360
  Look how their pike-points gleam and glimmer where
  The bright sun strikes through misty morning air!
  Darkly the mighty quadrilateral stirs;
  Afire for deeds, a thousand warriors
  Are waiting ready: judge what massive power
  Shall break our enemy in this great hour!

THE EMPEROR. So fine a sight has never met my eyes.
  An army such as this looks twice its size.

THE COMMANDER-IN-CHIEF. Of our left flank there is
    nothing I need say.
  The cliff stands sheer, brave fighters guard the way;   10370
  That precipice, where weapons glint, protects
  The vital path. The enemy expects
  To take the narrow rocky pass: but he
  Will come to bloody grief there, I foresee.

THE EMPEROR. So here they come, false cousins as they
    are,
  Who called me cousin, uncle, brother; far
  Beyond itself their insolence has grown:
  My sceptre's power is usurped, my throne
  Robbed of respect; against me all rebel,
  Though by their own feuds they have devastated   10380
  The Empire. The weak mob first hesitated,
  And now the current sweeps it on as well.

THE COMMANDER-IN-CHIEF. Approaching from the
    rocks, a trusty scout
  Comes to report: let's hear what he's found out.

FIRST SCOUT. By skill and by audacity
        We have penetrated and explored
        Hither and thither: would that we
        Could bring more favourable word!
        Many still plight their troth to you,
        But plead excuse: what can they do,   10390
        They say, amid this fermentation,
        This inner peril of the nation?

THE EMPEROR. Thus the old self-preserving attitude
    Flouts honour, duty, love and gratitude.
    But when their reckoning's made, can they not learn
    That in a neighbour's fire one's own house too may
        burn?

THE COMMANDER-IN-CHIEF. Our next man comes.
    Slowly, unsteadily
    He clambers down: how weary he must be!

SECOND SCOUT. At first we were content to view
        This wild rebellion's mad career;   10400
        But unexpectedly, a new
        Emperor suddenly was here.
        Where his false standards now unfold,
        The mob sets out across the plain;
        They meekly march where they are told;
        For sheep they are and will remain.

THE EMPEROR. A rival emperor is what I need;
    Now I feel I am Emperor indeed.
    I first wore arms merely as soldiers do,   10410
    But now I have a higher cause in view.
    My court was splendid, but from every feast
    Danger was absent—that was what I missed.
    I tilted at the ring, you counselled so,
    But my heart longed for jousting. Now I know
    That had I not on your advice abstained
    From war, a hero's glory I'd have gained.
    That fiery kingdom mirrored and revealed
    My true self: was I there not proved and sealed?
    Those dreadful flames besieged, surrounded me—
    Though it but seemed, how great it seemed to be!   10420
    My fame and conquests have been dreams, confused
    And idle; now I shall make good that time misused.

    [*The heralds are dispatched with his challenge to the rival
    emperor. Enter* FAUST *in armour, with his visor half
    closed, and* THE THREE MIGHTY MEN, *armed and
    dressed as above.*]

FAUST. Sire, we approach you, hoping we do right:
    Precaution's wise, even when the risk is slight.

Mountain folk,* as you know, live deep in thought;
By rocks, by Nature's runes, they are well taught.
Spirits, once denizens of the plains, have come
To make high mountains their more favoured home.
Through silent labyrinths working without rest,
The noble vapours, ore-rich gas they test,   10430
Analyse, separate, combine, intent
Ever to find some new thing to invent.
With gentle craft and spirit-power they build
Transparent shapes of crystal, and are skilled
Through these eternal quietudes to gaze
At the upper world and to divine its ways.

THE EMPEROR. All this I've heard and can believe; but
    how,
My good man, should it interest me now?

FAUST. The Sabine sorcerer from Norcia presents,
    Sire, his devoted loyal compliments.   10440
A hideous fate awaited him: he stood
There amid flickering flames and crackling wood,
Dry logs arranged around him, mixed with pitch
And sulphur-sticks that kindle at a touch;
From man, God, Devil, now no help remains—
The Emperor's hand sunders his glowing chains.
That was in Rome. Since then, most mightily
Indebted, he has watched your destiny
With anxious care: forgetful of his own,
He probes the stars, the depths, for you alone.   10450
At his command we hasten here to assist
Your Majesty. The mountains can enlist
Great powers; here Nature works with sovereign skill—
Let dull priests call it magic if they will.

THE EMPEROR. Glad guests are welcome on a festive day,
    Who come to while a pleasant time away;
They give us pleasure, pushing, shoving, filling
Our hospitable halls to overspilling.
But yet more welcome is the valiant friend
Who on a fateful morning comes to lend   10460
His strong support, while peril still prevails

And our great issue hangs in even scales.
And yet, in this high moment I would ask:
Withhold your hands from your sword's willing task,
Honour this day when thousands march to fight
For or against me. It is right
A man should help himself! He who would sit
Upon a throne must prove he merits it.
This phantom rebel, emperor in name,
Who would possess my territories, would claim   10470
To be my vassals' feudal lord, and chief
Commander of my army—I'll dispatch this thief
Myself back to the shades!

FAUST.   To pledge your life
Is ill-advised, even in so great a strife.
Your sacred head, shielded by crest and plume,
Gives courage to us all. Could limbs presume
To act without a head? If that should fall
Asleep, they too must sink with it; they all,
If it is wounded, feel the wound; likewise
When it recovers, back to life they rise.   10480
At once the arm is strong, asserts its right,
Raises the shield to guard the skull aright;
At once the sword perceives its duty clear,
Wards off the blow, returns it without fear;
The stalwart foot then shares their battle-lust,
Treading the slain foe's neck into the dust.

THE EMPEROR. So speaks my anger; such his fate shall be;
    His proud head as my footstool I will see!

THE HERALDS [returning].
                Little honour, small esteem
                We were shown: nobly we spoke   10490
                Our message, but they dared to joke,
                Mocked it as an idle dream:
                'Where's your emperor? Answer where,
                Echoing mountains and thin air!
                He's a memory, an old story;
                Once-upon-a-time his glory!'

FAUST. This prudent answer will have satisfied
The loyal friends now standing at your side.
The foe draws near, your men are eager: tell
Them to attack, the moment augurs well.   10500

THE EMPEROR. I'll not be war-lord here or give commands.

[*To* THE COMMANDER-IN-CHIEF.]

Prince, I must lay your duty in your hands.

THE COMMANDER-IN-CHIEF. Let our right wing attack,
     then! They will meet
The enemy's left, which still is uphill-bound;
Before they reach that higher ground
Our brave young loyal troops will force them to retreat.

FAUST. Permit this lively hero, then, at once
To join them and take part in their advance,
To mingle intimately with their ranks
And there pursue his energetic pranks.   10510

[*He points to the right.*]

BUSTER [*stepping forward*].
The man who shows his face to me, before
He looks away I smash his cheeks and jaw;
The man who turns his back, I make his brain-pan dangle
Down from his neck at a queer angle.
I'll rage; just let your men keep pace,
And strike with sword and battle-mace.
By scores the enemy will fall,
Their blood will drown and choke them all. [*Exit.*]

THE COMMANDER-IN-CHIEF. Now let our centre
     quietly follow them
And match the enemy's strength and stratagem.   10520
Already, on the right, our men have fought
Back furiously, bringing their plans to nought.

FAUST [*pointing to his middle man*].
Then let this man follow your order too;
He'll quickly show them all what they must do.

BAGGER [*stepping forward*].
High valour in an army's mind
With lust for spoils should be combined.

Let our whole purpose now be bent
On the false emperor's well-stocked tent.
He'll not sit long on that proud seat;
I'll lead the phalanx on to his defeat.   10530

SNATCHER [*a camp-follower, attaching herself to him*].
Though we're not married, I confess,
He's my best sweetheart none the less.
What a fine harvest's now in store!
Women are fearsome when they're stealing,
They loot and plunder without feeling.
But victory's ours; all's fair in war! [*Exeunt.*]

THE COMMANDER-IN-CHIEF. Their right wing now,
     predictably of course,
Attacks our left with sudden desperate force;
That narrow pass on the cliff side, it must
Be held to the last man against their thrust.   10540

FAUST [*pointing to the left*].
Note this man too, sir; it will do no harm
To strengthen your strong troops with his strong arm.

HUGGER [*stepping forward*].
The left wing's safe; leave it to me!
To have's to keep, wherever I may be;
Possession's old, I make it last;
No thunderbolt can split what I hold fast. [*Exit.*]

MEPHISTOPHELES [*descending from uphill*].
Now from each gorge, from each ravine,
Armed men emerge and fill the scene,
Crowding the pathways in our rear;
Behind our army they appear,   10550
All armed and helmed, with sword and shield,
Forming a wall that will not yield;
They wait the signal to advance.

     [*Aside, softly, to those in the know.*]

No doubt you'll guess their provenance.
I of course have not hesitated:
A score of armouries I've evacuated.
All round they stood, footmen and horse,

Pretending still to be a ruling force.
Kings, emperors, lordly knights they were,
And now they're empty snail-shells, nothing more.   10560
Now phantoms dress up in them for a while,
Giving new life to medieval style.
It's mere demonic animation,
But quite a useful show on this occasion.

[*Aloud.*]

Hear how with bang and knock and rattle
They anticipate the coming battle!
And see, old standards fluttering! Those stale rags
Longed for fresh air to fly again as flags.
An ancient army stands again today,
Eager to join new wars that come its way.   10570

[*A fearsome trumpet-call from above; signs of disarray in
the enemy army.*]

FAUST. The horizon mingles with the dark,
And only here and there a spark
Flashes, a red and ominous light;
With glint of blood the weapons flare.
The rocks, the forest and the air,
The very heavens compound this sight.

MEPHISTOPHELES. The right flank holds, stoutly resisting;
I see Jack Buster's there, assisting
Them in his way; he's quick and tall,
That monster, he outfights them all.   10580

THE EMPEROR. Where there was one arm in that fray
I now see twelve, all raised to slay;
It seems unnatural to me.

FAUST. Have you not heard of clouds that drift
Along the coast of Sicily?
By day's light, shimmering, they lift
Into the middle air a high
And wondrous vision, mirrored by
Vapours of special quality.
There cities flicker to and fro   10590
And gardens rise up and sink low
As through the air the pictures go.*

THE EMPEROR. But look, how strange! On each tall spear
   I see a tip of light appear,
   And agile little flames that dance
   There on our phalanx, lance by lance.
   I do not like this spectral show.

FAUST. By your leave, Sire, these are the traces
   Left by long-vanished spirit-races:
   The Heavenly Twins send this reflection.   10600
   All sailors once sought their protection;
   You see here their last fading glow.*

THE EMPEROR. But who thus earns our thanks? Who
      made
   Nature herself come to our aid,
   Using her rarest powers so?

MEPHISTOPHELES. Who but our Master,* whose high art
   Protects your destiny! His heart
   Stirs at the peril you are in;
   In gratitude he means to win
   Victory for you in these wars,   10610
   Or gladly perish for your cause.

THE EMPEROR. The crowds cheered as I solemnly passed
      by;
   I thought: Now I am someone: let me try
   It out at once. And on an impulse: That
   Old greybeard's in a hot spot; why not set
   Him free? And so I spoilt the clergy's fun;
   They always bore a grudge for what I'd done.
   After so many years, am I indeed
   To reap the fruits of that light-hearted deed?

FAUST. A generous gift richly repays the giver.   10620
   Look at the sky! An omen will appear,
   Sent by the Master; take good note,
   And soon its meaning will be clear.

THE EMPEROR. I see an eagle in the heavens hover;
   A griffin comes in wild pursuit.

FAUST. Mark well! This sign is favourable.
   A griffin is a beast of fable:

What insolence to brave in fight
The king of birds' authentic right!

THE EMPEROR. See, in wide circles now they soar   10630
　　Around each other; all at once
　　They swoop to the attack, they pounce
　　To strike with beak, to rend with claw!

FAUST. Look, the vile griffin's proud endeavour
　　Now brings it low: plucked, pulled to bits,
　　It falls into the woods, with its
　　Lion-tail drooping, lost for ever.

THE EMPEROR. As you interpret it, so be it!
　　I accept the omen, though amazed to see it.

MEPHISTOPHELES [*looking to the right*].
　　　　　　They fall back, our deadly foes,   10640
　　　　　　Driven by a rain of blows!
　　　　　　Now uncertainly they fight,
　　　　　　Crowding over to their right;
　　　　　　Their main force, by this intrusion
　　　　　　On its left, is in confusion.
　　　　　　So our centre, thrusting hard
　　　　　　To its right, now finds their guard
　　　　　　Lowered; quick as lightning-flash
　　　　　　There it strikes, and with a splash
　　　　　　As of stormy waves, those powers   10650
　　　　　　Rage as equals, theirs and ours.
　　　　　　How magnificently done!
　　　　　　Now this battle we have won!

THE EMPEROR [*on the left, to* FAUST].
　　　　　　Over there, it seems to me,
　　　　　　Our men falter. I can't see
　　　　　　Rocks being thrown. They were to hold
　　　　　　That high ground! The pass is sold!
　　　　　　Look! The enemy outnumber
　　　　　　Us by far, and now they clamber
　　　　　　Up the cliff, and force their way   10660
　　　　　　Nearer still!—This fateful day,

   Crowns an impious campaign
   With success! Your arts are vain!

     [A pause.]

MEPHISTOPHELES. Here come my ravens; they will tell
 Bad news. Things can't be going well
 With us; I wonder what they've seen.

THE EMPEROR. Why have those ugly birds come here?
 Like black-sailed ships to us they steer,
 Straight from the cliffside battle scene.

MEPHISTOPHELES [*to the ravens*].
 Perch close, and croak into my ears.   10670
 Those you protect need have no fears;
 Good counsellors you have always been.

FAUST [*to* THE EMPEROR].
 You will have heard of doves that fly
 From distant countries through the sky
 Home to their nests to brood and feed.
 These are indeed dissimilar:
 The pigeon-post serves peace, in war
 The raven-post makes better speed.

MEPHISTOPHELES. Disaster threatens you: look there
 At our cliff-hanging heroes! Their   10680
 Position has grown perilous.
 The enemy has gained much height,
 And if they take the pass, things might
 Go very seriously with us.

THE EMPEROR. So you have tricked me at the last!
 A dreadful net now holds me fast,
 And you enticed me into it.

MEPHISTOPHELES. Courage! All's not yet lost. With wit
 And patience we'll still find a way;
 The darkest hour precedes the day.   10690
 My messengers are swift and true:
 Let me command your troops for you!

THE COMMANDER-IN-CHIEF [*approaching*].
 Sire, these are allies of your choosing.
 I never liked it; now we're losing

The war, thanks to their jugglery.
This battle's broken, I can't mend it;
These two began it, let them end it.
I hand back my authority.

THE EMPEROR. No, keep your staff for better days;
Our fortunes yet may change. I rather   10700
Shrink from this creepy fellow and his ways;
I don't like his tame ravens either.

[*To* MEPHISTOPHELES.]

I can't give you the staff; somehow
You don't seem quite the proper man.
But take command, and save us if you can.
I'll let things take their own course now.

[*Exit into the tent with* THE COMMANDER-IN-
CHIEF.]

MEPHISTOPHELES. Good luck to him with his stale old
    stick!
That thing's no use to us, my friend;
It had a cross stuck on one end.

FAUST. What must we do?

MEPHISTOPHELES.   It's done!—Be quick   10710
Now, my black servant-cousins, and take wing
To the mountain lake: my greetings to its daughters,
And I'd like an appearance of their waters.
Those nymphs, by some arcane womanish wonder,
Can make Being and Seeming come asunder,
So that you'd swear the illusion's the real thing.

[*A pause.*]

FAUST. Our ravens must have won the hearts
Of the lake-ladies by their flattering arts;
Look, there it comes, a trickling stream.
In many a dry bare rocky place it gushes;   10720
It grows and widens, swirls and rushes.
Their victory's become a dream.

MEPHISTOPHELES. Their bold rock-climbers now are
    meeting
A strange and disconcerting greeting.

FAUST. Now torrents multiply in downward course,
   Disgorged from gorges with redoubled force;
   A stream becomes an arching waterfall,
   Then all at once, caught by the cliff's wide ledge,
   It rushes foaming sideways, edge to edge,
   And drops cascading to the valley's call.   10730
   The enemy bravely but vainly strives
   To stand upright, engulfed in monstrous waves;
   Even myself such dreadful floods appal.

MEPHISTOPHELES. I can see nothing of these watery lies;
   They take effect only on human eyes.
   But I can relish this unnatural brawl:
   Hundreds of men in panic, running round
   With silly swimming motions on firm ground!
   Poor fools, they think they're being drowned,
   Though they're on dry land, snuffling safe and sound.   10740
   Confusion overwhelms them all.

       [The ravens have returned.]

To our high Master I'll speak well of you.
Now, if you would yourselves be masters too,
Then hasten to that glowing smithy where
The dwarf-folk, toiling tirelessly,
Strike sparks from stone and metal. There,
Using the same persuasive flattery,
Ask for a show of fire: a burst, a blaze,
A scintillation, such as plays
Within our Master's mind. The distant flicker   10750
Of the sheet-lightning, starlets falling quicker
Than thought, are any night's displays:
But lightning shimmering through the tangled wood
And stars that hiss across wet earth—these should
Still have some power to amaze.
Take no great pains then, but just ask, in fact
Just give the dwarves my orders so to act.

   [The ravens fly off; the prescribed phenomena take place.]

MEPHISTOPHELES. Dense darkness now engulfs the foe,
   They grope and stumble as they go;
   False fires beset them every way they turn,   10760

Or sudden flashing lights that burn
Their eyes out. Beautiful, indeed!
Now a tremendous noise is all we need.

FAUST. Those hollow warriors from dead armouries,
The fresh air seems to strengthen them—I hear
Them clanking, rattling loud and clear
Up there: what strange discordant sound it is!

MEPHISTOPHELES. Quite so! Now there's no holding
them; those knights
Bang away, fighting ceremonious fights,
As in the dear old times they used to do.   10770
Now empty greaves and brassards clash
Like Guelphs and Ghibellines, swift and rash
Their ancient quarrel they renew.
In the long-wonted ways set fast,
They are implacable to the last;
Their hubbub's spreading far and wide.
These devil's feasts, say what you will,
Thrive best on partisan hatred still;
Fine horror-fare it can provide.
Now hear it roar! The cliffs resound   10780
With hideous shrill satanic sound,
And all in panic dread are bound.

[*Warlike tumult in the orchestra, finally giving way to
triumphant martial music.*]

16 · THE RIVAL EMPEROR'S TENT

[*A throne, rich furnishings. Enter* BAGGER *and*
SNATCHER.]

SNATCHER. So here we are, the first to come.

BAGGER. Faster than ravens flying home.

SNATCHER. Ah, what a treasure-house we're in!
It's endless: where shall we begin?

BAGGER. The whole room's full, it's fit to burst;
I just don't know what to take first.

SNATCHER. That rug would be the thing for me;   10790
   I often sleep so wretchedly.

BAGGER. Here's a steel morning star, a thing
   I've always longed to hold and swing.

SNATCHER. A scarlet mantle hemmed with gold!
   This is a thing my dreams foretold.

BAGGER. I like this weapon; one quick blow,
   Out come the brains, and on you go.
   Why are you packing all that stuff?
   There's nothing there that's good enough.
   Just leave the junk behind! Our best
   Plunder would be that treasure-chest.   10800
   Its belly holds the army's pay
   In gold: let's spirit that away.

SNATCHER. But who's to carry, who's to lift?
   This weight the devil himself won't shift!

BAGGER. Bend down, be quick about it, stoop!
   Your back is strong, I'll hoist it up.

SNATCHER. Oh God, I've done it now, oh God,
   My back has cracked under the load!

       [*The chest drops and bursts open.*]

BAGGER. There's the red gold, spilt on the floor.
   Quick, pick it up, pick up some more!   10810

SNATCHER [*crouching down*].
   Quick, pick it up yourself and fill
   My lap with it! We've plenty still.

BAGGER. Enough now; hurry!

         [*She stands up.*]

        To hell with it!
   Your apron's sprung a leak, it's split!
   You're wasting treasure, scattering, sowing
   It all behind you as you're going.

GUARDS [*of our Emperor, entering*].
   What are you doing here? Who are you?
   This is State property: how dare you!

BAGGER. We risked our lives and limbs for you,
  We want our share of booty too.   10820
  An enemy tent's fair game, by rules
  Of war; we're soldiers and not fools.

GUARDS. That's not our way of thinking; we're
  Soldiers, not thieving riff-raff here.
  Our Emperor's served, we'd have you know,
  By honest men.

BAGGER.   Oh yes, quite so;
  Your honest trade we understand.
  It's known as: living on the land.
  Soldiers are all in the same game:
  War contributions is its name.   10830

            [To SNATCHER.]

  Get on with it, take what you've got.
  Who's welcome here? I see we're not! [Exeunt.]

FIRST GUARD. Why didn't you give him a good clout
  To shut him up? Insolent lout!

SECOND GUARD. I don't know, but I'd got a scare
  Somehow; they're like two ghosts, that pair.

THIRD GUARD. My eyes went queer, all flickering
  It was, I couldn't see a thing!

FOURTH GUARD. What's happening I can't rightly say.
  It's been so sultry-hot all day,   10840
  Stuffy and close, scary as well.
  The one man stood, the next man fell.
  We stumbled on and fought by luck:
  An enemy died each time we struck.
  You couldn't see through that strange mist,
  And your ears hummed and drummed and hissed.
  So it went on, and we're here now,
  And we ourselves, we can't tell how.

    [THE EMPEROR enters with four princes.* The
    GUARDS withdraw.]

THE EMPEROR. Well, be that as it may! The enemy has run
  Away into the plains, the battle has been won.   10850

Here stands the empty throne, and cluttered round it lies
Treasure that traitor stole, wrapped up in fineries.
By our own noble guards defended, we await
The nations' envoys here, in our imperial state.
Good news comes from all sides: the Empire's said to be
At peace again, and all swear fealty to me.
We did perhaps employ some trickery in these wars,
But in the end we fought only for our just cause.
Chance can help soldiers win their battles, as we know:
A meteor falls from heaven, or blood rains on the foe,   10860
Or rocky caves resound with dreadful symphony
Which lifts one's spirits but confounds the enemy.
Our adversary fell, whom all will now deride;
The glorious victor thanks God who was on his side.
All join in this *Te Deum*, though no command was given;
A million voices sing their gratitude to Heaven.
Yet chiefly my own heart, I find, deserves high praise,
And to it now, for once, I turn my reverent gaze.
A young and lively prince wastes days from his life's
    store,
But as the years go by, values each moment more.   10870
Therefore, to save my house, my court, my empire too,
I bind myself at once, four worthy lords, to you.

[*To the first.*]

Our army was well served, prince, by your dispositions;
Wise and heroic too your timely bold decisions.
Be active now in peace, as present time demands:
I place the Sword of State, Lord Marshal, in your hands.

THE IMPERIAL LORD MARSHAL. Your loyal troops, till
    now embroiled in civil strife,
At your frontiers shall yet defend your throne and life.
Then let the ancestral halls rejoice, our privilege be,
Amid a throng of guests, to feast your Majesty;   10880
And borne ahead of you or at your side, my Sword
Shall shine to honour you, great and all-conquering lord!

THE EMPEROR [*to the second prince*].
With charm and courtesy your courage is combined:
Be my High Chamberlain! A hard task, you will find,

To be the ruler of the whole domestic rout;
I am ill served by their perpetual falling out.
To please me and my court they've not yet learnt—but
    now
Let your honourable example teach them how.

THE HIGH CHAMBERLAIN. Favoured is he who serves
    your noble policy:
Help to the best, even to the least no injury;   10890
An undissembling calm, candour without deceit.
If you can read my heart, then my reward's complete.
I see you, Sire—if my mind's eye may be so bold—
Entering to that great feast: the golden bowl I hold,
I hold your rings, and you, upon that day of pleasure,
Refresh your hands; your look contents me in like
    measure.

THE EMPEROR. Though my new serious mood should
    banish festive thoughts,
I'll think them none the less; there's profit in such sports.

[*To the third prince.*]

You shall now be High Seneschal, to supervise
All our hunting-demesnes, farms, poultry yards; be wise   10900
And skilful to provide my choice of favourite fare,
In season month by month, furnished and cooked with
    care.

THE HIGH SENESCHAL. Now let strict fasting be my
    duty and my wish,
Till I have served you first, Sire, with some gladdening
    dish.
The cooks and I shall strive, as we prepare such cheer,
The season to advance, to bring the distant near.
Not to your taste the out-of-time, the exotic show:
You prefer wholesome simple nourishment, I know.

THE EMPEROR [*to the fourth prince*].
Since, my young valiant cousin, we are now concerned,
Only with feasting, as it seems: you must be turned   10910
Into an Imperial Cupbearer. Henceforth provide
Us with good wine now, see our cellars well supplied.

And yet be moderate yourself in celebration;
Resist the enticing opportunity's temptation!

THE IMPERIAL CUPBEARER. Sire, if you will but trust
    it, even youth can grow
Into full manhood, and more quickly than you know.
I too can see myself at that great banquet: there
The imperial buffet I grace with vessels rare
Of gold and silver; yet I choose above the rest,
To offer to your lips, a goblet of the best   10920
Venetian crystal, in which sweet contentment waits,
For it improves the wine, yet not inebriates.
Some men might trust too far a cup so magical;
Your Majesty's restraint protects us best of all.

THE EMPEROR. These honours I bestow on you you
    each have heard
Now solemnly announced by my imperial word,
Which you may trust, for it is mighty, and assures
All gifts; yet still they need the writing that endures,
Our noble signature. For this formality
The right man in good time approaches, as I see.   10930

[*The* HIGH CHANCELLOR ARCHBISHOP *enters.*]

THE EMPEROR. The last stone crowns the arch: a vaulted
    roof entrusting
Itself to such a key is built for everlasting.
You see four princes here: with them I have discussed
My household firstly, and my court, and how they must
Be governed. But the Empire as a whole, with all
Its weight and strength, now to your fivefold care must
    fall.
All five, outsplendouring others, shall be rich in lands:
Therefore I give to you the whole inheritance
Forfeit by all supporters of that reprobate;
And thus, my loyal friends, I enlarge now your estate   10940
With much fine land, which in due course you may
    augment
By purchase, by exchange, or such entitlement
As may arise. All feudal rights that here accrue
I also grant, without impediment, to you.

Your judgements shall be final, and against your high
Courts, your supreme tribunals, no appeal shall lie.
Rents, tithes and levies, tolls, safe conducts, these I join
To you, all salt and mining rights, the right to coin
Money likewise. For thus my gratitude I prove,
Setting you from my throne at only one remove.   10950

THE HIGH CHANCELLOR. I render deepest thanks for all
 of us; for our
Advancement will increase your Majesty's own power.

THE EMPEROR. The five of you shall have a higher
 privilege still.
While I yet live, I reign, and I live with a will:
But a long chain of forebears draws my thoughtful gaze
From present strivings back to troublous, threatening
 days.
I must leave you, my friends, later or earlier;
Your duty then's to elect another emperor.
Crown him, and on the sacred altar raise him high;
Then peace shall reign, and all our storms will have
 passed by.   10960

THE HIGH CHANCELLOR. With our hearts full of pride
 and humbly bowed we stand,
Princes before your throne, the noblest in the land.
So long as loyal blood stirs in these veins, we still
Are but the body moved entirely by your will.

THE EMPEROR. Finally, what we here have hitherto
 enacted,
Let it be for all time in written form contracted.
All these Electoral lands, of course, though to be held
Freehold by you, are indivisibly entailed,
And must, increased or not, pass (so we stipulate)
By primogeniture in undiminished state.   10970

THE HIGH CHANCELLOR. This weighty statute shall to
 parchment be committed
And gladly for your sacred signature submitted;
I'll charge my office with the engrossment, and the seal
Shall be affixed, for our and the whole Empire's weal.

THE EMPEROR. So, my lords, take your leave! that each
    of you now may
  Calmly and at his ease reflect on this great day.

    [*The temporal princes withdraw; the spiritual lord
    remains, and speaks in solemn tones.*]

THE ARCHBISHOP. The Chancellor has left, the Bishop
    lingers here,
  Impelled to utter a grave warning in your ear,
  Moved by concern for you, by fatherly distress!

THE EMPEROR. What so concerns you on this day of
    happiness?   10980

THE ARCHBISHOP. I see with bitter sorrow, in this very
    hour,
  Your sacred Majesty enthralled to Satan's power.
  Your throne now seems assured, but by the means you
    used
  The Holy Father's mocked, God himself is abused.
  When the Pope hears of it, a righteous doom will smash
  Your sinful Empire by his sacred thunderflash.
  He still recalls today how at your coronation
  You pardoned, at the point of death, that vile magician.
  Your crown's first ray of grace fell on that cursèd head;
  How many souls in Christendom that deed misled!   10990
  But strike your breast, and purge your guilty fortune's
    blight
  By rendering to Holy Church a moderate mite.
  Up on that broad hillside, there where you pitched your
    tent,
  Where evil spirits with your cause made covenant,
  Where to the Devil you gave ear—there found and make
  A holy priory, for your contrition's sake.
  Let it be set on those green slopes, which will provide
  Rich pasture; give it woods and mountains far and wide;
  Bright lakes well stocked with fish, numberless streams
    that pour
  Down swiftly winding to the valley; furthermore   11000
  The broad valley itself, its meadows, fields and dales.
  All this shall be your penance, which for grace avails.

THE EMPEROR. My grievous fault alarms me, I am much
    distressed.
Measure the boundary yourself as you think best.

THE ARCHBISHOP. First: we must cleanse the site from
    such defilement, by
Rededicating it at once to the Most High.
Soon the great walls rise up before my inner gaze;
The choir, already built, gleams in the morning's rays;
The growing structure spreads, a cruciform design;
The nave grows wide and high, the faithful hail this sign.   11010
See with what ardent joy they stream through the great
    gate,
As over hill and dale the bells' first notes pulsate,
Pealing from lofty towers that strive into the sky;
Summoned to a new life, the penitents draw nigh!
And on the day—may it be soon!—of consecration,
Your presence, Sire, shall be our triumph's
    consummation.

THE EMPEROR. May this great enterprise, this pious
    monument,
Glorify God, and purge the sin I now repent.
Enough! My soul's relieved, my heart begins to lift.

THE ARCHBISHOP. As Chancellor I now need a formal
    deed of gift.   11020

THE EMPEROR. Draw up a formal paper, then, that will
    assign it
All to the Church; bring it to me, I'll gladly sign it.

THE ARCHBISHOP [taking his leave, but turning round again
    at the door].
You will also assign the land's whole revenues
To this development; its rents, tithes, levies, dues,
In perpetuity. Costs of proper maintenance
Are high, and there will be administrative expense.
Some gold, too, from your booty—that will expedite
The building work itself, on such a barren site.
I must mention likewise the transports we shall need
Of timber, lime, and slate and suchlike; those indeed   11030
Can be brought by the people—we shall preach, of course,

That blest are they who serve the Church with cart and
  horse. [*Exit.*]

THE EMPEROR. This sin is very burdensome; I lent an ear
  To those damned magic-men, and now they cost me
    dear.

THE ARCHBISHOP [*returning again, with a deep bow*].
  Your pardon, Sire. That infamous man was granted land*
  On the Empire's coast: but he and it are cursed and
    banned
  Unless you also grant us that land's revenue,
  Its rents, tithes and so forth, as further penance due.

THE EMPEROR [*irritably*].
  But no such land exists, it's still under the sea!

THE ARCHBISHOP. Our right suffices, time provides,
    we'll wait and see.   11040
  Meanwhile your word remains your bond, Sire, as we
    know.
                                               [*Exit.*]

THE EMPEROR [*alone*].
  Why not just sign away the whole Empire at one go!

ACT FIVE

17 · OPEN COUNTRY

A WANDERER. There they are, so dark and strong,
               Those old lindens, as before;
               I have wandered for so long,
               Now I find them here once more!
               And the hut that sheltered me,
               Tempest-tossed as I was then,
               On the sand-dunes here I see:
               This is the same place again!   11050
               And my hosts? That fine old couple
               Rescued me with ready will:
               They were pious gentle people—
               Can I hope to find them still?
               They were old at our first meeting.
               Shall I knock or call?—My greeting
               To you, if the gods still bless
               You with your life of kindliness!

BAUCIS* (*a very old little woman*).
               Stranger dear, speak softly please,
               Softly! My old husband, he's   11060
               Resting still. He needs the length
               Of his nights, for short days' strength.

THE WANDERER. Dear old woman, is it true,
               Can I still be thanking you
               For my young life you and he
               Long ago saved from the sea?
               Baucis! You, who when death coldly
               Kissed me, warmed my freezing blood?

            [*The husband enters.*]

               You, Philemon, who so boldly
               Snatched my treasure from the flood?   11070
               Yours the hospitable fire,

Yours the bell with silver tone,
You, my rescuers from dire
Peril, you my help alone!
Now, to ease my heart's emotion,
I must look upon this shore;
I must kneel and pray once more,
Gazing on the boundless ocean.

[*He steps forward across the sand-dune.*]

PHILEMON [*to* BAUCIS].

Quickly now, let's lay the table
Here among the flowers and trees.   11080
Let him go; he'll stare, unable
To believe the change he sees.

[*Standing by* THE WANDERER.]

Look! Your enemies of old,
The fierce foaming waves, have been
Turned into a park; behold
Now this paradisal scene!
I was not young enough to lend
My helping hands to this endeavour;
Soon my strength was at an end;
The sea was further off than ever.   11090
Those wise lords, they sent bold slaves:
Dams and dikes built in a day
Stole the birthright of the waves
And usurped the ocean's sway.
Now green fields and gardens lie,
Woods and villages have grown
Up all round. But come, the sun
Will be setting by and by,
Let us eat. Those distant white
Sails seek haven for the night;   11100
Now like nesting birds they know
Here's a port where they can go.
Thus it is; you must look far
Now to find the sea's blue shore,
For dense between, on wide new land,
New human habitations stand.

[*The three sit at table in the little garden.*]

BAUCIS.   You are silent? And no food
           Has refreshed you, stranger dear?

PHILEMON. Tell him about the wonders; you'd
           Like to talk, he'd like to hear.   11110

BAUCIS.   Yes, the wonders. I'm still worried
           By strange doings we have seen.
           Things unnaturally hurried;
           Things not as they should have been.

PHILEMON. Can the Emperor sin? He named him
           Feudal lord of all the coast;
           Even a herald, marching past
           With his trumpet-call, proclaimed him.
           It began here near the dune,
           That first foothold on the flood;   11120
           There were tents and huts. But soon
           In green fields a palace stood.

BAUCIS.   Slaves toiled vainly: blow by blow,
           Pick and shovel made no way.
           Then we saw the night-flames glow—
           And a dam stood there next day.
           They used human sacrifice:
           Fire ran down, like rivers burning.
           All night long we heard the cries—
           A canal was built by morning.   11130
           He is godless, for he sorely
           Wants our hut, our clump of trees.
           As a neighbour he's too lordly;
           We must serve him, if you please!

PHILEMON. Yet a fine new house he's found
           For us on the polder-ground.

BAUCIS.   I'd not trust that soil for long.
           Stay up here where you belong!

PHILEMON. Come, let's watch the sun's last ray,
           When our chapel bell we've tolled.   11140
           Let us kneel there, let us pray,
           Trusting our God, as of old.

18 · A PALACE

[*A large ornamental park, with a long straight canal.*
FAUST *in extreme old age, walking about pensively.*
LYNCEUS THE WATCHMAN* *speaks through a*
megaphone.]

LYNCEUS. The sun sinks, the last ships appear,
   Gaily they pass the harbour bar,
   Soon a tall vessel will be here
   In the canal; how merry are
   Those fluttering pennants! Each one plays
   From a proud standing mast; the crew
   Are sharing the good fortune too
   That greets you in your latter days.   11150

  [*The chapel bell sounds from the sand-dune.*]

FAUST [*starting up angrily*].
   Damned bell! A treacherous wound that flies
   As from a sniper's shot behind me!
   Out there my endless kingdom lies,
   But this vexation at my back,
   These teasing envious sounds remind me
   My great estate's not pure! That line
   Of linden-trees, that little shack,
   That crumbling chapel, are not mine.
   On that green place I may not tread
   Another's shadow falls like dread;   11160
   It irks my feet, my eyes, my ear—
   How can I get away from here!

LYNCEUS THE WATCHMAN [*as above*].
   Now, in the evening breeze, all hail
   To this fine ship with swelling sail!
   How swift it glides, its load how high—
   Sacks, boxes, piled against the sky!

[*A splendid boat appears, richly loaded with a variety of*
products from distant lands. Enter MEPHISTOPHELES
and THE THREE MIGHTY MEN.]

CHORUS.   Welcome ashore!
               We're back again!
               Long live the master,
               Say his men!   11170

        [*They land; the cargo is brought ashore.*]

MEPHISTOPHELES. We have done well and had good
                    sport;
               We hope my lord will be content.
               We'd only two ships when we went,
               With twenty now we're back in port.
               Our cargo richly testifies
               To our great deeds that won this prize.
               The ocean sets one's notions free:
               Who's plagued by scruple out at sea?
               To catch a fish, to catch a ship,
               The only way is grab and grip;   11180
               And once three ships have come one's way,
               A fourth is easy grappling-prey.
               Then guess what chance a fifth will stand!
               For might is right, by sea or land.
               Not *how* but *how much*—that's what's counted!
               What seaman does not take for granted
               The undivided trinity
               Of war and trade and piracy?

THE THREE MIGHTY MEN. No thanks to meet us,
               No word to greet us!   11190
               Our master thinks
               Our cargo stinks.
               His face expresses
               Great displeasure;
               He does not like
               This princely treasure.

MEPHISTOPHELES. There's no more for you
               On the house.
               You took your cut,
               So what's the grouse?   11200

THE THREE. That's a mere penny
                        For our pains:
                        We ask fair shares
                        Of all the gains!

MEPHISTOPHELES. Go up there first
                        And set out all
                        The valuables
                        Hall by hall.
                        He'll see the richest
                        Show on earth;   11210
                        Then he'll work out
                        Just what it's worth,
                        Decide he can
                        Afford a treat,
                        And order a feast-day
                        For the fleet.

                        Tomorrow the pretty birds we'll see;
                        They're my responsibility.

                        [*The cargo is removed.*]

MEPHISTOPHELES [*to* FAUST].
                        Why these dark looks, this frowning brow?
                        Sublime good fortune greets you now: 11220
                        By your high wisdom, the sea-shore
                        And sea are reconciled once more;
                        Now from the land in easy motion
                        The ships glide swiftly to the ocean;
                        And thus, here in this royal place,
                        The whole world lies in your embrace!
                        Your kingdom started on this spot;
                        The first shed stood here, did it not?
                        Here the first shallow trench was tried
                        Where now the plashing oars are plied.   11230
                        Your lofty plan, our industry,
                        Have made you lord of land and sea.
                        From here—

FAUST.   *Here*! That damned word again,
                        The theme and burden of my pain!

You are no fool: I must tell you
It cuts my very heart in two,
I'll not bear it another day!
Yet as I say it, even I
Feel shame. The old couple must give way!
I chose that linden clump as my   11240
Retreat: those few trees not my own
Spoil the whole world that is my throne.
From branch to branch I planned to build
Great platforms, to look far afield,
From panoramic points to gaze
At all I've done; as one surveys
From an all-mastering elevation
A masterpiece of man's creation.
I'd see it all as I have planned:
Man's gain of habitable land.   11250

This is the sharpest torment: what
A rich man feels he has not got!
That linden-scent, that chapel-chime
Haunt me like some grim funeral-time.
My will, my sovereign command
Is broken on that mound of sand!
How shall I cure my mental hell
That rages at that little bell!

MEPHISTOPHELES. Indeed, such matter for distress
    Must turn your life to bitterness.   11260
    These cursèd tinkling sounds we hear
    Must stink in every noble ear.
    Ding-donging, tintinnabulating,
    Clear evening skies obnubilating:
    Every event of life it blights,
    From that first bath to our last rites—
    As if life were some dream-like thing
    That fades away from dong to ding!*

FAUST. Their stubbornness, their opposition
    Ruins my finest acquisition;   11270
    And in fierce agony I must
    Grow weary now of being just.

MEPHISTOPHELES. Why scruple then at this late hour?
      Are you not—a colonial power?

FAUST. Well, do it! Clear them from my path!—
      A fine new cottage, as you know,
      I've built, where the old folk can go.

MEPHISTOPHELES. We'll lift them up and whisk them to it;
      A moment's work, they'll scarcely know it.
      They'll suffer it with a good grace   11280
      And settle down in their new place.

   [*At his shrill whistle,* THE THREE MIGHTY MEN
   appear.]

      Come, we have orders from my lord;
      Tomorrow there'll be a feast on board.

THE THREE. We've had a poor reception here;
      A feast's an excellent idea. [*Exeunt.*]

MEPHISTOPHELES [*ad spectatores*].
      The same old story! No doubt you
      Have heard of Naboth's vineyard too. (*I Kgs.* 21)

19 · DEEP NIGHT

LYNCEUS THE WATCHMAN [*on the castle tower, singing*].
      A watchman by calling,
      Far-sighted by birth,
      From this tower, my dwelling,   11290
      I gaze at the earth:

      At the earth near and far,
      At the world far and near,
      At the moon and the stars,
      At the woods and the deer.

      A beauty eternal
      In all things I see,
      And the world and myself
      Are both pleasing to me.

      Oh blest are these eyes,   11300
      All they've seen and can tell:

Let it be as it may—
They have loved it so well!

[*A pause.*]

But I keep my watch so high,
Alas, not only for delight!
What dread terror of the night
Spreads its threat across the sky?
Fiery sparks are scattering, spraying
Through the twin-dark linden-trees:
Higher still the flames are playing,   11310
Fanned to heat by their own breeze!
Now the hut's ablaze all through,
That was moist and mossy green;
Too late now for rescue—who
Can bring help to such a scene?
Smoke will choke the good old couple,
At their hearth so carefully
Kept and tended, poor old people,
What a dreadful tragedy!
Flames lick up, black mossy beams   11320
Now are turned to burning red:
How grim this wild inferno seems!
Can they escape it? Have they fled?
Tongues of fearful lightning rise
Through those leaves and branches tall;
Dried-up boughs burn flickerwise;
Charred and breaking, soon they fall.
Cursèd eyes, why must I see?
Take your gift away from me!—
By their downward-crashing weight   11330
Now the little chapel's crushed;
Snaking pointed flames have rushed
Up to crown the tree-tops' fate.
Hollow trunks in fiery showing
To their very roots are glowing.

[*A long pause; singing.*]

Something lovely to behold
Has vanished like an old tale told.

FAUST [*on the balcony, looking towards the sand-dunes*].

> From overhead, what song of woe?
> Its words and music came too slow.
> My watchman wails: and inwardly   11340
> The impatient deed now vexes me.
> What if the linden-trees are gone,
> Their trunks half-charred, a direful sight—
> I'll quickly build a watch-tower on
> That place, and scan the infinite!
> I see the new house over there,
> That soon will shelter that old pair;
> They'll praise my generous patronage
> And pass a peaceable old age.

MEPHISTOPHELES and THE THREE [*from below*].

> We're back, sir, with due promptitude;   11350
> Regrettably, they misconstrued
> Our meaning, and some force was needed.
> We knocked and banged, but were not heeded.
> We rattled on, and banged some more,
> Till there it lay, the rotten door.
> We threatened them and made a din:
> They would not budge, or ask us in,
> And as is common in such cases
> They just sat on with stolid faces.
> On your behalf, our zeal not lacking,   11360
> We grabbed them then and sent them packing.
> They didn't linger long—the pair
> Dropped dead of terror then and there.
> A stranger, lurking with them, drew
> His sword and was soon dealt with too.
> The fight was brief and violent;
> Some coals were scattered, and up went
> Some straw; the merry blazing fire
> Is now a triple funeral pyre.

FAUST.   And this you claim to have done for me?   11370

> I said exchange, not robbery!
> Deaf savages! I curse this deed;
> Now share my curse, your folly's meed!

THE OTHERS, IN CHORUS. The moral's plain, hear it
> who can:
>> Never resist the powerful man.
>> Don't put up a bold fight, or you
>> Risk house and home, and your life too. [*Exeunt.*]

FAUST [*on the balcony*].
>> The stars have hid their gleam and glow,
>> The fire sinks and glimmers low;
>> A breeze still fans its embers free   11380
>> And blows the reek across to me.
>> A rash command, too soon obeyed!—
>> What comes now, like a hovering shade?

20 · MIDNIGHT*

[*Enter* FOUR GREY WOMEN.]

THE FIRST. My name is Want.

THE SECOND.   My name is Debt.

THE THIRD. My name is Care.

THE FOURTH.   My name is Need.

THREE OF THEM. The door will not open, we'll never
> get in.
> This is a rich man's house, there's no way in.

WANT. I am a shadow there.

DEBT.   I am as nothing there.

NEED. They pay no heed to me, for they need nothing
> there.

CARE.   You are locked out, sisters, you cannot stay.   11390
> But through his keyhole Care finds a way.

[CARE *vanishes.*]

WANT. Come then, my grey sisters, for you must begone.

DEBT. I'll follow you closely, sister, lead on!

NEED.   Need follows you, sister, as close as a breath.

ALL THREE. The dark clouds are drifting, the stars
      disappearing:
   From far off, from far off, another is nearing!
   Our brother is coming; he comes— brother Death.

                    [*Exeunt.*]

FAUST [*in the palace*].
   I saw four come, I only saw three go.
   What their speech meant I do not know.
   They talked of *debt*, and then another word   11400
   That almost rhymed—could it be *death* I heard?
   A dark and hollow sound, a ghostly sigh.
   I have not broken through to freedom yet.
   I must clear magic from my path, forget
   All magic conjurations—for then I
   Would be confronting Nature all alone:
   Man's life worth while, man standing on his own!

   So it was once, before I probed the gloom
   And dared to curse myself, with words of doom
   That cursed the world. The air is swarming now   11410
   With ghosts we would avoid if we knew how.
   How logical and clear the daylight seems
   Till the night weaves us in its web of dreams!
   As we return from dewy fields, dusk falls
   And birds of mischief croak their ominous calls.
   All round us lurks this superstition's snare;
   Some haunting, half-seen thing cries out Beware!
   We shrink back in alarm, and are alone.
   Doors creak, and no one enters.

                 [*In sudden alarm.*]

                               Is someone
   There at the door?

CARE.   You ask, need I reply?   11420

FAUST. And who are you?

CARE.   I am here, here am I.

FAUST. Go away!

CARE.   I am here where I should be.

FAUST [*at first angry, then calmer, to himself*].
    I must take care to use no sorcery.

CARE.   Though no human ear can hear me,
             Yet the echoing heart must fear me;
             In an ever-changed disguise
             All men's lives I tyrannize.
             On the roads and on the sea
             Anxiously they ride with me;
             Never looked for, always there,   11430
             Cursed and flattered. I am Care:
             Have I never crossed your path?

FAUST. I merely raced across the earth,
    Seized by the hair each passing joy,
    Discarded all that did not satisfy;
    What slipped my grasp, I let it go again.
    I have merely desired, achieved, and then
    Desired some other thing. Thus I have stormed
    Through life; at first with pride and violence,
    But now less rashly, with more sober sense.   11440
    I've seen enough of this terrestrial sphere.
    There is no view to the Beyond from here:
    A fool will seek it, peer with mortal eyes
    And dream of human life above the skies!
    Let him stand fast in this world, and look round
    With courage: here so much is to be found!
    Why must he wander into timelessness?
    What his mind grasps, he may possess.
    Thus let him travel all his earthly day:
    Though spirits haunt him, let him walk his way,   11450
    Let both his pain and joy be in his forward stride—
    Each moment leave him still unsatisfied!

CARE.   When a man is in my keeping,
             All his world is dead or sleeping;
             Everlasting dusk descending,
             Sun not moving, dark not ending.
             Though each outward sense be whole,
             Night has nested in his soul;
             Riches stand around him staling,

Unpossessed and unavailing;   11460
Gladness, sadness are mere whim,
Plenty cannot nourish him,
He delays both joy and pain
Till the day has passed again,
And on time-to-come intent
Comes to no accomplishment.

FAUST. Stop! You'll not put that blight on me!
I will not listen to such stuff.
Leave me! Your wretched litany
Can drive wise men to madness soon enough.   11470

CARE.   Shall he come or shall he go?
He can't choose, he does not know.
In the middle of the road,
See, he staggers, tremble-toed!
Wanders deeper in the maze,
Sees the whole world crookedways,
Burdening himself and others;
Still he breathes, yet chokes and smothers—
Not quite choked, yet life-bereft,
Stubborn, though with hope still left.   11480
Such a ceaseless downward course,
Bitter *may not, must* by force,
Now released, now re-pursued,
Restless sleep and tasteless food,
Binds him in a static state,
Makes him hell's initiate.

FAUST. Horrible phantoms! Thus you still conspire
Again against mankind and yet again;
Even indifferent days you turn into a dire
Chaotic nexus of entangling pain.   11490
Demons, I know, are hard to exorcize,
The spirit-bond is loath to separate:
But though the creeping power of Care be great,
This power I will never recognize!

CARE.   Suffer it then; for as I go
I leave a curse where I have passed.

Men live their lives in blindness: so
Shall even Faust be blinded at the last!

[*She breathes on him. Exit.*]

FAUST [*blinded*].
Night seems to close upon me deeper still,
But in my inmost soul a bright light shines.   11500
I hasten to complete my great designs:
My words alone can work my mastering will.
Rise from your sleep, my servants, every man!
Give visible success to my bold plan!
Set to work now with shovel and with spade:
I have marked it all out, let it be made!
With a well-ordered project and with hard
Toil we shall win supreme reward;
Until the edifice of this achievement stands,
One mind shall move a thousand hands.   11510

21 · THE GREAT FORECOURT OF THE PALACE

[*Torches.* MEPHISTOPHELES *as overseer leading a gang
of* LEMURS.*]

MEPHISTOPHELES. Come now, my lemur-goblins,
                patched-
        Up semi-skeletons,
        With mouldering sinews still attached
        To move your rattling bones!

LEMURS [*in chorus*].
        We came at once, sir, when you called;
        Is there—we did half hear of it—
        A plot of land here to be sold,
        And shall we get our share of it?

        Here are the chains, here are the posts
        To measure out the site.   11520
        Why did you summon us poor ghosts?
        We can't remember quite.

MEPHISTOPHELES. There's no need for these mysteries;
    Just use yourselves as measuring-rods!
    The tallest of you can lie down lengthwise,
    The rest stand round and cut away the sods.
    A rectangle of earth dug deep,
    A good old-fashioned place to sleep!
    From palace to this narrow house descending—
    That always was the stupid story's ending.   11530

LEMURS [*digging with mocking gestures*].
        In youth when I did love, did love*
        Methought 'twas very sweet,
        And night and day to music gay
        I danced with nimble feet.

        But Age with his crutch and cunning clutch
        Has come to trip me now.
        By a grave I stumbled, and in I tumbled;
        They'd left it open somehow.

FAUST [*comes out of the palace, groping at the doorpost*].
    The clash of spades: how it delights my heart!
    These are my many workmen; here they toil,   11540
    The alienated earth to reconcile,
    To keep the ocean and the land apart,
    To rule the unruly waves once more.

MEPHISTOPHELES [*aside*].
    And yet it's us you're working for
    With all your foolish dams and dikes;
    Neptune, the water-devil, likes
    To think of the great feast there'll be
    When they collapse. Do what you will, my friend,
    You all are doomed! They are in league with me,
    The elements, and shall destroy you in the end.*   11550

FAUST.   Overseer!

MEPHISTOPHELES. Sir!

FAUST.   I need more workers; bring
    Them to me by the hundred! Use persuasion,
    Cajole or bully them, try everything,
    Inducements, money, force! This excavation

Must go ahead; the ditch I've now begun—
I must know daily how much has been done.

MEPHISTOPHELES [*sotto voce*].
The digging has gone well today;
No ditch or dike, but dust to dust, they say.*

FAUST. A swamp surrounds the mountains' base;*
It poisons all I have achieved till now.   11560
I'll drain it too; that rotten place
Shall be my last great project. I see how
To give those millions a new living-space:
They'll not be safe, but active, free at least.
I see green fields, so fertile: man and beast
At once shall settle that new pleasant earth,
Bastioned by great embankments that will rise
About them, by bold labour brought to birth.
Here there shall be an inland paradise:
Outside, the sea, as high as it can reach,   11570
May rage and gnaw; and yet a common will,
Should it intrude, will act to close the breach.
Yes! to this vision I am wedded still,
And this as wisdom's final word I teach:
Only that man earns freedom, merits life,
Who must reconquer both in constant daily strife.
In such a place, by danger still surrounded,
Youth, manhood, age, their brave new world have
    founded.
I long to see that multitude, and stand
With a free people on free land!   11580
Then to the moment I might say:
Beautiful moment, do not pass away!
Till many ages shall have passed
This record of my earthly life shall last.
And in anticipation of such bliss
What moment could give me greater joy than this?

    [FAUST *sinks back, the* LEMURS *seize him and lay him
    on the ground.*]

MEPHISTOPHELES. Poor fool! Unpleasured and unsatisfied,
Still whoring after changeful fantasies,

This last, poor, empty moment he would seize,
Content with nothing else beside.   11590
How he resisted me! But in the end
Time wins; so here you lie, my senile friend.
The clock has stopped—

CHORUS.   Has stopped! Like midnight it is
     stilled.
The clock-hands fall.

MEPHISTOPHELES.   They fall. All is fulfilled.*

CHORUS. All's over now.

MEPHISTOPHELES.   Over! A stupid word!
Why 'over'? What can be
'Over' is just not there; it's all the same to me!
Why bother to go on creating?
Making, then endlessly annihilating!
'Over and past!' What's that supposed to mean?   11600
It's no more than if it had never been,
Yet it goes bumbling round as if it were.
The Eternal Void is what I'd much prefer.

22 · BURIAL RITES

A LEMUR [*solo*].
              Why is the house so poorly made,
              And hempen the shrouding-sheet?

LEMURS [*in chorus*].
              'Twas built with pickaxe and with spade,
              And for such a guest 'tis meet.

A LEMUR [*solo*].
              Who furnished it so ill, who took
              The table and chairs away?

LEMURS [*in chorus*].
              Not yours to own, 'twas all on loan,   11610
              The creditors came today.

MEPHISTOPHELES. The body's down, the spirit I'll soon fix,
     I'll show him his own blood-scribed document*—
     Yet souls come hard these days, their friends invent

Loopholes, and try to play the Devil tricks.
Our older methods gave offence,
Our new ones don't commend us greatly;
I used to do it all myself, but lately
I've had to send for adjutants.

Things are no longer what they were!   11620
Traditional custom, the old rules inspire
No confidence now; there's nothing one can trust.
In former times a man would breathe his last,
Out popped the soul as quick as any mouse,
And snap! my waiting claws would close on it.
But nowadays it hesitates to quit
The gloomy corpse, its dark disgusting house;
Till in the end the elements at strife
Drive out the wretched scrap of life.
I rack my brains about it night and day: 11630
When, how, and *where*'s the question—who can say?
Old Death has lost his old decisive style;
Even the *whether*'s doubtful a long while.
Often I've watched stiff limbs with lustful eyes—
Sham-dead again! They twitch and squirm and rise.

> [*He makes fantastic summoning gestures, like a flank-man
> drilling troops.*]

Come on then, at the double now, my friends,
Straight-horns and crooked-horns! Good solid fiends
Of the old school. And bring the jaws of hell,
Please, gentlemen, along with you as well!
Hell has a multiplicity of jaws, it's true,   11640
And swallows up by rank and by degree;
Although in future those rules too
Will be relaxed, presumably.

> [*The frightful jaws of hell open up on the left.*]

The fangs gape; through the arching orifice
Hell's maw spews up a fiery ocean,
And in the seething murk of the abyss
I see the Infernal City's ceaseless conflagration.
The red surf surges to the teeth: 'At last',

Think damned souls, swimming up, 'here's rescue!' But
   the vast
Hyena-crunch reclaims them; with dismay   11650
They must pursue their incandescent way.
Amusing those odd corners look as well;
What horrors a small area can contain!
It's supposed to scare sinners; they remain,
However, total sceptics about hell.

[*To the fat devils with short straight horns.*]

Now, you pot-bellied red-faced rascals, you!
How fat you are! Hot brimstone in your guts,
No doubt; you stiff-necked lumps, you no-necked clots!
Watch here for a sudden phosphorescent glow:
It's called the soul, 'Psyche'—pull off its wings!   11660
Without them, souls are nasty worm-like things.
I'll stamp it with my seal; off with it then
Into the fire-storm!

                You, the gentlemen
Resembling bladders, guard his lower parts!
Don't let our prey squeeze out there—we don't know
Exactly, but it might live where he farts;
Perhaps its whimsy takes it to do so—
Or in the navel maybe; that's a place
It likes. Watch that, or you'll be in disgrace!

[*To the thin devils with long crooked horns.*]

You, flanking giants, you tall gangling fools,   11670
Snatch at the air—keep practising, and keep
Your arms straight! Spread your claws, they're good
   sharp tools;
Don't let our fluttering bird give you the slip!
It must be tired of its old lodging now;
And genius, too—that must soar up somehow.

[*A flash of glory from above right.*]

THE HEAVENLY HOST. Follow, bright envoys,
               Companions of heaven,
               Unhurriedly soaring:
               Let sin be forgiven,

          Earth-creatures restoring,   11680
          All natures partaking;
          Let each feel the trace
          As you pause at the place
          Of your hovering grace!

MEPHISTOPHELES. Now what cacophony is this, what
    jangling
Noise from above, unwelcome as that light?
A boyish-girlish callow twing-a-twangling,
Fit for some pious nun or acolyte!
In vain we hatched that supersubtle plot
To lay the human population waste;   11690
Our most outrageous trick, just fancy what?
Exactly suits their dim religious taste.
The hypcrites, the riff-raff! Here they are!
That's how they've cheated us of many a prize;
They fight with our own weapons in this war—
They're devils too, but in disguise.
You there! Hold firm, on your eternal shame!
Stand round the grave, and guard it like hell's flame!

CHORUS OF ANGELS [*scattering roses*].
          Roses resplendent,
          Roses balm-redolent,   11700
          Floating and hovering,
          Stem-wing and petal-wing,
          Rosebuds reopening,
          Blossom recovering,
          Secretly succouring:
          Hasten to him and bring
          Crimson and green of spring,
          Make him a paradise
          Here where he lies!

MEPHISTOPHELES [*to the demons*].
What's all this flinching, twitching? Did they teach   11710
You that in hell? Stand fast, and let them throw
Bouquets about! To battle-stations, each
Ugly man-jack of you! They think they'll snow
Hot fiends up under flower-power! Blow,

And they'll all wither, they'll all fade and bleach!
Snuff them out, snuffle-snouts!—Enough, enough!
The whole flight's blighted with your stinking puff!
Just take it easy! Shut your mouths and noses!
Damn you, you're blowing far too hard!
Can't you learn moderation? Look, those roses,   11720
They're not just withering, they're all black and charred—
They're burning! Here they come, the poisoned flames.
Stand and resist, in the three devils' names!—
They're losing heart, they might as well retire.
My devils smell a new, insinuating fire!

ANGELS [in chorus].

        Flowers of blessedness,
        Flames with your dancing light,
        Spreaders of happiness,
        Powers of love that bless,
        Givers of heart's delight: 11730
        True words that shine and last,
        Brightness in ether lost,
        For the eternal host
        World without night!

MEPHISTOPHELES. Damn you, my satan-wimps! Now,
    by my wrath,
They're standing on their heads; oh, shame on you!
The louts are turning cartwheels—the whole crew
Goes plunging arsewise back into perdition.
May you enjoy your well-deserved hot bath!
But I'll not budge from my position.   11740

    [Striking out at the roses as they float down.]

Begone, will-o'-the-wisps! You're bright lights, yes,
But once I catch you, you're a sticky mess.
Ugh! Get away from me, you fluttering pack!—
They cling like pitch and sulphur to my back.

ANGELS [in chorus].

        What has no part in you
        You have no need of it,
        What frets the heart in you
        Do not take heed of it.

       If the defences fail
       Our strength must then prevail.   11750
       Love: for by love alone
       Heaven is won.

MEPHISTOPHELES. My head's on fire, my heart and guts
    as well:*
  This is worse than the flames of hell!
  Some superdiabolic element
  Is piercing me. Is this the pain that's meant,
  Why unrequited lovers wail Alas!
  And crane their necks to see their mistress pass?

  Even I! What twists my head towards them somehow?
  I was their mortal enemy till now: 11760
  Even the sight of them was more than I could bear.
  Am I possessed, then, by some alien force?
  I like the look of these nice boys—of course
  I do! What's this? Why can't I curse and swear?
  I'd like to know who's going to be
  The fool in future, if they make a fool of me!
  Young ruffians, how I hate them all! Yet I confess
  They're damned attractive none the less!—

  My dears, would I be wrong to guess you are
  By any chance cousins of Lucifer?   11770
  You're pretty! I must give you all a kiss!
  I think you'll suit me at a time like this.
  I feel so comfy and so natural,
  As if I'd seen you many times before;
  So curiously cat-randy, and the more
  I contemplate you, the more beautiful
  You get. Come closer, please! Just one sweet glance!

THE ANGELS. We are coming; why do you shrink as we
    advance?
  As we draw near, stand your ground if you can!

    [THE ANGELS *circle round, filling the entire stage.*]

MEPHISTOPHELES [*pushed forward to the proscenium*].
  You give us a bad name as sprites of hell,   11780
  And yet the witchcraft's yours: your goblin-spell

Seduces woman and seduces man!
Damn this for an adventure! Can this be
The element of love, can it be real?
I burn all over, I can scarcely feel
My burnt hump where those flowers got at me.
You dither about so, my dears: come down!
Those lovely limbs should move more worldly-wise.
It's true it suits you well, that serious frown;
But to see you smile would be a sweet surprise!   11790
Just once, please! It would give me such delight!
Just smile the little smile that lovers use—
A modulation of the mouth, that's right!
You tall boy there, now you I'd not refuse;
But why this unbecoming priestly air?
Give me a lustful look instead, ah yes!
And please, be all a little nakeder!
Those flowing robes are decent to excess.
They turn—the rear view is too tantalizing!
Delicious monkeys! ah, how appetizing!   11800

CHORUS OF ANGELS. Turn, burning flames of love,
                        Turn into clarity!
                        So to the self-condemned
                        Truth shall bring liberty;
                        Freed from the evil spell
                        They shall win through as well
                        Into the blessed throng
                        Where all belong.

MEPHISTOPHELES [*pulling himself together*].
What's wrong with me? I'm out in boils all over,
Like Job! A self-repugnant spectacle;   11810
And yet a triumph, when one sees the whole
Depths of oneself, and trusts them to recover.
My noble devil-parts are saved alive!
Those love-charms, as mere eczema they thrive;
The whole damned bonfire's now a burnt-out case,
And once again I curse the whole angelic race!

CHORUS OF ANGELS. Blaze, holy fire! These
                        Whom you surround here

Sweet life have found here
For all to share.   11820
With single voice now
Cry and rejoice now!
The spirit breathes
In a purified air.

[They soar upwards, carrying FAUST'S *immortal part.]*

MEPHISTOPHELES *[looking round].*

But what is this? They've gone! Where can they be?
You halflings, I've been caught off duty!
You've hovered off to heaven with my booty!
That's why they snuffled round this grave; I see!
I've lost my greatest, my most precious prize.
That lofty soul who pledged himself to me—   11830
Filched cunningly before my very eyes!
Now who shall I complain to? Who
Will give me justice, give me back what's mine?
Poor fool, at your age you've been tricked. A fine
Mess you are in, and well deserve it too!
I've misbehaved, there's no one else to blame,
I'm in disgrace. The whole investment lost;
All that good work for nothing! Common lust,
Absurd infatuation puts to shame
The hard-boiled Devil. And if even my   11840
Wisdom's no match for such tomfoolery—
Then to this strange love-madness I extend
My compliments, since it could catch me in the end!

23 · MOUNTAIN GORGES*

*[A wild rocky region in the forest. Holy anchorites have
settled at various heights among the clefts of the mountain
side.]*

CHORUS and ECHO. Woods, hitherwavering,
                  Rocks, cliffs, downburdening,
                  Roots close to roots they cling,
                  Trunk to trunk neighbouring.

The rushing waters leap,
The sheltering caves are deep.
Lions prowl round us, dumb,   11850
Gentle and shy to come
Into this holy place,
Sacred to love and grace.

PATER ECSTATICUS [*hovering up and down*].
    Joy of immortal fire
    Lovebond of hot desire,
    Heart's seething agony,
    Godspring of ecstasy!
    Arrows, pierce through me now,
    Spearpoints, subdue me now,
    Clubs, strike and break me now;
    Lightnings, unmake me now!   11860
    All that is vain and void
    Let it be all destroyed:
    Shine, star, for evermore,
    Love's everlasting core!

PATER PROFUNDUS [*in a lower region*].
The rocky precipice below
Weighs on a chasm still more deep;
A thousand streamlets shine and flow
Down to the foaming flood's dread leap;
By its own energy ascending   11870
The tree thrusts skywards straight and tall:
All these show forth the love unending
That shapes all things and shields them all.

How wild a roar is this, as if
The forest shook, the abyss were stirred!
Yet the great torrent from the cliff
Pours down like love, its sound half-heard,
To the valley's thirst; and by and by
Lightning has struck, its flame makes clean
The poisoned air, the sultry sky   11880
Where swollen thunder-clouds have been;

These are love's messengers! They tell
Of power all-making, all-surrounding.

Oh let it burn in me as well!
Bonds of dull sense, my mind confounding,
Torment and chill me: oh release
Me from these chains that bind so tight!
Oh God, between my thoughts make peace
And to my needy heart give light!

PATER SERAPHICUS [*in the middle region*].
Something hovers through the swaying   11890
Pine-trees' tresses: who can tell
What it is? A cloud of daying!
In it youthful spirits dwell.

CHORUS OF BLESSED BOYS.
Father, say, what is this place?
Kind friend, is it you who call?
Here we feel such happiness:
Life is gentle to us all.

PATER SERAPHICUS. Mortal children, midnight-born,
Minds half open, sense half dead,
From your parents' arms soon torn,   11900
To the angels given instead.
You have felt a lover near you:
Come to him! But, happy few,
Earth's rough journey was to spare you
And to leave no mark on you.
Enter into me, come down now
Into my earth-worldly eyes:
You can use them as your own now.
Look at this strange paradise!

[*He takes them into himself.*]

These are trees, and those are rocks;   11910
There a waterfall that gushes
Wildly from the height—it strikes
Its steep path, and down it rushes.

THE BLESSED BOYS [*from inside him*].
It is sad and gloomy here
Though these sights are great to see:
We are stirred with dread and fear.
Noble father, set us free!

PATER SERAPHICUS. Rise to higher spheres and grow
    Imperceptibly, as stronger
    Still God's presence there will glow,   11920
    Pure, eternal, dimmed no longer;
    For the spirits' nurture reigning
    In that free ethereal zone
    And their blessed hope sustaining,
    Is eternal Love made known.

CHORUS OF BLESSED BOYS [*circling round the highest*
  summits].
     Dance ring-a-ringing,
     All of us hand in hand
     Joyfully singing,
     Dance, sacred brother-band!
     Heed that wise teaching!   11930
     Him you revere,
     Pure hearts upreaching
     Shall see him here.

ANGELS [*hovering in the upper atmosphere, carrying* FAUST's
  immortal part].
    This noble spirit saved alive
    Has foiled the Devil's will!
    He who strives on and lives to strive
    Can earn redemption still.
    And now that love itself looks down
    To favour him with grace,
    The blessed host with songs may crown   11940
    His welcome to this place.

THE YOUNGER ANGELS.
    Holy penitents who gave
    Roses of their love to scatter,
    Helped us so in our great matter,
    As we fought this soul to save,
    Helped us gain this noble prize.
    Devils fled before our eyes,
    Hell's dark spirits shrank back daunted
    As we smote them with unwonted
    Heaven-fire of love's hot rain;   11950

Even old Satan felt that pain
Penetrate his master-mind.
We won! Rejoice, all angelkind!

THE MATURER ANGELS. An earthbound, immature
              And fragmentary,
              Fireproof yet still impure
              Burden we carry.
              When spirit-energy
              Captures the physical
              Elements powerfully,   11960
              No force angelical
              Can loose the subtle bond
              That has allied them:
              Only the Love beyond
              Time can divide them.

THE YOUNGER ANGELS. Spirits in nebulous
              Motion advancing
              Round this vertiginous
              Rock-peak are dancing.
              Now the cloud brightens: see,   11970
              A happy company
              Circling together, new-
              Freed from earth's burden—they
              Are blessed children, who
              In the spring's beauty here,
              In this new higher sphere
              Rejoice and play.
              Let him first be with these:
              To joy's, to truth's increase
              That is his way.   11980

THE BLESSED BOYS. Gladly we welcome this
              Chrysalid-aspirant:
              Ours now his heaven-bent
              New metamorphosis.
              Thus from his close cocoon
              We set him free:
              With angel-life so soon
              How fair is he!

DOCTOR MARIANUS [*in the highest and purest cell*].

How wide a view up here,
The soul to lift!   11990
What women now draw near?
Upwards they drift,
And in their midst, with stars
Crowning her splendour,
I see heaven's Lady pass—
Those lights attend her.

[*In ecstasy.*]

Queen and ruler of the world!
In this deep blue sky,
In thy tent of heaven unfurled,
Show me thy mystery!   12000
I must love thee as a man,
And my heart's emotion
Gives what sacred love I can:
Spurn not my devotion!

We who fiercely fight for thee,
Conquerors at thy bidding,
Gentle lovers we can be
If thou hear our pleading.
Purest Virgin, noblest Mother,
Queen of our election,   12010
Goddess yielding to none other
In thy great perfection!

Cloudlets surround her
Light as the elements:
These are her penitents,
Sorrowing and tender.
Drinking the ether,
Needful of mercy,
Suppliants besiege her.

Though inviolate, exempted   12020
In thy peerless glory,
Thou mayst listen to their story
Whom sweet sin has tempted.

They were weak, in thee they trust;
Who shall save them now?
Who can break the chains of lust?
Who will help but thou?
Easily the foot can slip,
Slide to swift destruction,
Ardent eye and flattering lip   12030
Breathe such strong seduction.

[*The* MATER GLORIOSA* *hovers into view.*]

CHORUS OF PENITENT WOMEN.*
              In the transcendent
              High regions soaring,
              Lady resplendent,
              See us adoring,
              Hear us imploring!

MAGNA PECCATRIX (*Luke* 7:36).
              By the love that on thy glorious
              Son's feet shed a balm so tearful,
              While the Pharisee's censorious
              Thoughts despised that homage fearful;   12040
              By the fragrance poured so gladly
              From the jar of alabaster,
              By my hair that softly, sadly
              Dried thy sacred limbs, oh Master—

MULIER SAMARITANA (*John* 4)
              By that well where once they tarried,
              Flocks by Abraham's shepherds tended,
              By the cooling draught I carried
              Which his dear parched lips befriended;
              By that pure rich fountain flowing
              Now through all the world, unceasing,   12050
              Ever in abundance growing,
              In its brightness still increasing—

MARIA AEGYPTIACA (*Acta Sanctorum*).
              By the holy place where they
              Laid to rest our Saviour mortal,
              By the arm that barred my way

As I dared approach its portal;
By my forty years awaiting
Pardon in a desert land,
By my last and blessed greeting
Written on the burning sand—   12060

ALL THREE. Such great sinners find a place
Near thee, by thy condescension,
And their penitent intention
Grows into eternal grace:
This good soul, who only once
Went astray and scarcely knew it,
Also seeks thy mercy—show it
As befits her innocence!

UNA POENITENTIUM *once known as Gretchen* [*pressing
     close*].

Virgin and Mother, thou
Lady beyond compare, oh thou   12070
Who art full of glory, bow
Thy face in mercy to my great joy now!
He whom I loved—oh see,
He is undarkened, he
Comes back to me!

BLESSED BOYS [*circling nearer*].

How soon with limbs of might
He has outsoared us!
We nurtured him aright,
He will reward us.
Out of life's music all   12080
Too soon death plucked us,
But he has learnt it all;
He will instruct us.

THE PENITENT *once known as Gretchen*.

Ringed by that noble spirit-chorus,
This neophyte of life unknown,
Scarcely awake, and strange before us,
Already makes our form his own.
See, how all earthly bonds discarding
He casts his outworn husk aside,

And an ethereal raiment parting   12090
His youth steps out refortified!
O Lady, grant me now to teach him!
He is dazzled still by the new day.

MATER GLORIOSA. Come! into higher spheres
                        outreach him!
                He must sense you to find the way.

DOCTOR MARIANUS [*prostrated in adoration*].
                Gaze aloft—the saving eyes
                See you all, such tender
                Penitents; look up and render
                Thanks, to blest renewal rise!
                May each nobler spirit never   12100
                Fail to serve thee; Virgin, Mother,
                Queen, oh keep us in thy favour,
                Goddess, kind for ever!

CHORUS MYSTICUS.
                All that must disappear
                Is but a parable;
                What lay beyond us, here
                All is made visible;
                Here deeds have understood
                Words they were darkened by;
                Eternal Womanhood   12110
                Draws us on high.

SELECTED PARALIPOMENA*

*(a) Unpublished note (1797) for an overall scheme of Parts One and Two
    (paralipomenon BA 5*)*

Ideal striving to achieve interaction and empathy with the whole of
Nature.

Apparition of the Spirit as the genius of the world and of deeds.

Conflict between form and the formless.

Formless content preferred to empty form.

Content brings its form with it, there is never form without content.

These contradictions to be made sharper instead of reconciling them.

Clear cold scholarly striving: Wagner.

Naïve warm scholarly striving: the Student.

[*deleted*: Life Activity Essence]

Personal enjoyment of life viewed [?sought] from without   Part
   I   In naïvety passion.

Enjoyment of activity outwards   Part II   Enjoyment with con-
   sciousness, beauty.

Enjoyment of creativity from within. Epilogue in Chaos on the way
   to Hell.

*(b) Unpublished synopsis (1816) of an early conception of Acts I, III, and IV
    (paralipomenon BA 70*)*

At the beginning of the Second Part Faust is discovered asleep. He
is surrounded by choruses of spirits, who with visible symbols and
agreeable singing conjure up for him the pleasures of worldly
honour, fame, power, and sovereignty. They disguise their in fact
ironical propositions in flattering words and melodies. He wakes, all
his previous dependence on sensuality and passion have disappeared.
His spirit purified and refreshed, striving towards supreme heights.

Mephistopheles enters and gives him a light-hearted and stimulat-
ing account of the Imperial Diet at Augsburg which has been
convened by the Emperor Maximilian; he makes believe it is all
taking place in the square outside the window, although Faust can
see nothing. Finally Mephistopheles pretends to see the Emperor in

a window of the town hall, talking to a prince. He assures Faust that the Emperor has been enquiring after him, asking where he lives and whether he might perhaps be presented at court. Faust lets himself be persuaded, and the magic cloak expedites their journey. In Augsburg they land before a solitary hall, and Mephistopheles goes to explore. Faust in the meantime reverts to his earlier abstruse ruminations and lofty demands upon himself, and when his companion returns, he makes the strange stipulation that Mephistopheles must not enter the hall but stay outside the door; and moreover, that in the Emperor's presence there is to be no trickery or juggling with appearances. Mephistopheles complies. We find ourselves in a banqueting room, where the Emperor, who has just risen from table, steps to the window with one of the princes and confesses that he would like to have Faust's magic cloak, which would enable him to go hunting in Tyrol and be back next day to attend the session. Faust is announced and received graciously. The Emperor's questions are all concerned with earthly obstacles and how they can be overcome by magic. Faust's answers hint at loftier goals and loftier means. The Emperor does not understand him, still less the courtier. The conversation becomes confused, falters, and Faust in embarrassment looks round for Mephistopheles, who immediately steps up behind him and answers in his name. This enlivens the dialogue, several other people join in, everyone is pleased with the strange guest. The Emperor demands apparitions; Faust and Mephistopheles consent. Faust absents himself to make the necessary preparations. At that moment Mephistopheles assumes Faust's shape, to entertain the older and younger ladies, who end by thinking him a most remarkable fellow, since he can cure a wart on one's hand with a light touch, or a corn on one's foot by treading on it a little more roughly with his disguised cloven hoof; and one blonde maiden even permits him to dab at her face with his long skinny fingers, assured by her looking-glass that this is making her freckles disappear one after another. Evening falls, and a magic theatre rises from the ground of its own accord. The figure of Helen appears. The comments of the ladies on this beauty of beauties animate the otherwise awesome spectacle. Paris enters, and is given the same treatment by the men as his partner received from the women. The disguised Faust agrees with both parties, and a very entertaining scene develops.

There is some dispute about what the third apparition should be, and the already conjured spirits become restless; several important phantoms appear together. Bizarre complications ensue, and finally the theatre and the spirits disappear simultaneously. The real Faust lies in the background in a swoon, with three lamps shining on him; Mephistopheles takes to his heels, the onlookers begin to suspect that there are two of them, and there is a general feeling that things are not as they should be.

When Mephistopheles meets Faust again he finds him in a most passionate condition. He has fallen in love with Helen, and now orders his magical factotum to summon her up and deliver her into his arms. There are difficulties about this. Helen belongs to the underworld, and although magic arts can draw her out of it, they cannot hold her. Faust insists; Mephistopheles undertakes the task. Infinite longing on Faust's part for the supreme beauty he has now recognized. An old castle is chosen as the residence of the latter-day Paris; its owner has gone to the wars in Palestine, but its keeper is a magician. Helen appears: her bodily form has been restored to her by a magic ring. She believes she has come from Troy and is just arriving in Sparta. She finds everything lonesome and longs for company, especially male company which all her life she could never do without. Faust appears as a German knight, a likeness most strangely contrasting with the heroine from antiquity. She finds him odious; but since he has a flattering tongue, she gets used to him little by little, and he becomes the successor of so many heroes and demigods. The offspring of this union is a son, who is no sooner born than he dances, sings and hews the air like a fencer. It must be mentioned that the castle is surrounded by a magic circle, and these half-real beings can survive only if they remain within this enclosure. The rapidly growing boy is the joy of his mother's heart. He may do whatever he pleases, being only forbidden to cross a certain stream. But one festive day he hears music from the other side and sees the country people and the soldiers dancing. He crosses the boundary-mark and mixes with them, becomes involved in a brawl, wounds a number of people, but is finally killed with a consecrated sword. The castle magician retrieves his body. His mother is inconsolable, and as she wrings her hands in despair she rubs the ring off her finger and falls into Faust's arms, but he embraces only her empty robe. Both mother and son have vanished. Mephistopheles, who has in the meantime assumed the shape of an aged housekeeper-woman and witnessed all these events, tries to console his friend and tempt him to a desire for riches. The lord of the castle has perished in Palestine, monks try to seize the property, their benedictions dissolve the magic circle. Mephistopheles advises Faust to resort to physical force, and provides him with three helpers and servers called Buster, Bagger and Hugger. Faust now judges himself to be sufficiently equipped and dismisses Mephistopheles and the castellan; he makes war on the monks, avenges his son's death and wins great possessions. In the course of all this he grows old, and how the story continues will be seen when at a future date we assemble the fragments, or rather the separately composed passages of this Second Part, and thereby preserve some material that will be of interest to our readers.

(c) Unpublished synopsis (1826) of an early conception of Act II (from paralipomenon BA 73*)

(. . .)The old legend tells us (and the scene is duly included in the puppet play) that Faust in his lordly arrogance requires Mephistopheles to procure for him the beautiful Helen of Greece, and that Mephistopheles after some demur consents to do so. In our own version we felt in duty bound not to omit so significant a motif; it is hoped that the following pages may serve for the time being as an account of how we have sought to discharge this obligation, and what we have judged to be a fitting introduction to the theme.

During a great feast at the German Emperor's court, Faust and Mephistopheles are commanded to conjure up spirits; unwillingly, but having no choice, they evoke the required apparitions of Helen and Paris. Paris enters, and the ladies are in ecstasies; the men vainly seek to cool their enthusiasm by criticizing him on this point and that. Helen enters, and the men are beside themselves; the women examine her closely, and contrive to cast a derogatory light on this splendid figure by mocking the heroic size of her feet and her ivory complexion which is in all probability painted on, but above all by casting dubious aspersions which are indeed only too well founded in her true history. Paris stoops to embrace her, and Faust, carried away by such sublime beauty, overboldly tries to thrust him aside;

a thunderclap fells him, the apparitions vanish, and the feast ends in tumult.

Faust lies in a long and heavy trance-like sleep, during which his dreams are visibly and circumstantially enacted before the eyes of the audience; but he is recalled to life, steps forward in an exalted state, entirely absorbed by a lofty vision, and vehemently demands from Mephistopheles the possession of Helen. Mephistopheles, not liking to admit that he has no competence in the classical Hades and is not even a welcome visitor there, resorts to his former well-tried method of driving his employer hither and thither in all directions. This leads to all manner of remarkable developments, and in the end, to allay his master's impatience, Mephistopheles persuades him to pay a visit—*en passant* as it were and *en route* to his destination—to Professor Doctor Wagner (for such is now the latter's academic status). They find him in his laboratory, crowing triumphantly over the success he has just had in bringing a chemical mannikin into existence.

This creature now immediately shatters his luminous glass retort, and emerges from it as an active, well-formed little midget. The recipe for his progeniture is hinted at in mystical terms; he gives demonstrations of his talents, and in particular it becomes clear that his head contains a general historical universal calendar, for he can at any given moment state what has happened in human affairs whenever, since the creation of Adam, there has been the same configuration of the sun, moon, earth and planets. And sure enough, he at once shows off this talent by announcing that the present night exactly coincides with that in which preparations were made for the battle of Pharsalus and on which neither Caesar nor Pompey slept a wink. On this point he falls into an argument with Mephistopheles, who on the evidence of the Benedictine fathers will not accept that that great event occurred at this hour, but declares it to have been several days later. In reply it is pointed out to him that the Devil has no business relying on the statements of monks. But since he obstinately insists that he is right, the dispute seems likely to disappear into irresoluble chronological controversy; the chemical mannikin, however, now gives further proof of his profound historical-mythical nature, and draws attention to the simultaneous occurrence of the Classical Walpurgis Night, which since the beginning of the mythical world has always been celebrated in Thessaly, and which in accordance with the basic epochal coherence of world history was indeed the real occasion of the disaster they are discussing. The four of them decide to go there, and Wagner, for all his haste, does not forget to take a clean glass phial with him, hoping that with luck he may be able to collect here and there the elements needed for the making of a little chemical woman. He puts the glass in his left and the chemical mannikin in his right breast pocket, whereupon they entrust themselves to the travelling cloak. A flying commentary from the pocketed mannikin provides them with an unending flood of geographical and historical detail on every place they pass over; and this, together with the lightning speed of their conveyance, quite distracts their minds until at last they set foot on the plain of Thessaly, under the bright but waning moon.

Here on the desolate heath they first encounter Erichtho, who is greedily breathing in the inextinguishable smell of decay that hangs over these fields. She has been joined by Erichthonius, and we are now given etymological proof of the close kinship between these two, of which the ancients knew nothing. Unfortunately, since he is rather lame, she is often obliged to carry him on one arm, and even, when the young prodigy displays a peculiar passion for the chemical mannikin, to take the latter on her other arm too—a matter on which Mephistopheles does not fail to make malicious comment.

Faust has become involved in conversation with a sphinx which is sitting there on its back paws, and they embark on an endless exchange of the most abstruse questions and enigmatic answers. Nearby, in the same posture, sits a watchful griffin of the gold-guarding species, who interrupts them from time to time, though without shedding the least light on anything. A colossal ant, also a gold-hoarder, has joined them, and confuses the discussion still further. But with our minds already at such desperate odds, we must now lose faith in our senses as well. Empusa appears, having put on an ass's head in honour of today's feast, and proceeds to change into further shapes, thereby provoking the other well-defined figures to restless impatience, though not to self-transformation. Sphinxes, griffins, and ants now appear in infinite profusion, developing out of themselves as it were. We see indeed all the monsters of antiquity, swarming and running to and fro: chimeras, goat-stags and half-human hybrids, together with numerous many-headed snakes. Harpies flutter and flit about like bats, circling uncertainly; even the dragon Python appears in the plural, and the Stymphalian birds of prey, with their sharp beaks and webbed feet, come whizzing past one after another as quick as arrows. But suddenly, hovering over them all like a cloud, comes a procession of sirens, singing and making music: they plunge into the Peneus and bathe, plashing and piping, then settle on the trees by the riverside and sing the sweetest of songs. Nereids and Tritons now begin by excusing themselves, since they are prevented by their bodily shape from joining in this feast, notwithstanding the proximity of the sea. But they then invite the whole company very pressingly to come and take their pleasure in the various waters and gulfs and islands and coasts of the neighbourhood; part of the crowd follows this enticing invitation and plunges seawards.

Our travellers, however, being more or less accustomed to such spook-shows, scarcely notice all this as it hums around them. The chemical mannikin, creeping about on the ground, picks out of the soil a whole lot of phosphorescent atoms, some radiating blue light and others purple. He conscientiously hands them over to Wagner for his phial, though he doubts if they can ever be used to make a female chemical midget. But when Wagner, to inspect them more closely, gives them a good shake, whole cohorts of Pompeyan and Caesarean troops appear, eager perhaps to retake the component parts of their individualities by storm and thus achieve legitimate resurrection. And indeed they nearly succeed in reassuming these inanimated corporealities; but the four winds, which have been buffeting each other all night, protect the present owner, and the phantoms hear from every side the unwelcome message that the remnants of their Roman greatness have long ago been whirled away in all directions and taken up into a million creative processes to be formed anew.

The tumult is not lessened, but so to speak appeased for a moment, when attention is drawn to an event in the middle of the wide plain. There the earth first quakes, then swells up, and a mountain range is formed, running right up to Scotusa and down to the Peneus, even threatening to block the river. The head and shoulders of Enceladus thrust themselves out of the ground, for sure enough, he has been burrowing along under sea and land to join the important celebration. Flickering flames come licking up out of various chasms. Natural philosophers, likewise inevitably present on this occasion, begin vehemently disputing the phenomenon, Thales ascribing everything to water and moisture, Anaxagoras seeing molten and melting masses everywhere. They mingle their solo perorations with the rest of the choral hubbub; both quote Homer, and each calls the past and the present to witness. Thales, in a rolling didactic flood of self-complacent argument, relies vainly on spring tides and diluvial cataclysms; Anaxagoras, wild as the element that rules him, speaks with greater passion, and prophesies a rain of meteorites, whereupon one immediately falls down out of the moon. The crowd hails him as a demigod, and his adversary is obliged to retreat to the sea-shore.

But before the mountain ravines and summits have even settled into their firm shapes, swarms of pygmies emerge from the gaping chasms round about: as the giant is still heaving himself upwards, they take possession of his upper arms and shoulders and use them as dancing-floors and playgrounds. At the same time countless hosts of cranes circle with shrill cries round the hairy summit of his head, as if they were flying over dense forests, and this promises a delightful warlike spectacle before the end of the festivities.

These many events and others as well we must imagine, if we can, as simultaneous, for that is how they happen. Mephistopheles in the meantime has made the acquaintance of Enyo, whose grandiose ugliness has so startled him that he has nearly lost his composure to the point of uttering rude and offensive exclamations. But he pulls himself together, and bearing in mind that she has lofty ancestors and is influentially connected, tries to win her favour. They understand each other and come to an agreement, the stated terms of which do not seem to amount to much, but which has hidden implications that are all the more remarkable and fraught with consequence. Faust for his part has sought out Chiron, who lives in the mountains nearby and is making his usual round. A serious tutorial interview with this primeval pedagogue is disturbed, if not interrupted, by a group of Lamiae, who continually circle in and out between Chiron and Faust: attractive women of all kinds, blonde, dark, tall, short, dainty and buxom, each of them speaking or singing, walking or dancing, darting or gesticulating, so that if Faust had not received into his heart the supreme image of beauty, he would inevitably have been seduced. And Chiron meanwhile, old and incorruptible as he is, seeks to explain to his new and intelligent acquaintance the principles he has applied in educating his noble heroes; thus we hear the story of the Argonauts, with Achilles as the climax. But when the pedagogue comes to describe the results of his efforts, it is not a very cheerful one; for they have just gone on living and acting as if they had not been educated at all.

Now when Chiron hears what Faust desires and intends, he is delighted once more to encounter a man who demands the impossible, for that is what he has always encouraged in his pupils. He also offers the modern hero assistance and advice, carries him on his broad back criss-cross over all the fords and pebbled shores of the Peneus, leaves Larissa on his right, and shows his rider only this or that place where the ill-fated king Perseus of Macedonia rested for a few minutes on his perilous flight. And thus they make their way downstream to the foot of Mount Olympus; here they come across a long procession of Sibyls, more than twelve in number. Chiron describes the first few who pass them as old acquaintances, and commends his protégé to Manto, the wise and well-disposed daughter of Tiresias.

She reveals to him that the path to the underworld is about to open, since now is the hour at which long ago the mountain had to gape wide to allow so many great souls to pass below. This indeed happens, and favoured by the horoscopic moment, they descend silently together. Suddenly Manto covers her protégé with her veil, thrusting him off the path and against the rocky wall, so that he fears he will choke to death. Releasing him a few moments later, she explains this precaution: the head of the Gorgon, growing ever bigger and wider with the passage of centuries, was moving up the chasm towards them; Persephone tries to stop it showing itself on the plain, for the phantoms and monsters gathered there for the feast would be driven distracted by its appearance and scatter immediately. Even Manto herself, wise as she is, does not dare look at it; and if Faust's eyes had fallen on it, he would have been at once destroyed, and no trace of his body or spirit ever found again in the entire universe. At last they arrive at the court of Persephone, immeasurable in its size and thronging with the countless figures of the dead; here there is boundless scope for incident, until finally Faust, presented as a second Orpheus, is well received, though his request is considered rather strange. The speech of Manto as his sponsor will of course be impressive: she relies first on the force of precedents, adducing in detail the favoured cases of Protesilaus, Alcestis, and Eurydice. Helen herself, she points out, has once already been given leave to return to life, to unite herself with Achilles, her early love! We must not here disclose the remainder of this speech and its eloquence, least of all its peroration, upon which the Queen is moved to tears and gives her consent; she refers the petitioners to the three Judges in whose adamantine memory all things are engraved as they roll past their feet in the stream of Lethe and seem to vanish away.

It here comes to light that on the previous occasion Helen was permitted to return among the living on condition that she remained on the island of Leuce. With a similar restriction she is now to return to the territory of Sparta and to appear there as truly alive in an imaginary palace of Menelaus; it must then be a matter for her new suitor to see whether he can so influence her changeable mind and sensitive temperament as to win her favour.

The intermezzo I have announced begins at this point; it is of course sufficiently integrated with the course of the action, but for reasons that will later appear, I am here publishing it on its own.

This brief scenario should of course have been offered to the public in a form elaborated with all the embellishments of poetry and eloquence. But for the time being let it serve, just as it is, to make known the antecedent circumstances (*Antezedenzien*) of the forthcoming 'Helena: A Classic-Romantic-Phantasmagorical Intermezzo to *Faust*'; for as its prelude they deserve close acquaintance and careful attention.

EXPLANATORY NOTES TO
INTRODUCTION, TEXT, AND
SELECTED PARALIPOMENA

xii *Helena*: Goethe's diaries of 1826 even refer to *Helena* and *Faust* as if they were separate works which he happens to be writing simultaneously.

early version of Helen story: in 1826 Goethe wrote to Wilhelm von Humboldt that '[*Helena*] is one of my oldest conceptions; it is based on the puppet-play tradition' (letter of 22 October 1816; similarly to Boisserée on the same date). To Knebel he called it in 1827 'a product of many years' which now is as impressive to him as the tall trees in his garden in Weimar (which he had planted himself in the mid-1770s) (letter of 14 November 1827). In 1828 he told a visitor: '[*Helena*] is a fifty-year-old conception. Some of it dates from the earliest days when I first began writing *Faust*' (conversation with Kraukling, ?31 August 1828).

Faustus legend: see Part One, Introd., pp. xiii ff. The Helen motif was made memorable by the famous passage in Marlowe's dramatized version in which Faustus, seeing the apparition of Helen, exclaims:

> 'Was this the face that launched a thousand ships
> And burnt the topless towers of Ilium?' etc.

xiii *comedy*: in two of his last letters (to Boisserée, 24 November 1831, and Wilhelm von Humboldt, 17 March 1832) Goethe expresses regret that, having decided not to publish Part Two in his lifetime, he will not be able to enjoy his friends' appreciative response to 'these very serious jests'. The comic element in the text, of which Goethe was well aware, has been greatly underemphasized by critics.

xiv *Wager and Part Two*: this applies particularly to lines 9381 f. and 9411–18 of the central scene of Act III (see Introd., p. xliv). The Gretchen tragedy was written between 1771 and 1775, the scene of Faust's Pact and Wager with Mephistopheles between 1797 and 1801, and Goethe did not begin writing Part Two, except for a few fragments, until 1825. The problem of how the Wager is related to the rest of Part One is discussed in the Introduction to Part One, pp. xxxvi ff., xliv f.

composition of Part One: See Part One, Introd., esp. pp. lvi f.

xv *epic and lyric features*: see for example Part One, Sc. 5 ('Outside the town wall'), the latter part of Sc. 4 ('Night'), and most of the two scenes called 'Faust's study' (Sc. 6, 7).

xv *Goethe and Schiller*: see Part One, Introd., pp. xxvi f.

xvii *epic mode*: discussing his current work on Act IV, Goethe remarks
that this Act will have 'a character all of its own' and be 'joined to
the whole only by a tenuous connection with what precedes and
what follows it'. Eckermann credits himself with the further obser-
vation that this will mean that it is entirely in keeping with many
other scenes and episodes in the two parts of *Faust*, which 'are all
just little worlds existing on their own, circumscribed within them-
selves, and affecting each other no doubt, but yet having little to do
with each other. The poet's concern is to express a manifold cosmos,
and he uses the story of a famous hero merely as a thread of
continuity so to speak, threading one thing after another onto it as
he pleases. That is just how it is in the *Odyssey* too, and in *Gil Blas*'.
Goethe replies: 'You are absolutely right. And in such a composition
the most important thing is that the individual masses should be
significant and clear, although as a whole it must always remain
incommensurable; but that is the very reason why, like an unsolved
problem, it will always invite people to study it afresh' (conversation
of 13 February 1831).

damnation of Faust: see Part One, Introd., pp. xiv ff. In Marlowe's
'Tragical History', and of course in all the popular Faust chapbooks
from the late 16th century onwards, devils carry the infamous hero
off to hell on the expiry of an agreed period. Before Goethe, the
only precedent for saving him seems to have been a lost fragmentary
drama by Lessing, Goethe's precursor in the humanistic revival of
German literature in the later 18th century. The traditional denoue-
ment is revived and impressively modernized by Thomas Mann in
his tragic novel *Doctor Faustus*, written during the Second World War
(see pp. lxxix f.).

xviii *entelechy*: see pp. xxx, lxxii and note, lxxvi.

ironic distance: see Part One, Introd., pp. xxxi f., xxxvi f.

xix *historicist-genetic method*: see Part One, Introd., pp. x f.

xxi *paralipomena*: four years after Goethe's death, Riemer and Eckermann
published a heavily edited short selection from this posthumous
material; borrowing a word that Goethe had sometimes used, they
called these the 'paralipomena' ('left-overs'), and this designation has
been adopted by *Faust* editors ever since. The paralipomena were
not assembled methodically until 1887–8, when Erich Schmidt in-
cluded them in the *Faust* volumes of the Weimar edition (Weimarer
Ausgabe, WA; see Preface).

Berlin edition (Berliner Ausgabe, BA): see Preface. The 'Selected Paralipomena' in the present edition are BA 5, BA 70, and BA 73, corresponding to WA 1, WA 63, and WA 123.

xxii *conversation with Eckermann*: Eckermann reports that Goethe made this and other comments to him on the elf scene just after writing it; this conversation is wrongly dated 12 March 1826 in many editions. Its date is uncertain, but it cannot have taken place before the early summer of 1827 if the scene was written then (see 1st note to p. 3).

genesis of elf scene: the role of the spirits as tempters beguiling Faust with the thought of great deeds is in keeping with the theme of activity which Goethe frequently associated with Faust. He evidently retained this scenario until a late stage, since it reappears in a short manuscript sketch for Act I (paralipomenon BA 76) which has been dated to May 1827, only a month or two before the probable date of the elf dialogue (June or July 1827). This point is made by Wolfgang Schadewaldt in his study of the scene; he also suggests, however, that over the years Goethe had become dissatisfied with the old conception. An important stimulus to his change of plan and adoption of the profounder theme of the healing processes and cycles of nature had been Goethe's interest in Chinese poetry during 1827; this also bore fruit in his late cycle of lyric poems *Chinese-German Hours and Seasons*, one of which is strikingly similar to the elf chorus (4634–65).

xxiii *Doppelgänger*: an element of this motif is curiously retained in Sc. 2 of the final version, where Mephistopheles plays prompter to the Astrologer (4947–72, 5048–56), rather as if the latter were Faust in disguise, though the final text does not seem to allow this; the ambiguity may have arisen because Goethe contaminated an earlier and a later conception.

xxiv *ancien régime*: a veiled reference, here as elsewhere in Goethe's work, to the contemporary political upheavals in France seems especially probable. In particular, the role of Mephistopheles at the Emperor's court has been compared (see Williams, 1987, 126 f.) to that of the charlatan 'Count' Cagliostro, who is thought to have gained the favour of Marie Antoinette and to have played a leading part in the affair of the diamond necklace in 1785. Goethe wrote a satirical comedy based on this scandal (*The Grand Kophta*, 1792), which he saw as symptomatic of a society ripe for revolution.

paper money: it is clear from one of his conversations with Eckermann (27 December 1829) that in the paper money episode Goethe is alluding to a talking-point of the day. Some of the historical precedents are listed by Williams (1987, 128), who points particularly to the suggestion of buried ecclesiastical treasure in 5018–32 and to the sequestration of church assets and property in 1790 by the French revolutionary government as backing for the so-called *assignats*, a form of paper currency which was issued with inflationary consequences.

xxv *roles in the Masquerade*: in a conversation of 20 December 1829 Goethe remarks to Eckermann: 'You will have noticed that the mask of Plutus is worn by Faust, and that of Avarice by Mephistopheles. But who is the Boy Charioteer?' Eckermann's account continues: 'I hesitated and could not answer. "It is Euphorion!" said Goethe. "But how", I asked, "can he be appearing here already in the Carnival, when he is not born until Act III?" "Euphorion", Goethe answered, "is not a human being, only an allegorical figure. He is the personification of poetry, which is not bound to any time or place or person. The same spirit who later chooses to be Euphorion now appears as the Boy Charioteer, and in this respect he is similar to ghosts, who can be present anywhere and manifest themselves at any moment." '

xxvi *Charles VI*: the *Historical Chronicle* by Johann Ludwig Gottfried (1619) tells of a masked ball at the court of Charles VI of France in 1394, at which the king was disguised as a wild man with hemp and pitch; this costume caught fire when the Duke of Orléans came too near him with a lighted torch. Four courtiers were burnt to death, and the king became mentally deranged. Goethe had read this book as a child in an edition illustrated with woodcuts.

Arabian Nights motifs: one (a favourite in the *Tales*) is that of treasure hidden underground; this indeed was also a main theme in Sc. 2 (4890–4, 4927–38, 5007–46). Typically, the treasure is found or promised as a reward for virtue (in a ruler who reforms his prodigality, for instance) or is associated with greed and its punishment. In one story a magician shows a young man how to use a paper inscribed with magic words to gain access to a treasure-chamber under a fountain; Mommsen thinks that this is not unlike the 'magic' paper money (6157) and Faust's fiery treasure-fountain. Other tales tell of illusory fires and floods conjured up by a magician to educate a ruler, even of a ruler whose beard catches fire in one such case. Another *Arabian Nights* motif is that of battles between spirits who constantly change their shape (5471–83); another is that of kingdoms under the sea (6013–26).

xxvii *Mothers*: Goethe claimed (conversation with Eckermann, 10 January, 1830) to have found a reference to 'goddesses who are called Mothers' in Plutarch (it occurs in the *Life of Marcellus*) and to have invented the rest himself; certain other passages in Plutarch's writings, however, seem to be echoed by Mephistopheles' descriptions. (In the essay *On the Cessation of Oracles*, for instance, we read: 'There are a hundred and eighty-three worlds. These are arranged in the form of a triangle . . . The area within the triangle is to be regarded as a centre common to all of them, and is called the Field of Truth. In it lie motionless the causes, shapes and prototypes of all things that have ever existed and will yet exist. They are surrounded by eternity, out of which time overflows into the worlds'.) Williams (1987, 137 f.) is inclined to emphasize the element of irony which is also detectable in Goethe's presentation of this mythic theme, continuing perhaps Mephistopheles' role as a Cagliostro-like figure (see 1st note to p. xxiv); Faust himself (6249 ff.) calls him a 'mystagogue' who tries to deceive his neophytes with elaborate ritual and verbiage.

xxviii *where Helen really belongs*: at the level of the autobiographical allegory we may compare Faust's escape from the Emperor's world to Goethe's withdrawal from frustrating political involvements at Weimar, a frustration expressing itself in his sudden 'flight' to Italy in 1786 in pursuit of his poetic and scientific development (cf. pp. xxiv, xxxv f.).

Greek mythology: Goethe's main source for Greek mythological material, in the 'Classical Walpurgis Night' and elsewhere, was Benjamin Hederich's *Gründliches Mythologisches Lexikon* (Complete Lexicon of Mythology), 2nd ed., 1770. He was also able to consult Riemer, his resident adviser on all matters of classical scholarship.

xxix *Pharsalus*: the text also recalls (7465–8) another decisive battle: the total defeat of Perseus of Macedon at Pydna, in 168 BC, by forces of the Roman Republic (7468). With the fall of the last successor of Alexander the Great and with him of the Macedonian kingdom, all effective Greek resistance to Roman power was at an end. This event is symbolically balanced by the victory of Caesar at Pharsalus 120 years later, as a result of which the whole Greek world became a province of the Roman Empire by the end of the 1st century BC.

homunculi: Goethe is thought to have had in mind the method advocated by Paracelsus (1493–1541): 'Let the sperm of a man by it selfe be putrefied in a gourd glasse, sealed up, with the highest degree of putrefaction in Horse dung, for the space of forty days, or so long until it begin to bee alive, move, and stir, which can easily be seen. After this time it will be something like a Man, yet transparent, and without a body. Now after this, if it bee every day warily, and prudently nourished and fed with the Arcanum of Mans blood, and bee for the space of forty weeks kept in a constant, equall heat of Horse-dung, it will become a true, and living infant, having all the members of an infant, which is born of a woman, but it will bee far lesse. This we call Homunculus, or Artificiall. And this is afterwards to be brought up with as great care, and diligence as any other infant, until it come to riper years of understanding' (quoted by Gray, 1952, 205 f., from the English translation of 1650). Goethe could also read about homunculi in the *Anthropodemus Plutonicus*, a 17th-century demonological treatise by Johannes Schultze ('Johannes Prätorius') which yielded much material for *Faust*. The motif of bottle-imps and similar creatures is widespread in folklore, and is to be found in the *Arabian Nights*. Goethe is also known to have read and admired Sterne's *Tristram Shandy*, where he would have found a humorous, if obscure, reference to 'the Homunculus' in ch. 2 of book I.

xxx *entelechy*: from an undated conversation reported by Eckermann to Riemer and by Riemer to one of the early *Faust* editors who published it in 1857 (see Williams, 1987, 144 and note). For further reference to Goethe's conception of the entelechy and its survival, see pp. lxxii and note, lxxvi f.

xxxi *Mephistopheles and the Homunculus*: in a conversation of 16 December 1829 Eckermann 'cannot help thinking that [Mephistopheles] has secretly helped the Homunculus into existence', and Goethe replies: 'You appreciate the position very correctly. It is in fact so, and I have already considered whether I should not put a few lines into the mouth of Mephistopheles, while he is visiting Wagner and the Homunculus is developing, which would make it quite clear to the reader that he has had a hand in it.' Eckermann points out that there is already a hint to this effect in 7003 f., and Goethe replies: 'You are right. For the attentive reader this might almost be enough; still, I shall try to think of a few lines nevertheless.' No such lines were in fact added.

Faust's dream: both in this passage and in Faust's later vision by the Peneus (7271–312), what Faust sees is not Helen herself but her biological antecedents as it were, the begetting of her by the divine swan. In the conversation of 16 December 1829 Eckermann comments very perceptively on the former passage (the other had not yet been written), admiring the way in which 'in a work of this kind the particular parts refer to each other, affect each other, and complement and enhance each other. It is really only this dream about Leda, here in the second Act, that lays the true foundation for the subsequent Helena episode. In the latter, we keep hearing about swans and about a woman begotten by a swan, but here that very action is presented and seen; and when we later come to the "Helena" full of the sensuous impression of such a situation, how much clearer and more complete it must then appear!' Eckermann adds: 'Goethe agreed with me, and it seemed to give him pleasure that I had noticed this.'

Homunculus in glass vessel: in a conversation of 20 December 1829 Eckermann wonders how the role of the Homunculus in Wagner's laboratory could be represented on the stage; Goethe suggests that Wagner 'must not let the flask out of his hands, and the voice would have to sound as if it were coming out of the flask. It would be a part for a ventriloquist; I have heard them perform, and I am sure one of them would make a good job of it.'

xxxiv   *transitions*: in an undated conversation (?1831) Goethe remarks to Riemer that the essential meaning of Part Two as a whole seems to him to be sufficiently clear for an intelligent reader, 'even if there are transitions enough that he will have to supply'. Another such hiatus occurs at the end of Act IV, again because Goethe omitted to write an intended scene, in this case that in which Faust receives from the Emperor a formal grant of the coastal land under the sea.

xxxvi   *'neptunism' and 'vulcanism'*: according to the 'neptunist' or 'diluvianist' theory, the earth's crust had been shaped and modified by the gradual sedimentation of rocks in the oceans, whereas the 'vulcanists' or 'plutonists' regarded volcanic or seismic activity as the primary factor. Goethe also saw this scientific controversy as a political allegory, in which the two opposing principles were reforming gradualism on the one hand and violent revolutionary change on the other. He was temperamentally inclined to a gradualist, evolutionary view in both the geological and the political spheres; in particular he abhorred the French Revolution, and dreaded all his life the recurrence of similar upheavals in Europe (cf. p. lix f.). Both the episode of Anaxagoras's mountain suddenly brought into being by an earthquake (7503–689, 7801–950) and the geophysical discussion between Mephistopheles and Faust in Act IV (10072–127) are satirical developments of the same allegorical theme; and the Homunculus's preference for the counsels of the 'neptunist' Thales represents Goethe's refusal to be involved in the world of politics, escaping instead into the study of the slow and orderly processes of nature.

xxxvii   *essay*: 'On Simple Imitation of Nature; Manner; Style' (1789).

xxxix   *magical power*: in a conversation of 16 December 1829 Eckermann remarks (and Goethe agrees) that in 'Helena' Mephistopheles 'always seems to be playing a secretly active part'. It is indeed notable that throughout most of Act III Phorcyas-Mephistopheles appears to be magically in charge of all that is going on. He describes Faust's castle to Helen, undertakes to 'surround her' with it instantly (9049), and the scene changes to it as soon as she consents. Earlier, he claps his hands and summons up 'masked dwarf-like figures' who obey his instructions like magic slaves in a *Märchen*, as he supervises with comic relish their preparations for the ritual slaughter of Helen (8936–46). He is, as it seems, running the whole show, rather as if it were indeed a show, a play within a play like the 'Walpurgis Night's Dream' in Part One. This is partly (as Mommsen argues) a technical device on Goethe's part: given the difficulties of stage presentation of magical events, an epic, fabling element is needed; it takes the form of Mephistopheles-Scheherazade's fantastic narratives, which describe what is happening, or indeed cause it to happen, and which at the same time, in effect, demonstrate and celebrate the power of poetic imagination.

xli *precedent*: in his final version (Acts II and III) Goethe alludes twice (7435 f., 8876–9.) to the posthumous encounter of Helen and Achilles, thus lending plausibility to Faust's own enterprise; in the first case, rather curiously, he deliberately alters their meeting-place from the island of Leuce to the Thessalian city of Pherae, in order to contaminate the Leuce motif with the similar but better-known story of Alcestis, who was brought back from the dead after nobly sacrificing herself for her husband Admetus, king of Pherae (see Index, **Pherae**).

Euphorion: the old German Faust books also mention a son born to Faust and Helen by their diabolic union; the boy's name is Justus Faustus, and he disappears after his father's sudden death, prompting one 17th-century commentator to wonder whether he had been properly baptized. For details of the Greek Euphorion story, see Index. One of the most interesting of the paralipomena to Goethe's version is the discarded draft (BA 196) of a speech for Phorcyas-Mephistopheles, evidently written in a relaxed mood, in which Goethe makes fun of his own treatment of the Euphorion story and even of the venerable iambic trimeter. As part of her narrative to the Chorus at the beginning of Sc. 13, Phorcyas describes the boy's birth and alludes to his mythological provenance: Faust and Helen, she explains, will presently emerge from their underground grotto

> Wedded parentally by a charming little boy,
> Whom they have called Euphorion; that was long ago
> His step-stepbrother's name, now no more questions please!
> Enough, you soon will see him; though this case is worse
> Than on the English stage, where gradually some brat

Can grow from tiny stature to heroic size.
Here it's still crazier: only just been begotten and at once he's born.
He leaps, he dances, he can fence already! Though
Some say that's nonsense, others think: this must not be
Humdrumly understood, there's some deep meaning here.
They smell a mystery, no doubt, perhaps they even smell
Mystification, Indian and Egyptian lore;
And to know how to clip it all together, how
To make a proper brew, an etymological
Dance—to enjoy all that's the mark of scholarship.
And so say we; profoundly it convinces us,
Such neo-symbolism and its faithful neophytes.
But now I am no longer useful in this place.
Poetic fiction's ghostly thread spins on and on
Till in the end it tragically breaks.

stipulation: the rule requiring Helen to remain in Sparta is not made explicit in the final 'Helena' text, but is mentioned several times in the later paralipomena, notably that of 1826 (BA 73), where Persephone imposes this condition on her in the unwritten Hades scene.

monks: this anticipates the role of the clergy in the war of Act IV, where Goethe continues his familiar line of anticlerical satire (see p. lviii). The three giants with whose assistance the Faust of BA 70 defeated the monks are also featured in Acts IV and V. In his illuminating article on Faust's political role in the last two Acts, Vaget (1980) states not quite correctly that the war with the monks takes place in Greece (in fact the BA 70 version of the Helen story is located entirely in Germany).

xlii *classical-romantic*: Goethe tends to use the term 'romantic', as here, to mean 'modern' in the widest sense, that is to say as including the Middle Ages but not classical antiquity; belonging, in other words, to the Christian era, and having more to do with northern than with southern Europe. The paradoxical description 'classical-romantic' points to the mixture of ancient and modern styles in the piece and to the idea of a synthesis of two historical cultures, as well as perhaps to Byron, in whom such a synthesis is in some ways personified.

Faust's education: this point has been made by Williams (1983, 'Faust and Helen,' 30 f.); in the light of it, the critical dispute over the degree of reality or illusoriness to be attributed to the Helen of Act III becomes otiose.

xliii *classical metres*: ancient Greek verse was 'quantitative' in the sense that the syllables were either 'long' or 'short', and the lines were regulated structures of such syllables, with stress accent playing no part. Modern German or English verse is 'accentual', with stress as

the chief factor. Subject to this basic difference, some impression of
the specific character of Greek versification can be given by modern
(and especially German) accentual imitations which substitute
stressed and unstressed syllables for longs and shorts respectively. In
Faust Goethe imitates above all the 'iambic trimeter' of the classical
drama, a line consisting basically (with certain permitted variations)
of three metrical units each of which is in principle a double iambus
($\cup- \cup-$). It therefore tends to have twelve syllables like the modern
alexandrine; but there is a certain difference of rhythm between these
two lines, more easily conveyed in German than in English. The
other 'Greek' line in Act III, used especially by the Chorus, is the
'trochaic tetrameter' of four double trochees ($-\cup -\cup$). The Chorus
also uses odes with repeating patterns of strophe, antistrophe, and
epode, in which the first two are metrically identical and the third a
variation (e.g. 8610–37). Goethe imitates these forms with some
accuracy and subtlety.

xliii *Behramgur*: this hidden allusion is not the only example of Arabic-
Persian influence in these scenes, as Mommsen has shown: the whole
style of Faust's courtship of Helen, whether direct or by proxy
through Lynceus, is essentially that of an Oriental prince (the
watchman who fails to notice the royal guest's approach is not only
condemned to death but must be instantly executed unless she
pardons him; all the jewels and treasures in the world cannot
compare with her beauty, etc.).

xliv *Marianne von Willemer*: Goethe first met Marianne in July 1814 while
revisiting his native city of Frankfurt and while engaged on the
writing of the *West-Eastern Divan*; his emotional involvement with
her was perhaps the profoundest of all his attachments to women,
and inspired some of his greatest poetry. The then 30-year-old
Marianne Jung, a former actress of considerable literary and musical
talent, had in 1800 become the protégée of Johann Jakob von
Willemer, a rich Frankfurt banker twenty-four years her senior; their
marriage, officially formalized in September 1814, remained childless
and unhappy. The mutual love and understanding between Marianne
and Goethe was at its height during his further visit in the late
summer of 1815 to Willemer's country house near Frankfurt, and
again during the brief meeting in Heidelberg in September which
was to be their last. They often communicated by allusions or
numerical references to the newly written *Divan* poems, adopting
the personae of 'Suleika' and 'Hatem', and Marianne herself con-
tributed several of the poems, which Goethe retouched and adopted
as his own. He was evidently alarmed, however, by the depth of the

passion he had come to feel for her and had aroused in her. Shortly after the death of his own wife Christiane in June 1816, he set out in a state of mental conflict to visit Frankfurt once more, but two hours after leaving Weimar his carriage overturned, a mishap which he interpreted as an omen; he returned home and decided to break off the relationship without explanation. For years he maintained a cruel silence, despite Marianne's consequent nervous illnesses and desperate pleas, and despite the entreaties of Willemer himself, who was flattered by the great poet's attentions to his wife and later even went so far as to propose that Goethe should leave Weimar and move permanently back to Frankfurt, living with them in a *ménage à trois*. In 1819 Goethe began again to reply to Marianne's letters, and an affectionate correspondence was resumed; but between 1815 and his death he avoided any further meeting with her. Marianne, though she lived until 1860, never really recovered from the shock of losing Goethe, and his emotions too were never quite extricated from the experience. Three weeks before his death Marianne received a packet which he asked her to leave unopened 'until the uncertain time comes'. It contained all her letters to him and a short poem entitled 'A Legacy':

> To my darling now I send them,
> Back into the hand that penned them—
> How I waited for them, burning
> With the love they were returning!—
> To her heart they poured from, may
> These her letters find their way,
> Ever ready to recall
> There the loveliest time of all.

Wager. See above, pp. xiii f.

xlvi *Byzantine Hellenic revival*: as one authority has put it: 'The rise of Mistra was almost the only bright spot in the history of the Peloponnese during the 14th century' (Woodhouse, 1986). Mystra became, among the few centres of culture remaining under Byzantine control (others were Constantinople itself, Thessalonica and Trebizond), especially prominent during the lifetime of Gemistus Pletho (c.1360–1452; his adopted name was modelled on 'Plato'). Pletho settled in Mystra around the turn of the century, and became an influential and controversial teacher, enjoying the protection of the enlightened Imperial family and living to a remarkable age. His views went well beyond the official discreet coexistence of humanistic classical learning with Orthodox Christianity, and indeed amounted to an outright neo-paganism. In 1438–9 he visited Italy,

officially as a member of the Imperial delegation to the ecclesiastical
Council of Florence; his lectures to Italian scholars were heard with
enthusiasm, and contributed to the Renaissance in Italy by helping
to pioneer the study of Platonism there. He became so admired a
figure that twelve years after his death a cultured Venetian *condottiere*,
on an expedition against the Turks in the Peloponnese, removed his
body from Mystra and brought it back to Rimini for honorific
reburial; this was not long after Pletho's most daring book, posthu-
mously brought to light, had been formally burnt in Constantinople
by order of the Patriarch. (Cf. also Runciman 1970, 1980).

xlvi *Menelaus*: it has been argued that, historically, the Greeks of late
antiquity and the Dark Ages neglected the cities and regions of the
former classical culture, allowing them to be overrun by the
barbarians, and that the Byzantines later did the same, thus giving
the Franks their opportunity to occupy the peninsula. Faust may then
be thought of as engaged on an operation to rescue the threatened
'Helen' from the Greeks themselves; her lawful custodian Menelaus
thus becomes the representative of post-classical Greece and Byzan-
tium. On this view, his threatened attack stands for the imminent
Byzantine reconquest, and the credit for the preservation of the
Hellenic heritage goes not to the Byzantine culture of Mystra and
elsewhere, but to Western and in particular (however implausibly)
Germanic peoples (*sic* Beutler and D. Lohmeyer).

xlvii *Faust's Arcadia*: the pastoral or 'bucolic' tradition here represented
goes back to antiquity, beginning in Greek poetry with the idylls of
Theocritus (3rd century BC) and in Latin with Virgil (70–19 BC), the
latter making 'Arcadia' (see also Index) its central symbol. In Faust's
description of the ideal landscape Goethe deliberately uses the
characteristic imagery of Virgil's *Eclogues* (mountain pastures, shady
trees and caves, flocks and streams, reference to Pan and Apollo,
etc.). Apollo (9558 f.; see Index) in fact adopted the disguise of a
shepherd not in Arcadia but in Thessaly.

xlviii *Arcadian refuge*: the secluded Arcadian setting of Faust's brief union
with Helen suggests to Boyle (1982–3, 138) Goethe's attempt (vainly,
as he himself came to see) to establish classical forms and classical
taste in a kind of idyllic isolation from the revolutionary politics and
wars that preoccupied the rest of contemporary Europe and trans-
formed the face of Germany; cf. also pp. xxvii, xlii f.

l *Act IV soliloquy*: the symbolic significance of the cumulus and cirrus
cloud formations observed by Faust is made clear in a short
manuscript sketch of Act IV (paralipomenon BA 106), where Goethe

writes 'Half the cloud rises south-eastwards as Helen, the other half north-westwards as Gretchen'. In his meteorological writings, under the influence of the English meteorologist Luke Howard, Goethe interpreted the movements and metamorphoses of clouds as a struggle between the higher and lower regions of the atmosphere, symbolizing the ascent of the human spirit from the moist, earthly level to the drier and 'purer' upper ether. For the similar cloud symbolism of Sc. 23, cf. p. lxxv.

li *the ending 'already written'*: see esp. conversation with Boisserée, 3 August 1815; cf. remark to Eckermann, 24 January 1830.

liii *Sc. 23*: Mason points out interestingly in this connection that the angelic choruses in Sc. 22 and 23 are metrically similar to the Easter choruses in Sc. 4 of Part One (written c.1800).

lv *entelechies of the Homunculus and Faust*: cf. pp. lxxii, lxxvi f.

lvii *'mountain people'*: Goethe had read about such gnome-like creatures in the *Anthropodemus Plutonicus* (see 2nd note to p. xxix). After Faust's mysterious speech, no further reference is made to them and his description of the 'mountain folk' (10425) does not seem to fit either the ghosts in the suits of armour or the unpleasant Three Mighty Men (see following notes) who now take over the battle.

phantom army: Goethe had read Walter Scott's *Letters on Demonology and Witchcraft*, which was one source for this widespread folklore motif.

three fighting-men: the biblical references alongside the text, here and elsewere, were probably added by Riemer. In Luther's translation of 2 Sam. 23 David's three champions have Hebrew names; 'Raufebold (Raubebold)' and 'Eilebeute' (the name of the camp-follower who joins the Three in Sc. 16) are from Isa. 8: 1. (cf. also Paralipomena, p. 244, and Sc. 18–19).

lviii *the Emperor*: it is notable that he here (10417–20) recalls his vision of fire which he described to Mephistopheles and Faust on the morning after the Carnival in Act I (5989–6002). The experience seems to have left a lasting impression on him, which again suggests that Goethe may have intended the magical later episodes of the Carnival scene as a symbolic education of the Emperor (cf. p. xxvi).

Golden Bull: Goethe had known this historic document since his Frankfurt days; a commentary on it, which he reread in 1831, had been published in 1766 by J. D. von Olenschlager, a friend of the Goethe family. By its provisions, the Electoral College was to consist of four temporal and three ecclesiastical princes (the King of Bohemia, the Duke of Saxony, the Margrave of Brandenburg, and the Count Palatinate of the Rhine, together with the Archbishops of Mainz, Cologne, and Trier). The Electors also held ceremonial court offices such as High Chamberlain, High Seneschal, and Imperial Cupbearer (as distributed to the three secular princes in Goethe's scene). These arrangements, which in effect represented the decentralization of the Empire, remained theoretically in force through the centuries, until the Empire was dissolved by Napoleon in 1806.

lix *enfeoffment scene*: a rough sketch of Act IV written in May 1831 (BA 107) mentions the grant of titles and lands to the four princes, then Faust's request to be granted 'the barren sea coasts', to which the Emperor accedes, 'glad to be able to fob him off so easily'. A curious point is that in another fragment (BA 219) the formal document read out by the Chancellor refers to Faust by name ('Faustus, the Fortunate as he is rightly called'), although in the rest of the Act there is no indication that the Emperor or anyone else has recognized him as the magician who introduced the paper money and whose name was known in that episode (6560).

lxiii *Philemon and Baucis*: in the comic theatrical 'prelude' of 1802 (its title *Was wir bringen*, literally 'What we are offering', is roughly equivalent to 'What you will' or 'As you like it') Mercury visits the couple disguised as a traveller, and offers them a magic carpet which will carry them from their tumbledown hut to a magnificent temple (representing the new theatre); 'Baucis' is reluctant to go, suspecting that the stranger is the Devil; Faust's magic carpet is even cited as a precedent. A further link between the Faust version and the classical story is perhaps the motif of the flood, with its biblical connotation of a new beginning to the world after divine punishment.

lxviii *Freud and Thomas Mann*: Freud, *New Introductory Lectures on Psycho-analysis*, 1933, lecture 31 (Standard Edition, vol. 22, p. 80); Mann, 'Freud and the Future', 1936 (*Essays of Three Decades*, p. 428). The parallel between Freud's simile and Faust's symbolic enterprise is noteworthy, though neither analogy can be pressed too far. Mann was probably influenced by the popular misconception that identifies the id (the world of primitive unconscious instincts) with the unconscious mind generally, and overlooks the unconscious functions of the ego. Freud's formulation should be seen in the context of his previous sentence: 'The purpose [of psychoanalysis] is after all to strengthen the ego, to make it less dependent on the superego, to expand its awareness and extend its organization, making it able to appropriate new areas of the id.' The note of conciliation and adaptation here is not quite in keeping with the image of resistance and antagonism which draining and damming imply; the 'sea' in Goethe's conception, notwithstanding line 11541 (which translates literally as '(to) reconcile the earth with itself') and lines 11221 f. ('the sea-shore and sea are reconciled'), seems to be thought of as a perpetual enemy.

lxix *last word on Faust*: this is pointed out by Williams (1987, 205).

lxxi *11934–41*: the first of these lines: 'This noble spirit saved alive' (*Gerettet ist das edle Glied der Geisterwelt*) has been indecently parodied in advance by Mephistopheles in Sc. 22, where he notes that although his sudden infatuation with the angel boys has brought him out in boils, no permanent damage has been done: 'My noble devil-parts are saved alive' (*Gerettet sind die edlen Teufelsteile*) (11813); in the German the play is on *Glied* (member).

lxxii *great entelechy*: Goethe further expounds this conception (which seems to amount to a theory of immortality-of-the-fittest by natural selection) in a conversation with Eckermann on 11 March 1828. The point about the diversity of entelechies, of which some are 'more powerful' than others, arises from their discussion of a phenomenon which Goethe calls the 'repetition of puberty': the retention or revival of youthful energy by certain men of genius in old age. Goethe remarks that

Every entelechy is a piece of eternity, and the few short years during which it is bound to an earthly body do not make it old. If this entelechy is of a trivial sort, it will exert scarcely any influence during its period of bodily obscuration; on the contrary, the body will predominate, and when the body grows old, the entelechy will not hinder its decay. But if the entelechy is powerful, as it is in all men of natural genius, it will pervade and animate the body, and not only will it have a strengthening and ennobling effect on the physical organization, but its superior spiritual strength will also be such that it will constantly try to assert its privilege of perpetual youth. That is why fresh periods of unusual productivity may still be seen to occur in exceptionally gifted men even when they are old; they seem from time to time to undergo a temporary rejuvenation, which is what I should like to call a repetition of puberty.

Also relevant in this connection is a conversation with Falk in 1813, in which Goethe expounds his theory of the entelechies at consider-able length; he here calls them 'monads', but it is clear from another statement to Eckermann (conversation of 3 March 1830) that he regarded the Aristotelian and Leibnizian terms as synonymous. According to Falk's account, Goethe talked of 'strong and powerful' monads which seize any lesser, insignificant ones that approach them, and draw them into an organic union with themselves. (The words of the angels in 11958 ff., where the 'spirit-energy' of Faust's entelechy 'captures the physical elements powerfully', are reminiscent of this train of thought.) Death is the natural process of dissolution in which the dominant monad releases its subordinates from this union. Goethe seems to imply here that although all monads are immortal, some are more immortal than others: there is a hierarchy in which some have a much stronger potential to participate in the process of creation, as well as to maintain themselves in existence. 'I myself', he adds, 'am sure that I have existed a thousand times already and may hope to return a thousand times again' (conversation with Falk, 25 January 1813).

lxxiii *'Mountain Gorges' and 'Classical Walpurgis Night'*: see Williams, 1976, 659–63; also 1987, 145, 162, 209.

lxxiv *castrato boys*: commentators have for some reason been strangely resistant to this obvious reading of these four lines; one eminent Catholic Goethe scholar (Beutler) wildly guesses that the devils' 'most outrageous trick' (11691) was the crucifixion of Christ.

lxxv *Pater Profundus, etc.*: the Latin epithets do not seem to intend any specific identification of these archetypal desert fathers, though in medieval times 'Pater Profundus' and 'Pater Seraphicus' were names given to St Bernard of Clairvaux and St Francis of Assisi, respectively. 'Doctor Marianus' was a title of honour given to scholarly contemplatives who excelled in devotion to the Mother of God.

lxxvi *Blessed Boys*: the idea that the contemplative lends his physical senses for spirits to use is derived from the Swedish mystic Emanuel Swedenborg (1688–1772), with whose *Arcana Coelestia* Goethe had been familiar since his youth.

integument: the '*Flocken*' in this line are usually interpreted as something like the cocoon of a chrysalis; but in his meteorological work Goethe uses the same word to suggest a fleecy cloud dissolving as it rises, and this image is probably also intended here, as Karl Lohmeyer (1927, 117) points out.

Luna: see Williams, 1976.

lxxvii *Goethe and Christianity*: Luke, 'Goethe's attitude to Christian belief' (*Publications of the English Goethe Society*, 59, 1988–9).

lxxviii *Götternebenbürtig*: the literal translation of 7440 (in Faust's description of Helen to Chiron) is 'the eternal being, born the equal of gods'.

unzulänglich: as Staiger points out (1959, 466), *unzulänglich* (which in modern German means 'insufficient' or 'inadequate') was used in the sense of 'inaccessible' in the 17th century and earlier; the mystical devotional writer Zinzendorf, for example, refers to God dwelling '*in einem unzulänglichen Lichte*' (*in lumine inaccessibile*), and other instances are given in Grimm's authoritative historical dictionary of the German language. Goethe's occasional retention of the older usage is documented in line 9083 of *Faust*, where *unzulängliche Mauer* (unassailable wall) appears to be what he wrote, though it was altered by the WA editor Erich Schmidt to *unzugänglich*, a 'correction' generally adopted. The use of *Ereignis* in the sense of '*Eräugnis*' (manifestation) in the next line of the Chorus Mysticus is also attested in Grimm.

Mahler: Gustav Mahler's setting (composed in 1906) of 'Mountain Gorges' constitutes the second and major part of his Eighth Symphony, a choral work in two long movements. Mahler includes most of Goethe's text, using vast orchestral and vocal resources and leading up to the 'Chorus Mysticus' as a massive climax.

3 [*Prologue*]: although not so called by Goethe, this scene has the character of a prologue designed to mark the transition from the world of Part One to that of Part Two. Its date of composition is uncertain, but has been shown by Schadewaldt to be very probably March or April 1826 for Faust's soliloquy (4679–727) and June or July 1827 for the elf dialogue (4613–78). In Goethe's original conception, represented by the 1816 scenario (paralipomenon BA 70) and by a jotting as late as May 1827 (BA 76), spirits tempt the sleeping Faust to pursue worldly glory by devoting himself to action in the public sphere, for which more austere purpose he must put the private world of 'sensuality and passion' behind him. This theme in its turn seems to echo the obscure schema of 1797 (paralipomenon BA 5), in which Goethe distinguishes between passionate personal enjoyment of life (*Lebensgenuß*) as the theme of Part One and enjoyment of deeds (*Tatengenuß*) as that of Part Two. The function of the attendant spirits was then changed, for reasons already further discussed (see Introd., pp. xxii f.).

Ariel: as in the 'Walpurgis Night's Dream' of Part One (Sc. 25), Goethe borrows the friendly elemental spirit Ariel from Shakespeare's *The Tempest*, though again without developing the Shakespearean connection in any way.

5 *How strong and pure* . . . : Faust's speech is in *terza rima*, the technically difficult and grandiose metre (with the rhyme scheme *aba bcb cdc* etc.) in which Dante wrote the *Divine Comedy*; Goethe hardly ever used it, the only other example being the great elegiac meditation on Schiller's skull ('*Im ernsten Beinhaus* . . .') written in September 1826—that is, probably a few months after Faust's speech. The

remarkable description of sunrise in the high mountains appears to be based on Goethe's memories of Switzerland, which he revisited in 1797. His account of this journey describes in particular the Rhine waterfall at Schaffhausen with a rainbow formed in its rising spray, a phenomenon he repeatedly returned to the spot to observe. The choice here of *terza rima*, with its ceaseless flow through a constant form, is particularly appropriate to the image of the rainbow, static in the moving water. On the symbolic level this image also continues the theme of healing and regeneration already embodied in the elf dialogue; Faust's inability to gaze directly at the sun and his gesture of turning to the rainbow instead (4715 ff.) are held together by the motif of renunciation. The passage, culminating in the much quoted and enigmatic final line ('*Am farbigen Abglanz haben wir das Leben*') which recalls Shelley's 'Life, like a dome of many-coloured glass, stains the white radiance of eternity' (*Adonais*, 1821), is usually interpreted in terms of the ancient metaphysical distinction between the perceptible, phenomenal world and an ulterior, divine reality. This reading appears to be supported by the various Neoplatonic echoes in Goethe's work, such as the remark in one of his scientific essays that 'The truth, being identical with the divine, can never be perceived directly by us, we only behold it in the reflection [*Abglanz*], in the example, the symbol, in particular and related phenomena' (*An Essay on Meteorology*, 1825). On the other hand, a dualistic interpretation is not clearly borne out by Faust's own words (4704–14), which seem to describe an overwhelming emotional or mystical encounter with the force ('what flame of love or hate') of life itself, rather similar to his encounter in Part One (Sc. 4) with the Earth Spirit, from which he also had to turn away. The essential difference, and the essential theme, is that he is now prepared to accept human limitations: he will study the phenomenon, love the similitude, rather than confront the terrible and impossible Absolute. Timelessness must not crush time into insignificance, but intersect with it, as the colours of the spectrum stand over the white moving spray, as art criss-crosses life in a synthesis 'changing yet ever still'. Such at least appears to be Faust's attitude in this speech. For purposes of this 'prologue' he is wise, philosophical, and mature; which is not to say, however, that Goethe portrays him as remaining consistently so throughout Part Two (cf. Introd., pp. xiii f., xviii f.).

6 *an imperial palace*: I have followed the Weimar edition in assuming that Goethe intends this location to be understood as a general heading for Scenes 2–7 of Act I, which all take place in various rooms of a palace or in its garden. *Pfalz* can be (as apparently here) an archaic

word for 'palace', or it can have the wider sense of 'palatinate', i.e., one of the various places of residence between which, since there was no official central 'capital', the medieval emperor would travel with his court.

7 *Mephistopheles*: Having somehow got rid (as Goethe indicated to Eckermann on 1 October 1827) of the official court jester, Mephistopheles takes his place, immediately propounding a riddle to which the answer is perhaps 'the Fool' or perhaps 'the Devil'.

9 *Ghibellines and Guelphs*: the two great factions in early medieval politics during the long struggle between the papacy and the Hohenstaufen emperors. The Ghibellines (the name is perhaps an Italianization of Waiblingen, the imperial family's place of origin) traditionally supported the Emperor and the Guelph (Guelf, Welf) party the Pope. The references to them here and in Act IV (10772) are anachronistic if we situate the dealings between Faust and the Emperor in the 16th century, but in this symbolic story of prodigal rulers and power conflicts no strict chronology is called for.

11 *gold in the earth*: Goethe here reverts to the folklore theme (which appeared more than once in Part One) that the Devil has knowledge of underground treasure (whether as veins of precious metal or as hidden gold and silver objects) and power to 'raise' or recover it (cf. Part One, 2675 ff., 3664–73).

12 *Astrologer*: on Mephistopheles' role as *souffleur* to the Court Astrologer, see notes to p. xxiii ('*Doppelgänger*') and p. 57. In the speech 4955–70 Mephistopheles wraps up his essential message (the advantages of possessing or magically acquiring silver and gold) in high-sounding astro-babble about the seven planets of the medieval system. Since the latter was geocentric, these included the sun and moon as well as the other five known moving stars, though the seven are here listed in the more correct Copernican order from the sun outwards. 'The Astrologer' alludes to the particular metals with which they were each traditionally associated or identified (the Sun with gold, the Moon with silver, Venus with copper, Saturn with lead, etc.) as well as to the mythical role of the deity after whom each was named (Venus as the love-goddess, Mars as the war-god, and so forth); the double prominence of Venus as morning and evening star is also mentioned (4958).

16 *Carnival masque*: see Introd., pp. xxiv ff. Goethe derived some of the costumed figures and other details for this court pageant from the Roman Carnival which he had seen and described in 1789, some from pictures such as Mantegna's 'Triumphs of Caesar' and Dürer's

'Triumph of the Emperor Maximilian', and a number from the book
by a Renaissance author, Grassini, describing the various triumphs
and masquerades in Florence at the time of the Medicis.

18 *Theophrastus*: a philosopher from Lesbos, *c*.370–287 BC, whose few
surviving works include a long treatise on plants.

20 *dialogues*: the reference in this and the next two stage directions to
unscripted spoken material may or may not mean that Goethe
intended to write it in but left the scene unfinished.

21 *Punchinellos*: the 'Pulcinella' was the stock figure of the clown in the
Italian popular comedy; Goethe uses this Italian form, of which
'Punchinello' (also shortened to 'Punch') was the corrupted English
equivalent.

Parasites: the παράσιτος (literally 'fellow-diner'), who flattered rich
people to earn free meals, was a popular figure in ancient comedy.

23 *Night and Graveyard poets*: Goethe alludes satirically to contemporary
'Gothic' fashions in German and English Romantic literature, which
he considered morbid and unnatural by contrast with the whole-
someness of classical Greek culture and mythology. For the 'Graces',
'Fates', and 'Furies' in the ensuing scene see Index.

26 *Asmodeus*: a demon in Persian or Hebrew mythology whose special
function is to stir up hatred and strife. He is mentioned again in 6961
by Mephistopheles.

mountainous beast: the allegorical elephant group (typical in Goethe's
Renaissance sources for this scene) has been variously interpreted. It
seems to be the last 'real' item in the procession; shortly after it, and
heralded by the arrival of Mephistopheles (5457; see next note), a series
of magical events begins which are not in the official programme and
which the Herald can no longer understand or control (5500–9).

28 *Zoilo-Thersites*: see Index (**Zoilus, Thersites**). Mephistopheles has
assumed the combined role of these two arch-mockers; he appears
in a back-and-front mask, with one face looking each way (these
two-way costumes were a feature of the Roman Carnival).

30 *splendid chariot*: the young driver of the chariot and the regal older
man who rides in it give the impression of being father and son,
symbolically at least (5629, in which Goethe seems to allude to the
words of God heard at the baptism of Jesus (Mark 1:11)). The young
Charioteer, in his initial *badinage* with the Herald (5528–51), explains
that he is himself an allegory of Poetry (5573), and that the father-like
figure is Plutus, the god of wealth (5569). For the information that
Plutus is in fact Faust, we have to go outside the text itself to Goethe's

conversation with Eckermann on 20 December 1829, from which we also learn that the young Charioteer, by magical anticipation, is Faust's son Euphorion who will appear in Act III and who also allegorically personifies Poetry; in his original MS Goethe even wrote 'Euphorion' instead of 'the Boy Charioteer'. These connections are further discussed in the Introduction (pp. xxv f. and note).

34 *the Skinny Fellow* (= 'the Miser' at line 5767): as Goethe also explained to Eckermann on 20 December 1829, the figure of Avarice is a further manifestation of Mephistopheles, contrasting here with the prodigal generosity of the Charioteer and Plutus (Euphorion and Faust); cf. Introd., pp. xxv f. His modelling of the gold into a phallic shape is possibly an allusion to the use of a golden phallus in ancient triumphal processions, as well as a diabolic synthesis of the anal and phallic aspects of gold.

38 *Great Pan*: the 'secret' (5805, 5809) appears to be the fact, known to some of those present, that it is the Emperor himself who is masked as Great Pan (6067). As Pan (see Index) he is accompanied by suitably wild companions, who probably represent various aspects of court life (fauns, satyrs, giants, nymphs); the gnomes revert to the theme of underground treasure waiting to be mined.

42 *his beard*: the final episode, in which the gold sets fire to the Emperor's beard, is discussed in the Introduction (p. xxvi and notes).

44 *prince of a thousand salamanders*: the Emperor's vision of a palace or temple of golden fire stands out as a poetically remarkable passage, as does Mephistopheles' reply. The latter's flattering fantasy (6025 f.) of the Emperor's union with the goddess Thetis (the mother of Achilles by Peleus; see Index, **Peleus**) has been seen by some commentators as a parallel to Helen's union with Faust as a modern counterpart to Achilles. Alternatively, or additionally, we might see the magnificent submarine palace to which Mephistopheles' imagination transports the Emperor as a hint of the motif, found in some versions of the Faust legend, of the Devil satisfying Faust's curiosity by conveying him magically to the heights of heaven and the depths of the sea. (In Thomas Mann's novel *Doctor Faustus* the hero tells of real or imaginary journeys he has made, by bathysphere and perhaps by spacecraft, with a mysterious cosmologist called Professor Capercailzie). Goethe is in any case also influenced in this scene by the *Arabian Nights* stories, which are specifically mentioned in 6032 f.; cf. Introd., p. xxvi.

48 *two worlds . . . happily united*: the Emperor appoints Faust and Mephistopheles as ministerial assistants to the State Treasurer, with

responsibility for locating the hoards and veins of gold which Mephistopheles has promised to extract from the earth as cover for the Emperor's debts. In 6139 f. the Emperor may be referring to the expected happy collaboration between the Treasurer, who is competent in ordinary matters above ground, and Faust, who will reveal subterranean treasures; alternatively, Goethe may be hinting at some more symbolic union of upper and lower worlds. The former reading is suggested by the Treasurer's reply in 6141 f., as he withdraws with Faust, leaving Mephistopheles behind; ironically, Faust seems to be regarded as the chief 'magician' and Mephistopheles as his unimportant subordinate.

51 *Mothers*: see Introd., pp. xxvi f. and note.

54 *buried treasure*: Goethe again hints in 6315 f. (as already in 6191 f. and 6197 f.) that the 'raising' of gold to cover the Emperor's paper money and the 'raising' of Helen for his entertainment are to be thought of as symbolically parallel enterprises (cf. Introd., pp. xxv ff.).

57 *the Astrologer*: Goethe takes up again the rather strange role of the court astrologer, whose speeches (as in Sc. 2) are really those of the 'prompter' Mephistopheles. As in Sc. 3, a narrator seems to be needed who will describe the events on the stage as they happen, rather as if the play were intended for readers and not spectators, and in any case giving the dramatic action in these scenes, such as it is, a half-serious, over-verbalized character, like a vaudeville or revue. It is not clear, however, why Mephistopheles could not equally well speak through the Herald, in this scene at least.

ready magic: as in the 1816 prose sketch, a stage is magically provided for the apparitions (cf. paralipomenon BA 70, p. 242).

61 *Compose yourself*: Mephistopheles only drops his role as prompter when a dramatic crisis develops, as Faust forgets his own part and passionately confuses semblance with reality (6487–500, 6544–63). Even Mephistopheles' spokesman the Astrologer finally intervenes in dismay (6560–3); it is curious that he here (perhaps because it is really Mephistopheles speaking) addresses Faust by name, the only time anyone ever does so in the first three Acts. The crisis itself is reminiscent of an incident in an 18th-century version of the Faust story: in Anthony Hamilton's *L'Enchanteur Faustus* (translated into German in 1778) Faust causes Helen, Cleopatra, and other notable beauties to appear before Elizabeth I of England, but when the Queen tries to embrace one of them there is an explosion, the scene disappears, and Faust is knocked unconscious. Whether or not Goethe used this source, the passionately rash behaviour of his Faust at this point remains problematical if we are trying to think of him

as a seriously developed and developing dramatic 'character'. This is the Faust of Part One rather than the supposedly mature Faust of the Part Two prologue, *A Beautiful Landscape* (cf. note to p. 5); once again, the allegory and the requirements of the particular episode seem to be what is important to Goethe, not a longer-term 'dramatic' view of events.

62 *only ten years old*: the story of Helen's beginnings as a nymphet who got herself kidnapped by the hero Theseus at the age of ten is also alluded to by Faust in Act II (7426 ff.) and by Mephistopheles and Helen herself in Act III (8848 ff.).

65 *bell*: the fact that the bell pulled by Mephistopheles at this point is not heard by Wagner until 200 lines later may mean, as Staiger suggests, that the (in any case episodic) scene between Mephistopheles and the Graduate was interpolated by Goethe at some later time. Alternatively, one could say that the bell rings simultaneously for the famulus Nicodemus (6620), for the Graduate (6727), and for Wagner (6819 f.): a curious device which Goethe will also use in the Classical Walpurgis Night, where the earthquake seems to happen simultaneously in lines 7254 ff., 7503 ff., and 7686 ff. It is in any case interesting that Mephistopheles claims (6727) that by ringing the bell he has himself summoned the Graduate.

66 *Wagner*: Faust's research assistant in Part One (Sc. 4 and 5); see Introd. to Part Two, pp. xxx f.

68 *Graduate*: Mephistopheles' visitor is of course (6686, 6702 ff, 6723, 6741 ff.) the Student who humbly sought his advice in Sc. 7 of Part One, mistaking him for Faust; he is now a Bachelor of Arts (*Baccalaureus*). Asked by Eckermann whether this figure satirically represents any particular contemporary idealistic school of philosophy, Goethe replies:

No, he personifies the kind of presumption that is especially characteristic of youth ... Every young person believes that the world did not really begin until after he was born, and that everything really exists for his sake. In fact there once really was a man in the East who made his servants gather round him every morning, and would not let them begin their work until he had ordered the sun to rise. But he had the good sense not to utter this command until the sun was actually about to appear of its own accord. (Conversation of 6 December 1829)

Despite Goethe's disclaimer, however, it is probable that this comical scene does indeed contain implicit satirical comment on the German idealistic school of metaphysics which flourished in the early 19th century; specific targets are perhaps Fichte (1762–1814) and especially Schopenhauer (1788–1860). Goethe had had some personal dealings with the author of *The World as Will and Idea* (1818), the polemical opening words of which are 'The world is my idea [*meine Vorstellung*]'; they had discussed Goethe's work on the theory of colour, and the young Schopenhauer had shown some degree of intellectual arrogance which Goethe treated forbearingly.

74 *the Homunculus:* see Introd., pp. xxix–xxxii and notes.

76 *romantic, classical:* see 1st note to Introd. p. xlii. The Homunculus is 'romantic' by his origins in medieval Christendom (to which alchemy and the Devil belong) and becomes 'classical' by the Greek sea-change that both he and Faust undergo.

Pharsalus: on the significance of the battle of Pharsalus (AD 48,) see Introd., p. xxix and note.

Asmodeus: see first note to p. 26.

77 *Blocksberg:* the mountain in central Germany on which the German 'Walpurgis Night' sabbath of the witches was supposed to take place (see Part One, Sc. 24).

Thessalian witches: Thessaly (the 'great plain where the Peneus flows' and where the battle of Pharsalus took place) was a region especially associated in antiquity with magic and witchcraft.

78 *one's own creatures:* see Introd., p. xxxi and note.

Classical Walpurgis Night: see Introd., p. xxix. Goethe's intention appears to have been to divide this long scene, or scene sequence, into four or perhaps five shorter scenes with subtitles such as 'The Pharsalian Plain', 'The Peneus', 'Rocky Inlets of the Aegean Coast', but the points of division are not clear and there is in any case some geographical licence. The titles 'By the upper Peneus' at 7080 and 'By the lower Peneus' at 7249 were inserted editorially in 1906 by Erich Schmidt, but do not seem necessary. (Goethe's ALH has merely 'The Peneus' at 7249.) The fluid and dream-like action of the sequence begins, in what I have called Scene 10a, on the battlefield of Pharsalus, some way south of the Peneus (see map), and then moves to the river itself. During his discussion with Chiron in Sc. 10b Faust is evidently carried downstream, to Manto's temple which Goethe situates near Olympus and the Aegean coast. Here they both disappear, and we return to the upper Peneus ('as before', at line 7495) for Sc. 10c; we are then taken downstream again for the Sea Festival in Sc. 10d.

Erichtho's speech: the sorceress Erichtho, who shuns the modern visitors, opens the scene in the grandiose iambic trimeter of Greek drama, which is not used again until Helen speaks at the beginning of Act III. On classical versification, see 1st note to Introd. p. xliii.

Pompey: Gnaeus Pompeius Magnus ('the Great'), the Roman general (106–48 BC) who became the rival of Caesar for supreme power in the Republic; he was finally defeated by him at Pharsalus and murdered shortly afterwards in Egypt.

79 *Caesar*: Gaius Julius Caesar (100–44 BC), the Roman general who after many victories over Rome's enemies abroad achieved autocratic power as consul and dictator, defeating his rival Pompey at the battle of Pharsalus in 48 BC, which decided the civil war (cf. Introd., p. xxix and note). The Roman Republic became a lost cause, and after a period of transition and further conflict Caesar's adopted successor Octavian became the first Roman emperor (Augustus Caesar). The family name became an imperial title, surviving into modern times as 'Kaiser' and 'Tsar'.

80 *You'll see a flash*: Mephistopheles' suggestion of separate exploration is accepted, but the signal for reunion is never in fact given, and this curious motif remains a loose end; Faust, left to his own devices, never communicates again with the Homunculus, and until Act III scarcely at all with Mephistopheles.

81 *greyfins*: the untranslatable word-play in 7092 f. is between *Greife* (griffins; see Index) and *Greise* (old men). It may or may not be relevant that in the Gothic typeface of the early editions of *Faust*, the two letters that Mephistopheles pretends to confuse appear almost identical (f, ſ). Both here and in the absurd etymological discussion that follows (7093–103), Goethe may be making some obscure satirical in-joke.

82 *Sphinxes*: see Index. The Sphinxes are symbolically associated with Goethe's conception, developed long ago in his essay *On Granite* (1784), of an absolutely stable, primal rock (*Urgestein*) uninfluenced by volcanic processes. They are thus related by contrast to the turbulent figure of Seismos, and belong with him to the whole thematic complex of neptunism-vulcanism (see Introd., p. xxxv f. and note).

think of a word: the Sphinx turns the riddle against Mephistopheles by describing the Devil.

83 *Sirens*: see Index.

84 *Chiron*: see Introd., p. xxxii and Index.

89 *Celestial Twins*: see Index, **Twins**.

91 *the Twins*: see Index.

91 *Pherae*: see Index.

92 *great fight*: the battle of Pydna (168 BC) in which Rome finally defeated Macedon; see note to Introd. p. xxix on Pharsalus and Pydna. Since Pydna is well to the north of Mount Olympus, Goethe's description of the battle as taking place between Olympus and the Peneus (7465 f.) seems inaccurate.

Manto: see Introd., p. xxxii and Index.

94 *Seismos*: (see Index). The whole episode (beginning here and continuing intermittently until line 7948) of the new mountain suddenly tossed up out of the earth by the earthquake-god Seismos, the creatures that begin swarming all over it, and the reactions of the Homunculus, Thales, and Anaxagoras to these phenomena, have usually been interpreted as a political allegory referring to the French Revolution of 1789, though an allusion to that of 1830 may also have been intended if Goethe wrote this part of the Classical Walpurgis Night in July of that year or later. In his fragmentary satirical narrative *The Journey of the Sons of Megaprazon*, written in 1792, he had already used a similar complex of imagery: an allegorical class-structured island suddenly blown apart by an earthquake, and the traditional war between the pygmies and the cranes or herons (the 'geranomachy', a motif from Greek mythology), representing the struggle between the mob and the aristocracy. The episode in *Faust* appears to be a reprise and elaboration of these allegorical themes, alluding to events in France as well as to the neptunist-vulcanist controversy. The fall of the meteor which wipes out the warring factions (7936–41) has been interpreted as the decisive intervention of Napoleon. It also seems probable, as Williams (1983, 'Seismos') has argued on textual evidence, that Goethe (never averse to a Rabelaisian jest) intended the various small inhabitants of the upstart mountain to be by-products of a gigantic fart by the earthquake-god; and furthermore, that the episode in which the Cranes of Ibycus (see Index) execute justice on the pygmies (7883–99) may represent the stern measures that Goethe in 1830 thought the governing classes should take against actual or threatened mob violence (Williams, 1984).

98 *Blocksberg, etc.*: Mephistopheles mentions various topographical features of the Blocksberg region (the Ilsenstein, the Heinrichshöhe, the Schnarcher, Elend) which occurred in the 'northern' Walpurgis Night scene (see Part One, Sc. 24).

102 *natural cliff*: in another indirect expression of Goethe's 'neptunist' view, the oread (mountain nymph) contrasts her authentic mountain, shaped by the slow processes of geological time, with Seismos's

unnatural 'lump' which, as Mephistopheles has noted (7808 ff.), was magically upheaved 'in just one night' and will vanish at dawn like a phantom.

105 *Anaxagoras's conjuration of the moon*: the Seismos episode, interwoven with the wanderings of Mephistopheles, the enquiries of the Homunculus, and the geological altercation between the philosophers Thales and Anaxagoras (see Index), reaches its climax in this speech which completes the ironic discrediting of the latter's views and of his pretensions as a rival mentor to the Homunculus. The 'vulcanist' Anaxagoras, in a literally lunatic vision, seeks to emulate the power of the Thessalian sorceresses to call the moon down to earth; the moon-goddess will perhaps save the pygmies ('my people', 7904) from the avenging cranes. His imagined success is explained by the fall of a meteor, seemingly originating from the moon (7939), which knocks away the top of the 'artificial' mountain and crushes both the pygmies and their enemies. The sudden and violent processes on which Anaxagoras pins his faith are thus parodied both by the formation of the mountain 'from underground' and by its deformation from above, all within a few hours (7942-5). The whole sequence of events is pronounced by Thales (7946) to have been mere 'fantasy'. The moon-meteor, whatever its political significance in the allegory, seems to be Goethe's variant on the Greek legend according to which the historical Anaxagoras correctly predicted the fall of a meteor from the sun. The invocation of the moon as both a heavenly and an underground (chthonic) power (7900-9) reflects the triune character of the moon-goddess, who was identified in Greek myth with Artemis (Diana) and the witch-goddess Hecate (7905). See Index, **Diana**; also Williams, 1976.

107 *resinous smell*: in the German text Goethe punningly associates the Harz Mountains with the homophonous but etymologically distinct word *Harz* (resin).

110 *the lofty Cabiri*: the bizarre episode of the 'Cabiri' (pp. 110 f., 113 ff.; see Index) was another of Goethe's afterthoughts exclusive to the final version. It appears to serve a thematic purpose: these mysterious Aegean deities, known only to the classically erudite, are introduced as honoured guests into the Sea Festival because their peculiar characteristic is to have not yet fully come into being. They too are still developing and even, like Faust, 'striving':

> By an onward urge obsessed,
> Hungry with a strange unrest
> For a goal beyond their reach.
> (8203-5)

Eckermann comments ruefully to Goethe on 17 February 1831 that *Faust* 'does contain some intellectual exercises', and that he had only understood this passage because he had read a book on the Cabiri by a contemporary scholar. 'I have always found', replies Goethe relentlessly, 'that to know things is a great help.'

112 *a poet's spell . . . three thousand years*: Nereus alludes to the Trojan War and to the semi-legendary poet who immortalized it (see Index, **Troy**). Homer (?8th century BC) is traditionally identified as the author of the two great epic masterpieces of Greek literature, the *Iliad* and the *Odyssey*; regarded as supreme among poets, his name is given to an age and to a whole corpus of heroic myth and legend.

120 *no Eagle, no Lion . . .*: see Introd., p. xl; the eagle, winged lion, cross, and crescent moon are respectively Byzantium, Venice, the Crusaders, and the Turks.

124 *Scene* 11: this first scene (8488–9126) of the 'Helen' Act closely imitates the style and metre of a classical Greek tragedy (cf. Introd., p. xliii and note). The iambic trimeter used by Helen and Phorcyas (Mephistopheles) is dominant; the Chorus uses ode forms with patterns of metrically related strophes, and at certain points the dialogue changes to trochaic tetrameter (8909–29, 8957–70, 9067–70). The exchange of invective between Phorcyas and the Chorus in alternating single lines ('stichomythia', 8810–25) is a further convention of the style.

135 *in duplicated shape*: see **Helen** in Index.

136 *A phantom to a phantom*: see **Helen** and **Achilles** in Index.

three-headed hell-hound: the monstrous (in some accounts fifty-headed) dog Cerberus who guarded the entrance to the underworld. Hercules (q.v.), as one of his Labours, dragged him up to earth and then returned him.

146 *fruit . . . ashes*: the so-called apple of Sodom, referred to by Milton (*Paradise Lost*, X, 560–6) and Byron (*Childe Harold's Pilgrimage*, III, 34: 'The apples on the Dead Sea's shore, all ashes to the taste'). The fruit (*calotropis procera*) outwardly resembles an apple, but is filled with hairy seeds, popularly identified with the ash from the holocaust of Sodom and Gomorrah.

147 *Faust's speech*: at this point the versification of the dialogue begins to change, and the metres of medieval and modern poetry (especially rhymed verse) become dominant until just before the end of the Act; cf. Introd., p. xliii.

158 *Arcadia*: see Introd., p. xlvi f. and note.

161 *daughter of Crete*: Mephistopheles-Phorcyas has claimed (8864 f.) to have been carried off into slavery by Menelaus on his expedition to Crete.

Hermes: Arcadia was especially associated with Hermes (Mercury), who was thought to have been born there. Goethe takes his catalogue of the god's exploits (9645-78) straight from Hederich's mythological lexicon (see 2nd note to p. xxviii).

166 *the young girl*: there is no agreed interpretation of this curious episode.

169 *'a well-known figure'*: the poet George Gordon, Lord Byron (1788-1824), had died of a fever in Greece while helping the Greeks in their war of liberation from Turkish rule. On the significance of Goethe's posthumous allegorical tribute to him by casting him as Faust's son, see Introd., pp. xlvii f.

Chorus: The Chorus's lament for 'Euphorion' (9907-38) refers in general terms to Byron's character and career (his aristocratic birth, early death, success with women, poetic genius, rebellion against conventional morality, adoption of the 'high purpose' of Greek liberation). In the course of their discussion of the Byron episode, Goethe asks Eckermann whether he has noticed 'that when the Chorus sing his lament, they are quite out of character? Earlier they are in the ancient style throughout, or at least they never cease to be a chorus of young girls; but here they suddenly become serious and full of lofty reflections, uttering things that they have never thought of and never could have thought of.' Eckermann replies that he had indeed noticed it, but that 'such small discrepancies cannot count against a higher beauty if they are the means to its achievement. The song after all had to be sung, there was no other chorus present, and so the girls had to sing it' (conversation of 5 July 1827). From 9939, after the music has stopped, both Helen and the Chorus revert to ancient metres.

170 *Phorcyas's speeches and unmasking*: the last words from Mephistopheles to Faust in Act III (9945-54) are a serious exhortation quite devoid of the speaker's usual cynical inflections; they are thus, as Goethe himself remarked of the Chorus's lament for Byron, 'quite out of character' (see previous note). It is perhaps a pity that no similar pronouncement by Goethe himself on 9945-54 has been recorded, as commentators might then have laid this point to rest. As it is, we have instead the already quoted conversation with Eckermann of 16 December 1829, in which Goethe endorses Ecker-

mann's impression that Mephistopheles exercises some degree of secret control (*Mitwirkung*) not only in the making of the Homunculus but throughout the 'Helena' action (see note to p. xxxix). Goethe had evidently decided to suggest that Mephistopheles, whether disguised as the court jester or as Phorcyas, is in some respects a representative of poetic inventiveness, considered as a kind of 'magical' creativity; hints of this, as we have seen, are already dropped in Act I (see Introd., p. xxvi), and the role of poet also at times appears to be given subliminally to Faust himself (see Introd., pp. xxvii and xxxvi f.). Here as elsewhere (see Introd., pp. xxxiii f.) Goethe seems to have been less concerned with consistency, with the construction of dramatic figures who would always speak 'in character', than with making a statement by means of a symbolic dramatic fantasy, in this case a statement about the nature of art. In Act III it is notable that Mephistopheles not only speaks unironically here about the ennobling effect of Helen (i.e., of classical beauty) on Faust, but also spoke similarly (9620–8) about Euphorion, the newly born personification of Poetry: 'the future master-maker of all beauty, through whose limbs the everlasting music is already flowing.' He reverts to his more usual cynical manner in his mocking speech (9955–61) about the dead Euphorion's garments and their promise of modish literary imitation; he then comes forward and sits down in the proscenium, and when the Chorus has sung the praises of 'the elements' and disappeared into them he rises, still outside the stage, like some gigantic master of ceremonies, and removes his actor's mask and actor's cothurni (the special leather boots that were worn as a symbol of the classical high tragedy). Phorcyas is revealed as Mephistopheles, ready with his unspoken last words on the 'drama' (*Stück*) that we have witnessed. By this ironical final stage direction, Goethe seems to suggest that the whole solemn and stylized 'Helena' action still has, as originally intended, something of the character of an intermezzo, a second-order 'play within a play'; and that art has two aspects or natures, that of timeless monumentality and that of illusion.

175 *Faust's soliloquy*: see Introd., p. l and note.

176 *Eph. 6: 12*: Goethe associates Mephistopheles' reference to the infernal host's 'lordship of the upper air' with St Paul's warning that our real enemies are not of flesh and blood, but evil spiritual powers of all kinds, including (the point is obscured by the Authorized Version but clearer in the Greek or in Luther's German) 'wicked spirits in the celestial regions'. Mephistopheles seems to be saying (10091–4) that the unseen presence of demons in the earth's atmosphere is something that mankind has taken a long time to discover.

177 *Moloch's hammer*: 'Moloch' appears in the Old Testament as the name of a Canaanite god associated with human sacrifice; in Milton and his German imitator Klopstock he is a fierce demon in the service of Satan. In Klopstock's epic *The Messiah* (1848), which Goethe read as a child, he lives among mountains, and strengthens his defences by building new mountains round them (II. 354 ff.).

179 *Babylonian debauch*: Mephistopheles has been describing to Faust the luxurious life of a typical *ancien régime* ruler, surrounded by a pleasure-loving court and a large formal garden such as that of Versailles (which the German princelings of the 18th century strove to imitate). Faust's comment, literally translated, is merely 'Vulgar and modern! Sardanapalus!'. Sardanapalus (668–26 BC), reputedly the most decadent and corrupt of the ancient Babylonian despots, was eventually (like Louis XVI) dethroned by a rebellion. He was the titular hero of a drama by Byron (1821) which the latter had dedicated to Goethe.

183 *mountain people, Peter Quince, Three Mighty Men*: for the 'mountain people' and the three giants, see Introd. pp. lvii f. and notes. Peter Quince, in Shakespeare's *Midsummer Night's Dream*, is the leader of the group of naïve tradesmen who present the 'merry and tragical' play of *Pyramus and Thisbe* at the ducal court; the comparison of Mephistopheles' sinister 'rabble' to these characters seems inappropriate.

187 *mountain folk*: see preceding note.

191 *pictures in the air*: Faust rather implausibly explains the three strong men's demonically multiplied fighting powers to the Emperor by evocatively describing an atmospheric phenomenon sometimes observed in the Strait of Messina between Sicily and Italy. (This seemingly magical mirage effect became known locally as *fata Morgana* after Morgan le Fay, the sister of King Arthur whose legend was carried to Sicily by Norman settlers.)

192 *last fading glow*: the dancing flames noticed by the Emperor on the spear-points of his army are similarly explained by Faust in terms of the luminous electrical discharge sometimes seen on the masts of a ship during a storm. Seamen knew this as 'St Elmo's fire', after the saint whose protection they invoked; it was also associated with the tutelary 'Heavenly Twins' (see Index, **Twins**) whom Faust mentions in 10600.

our Master: the 'sorcerer from Norcia' whom the Emperor had pardoned (see 10439–52 and Introd., p. lvii); he now also sends the favourable omen of the eagle and the griffin (see Index, **Griffin**).

199 *the Emperor and four princes*: Goethe creates a slightly ponderous and comic effect by writing this concluding scene in alexandrine couplets, the old-fashioned metre used by German poets of the earlier 18th century in imitation of French classical drama. For the scene in general, see Introd., p. lviii and note.

206 *that infamous man was granted land*: Goethe originally intended to include a scene showing the formal grant of the coastal lands by the Emperor to Faust, as predicted by Mephistopheles in 10303–6 (see Introd., pp. lviii f. and note). The phrases 'land on the Empire's coast' (11035 f.) and 'the wide sea-strand' (10306; literally 'the limitless strand') may refer to the North Sea or Baltic coasts of the German Empire, but Goethe did not necessarily conceive this motif in terms of geographical realism; for that matter the 'high sea' noticed by Faust on his aerial journey back from Greece (10198) was presumably the Adriatic, where the Empire's coastline could hardly be described as extensive.

207 *Philemon and Baucis*: see Introd., pp. lxii ff. and Index, **Philemon**.

210 *Lynceus the Watchman*: see Introd., p. lxiv and text pp. 147– 51.

213 *from dong to ding*: Goethe is said to have had a particular aversion to the sound of church bells.

217 *Midnight*: on this scene generally, see Introd., pp. lxiv–lxvii.

221 *lemurs*: see Index.

222 *In youth when I did love . . .* : the songs of the Lemurs as they dig Faust's grave, here and on p. 224, are partly adapted by Goethe from the Gravedigger's song in Shakespeare's *Hamlet* (V, i), using the variant version published by Thomas Percy in his *Reliques of Ancient Poetry* (1765).

Mephistopheles' prediction: see Introd., pp. lxviii f.

223 *no ditch*: Goethe here puns untranslatably on *Graben* (ditch) and *Grab* (grave).

Faust's last speech: see Introd., pp. lxx f.

224 *All is fulfilled*: Mephistopheles deliberately echoes Luther's translation ('Es ist vollbracht') of the last words of Jesus on the cross (John 19: 30).

his own blood-scribed document: the Pact and Wager with the Devil which Faust signed in Part One, Sc. 7; on Goethe's less than wholly serious treatment of this motif, see Introd. to Part Two, pp. xiii f.

229 *My head's on fire*: on Mephistopheles' flirtation with the angels, his final discomfiture, and Sc. 22 generally, see Introd., pp. lxxiii ff.

231 *Mountain Gorges*: on this last scene generally, see Introd., pp. lxxv–lxxviii and notes.

237 *Mater Gloriosa*: the Virgin Mother of God revealed in glory, in contrast to the Mater Dolorosa of Gretchen's earlier prayer (Part One, Sc. 21).

Penitent women: the three leading penitents are the prostitute whose 'many sins' Jesus forgave when she anointed his feet in the house of Simon the Pharisee, and who is traditionally sometimes identified with Mary Magdalene (Luke 7: 36–50); the woman of Samaria with 'five husbands' to whom he talked at Jacob's well, promising her the water of eternal life (John 4: 7–29); and Mary of Egypt whose story is told in the *Acta Sanctorum* (a calendar of the histories and legends of the saints and martyrs, compiled by Catholic scholars from the 17th century onwards). This Mary, also a courtesan, had attempted to enter the Church of the Holy Sepulchre in Jerusalem, but an invisible arm barred her way; repenting her sinful life, she then did penance for forty years in the desert, and before dying wrote a message in the sand requesting the monk Socinius to bury her and pray for her.

241 *paralipomena*: see Introd., p. xxi and notes.

paralipomenon BA 5 (1797): this much quoted but cryptic jotting dates from the third or 'classical' period of Goethe's work on *Faust* (see Introd., pp. xiv ff.). It is the only surviving fragment or draft of a more detailed scheme for the drama as a whole, in all probability written at the same time as the *Prologue in Heaven* (summer 1797). The fragment is difficult to interpret owing to its highly condensed style, partial illegibility, and defective punctuation, but it indicates clearly enough that Goethe has now decided to divide his *Faust* into two parts. Most of the formulations refer to Part One, which he was completing at this time. The first two lines seem to summarize Faust's opening soliloquy and the conjuring of the Earth Spirit, the third and fourth possibly refer to his turning away from the Sign of the Macrocosm to that of the Earth Spirit (Part One, 454–61), signifying perhaps his choice of earthly experience and rejection of other-worldly vision. The seventh and eighth lines point to the symbolic affinity between Wagner and the Student as repudiated aspects of Faust; the tenth line recalls the Gretchen tragedy by which the rest of Part One is dominated. ('*Von außen gesehn*' is read as '*von außen gesucht*' by some editors, but both phrases remain obscure.) The movement of Goethe's thought, here characteristic of its 'classical' style under the influence of Schiller, is dialectical, operating in antitheses which are then resolved into syntheses, as in the fifth line; the sixth perhaps expresses a sense of the dramatic value (well understood by Schiller) of clearly polarized contradictions and conflicts. The last three lines again set up antitheses ('from without : outwards : from within', 'life : activity', 'naïvety : consciousness', 'passion : beauty'). The deleted words seem to relate in some way to the last three lines; the eleventh line in particular evidently adumbrates Faust's experiences in Part Two at the Emperor's court ('activity') and with Helen ('beauty'), episodes conceived at this time though not yet written. The last line probably also refers to the concluding phase of Part Two as Goethe now envisaged it, if we may take 'creativity' to refer to Faust's land-reclamation enterprise or something similar, and 'epilogue in Chaos on the way to Hell' as an indication of the eventual non-tragic ending foreseen in the *Prologue in Heaven*: in an answering 'epilogue' Faust is somehow to be rescued from the Devil at the last moment (which is in fact what happens in the comic eucatastrophe of Act V).

241 *paralipomenon BA 70 (1816)*: see Introd., pp. xxi f. and *passim*.

244 *paralipomenon BA 73 (1826)*: see Introd., pp. xxi, xxviii and *passim*. Having decided in 1826 to publish what is now Act III, the 'Helena' Act, as a separate drama, Goethe considered providing an explanatory preface for the general public who had not studied the Faustus legend and knew nothing of what had happened to Goethe's hero after the death of Gretchen. He planned to publish this preface, in advance of *Helena* itself, in his periodical *Art and Antiquity*, but evidently found it difficult to write. Three versions are extant, one consisting for the most part of a highly discursive synopsis of what was later to become Act II, especially the 'Classical Walpurgis Night'. The synopsis is preceded by a preamble in which he gives reasons for having at last decided to publish part of Part Two, and referring to the gap that must be bridged between the Faust of Part One and the 'higher regions' and 'more dignified circumstances' in which he encounters the classical Greek heroine. The much shortened version that actually appeared in *Art and Antiquity* omits the synopsis; I have here omitted the preamble and kept the lengthy but rather more illuminating synopsis. The relationship between this material and the finished Act II is discussed in the Introduction, see especially pp. xxx–xxxiv.

BIBLIOGRAPHY
AND INDEX OF NAMES

I. *Studies in English of* Faust Part Two *and* Faust *generally*

Boyle, Nicholas, 'The Politics of *Faust II*: Another Look at the Stratum of 1831', *Publications of the English Goethe Society*, new series 52 (1981–2), 4–43.

Boyle, Nicholas, '*Du ahnungsloser Engel du!*: Some Current Views of Goethe's *Faust*', *German Life and Letters*, new series 36 (1982–3), 116–47.

Gray, Ronald D., *Goethe the Alchemist* (Cambridge University Press, 1952).

Littlejohns, Richard, 'The Discussion between Goethe and Schiller on the Epic and Dramatic, and its Relevance to *Faust*', *Neophilologus*, 71 (1987), 388–401.

Mason, Eudo C., *Goethe's Faust: Its Genesis and Purport* (University of California Press, 1967).

Williams, John R., 'The Festival of Luna: A Study of the Lunar Symbolism in Goethe's *Klassische Walpurgisnacht*', *Deutsche Vierteljahrsschrift für Literaturwissenschaft und Geistesgeschichte*, 50 (1976), 640–63.

Williams, John R., 'Faust's Classical Education: Goethe's Allegorical Treatment of Faust and Helen of Troy', *Journal of European Studies*, 13 (1983), 103–10.

Williams, John R., 'The Flatulence of Seismos: Goethe, Rabelais and the Geranomachia', *Germanisch-romanische Monatsschrift*, new series 33 (1983), 27–41.

Williams, John R., *Goethe's Faust*, Allen and Unwin (London, 1987).

II. *Studies in German of* Faust Part Two *and* Faust *generally*

Arens, Hans, *Kommentar zu Goethes Faust II*, Karl Winter Verlag (Heidelberg, 1989).

Beutler, Ernst, Introduction and Notes to *Faust*, in Goethe, *Gedenkausgabe*, vol. 5, Artemis-Verlag (Zürich, 1953).

Hamm, Heinz, 'Julirevolution, Saint-Simonismus und Goethes abschließende Arbeit am *Faust*', *Weimarer Beiträge*, 38/11 (1982), 70–91.

Hertz, Gottfried Wilhelm, 'Zur Entstehungsgeschichte von *Faust II* Akt 5 (1825, 1826, 1830)', *Euphorion*, 33 (1932), 244–77.

Hohlfeld, A. R., 'Die Entstehung des Faust-Manuskripts von 1825–26 (VH2)', *Euphorion*, 49 (1955), 283–304.

Lohmeyer, Dorothea, *Faust und die Welt*, Verlag C. H. Beck (Munich, 1975).

Lohmeyer, Karl, 'Das Meer und die Wolken in den beiden letzten Akten des *Faust*', *Jahrbuch der Goethe-Gesellschaft*, 13 (1927), 106–33.

Mommsen, Katharina, *Goethe und 1001 Nacht*, Akademie-Verlag (Berlin, 1960).

Mommsen, Katharina, *Natur- und Fabelreich in Faust II*, de Gruyter (Berlin, 1968).

Pniower, Otto, *Goethes Faust: Zeugnisse und Excurse zu seiner Entstehungsgeschichte*, Weidmannsche Buchhandlung (Berlin, 1899).

Schadewaldt, Wolfgang, 'Zur Entstehung der Elfenszene im 2. Teil des Faust', *Deutsche Vierteljahrsschrift für Literaturwissenschaft und Geistesgeschichte*, 29 (1955), 227–36.

Schuchard, G. C. L., 'Julirevolution, St. Simonismus und die Faustpartien von 1831', *Zeitschrift für deutsche Philologie*, 60 (1935), 240–74, 362–84.

Staiger, Emil, *Goethe*, vol. 3, Atlantis-Verlag (Zürich, 1959).

Vaget, H. R., 'Faust, der Feudalismus and die Restauration', *Akten des VI. Internationalen Germanisten-Kongresses Basel 1980* (Berne, 1980), 345–51.

Williams, John R., 'Die Rache der Kraniche. Goethe, *Faust II* und die Julirevolution', *Zeitschrift für deutsche Philologie*, Sonderheft Goethe, 103 (1984), 105–27.

III. *Miscellaneous*

Freud, Sigmund, *Complete Psychological Works* (Standard Edition), vol. 22, Hogarth Press and Institute of Psycho-Analysis (London, 1964).

Mann, Thomas, *Essays of Three Decades*, Secker and Warburg (London, 1947).

Runciman, S., *The Last Byzantine Renaissance* (Cambridge University Press, 1970).

Runciman, S., *Mistra: Byzantine Capital of the Peloponnese*, Thames and Hudson (London, 1980).

Storr, Anthony, *Solitude*, HarperCollins (London, 1989).

Woodhouse, C. M., *Gemistos Plethon: The Last of the Hellenes* (Oxford University Press, 1986).

IV. *Goethe's conversations and correspondence (index of names)*

Boisserée, Johann Sulpice (1783–1854): a connoisseur and art collector who became one of Goethe's closer friends and advisers from about 1811 onwards, communicating to him in particular some of his passion for medieval art and architecture.

Eckermann, Johann Peter (1792–1854): Goethe's secretary and resident companion from 1823 onwards. His famous *Conversations* appeared after Goethe's death, between 1835 and 1848.

Falk, Johannes Daniel (1768–1826): a writer and philanthropist who lived in Weimar from 1798 onwards; his memoirs, published after Goethe's death, are not thought to be wholly reliable.

Förster, Friedrich (1791–1868): a Berlin writer, editor of various periodicals.

Humboldt, Alexander von (1769–1859): a distinguished scientist and explorer, with whom Goethe became acquainted in 1797.

Humboldt, Wilhelm von (1767–1835): brother of Alexander; a distinguished scholar and statesman, founder of the University of Berlin. His ideas on classical culture were closely akin to those of Goethe and Schiller.

Iken, Karl Jakob Ludwig (1789–1841): a writer, scholar, and translator from Bremen, whose correspondence with Goethe about 'Helena' showed considerable insight.

Kraukling, Karl Konstantin (1792–1873): a librarian from Dresden who visited Goethe in the late summer of 1828.

Luden, Heinrich (1780–1847): a professor of history from Berlin who visited Goethe in 1806.

Meyer, Johann Heinrich (1760–1832): a Swiss painter and art historian whom Goethe met in Rome; he settled in Weimar, and both Goethe and Schiller were decisively influenced by his ideas.

Riemer, Friedrich Wilhelm (1774–1854): a classical scholar, who became the tutor of Goethe's son August in 1803 and lived in his house; Goethe relied on his advice on philological matters. He edited the poet's posthumous work in collaboration with Eckermann.

Schiller, Friedrich von (1759–1805): the dramatist, philosopher, historian, and poet who became Goethe's close intellectual companion and co-founder of Weimar Classicism; the development of Goethe's work on *Faust* owed much to his interest and influence.

Schubarth, Karl Ernst (1796–1861): a classical scholar and critic from Berlin who published a book on Goethe's work and met him in 1820.

Stapfer, Philippe Albert (1766–1840): writer and diplomat, translator of Goethe's dramatic works (including *Faust*) into French.

Zelter, Karl Friedrich (1758–1832): a composer and music teacher from Berlin who from 1799 onwards became one of Goethe's closest friends and set many of his poems to music.

I have not mentioned specific editions containing the letters and conversations quoted, since those who may wish to refer to the German text can nearly always identify them by their dates. There is no complete collection in English of Goethe's letters or conversations. The standard English translation of Eckermann's *Conversations with Goethe in the Last Years of his Life* is that by John Oxenford (1850; repr. Everyman's Library, London, 1930). See also *Conversations and Encounters*, ed. and trans. David Luke and Robert Pick, Oswald Wolff (London, 1966) and *Letters from Goethe*, trans. Marianne Herzfeld and C. A. M. Sym (Edinburgh University Press, 1957).

INDEX OF CLASSICAL GREEK AND ROMAN
MYTHOLOGY AND LEGEND

Achilles (91, 136, 249 f.): son of Peleus and the sea-goddess Thetis; the principal hero on the Greek side in the war against Troy, as described in Homer's *Iliad*, of which he is the central figure. According to one of the many stories about him, he became the lover of **Helen** (q.v.) after they were both dead (8876 ff.), and can thus be cited by Faust (7435) as a precedent for his own pursuit of Helen (see Introd., p. xli and notes).

Aeolus (104, 'Aeolian'): the god of the winds, who kept storm-winds imprisoned in a cave, thus generating explosive pressure.

Aesculapius (92): a semi-divine hero, the son of Apollo by a mortal woman; Apollo entrusted his education to the centaur **Chiron** (q.v.), and he was later worshipped as the god of healing and founder of medicine, thought even to be able to revive the dead. The names of his daughters—Iaso, Hygiea and Panacea—reflect his medical role. See also **Manto**.

Ajax (141): one of the Greek heroes besieging Troy, notable for his exceptional stature and the great shield he carried.

Alcestis (249): see **Pherae**.

Anaxagoras (103–6, 248): an Ionian philosopher of the 5th century BC, said to have written only one book, a treatise on Nature. According to his cosmology, a centrifugal motion initiated by primal Mind has hurled the heavenly bodies outwards from the earth like huge stones and heated them red-hot; they will fall back if this motion slackens. Anaxagoras was said to have foreseen the fall of a meteorite near Aegospotami in 467 BC, predicting that it would fall out of the sun. Goethe adopts him as a representative of the theory that fire is the formative principle of the world (7855, 7865–8; see Introd., pp. xxxv f. and note).

Antaeus (80, 160): a giant, the son of the sea-god Poseidon and the earth-goddess Gaia. His strength increased every time he touched the earth, so that Hercules could defeat him only by strangling him while lifting him in the air.

Aphidnus (135): a friend of **Theseus** (q.v.) and lord of Aphidnae, a stronghold in Attica.

Aphrodite (113, 119, 162): the Greek equivalent of Venus as the goddess of sexual love, also akin to the Oriental Astarte and Ishtar and the Egyptian Isis. She was said to have been a daughter of Zeus, but also to have been born of the sea foam (Gk. ἀφρός) and to have come to land at Paphos in Cyprus or on the island of Cythera off the Laconian coast; she is thus also called the 'Cyprian' (8146), 'Paphian' (8343), or 'Cytherean' goddess. In later sources she is the mother of **Eros** (q.v.).

Apollo (95, 157, 160, 162): the son of Zeus and the goddess Leto, and perhaps the most important of the Olympian gods after Zeus. He represented beauty of form, law and order, prophecy, medicine, archery, music, and the arts generally, being particularly associated with Delphi where his oracle spoke, and with the nearby Mount Parnassus, the home of the Muses. Under his epithet Phoebus ('shining') (7535) he became identified with the sun-god. Line 9558 alludes to the story of his year-long service as a herdsman to Admetus, king of Pherae, a penance imposed on him for killing Zeus's allies the Cyclopes.

Arcadia (157 f.): the mountainous region in the central Peloponnese. Greek myth associated it especially with the gods Hermes (9644) and Pan (9538), and the Roman poet Virgil later founded the tradition which idealizes Arcadia as a setting for the idyllic pastoral life in beautiful and fertile natural surroundings (cf. the evocation of these in 9514–61). Arcadia was also believed to be the earth's oldest inhabited land, older than the moon and hence the 'first land' (9565). Cf. Introd., pp. xlvi f. and note.

Ares (90): the Greek god of war, identified with the Roman Mars (4959).

Argonauts (89 f., 249): the heroes, in one of the most ancient of Greek legends, who sailed in the ship Argo to Colchis, at the eastern end of the Black Sea, to recover the Golden Fleece, a sacred trophy guarded by a dragon. The expedition was led by **Jason** (q.v.), but the names of the participants varied with later elaborations of the story.

Arimaspians (81): a legendary one-eyed people living at the north-eastern limits of the known world; they fought with their neighbours the **Griffins** (q.v.) to gain possession of the hoards of gold which the Griffins guarded.

Athene (later Athena; also known as Pallas Athene) (108, 124): daughter of Zeus and the wise goddess Metis. Fearing that his children by Metis might be wiser than himself, Zeus swallowed her when she became pregnant, and Athene was born out of his head fully armed. She personified wisdom and warlike qualities, and was thought of as the patron goddess of Athens.

Atlas (57, 94): one of the **Titans** (q.v.) who rebelled against Zeus; as punishment he was given the task of holding up the sky on his head and shoulders.

Bacchus (173): see **Dionysus**.

Boreads (90): the winged sons of Boreas, the god of the north wind.

Cabiri (110 f., 113 ff.): ancient pre-Hellenic deities, associated particularly with the islands of Samothrace and Lemnos in the northern Aegean, where they were from early times the object of an important mystery cult about which little is known. They were portrayed as young boys not fully grown, or as jars or pitchers with human heads, in the manner of some early Egyptian gods. There were said to be seven or eight of them (8194–9); this and other points of uncertainty were discussed by modern scholars whom Goethe read (Creuzer, *The Symbolism and Mysticism of*

Ancient Peoples (1811); Schelling, *The Deities of Samothrace* (1815)). The Cabiri were thought to be friendly to man and to protect seafarers from storms; Goethe alludes to this in 8176–85, but their relevance in the Faustian context seems chiefly to be their association with the motif of unfinished development and aspiration to higher forms of existence (8200–5).

Castor and **Pollux** (124): see **Twins**.

Chaos (95, 109): the original cosmic emptiness or formless matter, sometimes quasi-personified and said to have given birth to the primal deities Earth (Gaia), Night (Nyx), and Darkness (Erebus).

Chiron (85, 88–93, 248 f.): the divine semi-equine son of the ocean-goddess Philyra by Cronus the father of Zeus; Cronus approached Philyra disguised as a horse, and their son was born as the original centaur. He was benevolent and wise, being instructed by Apollo in medicine, prophecy, and other arts, and became the tutor of Aesculapius, Jason, Achilles, Hercules, and other heroes.

Cimmerian (140): in Homeric legend, the Cimmerians were the inhabitants of a land of mist and perpetual darkness at the limits of the known world.

Circe (112): in Homer, a daughter of the sun-god who lived on an island and practised evil enchantments, enticing strangers and turning them into animals; her spells were defeated by Ulysses, who became her lover (*Odyssey*, book X).

Clytemnestra (124): daughter of Tyndareus, king of Sparta, and of his wife Leda, and thus half-sister to Helen; she married Agamemnon, king of Mycene, the brother of Helen's husband Menelaus, but murdered him on his victorious return from Troy.

Cronus: leader of the Titans and predecessor of **Zeus** (q.v.).

Cyclops (112 ('monster with one eye'), 141): the Cyclopes were a race of giants having a single large central eye; one of them, Polyphemus, is blinded by Ulysses in book IX of Homer's *Odyssey*. In other contexts they appear as the forgers of the thunderbolts of Zeus or as workmen who built the walls of cities such as Mycene with massive natural stone blocks (9020 f.).

The **Cyprian** (112): see **Aphrodite**.

Cythera (124): an island in the gulf of Laconia, associated with the cult of Aphrodite.

Deïphobus (142, 153): a Trojan prince who after the death of his brother Paris became the lover of Helen, thus incurring the wrath of Menelaus.

Delos (94): a small island in the centre of the Aegean, supposed to have been the birthplace of Apollo and his twin sister Artemis (Diana). When Zeus's mistress Leto was about to give birth to them, his jealous wife Hera forbade all lands to receive her, but Delos (in the account adopted by Goethe) rose from the sea to give her refuge.

Diana (105): the Roman equivalent of Artemis, daughter of Zeus and the goddess Leto. She was chiefly thought of as goddess of hunting, but was also identified with the moon-goddess Luna (Selene) by association with her twin brother Apollo as sun-god, as well as with the goddess Hecate who was associated with sorcery and the underworld and said to have a threefold shape. Anaxagoras (7903 ff.) invokes the moon-goddess as three goddesses in one.

Dionysus (174): the son of Zeus and the Theban princess Semele; object of a very primitive or perhaps originally non-Greek cult as god of wine, viniculture, intoxication, and ecstasy. In 10011–38 Goethe evokes the 'mystery', or orgy, of his frenzied worshippers (satyrs, fauns, maenads, etc.), which involved promiscuous copulation and the tearing and devouring of the raw flesh of wild animals. Dionysus was also known as **Bacchus** (hence 'bacchant(e)s', 'bacchanalia'), and the Romans usually adopted this name for their wine-god; the Greeks also associated him with the Egyptian god Osiris.

Dorids (112, 120 f.): daughters of the sea-god Nereus by the ocean-nymph Doris; sisters of the Nereids, from whom Goethe's sources did not distinguish them.

Dryad (107): a tree-nymph (Gk. δρῦς, tree, oak-tree); see also their chorus, 9992–8.

Eleusis (91 'Eleusinian swamp'): a town on the Attic coast west of Athens, famous in antiquity as the site of a secret religious cult (Eleusinian Mysteries).

Empusa (100, 246): a shape-shifting, lascivious, blood-sucking monster with donkey's feet.

Enceladus (247): one of the giants who unsuccessfully rebelled against Zeus and the other Olympian gods; they were thought to be buried under volcanoes. In Goethe's final version of the 'Classical Walpurgis Night' his role is taken over by the earthquake-god **Seismos** (q.v.).

Endymion (61): see **Luna**.

Enyo (248): one of the **Phorcyads** (q.v.) (Pemphredo, Enyo, and Deino); cf. Introd., pp. xxxviii f. and text 7967–8033.

Erebus (133): see **Chaos**.

Erichtho (78 f., 246): a Thessalian sorceress, reputed to be a malignant blood-sucking monster, but able to prophesy and to conjure up the dead. According to Lucan's epic the *Pharsalia*, which Goethe read in 1826, Sextus Pompeius, the son of Pompey the Great, sought out this witch in her sepulchral retreats, and consulted her about the outcome of the impending decisive battle of Pharsalus between his father and Caesar.

Erichthonius (246): son of the fire-god Hephaestus (Vulcan) and the earth-goddess Gaia, who became king of Athens and was reputed to have dragon's feet. Goethe's etymological association of him with Erichtho is a facetious invention.

Eros (123, 162): the personification of the sexual drive (Gk. ἔρως, love). In earlier accounts he was a primal deity born out of the original Chaos, as the all-begetting and all-uniting life force; in 8479 Goethe expresses a similar conception. Later, in poetry and as his Roman equivalent Amor or Cupido (Cupid), he is seen as the youngest of the gods, the companion or son of Aphrodite, a cruel or mischievous boy who wounds gods and men with his arrows.

Euphorion (Sc. 13): son of Achilles and Helen, begotten when they met after death as ghostly lovers on the island of Leuce (or in the Isles of the Blest according to another version). His name (from εὔφορος, 'bearing good things') appears to refer to the fertility of his native soil. He was born with wings, and later attracted the amorous attention of Zeus, but fled from his advances; the god pursued him to the island of Melos, and there struck him dead with a thunderbolt. Some nymphs who took pity on him and buried him were turned into frogs. For Goethe's use of the name 'Euphorion' for Helen's son by Faust, see Introd., p. xli and notes.

Eurotas (125, 140, 143, 156): the river (see map) takes on a quasi-mythical character by its associations with Helen. She is born, or rather hatched (9517–21), beside it (presumably near the city of Sparta), and its 'grassy bank' in Yeats's poem 'Lullaby' is also where Leda conceived her. On returning from Troy, she lands (8538 f.) with Menelaus and his army at its mouth in the Gulf of Laconia (a place still called Skala, 'harbour').

Eurydice (249): see **Orpheus**.

Fates (Gk. Μοῖραι, Lat. Parcae) (24 f., 108, 139): the implacable goddesses of destiny, equivalent to the Norns of Nordic mythology; they were thought of as three old women spinning the thread of human life.

Fauns (39, 173): see **Satyrs**.

Furies (called in Gk. Ἐρινύες) (25 f.): spirits of vengeance who executed curses, pursued and tormented the guilty, and brought about famines and pestilences. In later sources there are three of them, with the names that Goethe uses, though he deliberately trivializes their roles.

Galatea (112, 120 f.): a sea-nymph, the favourite daughter of the old sea-god Nereus (q.v.), who thinks of her (8144–9) as inheriting the functions of Aphrodite (q.v.) and sharing her divinity. Galatea riding on a chariot of shells was a motif in paintings by Raphael which Goethe had seen in Rome. He introduces her at the climax of the sea-pageant as if to emphasize her special importance.

Gorgon (249): a female monster with terrifying attributes, such as snakes growing out of her head instead of hair and eyes that turned anyone who looked at her to stone. Homer mentions only one gorgon, other sources three (Sthenno, Euryale, and Medusa; see also **Phorcyads**). The hero **Perseus** (q.v.), with divine assistance, killed and decapitated Medusa.

Graces (23 f., 112): the goddesses personifying social charm and attractive-ness, usually three in number (Aglaia, Thalia, and Euphrosyne), but in Athenian tradition the name Hegemone is also found, which Goethe adopts possibly to avoid confusion with the Muse Thalia.

Graiae (131): see **Phorcyads**.

Griffin or **Gryphon** (Gk. γρύψ) (81, 96, 192 f., 246): a gold-guarding monster with the body of a lion and the head and wings of an eagle. The Griffins lived in the remote north-east of the known world, like their enemies the Arimaspians; the historian Herodotus compared them to pedantic, grumpy old men, a motif which Goethe adopts in 7093 ff. In medieval times the griffin was adopted as a heraldic animal (cf. 10625 ff., where its hybrid shape also befits the false emperor).

Hades (144, 171): the god of the underworld, whose name was later extended to refer to the underworld itself. Originally his domain fell to him by lot, as the brother of Zeus and Poseidon, who became gods of the sky and the sea respectively. Hades, who carried off and married Persephone, was also euphemistically called Pluto (Gk. Πλούτων, 'the giver of riches', because metals were found under the earth).

Harpies (134, 246): wind-demons who carried off persons or things (Gk. ἁρπάζω, 'snatch') and defiled food as it was being eaten. They were portrayed as winged women or birds with women's faces.

Hebe (90): a daughter of Zeus, who poured out nectar for the gods and personified eternal youth, like the Nordic goddess Freya. She conducted favoured mortals to Olympus and became the wife of Hercules when he joined the immortals there.

Hecate (105): see **Diana**.

Helen (**Helena**) (50, 60–3, 84, 90–3, Act III *passim*): a mortal daughter of Zeus, said to have been born of an egg (9521) laid by Leda, queen of Sparta, after Zeus had visited her in the form of a swan. She was reputedly the most beautiful of all women, and renowned for her fatal attractiveness to men. After marrying **Menelaus** (q.v.), who then became king of Sparta, she was abducted by the Trojan prince **Paris** (q.v.), thus occasioning the war of the Greeks against Troy; according to another story, however, Zeus allowed only a phantom of her to go to Troy, and removed the real Helen to Egypt for safe keeping during the war (8872 f.). Among many other legends about her and her lovers is that in which she and the hero **Achilles** (q.v.) are for a time miraculously united after death (8876 ff., 7435) and she bears him a son called **Euphorion** (q.v.)). For Goethe's use of this story and of the figure of Helen generally, see Introd., *passim*.

Helios (117, 173): the sun-god (Gk. ἥλιος, sun); see **Apollo**.

Hercules (Gk. **Heracles**) (84, 90, 135): the son of Zeus and Alcmena, a mortal woman whom the god seduced by impersonating her husband Amphit-ryon. Their son became the most famous of the Greek heroes, having legendary strength and endurance. He performed twelve seemingly impossible tasks (the 'labours of Hercules'), killed various monsters, and was eventually raised to Olympus and worshipped as a god.

Hermaphrodite (109): originally from the name (Ἑρμαφρόδιτος) of a son of Hermes and Aphrodite whose body became joined to that of a nymph; hence, a being having the physical characteristics of both sexes ('hermaphroditical', 8256).

Hermes (90, 144, 161 f.): son of Zeus and the goddess Maia, identified by the Romans with their god Mercurius (Mercury). He acted as messenger to the other gods and as guide of departed souls to the underworld (9116 ff.). He was thought to have been born in **Arcadia** (q.v.), and was especially associated with merchants, thieves, bodily agility, clever speech, and mischievous exploits (9644-78).

Hippocampus (117): a sea-horse with front hooves and a dolphin's tail.

Hours (4 (Gk. Ὧραι, Lat. Horae)): strictly, these were goddesses personifying the seasons or other fixed periods of the natural cycle. They were thought of as daughters of Zeus and attendants on the gods. Homer (*Iliad*, book v) describes them as the keepers of the gates of the sky; later they were especially associated with the sun-god.

Ibycus (98 ('Cranes of Ibycus')): the poet Ibycus was killed by bandits as a flock of cranes passed overhead; later, the murderers saw the birds again, and were stricken by this avenging omen into confessing their guilt. The story is told in one of Schiller's ballads.

Icarus (169): son of the legendary master craftsman Daedalus. He succeeded in flying with the pair of wings his father had made for him out of feathers and wax, but flew so near the sun that the wax melted and he fell into the sea.

Ilium (Ilion) (112): see **Troy**.

Jason (90): leader of the **Argonauts** (q.v.). His uncle Pelias had usurped his kingdom in Thessaly, but promised to restore it if Jason brought him the Golden Fleece from Colchis. The sorceress Medea, daughter of the king of Colchis, helped Jason to carry it off and eloped with him to Greece, where she took revenge on his enemies and later on Jason himself by killing their two children after he had deserted her.

Juno (108, 175): wife of Jupiter (see **Zeus**); she was identified by the Romans with Zeus's wife Hera.

Jupiter: see **Zeus**.

Lamiae (85, 99 ff., 248): vampire-like monsters who fed on human flesh and blood and took on attractive female shapes to entice their victims.

Leda (175): wife of Tyndareus, king of Sparta; loved by Zeus, who took the shape of a swan to visit her, and by whom she became the mother of Helen and the Dioscuri (see **Twins**).

Lemurs (Lat. *lemures*) (221–4): restless ghosts of the dead. Goethe had seen an ancient tomb near Naples on which they were portrayed as skeletons with still enough muscles and sinews to enable them to move.

Lernaean snake (Lernaean Hydra) (85): a monstrous water-serpent in the marshes of Lerna near Argos, with many heads, which multiplied as they were hacked off; it was killed by Hercules with the help of a companion who sealed the stumps with firebrands.

Lethe (3, 68, 250): in Virgil's *Aeneid*, one of the rivers of the underworld, whose water when drunk by the dead caused them to forget their earthly lives (Gk. λήθη, oblivion); hence, death or forgetfulness generally.

Leto (94): a goddess loved by Zeus, who became the mother of Apollo and Artemis (Diana); see **Delos**.

Leuce (250): an island in the western Black Sea on which the shade of Helen was allowed to meet that of Achilles, on condition that she did not leave Leuce (see **Euphorion**, **Pherae**).

Luna (61, 105): the moon-goddess (Gk. Σελήνη; see **Diana**). She was said to have loved the beautiful youth Endymion and descended to him as he lay asleep in a cave.

Lynceus (90, 147–51, 210 f., 214 f.): one of the Argonaut heroes, gifted with far sight; his name (Λύγκειος) is evidently derived from 'lynx' (λύγξ).

Maia (161): a goddess, the daughter of the Titan Atlas, who became the mother of Hermes by Zeus.

Manto (92 f., 249 f.): an aged prophetess or sibyl, also seen as a Thessalian sorceress paralleling Erichtho in her ability to raise the dead. According to the received mythological tradition her father was the blind seer Tiresias; but in his final version of Act II Goethe makes her a daughter of **Aesculapius** (q.v.), the god of healing, in order to emphasize her therapeutic role towards Faust (7446–51, 7487). He also invents her story of having guided Orpheus to the underworld (7493), as the Cumaean sibyl guided Virgil's Aeneas (*Aeneid*, book VI). (See Introd., pp. xxii, xxxv, xxxvii.)

Marsi (119): see **Psylli**.

Menelaus (124, 135, 140, 153): younger brother of Agamemnon, king of Mycenae; as husband of Helen he succeeded her putative father Tyndareus as king of Sparta. The elopement of Helen with the Trojan prince Paris provoked the expedition of the Greeks against Troy, which Agamemnon commanded.

Muses (Gk. Μοῦσαι, Lat. Musae) (95): the goddesses who inspired men to poetry, music (μουσική τέχνη, the art named after them), and other intellectual achievements. They were associated with **Apollo** (q.v.) and **Parnassus** (q.v.), but their number, names, and attributes varied.

Neptune (114, 117, 222): see **Poseidon**.

Nereids (44, 110, 113 f., 247): sea-nymphs, daughters of **Nereus** (q.v.).

'all' (πᾶν), he was sometimes understood as some kind of universal god. The Emperor is disguised as 'Great Pan' in the Carnival (Sc. 3).

Paphos (113): see **Aphrodite**.

Paris (50, 59 f., 112, 142): a son of Priam, king of Troy, to whom it was prophesied that the child would bring destruction on the city; he was exposed in the mountains but rescued, and spent his youth as a shepherd (6459). In the story known as the 'judgement of Paris' he was called upon, as the most beautiful of mortal men, to settle a beauty contest between the goddesses Hera, Athena, and Aphrodite, and awarded the prize to Aphrodite who had promised him the love of the most beautiful of mortal women. Restored later to his family, he was sent on an embassy to Sparta, where King Menelaus's wife **Helen** (q.v.) fell in love with him and fled with him to Troy. This brought about the Trojan War, at the end of which Paris was fatally wounded by a poisoned arrow.

Parnassus (95): the high mountain near Delphi, the site of the famous 'Delphic oracle' of Apollo; the whole mountain was sacred to Apollo and the Muses, as was the spring named after the nymph Castalia, who threw herself into it when fleeing from the god. The stream runs between two peaks which were sometimes thought of as the mountain's twin summits (to which Goethe here refers), though the real summit (2460m) is in fact high above them.

Patroclus (135): in Homer's *Iliad*, the beloved friend and companion-in-arms of **Achilles** (q.v.). While the latter, having quarrelled with Agamemnon, remains in his tent refusing to fight, the Greeks come close to defeat, and Patroclus begs his friend to allow him to rejoin the war on his behalf. Achilles lends him his own armour to terrify the Trojans (hence 'lookalike', 8855), but Patroclus is killed by the Trojan leader Hector. The grief-stricken Achilles turns his rage against Troy, and fights and kills Hector, which seals the fate of the city.

Peleus (44): a mortal descended from Zeus who became king of Phthia in Thessaly and married the sea-nymph Thetis, daughter of the old sea-god Nereus; their only child was Achilles, who is frequently referred to as 'the Peleid'.

Pelion and **Ossa** (95): two high mountains south-east of Olympus; giants rebelling against Zeus piled the one on top of the other and both on Olympus, in an attempt to scale the heavens.

Pelops (166): a descendant of Zeus who became the ruler of the whole southern peninsula of Greece, thereafter known as the Peloponnese (Πέλοπος νῆσος, 'island of Pelops'); see map.

Peneus (76, 86, 93): as the principal river of Thessaly (see map), the Peneus becomes a symbolic point of reference for the 'Classical Walpurgis Night' scenes, eventually leading down to its outflow into the Aegean for the last of these (cf. note to p. 78, 'Classical Walpurgis Night'). It is personified as a god (7249–56) and attended by nymphs and sirens. Faust's lines 7271–306 associate it in a dream-like way with the begetting of Helen and thus with the river **Eurotas** (q.v.).

Persephone (Lat. Proserpina) (93, 170 f., 249): daughter of the earth-mother Demeter; Hades (Pluto) carried her off and made her queen of the underworld. She was allowed to return to her mother during part of every year, her story thus symbolizing the annual growth of corn and the cycle of death and life.

Perseus (xxxix): a son of Zeus by Danae, a princess imprisoned in a tower to whom the god descended in the form of golden rain. His most famous exploit was the killing of the monstrous **Gorgon** (q.v.) Medusa; Goethe seems to have liked this story, to which Mephistopheles alludes twice in Part One (4194, 4208).

Pherae (91): a city in Thessaly, ruled by Admetus, whose wife Alcestis was brought back from the dead by Hercules after voluntarily sacrificing her life for her husband. By substituting 'Pherae' for 'Leuce' in 7435, Goethe deliberately associates this well-known story with that of the post-mortal encounter of Helen with Achilles on the island of **Leuce** (q.v.), which he uses as the main parallel to Helen's union with Faust and to which he refers elsewhere, mentioning the traditionally correct venue (see **Euphorion, Leuce**). In 7435 Helen and Achilles meet 'on [*auf*] Pherae'; the preposition, which suggests an island, is possibly an oversight.

Philemon and **Baucis** (Act V, Sc. 17–19): Ovid (*Metamorphoses*, book VIII) retells the Greek story of how Zeus and Hermes were travelling incognito in Phrygia and were refused hospitality by everyone until a poor but pious couple took them in. The gods punished the rest of the people by causing a flood to engulf the land, but rewarded Philemon and Baucis by turning their hut into a temple and granting their wish to die together; the husband was turned into an oak and his wife into a linden-tree. For the indirect connection between this story and the opening scenes of Act V, see Introd., p. lxiii and note.

Philyra (88): an ocean-nymph who became the mother of the centaur **Chiron** (q.v.); appalled at having given birth to a monster, she asked to be turned into a linden-tree (φιλύρα).

Phoebus (94): one of the names of Apollo, associating him particularly with the sun.

Phorcyads (107 ff.): three hags, also known as the Graiae, representing extreme old age and ugliness; they lived in a remote, dark place, sharing one eye and one tooth between them. Like their sisters and neighbours the **Gorgons** (q.v.), they were daughters of the sea-ancient Phorcys or Phorcos; Goethe varies the usual Greek form of their name (Φορκίδες, Lat. Phorcydes) to *Phorkyaden*, which I have imitated as 'Phorcyads'. For his use of the myth generally, see Introd., pp. xxxviii f.

Phorcyas (130–43 and Act III, *passim*): Mephistopheles in the shape (8027) of one of the **Phorcyads** (q.v.). Goethe uses '*Phorcyas*' (his adaptation of the Greek singular form Φορκίς, 'daughter of Phorcos') virtually as a proper name, instead of 'the Phorcyad'; his procedure in the case of '(the) Homunculus' seems to be similar.

Phorcys, Phorcos (131): see **Phorcyads**.

Pluto (43, 104 ('Plutonian')): see **Hades**.

Plutus (31–43): a god personifying riches (Gk. πλοῦτος, wealth; see **Hades**). Faust assumes the disguise of Plutus in the Carnival (see Introd., pp. xxv f. and note), but Goethe has ignored the tradition which represents Plutus as blind.

Poseidon (124): the brother of Zeus and Hades, to whom it fell by lot to be the ruler of the seas, though he was also responsible for earthquakes (in Homer he is 'the earth-shaker'). As an important god embodying and controlling elemental forces, he enjoyed an ancient and widespread cult; the Romans came to identify him with their water god Neptune. He was represented as stirring up the ocean with a trident, or riding across it with brazen-hooved horses. He was said to have fathered various monsters, including the one-eyed 'Cyclops' giants encountered by Ulysses during his voyage.

Protesilaus (249): a Thessalian prince who after his death in the Trojan War was allowed to return to his grieving wife for three hours.

Proteus (113, 115–19, 122 f.): a sea-god subordinate to Poseidon. He was gifted with knowledge and prophecy, and particularly noted for his constant self-transformations, which he often used to avoid questioning; he would answer if caught and held long enough to resume his true shape.

Psyche (226): the personified human 'soul' (Gk. ψυχή, literally 'breath'), represented in art as a human figure with butterfly's wings, or simply as a butterfly, which Mephistopheles describes as a winged worm.

Psylli (119): the Psylli and Marsi were ancient peoples from Libya and central Italy respectively, who had in common a reputation for snake-charming and skill in the healing of snake-bites. Goethe, using other sources and his own invention, moves them to Cyprus, and makes them priestly guardians and escorts of the nature-goddess Galatea, fulfilling an eternal, cyclic function which unobtrusively continues (8370–8) despite successive conquests of the island by warring human civilizations. If Goethe regarded snake-charming as relevant to this theme, he does not make the connection clear.

Pythian priestess (145): the prophetess of Apollo's oracle at Delphi was known as the 'Pythia', from the epithet 'Pythian' which the god had acquired after killing the serpent Python when he first came to Delphi, thus defeating the earth-goddess who preceded him there.

Rhea (108, 139): the sister and wife of Cronus and mother by him of Zeus and the other Olympian gods; sometimes identified with the Phrygian mother-goddess Cybele. The Roman equivalents of Cronus and Rhea were Saturn and Ops (7989).

Rhodes (Rhodos) (117): this island in the south-eastern Aegean was said to be specially favoured by the sun-god, who dispelled all clouds here as soon as they gathered (8293–8); the 'Colossus of Rhodes' was his statue, and a cult of Apollo was practised. Lines 8290–302 invoke Apollo as brother of the moon-goddess (8287 ff.; see **Diana**).

Samothrace (110): an island in the northern Aegean particularly associated with the mystery cult of the **Cabiri** (q.v.).

Satyr(s) (39, 86, 174): the companions of the revelry of **Dionysus** (q.v.) (see 10011–38), represented as partly human and partly animal and symbolizing wild uninhibited natural life. The Romans knew them as fauns (5819–28, 10018), Faunus being their equivalent of **Pan** (q.v.), to whom the satyrs are comparable; see also **Silenus**.

Scylla (133): a monster with six heads who lived in a cave at one side of a narrow sea passage, opposite the whirlpool Charybdis. In Homer's *Odyssey* (book XII), Ulysses' ship is forced to pass close to the cave, and Scylla seizes and devours six of his men. She was a daughter of **Phorcys** (q.v.) and therefore 'sibling' to Phorcyas.

Seismos (Gk. σεισμός, earthquake) (94 f.): Goethe's personification of the earthquake and volcanic forces generally; see Introd., p. xxxvi and note.

Sibyl (Gk. σίβυλλα, Lat. sibylla) (92, 249): a general name for various prophetesses in the ancient world, whose ecstatic utterances were thought to be inspired by a god and recorded as precious oracles. Later, they were sometimes adopted by Christian teaching and art as having the same status as Old Testament prophets. Goethe's use of such a figure in the 'Classical Walpurgis Night' thus reinforces the theme of Faust as a link between ancient and medieval culture.

Silenus (174): a kind of forest-god or nature-spirit, half human and half animal like **Pan** (q.v.) and the satyrs or fauns, though represented as an old man, drunken but gifted with wisdom.

Sirens (83 ff., 93 f., 109 f., 247): female demons whose magical singing lured seafarers to destruction. In Homer's story (*Odyssey*, book XII), Ulysses stops his men's ears with wax, but listens himself as the ship passes the rocks; he is enticed by the Sirens' promise to tell him everything he wants to know (7204 f.), but has ordered his men to lash him to the mast (7210) and on no account to release him until they are out of danger. In art the Sirens were depicted as half women and half birds, a shape which Goethe seems to adopt for them (7152 f.), though he moves them from the rocky coast to more innocuous locations in Sc. 10a (the plain) and Sc. 10c (by the river) and in general reduces their sinister mythological role.

Sparta (124, 155, 157): capital city of the kingdom ruled by Helen's putative father Tyndareus (see **Leda**) and then by her husband Menelaus. In historical times Sparta became an important military state with a distinctive, austere culture. It was also called **Lacedaemon**, a name which in its alternative Latin form Laconia is still that of the corresponding region in the southern Peloponnese, of which Sparta is the administrative centre.

Sphinxes (82–6, 94 ff., 246): the sphinx, a monster originating in Egyptian mythology, was a winged lion with a human head; in Greek literature it is female. The function of Goethe's sphinxes in these scenes is less than consistent, but they seem in several passages, by association with the colossal stone sphinx at Giza, to represent proud monumental antiquity and stability (7241–8, 7528 f., 7574–81); cf. 1st note to p. 82.

Stymphalids, or 'Stymphalian Birds' (85, 247): monstrous birds infesting the forest round Lake Stymphalus in Arcadia; they were destroyed by Hercules as one of his twelve labours.

Telchines (pron. 'Tel-khī-nēs') (117): legendary inhabitants of Rhodes, said to have magical powers and to be skilled metal-workers (as in the making of statues of the gods, 8299 ff.).

Thales (103–6, Sc. 10c *passim*, 247 f.): Thales of Miletus, according to tradition, was the first of the Greek philosophers (*c.*600 BC). He was credited with various discoveries, and said to have taught that all things are modifications of one eternal substance, which Thales held to be water. Goethe adopts him as the representative of the 'neptunist' doctrine (see Introd., p. xxxvi and note).

Thebes (141): the principal city of Boeotia, supposed to have been the birthplace of Dionysus and of Hercules and the scene of many other famous myths, notably those involving Oedipus and his family. Goethe's allusion is to the legend of the seven champions who attacked the city, led by one of the warring sons of Oedipus; these were the subject of Aeschylus's tragedy *The Seven Against Thebes*.

Thersites (28): in Homer's *Iliad*, an ugly low-born Greek noted for his cynical and scurrilous abuse of the heroes besieging Troy; he also appears in Shakespeare's *Troilus and Cressida*. (Cf. **Zoilus**.)

Theseus (135): a mythical king of Athens, the son of Aegeus (after whom the Aegean Sea was named); he was thought of as a parallel figure to Hercules (8849) and credited with a number of similar heroic exploits, including the killing of the monstrous Minotaur of Crete. Goethe's allusion is to the story according to which Theseus abducted Helen when she was a child, carrying her off to Aphidnae in Attica, where she was rescued by her brothers the Dioscuri (see **Twins**).

Thessaly (109, 246): the fertile plains of Thessaly were reputed, in mythical times and later, to be full of sorcerers and witches, able to predict the future and conjure the moon down to earth. ('Thessalian witches', 77, 106; 'Thessalian hag', 171).

Thetis (44): see **Peleus**.

Thyrsus-staff (101): a wand wreathed in ivy and vine-leaves, with a pine-cone at the top, carried by the worshippers of Dionysus.

Tiresias (133, 249): a Theban seer, appearing in many stories, who was blind but gifted with prophecy and a sevenfold or ninefold life-span (hence typifying extreme old age).

Titans (95): the original generation of gods, preceding **Zeus** (q.v.) and the other 'Olympian' deities. In the Greek myth, as in others world-wide, they were children of the Sky (Uranus) and the Earth (Gaia). Cronus, the youngest, overpowered and castrated his father Uranus, married his sister Rhea, and by her was the father of Zeus and his siblings, who in their turn eventually overthrew him and the other Titans after a ten-year war (the 'Titanomachy').

Tritons (110, 113 f., 247): originally 'Triton' was the name of an individual son of the sea-god Poseidon, half human in shape but resembling a fish from the waist down; he is then pluralized in some stories. Goethe's 'nereids and tritons' correspond to mermaids and mermen.

Troy (Troia) (62, 112, 124, 128, etc.): an ancient fortified city in north-west Asia Minor, also called **Ilium**, and chiefly famous as the semi-legendary theme of the *Iliad*, the heroic epic poem traditionally attributed to Homer. The poem describes the last phase of the ten-year siege of Troy by an expedition of allied mainland Greeks, which ended in the city's destruction (Trojan War, ?13th or 12th century BC); modern archaeological excavations have suggested that this story may have some historical basis. A second epic (the *Odyssey*, also attributed to Homer) describes the adventures of Ulysses (Gk. Odysseus) in the aftermath of the war. (See **Helen, Menelaus, Paris, Achilles**).

Twins (89 ('Celestial Twins'), 91 ('Twins') 124 ('the twins Castor and Pollux')): the twin sons of **Leda** (q.v.), Castor and Polydeuces (Lat. Pollux). Zeus, the father of their sister Helen by Leda, was also said to have fathered one or both of the Twins, who were therefore known as the Dioscuri (Διὸς κοῦροι, 'sons of Zeus'). Their exploits included an expedition to rescue their sister (7416) when she had been abducted by Theseus, and they were also said to have sailed with the Argonauts (7369). Later tradition associated them with the Cabiri and with the protection of mariners (10,600 f.); they also appear as the zodiacal constellation of Gemini (the 'Heavenly Twins').

Tyndareus (124, 140): king of Sparta, husband of Helen's mother Leda.

Ulysses (a generally adopted later spelling of 'Ulyxes', the Latin form of the original Greek name Odysseus) (85, 112): the hero of Homer's *Odyssey* and a prominent figure in the *Iliad* (see **Troy**). Goethe alludes here only to his adventure with the **Sirens** (q.v.) (*Odyssey*, book XII).

Venus (108, 112): see **Aphrodite**.

Zeus (82, 121, 128, 162, etc.): the supreme god, identified by the Romans with Jupiter. His father, the **Titan** (q.v.) Cronus, feared his own overthrow, and swallowed all his offspring except Zeus, who was hidden from him and grew up in Crete, eventually defeating and dethroning Cronus and casting down the other Titans. He then divided the world by lot with his brothers Poseidon and Hades, these taking the sea and the underworld respectively, while Zeus ruled the heavens, commanding thunderstorms and the weather generally, like other sky-gods of world mythology; the 'thunderbolt', wielded only by him, signifies his supreme power. He is called 'the cloud-gatherer' by Homer, and lives on or above high mountain-tops, holding court especially on Mount Olympus. He is also the supreme representative of impartial justice. Although his official partner was his sister Hera (Juno), he loved many other goddesses and mortal women, and was called 'father of gods and men' as being the only god who had himself fathered other important gods, as well as various human or semi-divine heroes. (see **Apollo**, **Diana**, **Dionysus**, **Helen**, **Leda**, **Twins**, **Hercules**, **Hermes**, etc.).

Zoilus (28): a philosopher and rhetorician (4th century BC) of the 'Cynic' school, notorious and indeed proverbial for his carping and rancorous attacks on writers of genius and especially on Homer. As a disguise for Mephistopheles in the Carnival scene, Goethe conflates him with Thersites, this double identity as 'Zoilo-Thersites' being appropriate to the negative and cynical outlook professed by Mephistopheles in *Faust* generally.

1 Map of Greece
for Acts II and III

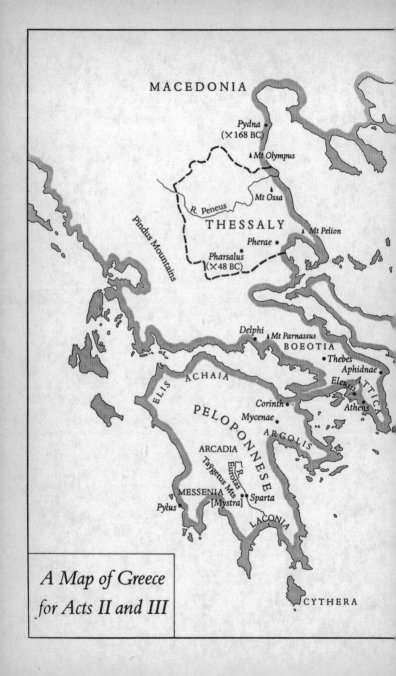

A Map of Greece
for Acts II and III